EDDIE PITTMAN

Missing Among the Stars

for Dad, my hero

for Aaron, my love

and for Taylor, my inspiration

Contents

V   The Extinction

Acknowledgments

This book couldn't have been possible without the lovely aid of numerous people. First, I want to thank my beta readers, especially my brother, Michael, who read the first ten chapters that I had drafted, and my partner, Aaron, who read the first draft in its entirety.

Lots of people have been kind in this process, and the self-publishing world is a daunting, relentless place. I have already begun work on the second book in this series, and plan for it to be a trilogy, but it may extend to four or five books. I also have some other projects I am working on, but right now this series is my primary focus.

My other beta readers also deserve mention, Elle (@elletay), Maddy (@maddy216), and Jen (@alacrityvirtual), all of who provided me with incredible feedback, and this novel would be wildly different without their input.

To any readers out there I want to thank you for just being a part of this journey with me. I am so excited to continue writing more worlds, stories, and branching into other genres (but I am first, and foremost, a science fiction author). If you can, please leave a review, that is the single best thing you can do for a self-published author. I love it when readers tell me their favorite scenes, where they hope to see the story go, and their honest feedback as it only strengthens me as a writer.

Prologue

In 2125, an alien signal with a single word reached the solar system. It said one word: "Hello." The simple message fractured Humanity. Sapien, a terrorist organization, opposed any communication with extraterrestrials. But curious Humans would not be stopped. They built a ship called *the Traveler* with the express purpose of finding the aliens.

Luke Mako, along with others, ventured aboard *the Traveler*. Their mission was simple—follow the signal's source. But *the Traveler* never returned, and no one knows what happened to the ship and her crew.

With *the Traveler* presumed destroyed, Sapien rose to power. They declared war on all those who built *the Traveler*. A long, bloody civil war erupted, called the Sapien War but colloquially called the "Human Civil War." Among those caught in the conflict was Luke's son, Kasey Mako.

In 2145 A.D., Kasey's commanding officer, Respow, dispatched Kasey on a rescue mission to Musk Station to save the son of the President of Mars, Leon Grace. The mission ended in catastrophe. A random attack from an unknown source left the station in ruins. The tragedy marked the end of the Sapien War.

When the dust settled, Humanity joined the Galactic Union. The GU welcomed Humanity, purely for their sheer numbers and resources. Ultimately, Respow secured his position as a Captain, just one heartbeat away from controlling all of Humanity. In an effort to stabilize Galactic-scale conflicts, Kasey joined the Peacekeeping Task Force (PTF), a coalition sworn to uphold galactic stability.

Introduction

Important Terms

Captains - Essentially the "vice president" of an entire species, second to Representatives.

Commission - Group of Three Lead Representatives that make decisions for the Galaxy as a whole. Lead Representatives are Petra for Psys, Tsperi for Orchi, and Respow for Humans.

Comms - Part of a converter implant allowing communication over vast distances. Usually requires a pad or proximity to a Fusion Center.

Converters - Implants that convert language to the implantee's choice. They affect vision as well, however, this component speculates a potential meaning. Adding languages after installation is painful but common.

Dyson Sphere/Swarm/Plates - Solar panels that surround a star to gather its energy. A Dyson Sphere completely closes off a star, whereas a Swarm is a series of non-connected panels. Further variants exist, such as Dyson Plates and Rods.

Fusion Centers - Buoys acting as way-points for interstellar communication. Depending on distance, this can take a few seconds or days.

Hybrids - Humans with mechanical enhancements exceeding 10% of the entire body.

Jasoosi - An alleged Orchi spy organization. The Psys have extensive documentation of their existence and meddling in Psys' affairs, but most Orchi deny it.

Navigators - Smaller ships (around 80 cubic meters) that travel a significant percentage of the speed of light.

Pad - The generic name of a device developed individually by different species acting as an advanced smartphone. The GU standardized them for ease of use and reliability.

Peacekeeping Task Force (PTF) - A group of twelve members tasked with keeping Peace in the Galaxy.

Point of No Return - (abbreviated and colloquially called PONR) The incurable state in which a Hybrid becomes so interwoven with technology they no longer feel emotions.

Representatives - Members that represent an entire species. Other species have a Representative, but they act as figureheads by bringing issues to Lead Representatives.

Rogue Planets - Planets roaming space without a host star.

Sapien - A large terrorist organization composed of only biological Humans seeking to alienate all extraterrestrials and view humanity as the best species.

Sapien War - Also referred to as the Human Civil War, the Sapien War raged on for years following the destruction of *the Traveler*.

Slart - A gun specialized for PTF members with non-lethal and lethal modes.

Tayir War - A short war that ended in the destruction of the Tayirs after they shot a Psys ship out of space.

The Traveler - A large ship sent to investigate the "Hello" signal with linguists, strategists, astrobiologists, and philosophers. Around one hundred Travelers were aboard, including Luke Mako.

Alien Species

Cerapto - A species dubbed the "artificial record keepers" for their love of information. They have endless data about the Universe, but their physical form is unclear.

Jasyx - Crab Centaur-like species who fear the Observers as primordial gods who intervene only when angered. Jasyx rest on four legs and have a pair of arms in addition to a pair of claws above them and four small black eyes.

Nyary - Quadrupedal lizards with elephant ear-shaped collars around their necks.

Orchi - Bipedal humanoids with striking purple eyes and scarlet skin. Most have spiral hair and long curls, however some are bald with lighter pink skin. They're the only known species of sentient life to exhibit bisexuality among every member.

Psys - Feline, bipedal species constantly in civil war. Several sub-species exist and have assigned clan names with two main ruling clans: Hyoose and Nima. They age past most sentient species, up to around 250 years.

Shura - Several spherical beings that compose "one" being. As each being must assent to what the entire being says, they speak in one-word sentences.

Tayirs - A species of large birds or bats depending on sub-species. They were eviscerated by the GU in the Tayir War. Unlike Jasyx, they worshiped the Observers as a benevolent race.

The Observers - A rumored species of aliens thought to be Gods that intervene when necessary. Purported evidence of their existence includes objects found scattered across the Galaxy, however their purpose is unclear. Assumed extinct.

Venori - Tall humanoid aliens with thin bodies, long limbs, and gray skin. Three or four tendrils arch out of their back, which they have full control over. Venori languages are complex, having words for everything. Several converters use as much vocabulary as possible to decode their sentences, making it difficult to understand.

Zayzay - Aliens in full suits that rarely interact with the GU. It is suspected they scout and perform experiments on species without interstellar travel. Some Humans even claim that Zayzay abducted them, however, no credible evidence links the two.

Acronyms

GU- Galactic Union
    GUM - Galactic Union Military
    MSAS - Military Standard Assault Shooter (also called "the Misses")
    PONR - Point of No Return
    PTF - Peacekeeping Task Force

Points of Interest

Bustan - The homeworld of the Tayir. Destroyed during the Tayir War.

Domus - The homeworld of the Orchi. Domus enacted an embargo six years ago in 2144 A.D. It is unclear why, and several smugglers sneak people onto the planet.

Earth - After modern space flight, Earth's population dwindled to a staggering billion people, spread across the once-overpopulated cities and continents.

Katree - The homeworld of the Psys. Three large continents sprung up life, with convergent evolution making three distinct types of Psys.

Kyros - A mega-ship composed of several "Panels" with different living conditions for each species. Panel C is the general Panel for most species.

Mars -After the construction of Musk Station, Mars had only colonies living under domes of protection until the Terraforming Committee found a way to replicate a magnetic field to keep control of the atmosphere. Now housing over 600 million people, Mars is one of the most diverse worlds among Humans.

Planet Exo- A Rogue Planet captured by a supermassive star that ultimately smothered half of it and froze the other half.

Porygar - The planet of the first mixed-species colony, including Psys, Humans, Hybrids, and Orchi. Tidally locked, the colony lived along the small ring of the planet cloaked in eternal twilight. Although several races were invited to join the colony, many cited tensions between Orchi and Psys as reasons for not going.

Poseidon - One of many "water worlds" where water composes at least 90% of the surface area. The planet has become a resort destination.

Ryland - Considered the "political" capital of the GU, Ryland is where hundreds of decisions are made. Originally founded by the Orchi.

Tyol - A large planet selected by Gyras Corp for mining operations for rare metals. The planet was tidally locked until terraformed through several asteroid impacts.

Venus - A planet containing nature preserves, housing Earth and alien life alike.

Major Characters

Amber Juno - A Hybrid who served in the Sapien War, and joined PTF as one of three Hybrids willing to join. The Seventh Member of the Peacekeeping Task Force.

Benjo Chun - A Hybrid who served in the Sapien War, and joined PTF as one of three Hybrids willing to join. The Fourth Member of the Peacekeeping Task Force.

Captain Respow - A stern man with a scar going from his chin past his milky eye. Iron fist, strict, but fair as some would say. Humanity's sole Captain, one step below Representative.

Falisto Nima - A Psys from the war-torn Nima Clan. Joined PTF to slow down life and regretted leaving the fighting world. The Second Member of the Peacekeeping Task Force.

Kasey Mako - Human PTF member who saved the son of the President of Mars on Musk Station. The First Member of the Peacekeeping Task Force.

Luke Mako - A Human Traveler aboard *the Traveler* twenty-five years ago in 2125. Father of Kasey Mako. (Presumed deceased).

Mariposa "Riley" Rodriguez - Called Riley by most, she serves as a linguist and one of few Hybrids aboard *the Traveler*. (Presumed deceased).

Private Powers - A Traveler known for technological and linguistic capabilities aboard *the Traveler*. (Presumed deceased).

Shamp Jajawush - A Venori PTF member, searching for a new homeworld for another Venori. The Twelfth Member of the Peacekeeping Task Force.

Tsarena Noelani - An Orchi who served in the Tayir War as a technological surveyor to determine the state of technology of the Tayirs. The Eighth Member of the Peacekeeping Task Force.

Tsoki Vanjo - An Orchi who served in the Tayir War as an information specialist. The Third Member of the Peacekeeping Task Force.

Minor Characters

Captain Bigon - Hyoose Captain who serves under Representative Petra.

Captain Qiula - Falisto's mother and Captain of the Psys. Deceased.

Chike - The Tenth Member of the Peacekeeping Task Force. A Nyary.

Donna - The Sixth Member of the Peacekeeping Task Force. A female Human in charge of guarding Earth.

Drake - The Ninth Member of the Peacekeeping Task Force. A PONR Hybrid.

Representative Petra - Leader of the Psys. Only Representative to have two Captains, Captain Qiula and Captain Bigon.

Representative Tsperi - Leader of the Orchi.

Shalotte - The Eleventh Member of the Peacekeeping Task Force. A Shura.

Tunde - A person known to have "information" about nearly everything.

Yvijon - The Fifth Member of the Peacekeeping Task Force. A female, Hyoose Psys assigned to protect the Psys cluster of planets.

Humanity Timeline

The Dying Earth 2075 A.D.

United Korea and Australia form the first successful Hybrid creations under the program "SHAMA," or Space Human and Mechanical Astronauts. Originally meant as a way to prolong Human life for long space travel, Hybrids are sent to Alpha Centauri to colonize planets there. Several volunteers die during the first journeys, but those that survive go out to the stars and form colonies. Eventually, these colonies create their own Human government too far removed from Earth's influence. After a cataclysm, the colonies are destroyed. Their advancements in space travel, however, propel the beginning of the Space Age.

The Beginning of the Space Age 2080 A.D.

Signals are sent throughout space with Human information. FTL drives are finally realized with the discovery of exotic matter on Mercury. Several corporations of Earth terraform nearby planets, including Mars and Venus, and moons like Europa. Titan, however, is found to have microbial life and is left undisturbed. On Earth, Human supremacists formalize a group called "Sapien." Their members speak out against signals sent into space, citing several forms of contact that could lead to species-wide conflict.

The Hello Signal & *The Traveler* 2125-2126 A.D.

Humans receive a signal saying "Hello" from several light-years away. It is in every language, both spoken and written, and comes from one discernible source. Sapien, now a fully political organization, launches terrorist attacks preventing construction on *the Traveler*. Despite the divide in humanity, *the Traveler* is sent after the signal.

The Sapien War and Musk Station Destruction 2127 A.D.

The Traveler is deemed lost, destroyed, or otherwise a lost cause, and Sapien declares a full Human Civil War. Massive starships are destroyed, and colony worlds quickly fall into tyranny.

The Galactic Union 2135 A.D.

Captain Respow, pilot of the *S.S. Gravity*, discovers a Megastructure twenty thousand light years away from Earth after using experimental worm-hole technology allowing further travel than conventional FTL. The Galactic Union makes itself known as a friendly entity and allows humanity to join as one of the many species. The Human population is over 30 billion people, across several planets, having more pull than other species.

Musk Station Incident 2145 A.D.

Still in the Sapien War, Kasey Mako goes on a mission to retrieve the son of the President of Mars. An unknown entity strikes the ship, but Kasey saves the target nevertheless. Trust and hope in Sapien shatters with the loss of innumerable Sapien supporters. The war rages on until 2146.

Human Acceptance 2149 A.D.

After realizing how much influence Humans have, the GU offers humanity membership and Representativeship in 2147. Kasey Mako becomes a PTF member in 2148, with his mission on Tyol in 2150.

I

The Sickness

Chapter 1

Kasey

Fact: user error accounted for over half of all spaceship crashes. It didn't matter if the ship was a tiny transport like the Navigator they rode in or a dreadnought like *the Irene.* It was almost always the pilot's fault.

This "fun" fact haunted Kasey as the Navigator's pilot played bumper cars with loose asteroids sprinkled in their path. Kasey's palms dripped with sweat, and his fingers fidgeted. When his team's eyes weren't focused on him, he cradled himself back and forth.

The crew didn't suspect his astroaerophobia. Most didn't. Diligent eyes detected his sweaty palms covered by the black military unitard, and the water wheel in his stomach spun faster with each bump. But Falisto and Tsarena—the two aliens under his command of the Peacekeeping Task Force—hadn't said anything about his yelps and jolts when flying.

"I don't know how he got out of basic," Falisto groaned under his breath, loud enough for Kasey to hear but low enough the pilot's headset wouldn't catch the snide remark. Whiskers stretched out under Falisto's nostrils, and his fur rustled from an air conditioning vent above him.

"He's a kid," Tsarena said, her purple eyes glistening under the overhead lighting.

"They could've let me fly."

Kasey wanted to interject, but a stomach rumble told him to stay as still as possible. Instead, he stared out the window as the Navigator pierced the atmosphere of their target planet—Tyol.

Tyol, a supposed "paradise," looked more like a desert hell. Dunes stretched far, covering the ground in a blanket of sand, with an occasional rock formation dotting the golden sea. Hills rolled, and a derelict path for transport was the only landmark for miles. The red giant star scorched the surface, and the only thing interesting to Kasey was the lush moons in orbit.

"Pretty empty." Falisto's chocolate and caramel fur writhed under the vent's air.

"The actual city is on the other side." Kasey turned to face him with his stomach innards slushing around. Using his pad, Kasey pulled images of what corporations advertised as Tyol. One set of photos showed soil cultivating all types of vegetation, both Earth-based and non-Earth-based. Basji sprouted out with dark leaves under the protective shade of looming trees. Another set of pictures flashed images of gray fish swimming in schools near the wetlands. The last set was of Tyol's capital and only established city, Neosalm.

"And they couldn't build all that near the mine," Falisto snickered.

"Can't imagine commuting every day," Tsarena hummed. She craned her head closer to the window and pointed with one of her four fingered hands. "So they have housing but no medical center?"

Kasey held his stomach as he joined the conversation. "Hybrids aren't gonna get hurt in a mine." Hybrids were a fancy term for Humans with cybernetic enhancements. Sometimes a metal arm or leg with ten times the strength of a biological one. Other times it came in the form of enhanced senses.

Tsarena shrugged. "But we're here because they're getting hurt."

"No they're getting sick," Falisto chuckled. "Some virus they found underground."

"This is your pilot," the pilot's young voice shouted through their converters under their ears. "We're getting ready to descend. Back to *the Irene* in three hours." His voice cracked towards the end in a higher pitch.

Crimson, fiery bursts sputtered from the ship's boosters, causing a layer of sand to encircle the ship as it finished its descent. When the door opened, sand accosted them, swirling in and attempting to wreak havoc on unprotected bits of skin. Instantly, their unitards shot protective sheaths across their faces, blocking hits from rocks floating from dust kicked up by the Navigator.

Kasey still flinched. It didn't matter if the military-grade uniforms were made from materials gathered across the galaxy. Far too frequently, Kasey's suit conveniently failed to absorb impact just as pellets hurled at him. A little scar on his left cheek was proof of that.

But, at least he was on land. Getting attacked with rocks was a small price to pay to not have to go back on a Navigator for a few hours. Maybe he wouldn't vomit his lunch.

The hot air surrounded Kasey. His skin secreted sweat that his unitard absorbed.

"Masks on," Kasey commanded. The team of three placed their masks along their mouths and noses.

"We don't *need these*," Falisto scolded, his voice muffled from the cloth. He tugged at the mask like a cat irritated with a cone around their neck.

"And we don't *need* antibiotics, but we sure as hell still take them." Kasey turned to Falisto, ensuring his mask wrapped around his mouth and nose. "Last thing I want is to have to report that one of my team got sick because they refused to wear a mask."

"Pathogens spread quick, Falisto," Tsarena added, her voice sounding gargled.

After a few minutes of lagging behind schedule, the group came to a tent stationed outside the mine. Winds from southward gave Kasey a chill, and they increased to the point that Kasey's boot prints were obscuring.

Robotic nurses and doctors, along with a handful of Humans, guarded the tents. One supervising doctor, a Human with brown skin and short black hair, wrote on a pad, using his stylus on the holographic screen. His pad converted his chicken scratch into Galactic Times font, point 13. Although still foreign to Kasey, his converter morphed the letters to Martian. Behind the doctor, a few medical professionals tended to others, with many robotic ones stationed at tents with the dead.

"Doctor." Kasey slid his hands into his pockets by the holster of his gun.

"Kinda busy at the moment," he responded, not looking up. He continued to write. Not sentences—not even phrases—just words Kasey could barely make out after translation. *Sick. Deadly. Mutating. Fast. Hybrids.*

"Captain Respow sent us," Kasey interrupted. The doctor's body stiffened, his legs hinging at the knee and hip before pulling his back upright. His grip on the stylus got tighter, and his fingers squeezed around the tip while in the middle of a word.

He gulped before a nervous laugh escaped his mouth. "Where's Captain Respow?" For a moment, he looked around for him, expecting the tall, gray-haired man waiting for him.

"On the *Irene*." Kasey pointed his finger skyward toward the ship. From their vantage point, the four-ring ship was visible, albeit not entirely discernible without a telescope or enhanced vision. Countless Navigators traveled to and from the ship, headed to Neosalm or back to *the Irene*.

A nurse aide strutted over, holding his own pad with a variety of text colors and doodles along the artificial margins. Kasey's converter struggled to decode it, generating a snide question mark next to each doodle.

"Eight more trapped in the mine." He handed a printed paper to the doctor, then another to Kasey.

"Eight more? Respow said you had something in the thousands?"

Before either responded, Kasey's eyes looked beyond the doctor and nurse, staring at countless gurneys housing humps of metal and Human skin. Some were covered by stained white sheets that turned into a cherry red. Most weren't covered. Arms, both metal and organic, hung low from the gurneys, all of them lifeless.

"God," Kasey whispered.

"It's bad," the doctor sighed. "Real bad."

"We have our converters, are they susceptible to the virus?" Tsarena asked.

"No." The doctor grabbed a few loose papers on a desk next to him. After a glance, he handed them to Kasey. "Only affects Hybrids. You should be fine."

"Should be?" Kasey asked.

"That's reassuring," Falisto muttered.

"Read it," the doctor said.

Kasey perused the report, skipping data tables and other sections labeled as definitions and disclaimers. He didn't want superfluous information, just the answer to his question. Towards the middle, the findings section revealed the first description of the virus.

Findings: Patient reports feeling sick after mining lower left quadrant of the Gyras Mine. Synthetic parts impacted first, now causing cough, blurry vision, and aches. Patient reports her bones feel like they are "on fire." Biological portions of body unaffected. Blood draw reveals a virus not recorded. Seemingly no cross-species risk. Hybrids only impacted, not Normal Humans.

Kasey grimaced at the modifier "normal." An addendum, added just fifteen minutes later, finalized the report.

Patient died shortly after administering nanotech blood. -Doctor Hamza.

Kasey reexamined the symptoms, cough, blurry vision, and fiery bones. "I need to report to Captain Respow," Kasey murmured. Hastily, he pulled out his pad, fumbling it and nearly dropping it into the ocean of shaded sand.

Falisto swiped a paper from Kasey's side of the table, his caramel fur drenched in sweat. He scanned it, reading each line with his marigold eyes, gliding right over words and punctuation to the meat of every sentence.

"So, we don't know anything about it?" Kasey continued to type his message.

The nurse stretched his arms. "We know more than earlier."

Doctor Hamza sighed, "Not enough to save thousands."

"How long does it take the virus to become lethal?" Kasey asked, not looking up from his pad.

"If you're under 70% Hybrid, it takes a few hours." Hamza wrote on his pad again. "But most in that mine are PONR."

Kasey's eyes widened. "Where in the mine are they?"

The doctor pulled a map on his pad, projecting it upwards. Pinching his fingers, he zoomed to the interior of the mine. Circled in blue highlight, he pointed to the rhodium quadrant. "Here." After a moment, Doctor Hamza procured another piece of parchment to Kasey. "Read it, in case you find any alive."

Kasey snuck a peek at the document. Much of it was uninteresting, giving tiny bits of irrelevant information, until the ending. His jaw hit the ground and his heart thumped against his chest. This had to be some sort of weird, fucked up joke.

"You can't be serious," Kasey stuttered, his smile weak and frightened. "You're joking."

"It's the way to slow the virus," the doctor said.

"It's barbaric."

"But it works," the nurse said. He held up his arms, adorned with scratches and cuts. "Just don't go too deep."

Chapter 2

Kasey

Gyras Mines were known for their gaudy entrances—giant wooden gates, humming with machinery and showmanship.

But this entrance didn't have any of the fun fixtures Kasey expected. Instead, the entrance was just a crude hole carved into a mountain of stone. Inside, decaying signs pointed to different sources of elements between gold, copper, and rhodium.

"No torches?" Tsarena asked.

"Hybrids don't need them," Kasey said. "Eyes are a cheap upgrade."

"You ever get the fancy eye surgery?" Falisto asked.

"Not for me," Kasey said. "Converter is my limit." Kasey tapped the area right below his ear where the converter rested.

At first, the dim lighting didn't bother Kasey. But the deeper they traveled, Kasey began tripping and bumping into the shrinking tunnel. Eventually, Kasey slipped open his pouch and retrieved a handful of glow sticks, fluorescent green in color. With his other hand, Kasey tapped his gun. "Use your Slart for lighting."

Slarts were the unique guns given to the Peacekeeping Task Force. It was supposed to be recognizable, like a badge of honor that screamed rank. In reality, it was nothing more than a gimmicky gun with sleep darts and lethal bullets, depending on the option the situation called for. But for now, it was a fancy flashlight. He cast the light to the ground.

That's when Kasey saw it.

Fresh prints carved a maze through the still, undisturbed air of the mine.

But they weren't prints Kasey recognized. No Human or Orchi feet, nor paws from Psys. Granted, there were several alien species it *could* have been. These prints resembled an ant hill with the textured sand. Kasey raised an eyebrow, and rather instinctively, he switched his Slart to lethal mode. Kasey dropped a glowstick.

"Not even sure why Respow sent us here," Falisto mumbled. "Doesn't Respow have work on tropical planets?"

"The virus is killing Hybrids," Kasey said, gripping onto the Slart. "We have to help them."

Falisto mumbled, "Yeah, but they're Hybrids."

Kasey recoiled. "They're people. Hybrids or not."

Falisto chided, "You're sounding like a cyborg sympathizer."

Kasey stopped dead in his tracks. "When I'm team lead, you don't talk like that." Kasey's nostrils bulged and with his wide, bloodshot pupils he stared into Falisto's cat eyes glistening in the darkness. "Do I make myself clear?"

Falisto waved it off and rolled his eyes. "Got it."

For a while, no one spoke, letting the tension linger like an odor. Heat blasted Kasey, not from the mine, but from residual rage churning in his body.

"What's that?" Tsarena pointed the light from her Slart to a glowing hue peeking out between cracks in the wall. Cobalt light shimmered, running in direct competition with white rays from their Slarts.

Kasey stepped forward and crunched pieces of rock under his boot. Cold air seeped through the hole. He turned back to Tsarena then jabbed the hilt of his gun into the crack until a head-sized hole appeared. More blue light poured inside the mine, illuminating Kasey's tan face and dark brown hair.

Craning his head over and under, Kasey peered inside the orifice. He couldn't see the source, but rather a dense fog reflecting the light.

"What is it?" Tsarena nudged Kasey.

"Maybe just some phosphorus, but I don't really know," Kasey admitted. "A fog, maybe?" Kasey dropped a glowstick and motioned them forward.

The further in, the more the walls condensed into a singularity. Heat from below simmered, inviting sweat beads to dot Kasey's face. Constriction brought them closer, but it didn't resolve the lingering tension that only festered with the claustrophobia.

"Anyone down there?" Kasey screamed. The echoes bounced off the walls, soaring further until dissipating. Kasey waited for a moment, hoping to hear something, anything. He labored a breath and sipped lukewarm water from a canteen.

"Help!" A voice bounced back, amplifying the further it traveled.

Kasey lit up. "We're coming!" He dropped a glowstick.

"Sounded like the person was below?" Tsarena said, sounding dumbfounded.

"Yeah it sounded—" The ground swallowed him. Rocks collapsed and he fell to his knees, sliding down a steep incline. The fall flung his body along the constricted walls. Each bounce evoked a yelp from him, and his mask failed to protect him from jagged pebbles fighting to make a new scar on his face. His speed generated dust from all sides and formed clouds of dirt and sand. He gagged from smoke clouding his lungs and vision. When his feet hit the ground, he rolled out of the way, scratching up his unitard from the jagged rocks around him.

Tsarena and Falisto followed, each of them screaming before they piled on top of each other amid the pile of Kasey's glowsticks. Falisto grunted, lifting himself on all fours and shaking every strand of fur like a wet dog. Kasey stood despite a sharp pain climbing his thigh. Tsarena gargled sounds, her voice labored and difficult.

After a singular step forward, Kasey collapsed again. Standing was too advanced for him now. Instead, he crawled towards them, the smoke cloud evaporating with each beat of pain. Summoning all the strength he could muster, Kasey walked off the injury. The unitard absorbed most of the impact. "You guys okay?"

"No," Falisto roared. "That fucking hurt." After finishing his whole body shake, he turned to each leg individually as if to rid it of something sticky.

"I'm fine." Tsarena gritted her teeth. "Reminds me of when you took us skiing." She coughed, lifting herself.

"I don't remember falling down a hole when we went skiing," Falisto countered.

Sobbing from a few meters away caught Kasey's attention. "You guys hear that?" Kasey whispered.

He took his Slart out in both his hands. The light shined along the ant-like footprints that multiplied down here. Tsarena and Falisto followed, both of them gripping their Slarts too.

They tiptoed towards the cries. Kasey looked back towards Tsarena and Falisto. Tsarena wore a pained expression mixed with a sense of anticipation. Falisto, however, had a grin with his lipless mouth curved upward.

They came to a wall of blue boulders that blocked off the cries. Kasey pressed his back to the boulders, letting the sharp edges dig into his body. He glanced at Tsarena and Falisto before peering past the rocks.

A mass—a Hybrid body—coughed with fresh blood dribbling down his lip. Silver cybernetics accentuated his masculine features with implants decorating his broad shoulders and arms. Dust covered his face and more boulders blocked off any possible direction. He was stranded.

Kasey rushed over to the man, sliding along his knees to the body. "Hey, hey, you're okay!" Kasey gripped his hand, with the Hybrid's grip burning hotter than Tyol's sun. Kasey ignored the searing pain and instead took out his combat knife.

"What are you doing?!" Tsarena shouted. "We gotta get him out of here!"

"We will," Kasey soothed, ignoring the ache plaguing his body. "But we gotta slow the virus." He peeled back the unitard covering his palms. Kasey prayed Doctor Hamza was right. His fleshy palm trembled and with his other hand, he gripped the knife.

Kasey slashed his palm.

Chapter 3

"What are you doing?!" Tsarena shouted again.

"The way to slow the virus," Kasey paused, gritting his teeth, "is by adding organic matter." He placed his bleeding hand near the mouth of the Hybrid, his pale lips bursting with color after each drip. "I know it's disgusting, but it's gonna help."

The near-unresponsive Hybrid sipped drips of blood slowly. Then faster. Faster. Faster. As if it were some elixir, he sucked out his blood, and a yelp escaped from Kasey as the Hybrid nearly sunk his teeth. Kasey kept up with the Hybrid's appetite and tightened his grip, squeezing more out before seizing his hand back. The Hybrid sent his tongue out of his mouth, seeking any remaining drops that dotted the side of his mouth.

Using his other hand, Kasey cut a section of his unitard and then secured it around his wound. Tsarena didn't hesitate after color returned to the Hybrid. She slashed her hand as well, joining in the ritualistic healing.

"Falisto?" Kasey asked. With his gold eyes, Falisto trembled. He hadn't brought his knife out yet, and instead of coming forward, he took a step back.

The Hybrid tugged Kasey, his metal practically boiling. "The others," the Hybrid coughed, choking on someone's blood. "They're dead." His metal finger quivered, pointing to an array of boulders. "There was *something* down there."

Kasey took a breath. "What?"

"A monster."

Kasey's blood ran cold. It was supposed to be a virus, not something down here unleashing it. That's what all reports pointed to: some biological pathogen, not an attacker.

"What was it?" Kasey pressed. But the man turned unresponsive. Tsarena squeezed more of her crimson into his mouth.

Kasey glanced back to Falisto. "We gotta get him out of here."

Falisto snapped out of whatever trance he entered and offered his paw. He shouldered the weight of the man, all four of his limbs unscathed from his combat knife. The Hybrid's weight anchored Falisto and Kasey.

The Hybrid wailed, "I can't! Please, I can't!" He sobbed, his face a scrunched mess of tears and blood. His lips shook and he shriveled back on the floor like a slug in sunlight.

"It's alright," Kasey soothed, running his hand along the man's arms. Forehead sweat from Kasey dripped onto the man's cybernetics, sizzling on impact.

"What's your name?"

"Oliver," he whimpered. His dark hair picked up gray dust, aging him a few years.

"Oliver, I need you to trust me, can you do that?"

The man's eyes pleaded for help. "Yes."

"It's not gonna be a cakewalk, but we're getting you out of here."

Kasey powered the energy setting on his combat knife. Golden light, the same shade as Falisto's eyes, encircled the blade. "I'm gonna amputate your metal parts."

Oliver's eyes shot open. His mouth widened, shouting in horror.

"Falisto, hold him down! Tsarena, you too!"

Kasey mounted Oliver, placing his knees over Oliver's Human hand and pinning it to the ground. The full metal arm fought off Tsarena, wiggling about and striking with a newfound second wind of energy. Oliver protested, revoking the trust he'd bestowed moments earlier. Kasey aided Tsarena with his free hand, holding it down and stopping it from punching them.

Falisto locked eyes with Kasey before gazing at a rag to the side, soaked in blood and coated with dust. "Use it," Kasey commanded. Falisto nodded, shoving the gag into Oliver's mouth, muffling his pleas. Oliver's cybernetic legs fought against Kasey. Oliver narrowly missed the 70% cybernetic Point Of No Return, or PONR, as they called it.

With a nod to the group, Kasey sliced through the metal arm, removing all but an inch of the components to the shoulder. Bits of Oliver's screams escaped from the rag's gag order and flooded the cavern, causing tiny rocks to fall around them. Falisto covered his mouth, silencing the screams further, and shushed him with his other paw. Bits of his brown fur mixed in with the blood-drenched rag, choking him on both.

The once metallic silver adorning Oliver's body resembled a muddied brown with dots of the original shine peering through the veil of blood-coated rust. The coils and gears decomposed against the virus's hunger, the tiny disease injecting its instructions for the metal to disintegrate, rust, or short circuit. Portions of the cybernetics had their own veins now, the illness spreading the pathogen and metastasizing to his organic parts.

Kasey dug his knife into infected metal portions of one of the legs. The virus stemmed from his extremities before moving inward, but it sped with each passing second. It crawled along electrical cables and nanotechnology, its poisonous spark jolting every conductor it came across. Kasey maneuvered towards the other leg, making quick work of it.

When the last metal piece fell with a *thud*, Oliver spit out pieces of the rag. Strands of cotton and nanotechnological-infused fabric coiled out, with some sticking in his teeth like dental floss. Whatever blood soaked into the rag, Oliver sucked out. Kasey wasn't sure how much pain Oliver endured, but judging by the blank stare, the mental trauma was far more damaging.

Kasey and Falisto helped Oliver up, with both legs and one arm severed, the Hybird would have to be carried. Falisto shouldered the weight alone. The slide of dust they fell down would be the most daunting portion of their return journey, but they had no other choice.

"This is gonna suck." Kasey groaned.

"I'll get up there." Falisto shifted the full weight of Oliver to Kasey. "Maybe we pull him up?"

"Do we got something to put him on?" Tsarena asked.

"Use the tarp," Oliver murmured. Kasey's eyes darted to a blanket decorated with fresh holes from fallen rocks, making it more of a fishnet.

"It'll have to do." Kasey grabbed the tarp and strung it together, passing off stakes to anchor it.

When it passed Kasey's safety test, Falisto climbed the slide, grabbing onto rocks protruding from the narrow sides of the tunnel and digging his claws into weakened sections. He inched his way with the rope on his back. One of the sharper rocks lacerated his hind leg and he winced in pain, losing his footing.

"Careful!" Kasey shouted.

By the time he reached the apex, Kasey and the others placed Oliver down on the tarp. Falisto wheezed, expelling dust and sand from his lungs. He took three stakes and secured his end of the rope, drilling it into the ground. Tsarena joined him seconds later, following the path Falisto scaled.

Together, the two pulled Oliver up, grunting with each forceful hand-over-hand (or, in Falisto's case, paw-over-paw) motion they made. Kasey's eyes never left the rope. He stood underneath the pulley, his hands stretched and his stance firm, ready for the worst.

"Got him!" they shouted from above, their voices still echoing.

Kasey turned behind him, hearing sounds of something like a large insect skittering across the rocky ground. But before he could take a moment to look, more rocks rained, and Kasey climbed the rope.

Doctor Hamza waited outside the mine with a few loitering robots. A cigarette dangled from his mouth, and he puffed circles of water-vapor. The Hybrids who survived the premature collapse of the mines and virus outbreak rode aboard Navigators shining brighter than the stars in the night sky. *The Irene* had plenty of space for them.

Doctor Hamza wrote on his tablet, typing on the holographic keyboard without making eye contact with the keys. When Kasey and the others emerged, he put out the cigarette, stomping on it the second it hit the floor. No one took doctors who smoked seriously in this day and age.

"Back in one—" Hamza started, as Kasey and Falisto levied the body of

Oliver. He wasn't dead, but he certainly wasn't alive. "—Piece."

Doctor Hamza yelled out, "Get him to the table!"

The robots ceased their slow pace, their eyes flashing red and dashing to the tables in accordance. They trailed behind Kasey who left a river of sweat as the team trekked through the sand.

Doctor Hamza slapped a nearby machine, causing plastic wraps to envelope his hands. The group dropped Oliver's body, and robots immediately jabbed IVs in his only remaining appendage and hooked him to standard equipment monitors. The Human nurse from earlier dashed from another tent, his blonde hair a mashed sphere of sweat and dirt.

"Heart rate is low," Doctor Hamza shouted. "I need the defibrillator powered up!" One of the robots opened its chest compartment revealing two electrical paddles and various settings.

"God, I hope we don't have to use that," he sighed. "Pump in the painkillers, and get a blood transfusion."

The other robot, red in color, opened its chest compartment, revealing a slim number of blood bags hanging from a silver hook. Usually, these robots overflowed with resources. "Here you are, sir."

The nurse hooked the bag to his arm, flooding his systems. The oxygen content increased steadily, and Hamza sighed with relief when an oxygen mask did the trick. After a few moments of the steady beat, he cracked a smile and closed the door of the robot's defibrillator.

"Phew." A grin broke his stoic face, and the robots began to loiter again. Doctor Hamza took note of the cut hands of everyone. "Told ya it would work."

"Followed more than just the single piece of advice," Kasey said.

"Is he gonna be okay?" Tsarena asked.

"He will," he said, having a residual smoke-induced cough escape his lungs. "Probably take him to Kyros. They'll give him new replacement parts when a vaccine is made."

"When a vaccine is made?" Kasey asked.

"He's gonna have to go on quarantine soon." Doctor Hamza wiped his mouth.

"Wait, why?" Falisto asked. "We just removed the infected parts?"

"The virus is in his body now." Hamza examined Oliver's body. "Anything metal we align just gets reinfected."

Oliver coughed. The shoulder of the severed arm twitched like he tried to move his arm that wasn't there. Kasey read about those—phantom limbs. Oliver tried a few times before resorting to his Human arm that dangled on the side of the table with three different veins punctured by the equipment.

A low-pitched ring came through Kasey's implant, the ringtone signaling a call from Captain Respow.

"Got a call," Kasey said, meandering away from the tent with blood and sweat drenching his unitard. Kasey took a quick inhale before answering the call.

"*Captain*," Kasey greeted, holding his index finger on his ear and turning to an empty side of the tent.

"*Mako*," he roared. "*You done down there yet?*"

"*Got one alive*," Kasey sighed. "*The others didn't make it.*" Kasey paused for a moment. "*The survivor we got said there was a monster down there? Are you sending reinforcements?*"

Respow ignored the question. "*Tyol's Government decided to do a full-scale evacuation, the mines are getting sealed then bombed.*"

"*What? Why?*"

"*Mako*," Respow tried to calm him. "*I'll explain more here. Check your messages. We got a bigger problem on our hands.*"

Chapter 4

Kasey

Flames erupted from the Navigator's boosters. Kasey took his seat, laying his back against the cushion. Though Tsarena and Falisto both rode the Navigator, several refugees from Tyol crowded the ship, separating the group. A family of three sat next to Kasey, squeezing him against the window of the Navigator.

Kasey swiped out his pad. After pressing a few combinations on the interface, it illuminated to life. The screensaver of Peyton and Kasey greeted him. His heart fluttered at the photo and he flashed it a weak smile. For a brief moment, he held his finger above the photo they took on a hike through the Mars Jungles. He could smell the dewy grass and taste the wet air.

He shook his head free of the thought and went to his messages. Four documents from Respow appeared, attached to an email with the subject line: *Roanoke*. Kasey raised an eyebrow, the word meaning nothing to him. Ignoring it, Kasey looked at the documents. The first, labeled "Team Assignment," caught Kasey's attention.

The document had the dossiers of four members assigned to the mission. The first three were unsurprising. Kasey, Falisto, and Tsarena. Kasey made a face at the fourth page and wondered who else got paired with them.

When his eyes read the name "Benjo," they rolled. Kasey knew about him, but he didn't "know" him. What Kasey was confident about was the stories he'd heard. Benjo was Respow's lapdog and personal errand boy, the poster child of "mission first."

Kasey's dossier sang to him like a siren, and his eyes shifted away from the other three in the document. Everyone in the Peacekeeping Task Force said the same thing: don't look at your dossiers. All the resumes did was highlight your achievements, but unlike a resume, these included your faults, your shortcomings, your flaws.

But Kasey couldn't help himself.

"Kasey Mako," he said aloud. Some Hybrids hitching a ride turned an eye to him. Not fans of speaking aloud, apparently.

Kasey stifled a laugh at a wrong fact that glared at him. He could forgive small errors, but his full name wasn't something he expected the dossier to miss. His name wasn't just Kasey Mako, it was Kasey Bijan Mako.

He continued to read data points. Each one tabbed to the middle, a black dot on the margin indicating a blurt of information. They were quick facts, no room for interpretation. Simple, immutable, and clear. Only child, late twenties, Veteran of the Sapien War, and no family. Kasey winced from the sting of the final point.

No family as a fact was harsh. His father—Luke—had a reputation as one of the most honorable men who perished on *the Traveler.* Maybe *that* deserved a mention instead of "only child."

At the bottom were "red flags," things a Captain, team lead, supervisor, etc, needed to know before missions. A Captain wouldn't send a PTF member to a planet to negotiate with a race they've never met. His finger kept the section hidden. This was what everyone said to avoid. If you had to read your own dossier, avoid this section like a plague.

"I'm not this boring," he hushed to himself. The dossier missed all the good stuff! No mention of his hikes, paintings he sold, how he spoke three languages fluently. Kasey pulled the keyboard up. If they left out the fun details, he'd add them.

- Hiker
- Avid painter
- Fluent in Martian, Koreish, and Modern Standard English

Satisfied, he hit the enter key, forever marking himself as the guy who hiked, painted, and spoke a lot. Along the bottom, the red flag blinked. Without another thought, Kasey clicked it open.

He narrowed his eyes at the alleged flags. Mouthing the words he read it to himself, *sole survivor of Musk Station.* He shut off his pad. He shouldn't have checked.

The Navigator shot out of the atmosphere of Tyol, leaving it behind and approaching *the Irene.* Kasey gazed out of the window, peering back to Tyol. Swirls of cerulean at the poles turned into wisps and eventually dots along the planet's surface. Kasey's stomach growled—not from hunger, but from the Navigator's erratic path. He focused on the various shades of periwinkle and teal metamorphosing into sea foam green. Another technique he read in an article that just didn't seem to work for him.

As they reached *the Irene,* four black arms extended from the dreadnought. Each arm took a side of the Navigator, clamping and magnetizing it to the appendages while yanking it into its gravitational field.

Even though he, Tsarena, and Falisto were stationed there, *the Irene* still enamored Kasey. It had everything a person wanted: Orchi symphonies filling halls and corridors; food from Psys including their sushi delicacies; and technology from the Galactic Union Military. Kasey's love for the ship never wavered, not even when he ate a revolting roll of sushi made by a Psys with a reputation for hating Humans.

When the Navigator settled in and the doors flung open, Kasey darted out before anyone had the chance. Respow didn't like waiting and Kasey sure as hell didn't like an unhappy Respow.

The inner portion of *the Irene* was designed by the Orchi and served as a hub for ships and common areas. Symbols of Orchi influence covered the walls with religious depictions of what they called the Observers. Kasey liked their religion. Most of the time, religious depictions in the GU made Kasey apprehensive, but Orchi teachings were pure and simple. The Observers were progenitors—a species long, long, long ago, that did just that: observe. They didn't interfere, just watching from the sidelines.

Human funding of *the Irene* was expressed in the heavy metals of the ship and luxury implemented in each facet possible. Parts of it made Kasey feel more at home, the way the faucets turned on via motion detector and chairs catered to knees bending a certain way. But it also alienated him—pristine whites with golden trim, marble counters, televisions for large screen viewing—all things out of his reach. His familiarity flirted with hospitals, sterile scents, and chemotherapy rooms with his mother.

The only race that didn't have a clear influence despite their funding, was the Psys. The cat-like aliens instead contributed covertly. All thirty missions planned at the beginning of the docket revolved around them. First and foremost: finding a new world for hunting. Unfortunately, that docket paused when the Tyol situation went from bad to worse.

Along the walkway, Kasey couldn't hear the Orchi melodies that usually played. Instead, an automated voice message played, over and over in different languages. Kasey's converter repeated it in Martian, just with a different twang each time.

Large windows crafted from industrial glass and triple-insulated material looked over Tyol. The planet, once a desert world, likely didn't originate in the Indus System that they were in. The origins didn't bother scientists, instead, that accolade belonged to the virus.

Kasey passed scientists in the hub, all huddled around virtual drawing boards. Common areas contained far too many people violating whatever fire code *the Irene* had, but Kasey had to pass through them if he wanted to get to Respow quicker.

Hybrids dotted the ship everywhere: sitting along walls, holding one another while they cried in the middle of walkways, and even inside rooms and convenience stores. Some sobbed silently, others wailed. Kasey tried not to lock eyes with them, but he couldn't hide from their painful gazes.

After getting to the end of the cylinder portion of *the Irene*, Kasey came to the "X" shape bridge connecting the rings. A handful of Hybrids hustled in, trying to find a room to claim as their own for the time being.

Noticing the influx, Kasey activated his face mask, the cloth and fabric springing from his suit and snapping around his face. Briskly, he walked past Hybrids looking out at the stars around them.

In the distance, a lime bursted from a ship's engine heading towards Tyol. The design was unmistakably Psys; it was a vibrant red torpedo ship, piercing forward to the planet. Behind, several missile-shaped vessels headed to the planet.

"Monsters," a crying Hybrid muttered. Her robotic hands held onto the railing, and a tear fell down the side of her cheek. "There's still people down there and they're already colonizing." Kasey lowered his head as the woman continued to curse.

When Kasey reached the end of the bridge, he entered the PTF ring which noticeably dwarfed in comparison to the others. All four rings of *the Irene* had specific purposes. One housed all of PTF, one dedicated to casual travel, one contained all permanent residents, and one changed regularly for mission based objectives. In this case, refugees.

Kasey turned and headed into his room, wedged between Falisto's and Tsarena's. PTF gave him a studio, something he requested. He didn't need space for more than just one person.

He lowered his mask and grabbed his sepia satchel from a hook. He'd planned to gather some sodas before too many shopkeepers gouged their prices. Even the commissary neglected common decency.

Closing the door behind him, a video frame along his dresser caught his eye. Peyton got it for him for their first anniversary. At the time, Kasey thought it was tacky—having photos and videos of a couple scattered in the place they lived. Now, he wished he could fill the room with them, turn the walls into media players and play loops of him and Peyton together. He watched the video in full this time.

Peyton took Kasey to the highest point on Mars, Olympus Mons. The already man-made atmosphere barely let them breathe, so they wore apparatuses. They looked goofy back then, both bald and brushing against one another. Kasey slowly closed the door, stealing another watch of the video loop.

Captain Respow pinged him, asking for his location. Kasey updated his ETA—four minutes standard. The standard time followed the Psys's normal schedule— another demand the Psys made when funding *the Irene*.

An easy concession given converters automatically transformed it for the user. No one ever needed to say "standard hours" or "standard times," the computers inside in converters did that.

Kasey continued until he reached the biometric scanner of Respow's office. The lock mounted next to the door demanded a handprint for access. Slowly, he placed his hand along the lime green outline. The frigid cold sent an involuntary shiver down his spine, and the viridescent ray traced his hand, reading each ridge and mark, even noting a scar on the pinky's surface.

"Access granted. Kasey Mako."

Three locks moved together, with the door parsing aside. Kasey walked through, taking stairs that taunted him the moment the door opened. It was an unholy sight whenever Kasey came back from an intensive mission that shot his legs just to immediately have to scale *the Irene's* Mount Everest. At the top, Kasey came into a cockpit-like area. Captain Respow wore his white Captain suit, accessorized by pins and medals of valor, including the first contact badge. That was how most Humans knew him. The Captain of the *S.S. Gravity*, turned prominent political leader of Humanity.

Three workers completed other tasks inside, not turning to Kasey. Two of them looked at a holograph of planets in the system, with four habitable Earth planets surrounding the red giant of the Indus System. One worker zoomed into view of the planet closest to the sun, Indus, and further honed into a grassy stretch of land.

"Could work," he suggested. He typed things into a keyboard projected in front of him. "Soil could be bad, though."

Captain Respow came to Kasey, leaving his view of the star and planets from his station. "Mako," Captain Respow roared. "You're late."

"Came as soon as I could, sir."

Respow softened his face, letting the tension fade. Kasey held his hand in the salute position and he didn't shift his gaze. Respow had one of the faces that looked deceptively younger than he was. Allegedly, he'd been in service for thirty years, but he didn't look a day over forty with a head full of hair. He'd be just older than Kasey's father if he was alive. The mark that was quintessential to Respow was the diagonal scar that went from his left lower chin to his eyebrow, resulting in a milky, right eye.

"At ease, soldier," he said with a smile.

After relaxing slightly, Kasey asked, "What's the mission? Is it about the virus?"

"No." He looked out the window, lowering his head. "No, it is not."

"It's not?" Kasey's eyes narrowed. They'd *just* arrived in the Indus System. Kasey was no math genius but there was no way in hell they'd evacuated the entire planet.

"That situation is..." Captain Respow searched for the right words. "Handled."

Kasey's eyes nearly exploded. Handled? He had to stop himself from scoffing at such a preposterous statement. How was it handled? The planet had thousands dying by the second with a virus spreading across the surface.

Respow must've sensed Kasey's disbelief. "Okay, we're handling it. We'll find a treatment soon."

"What about a cure?"

"Look," Captain Respow interrupted. "Frankly, I don't know about the science. The Commission thinks we'll find a way to deal with it."

Kasey thought for a moment about the Hybrids. The woman watching as her new home became someone's newer home, Oliver living without limbs for years, Doctor Hamza performing amputations like the dark ages before antibiotics. Respow and the Commission may *think* it was contained, but the millions displaced and the thousands dead would disagree. Kasey certainly did.

"Have you ever heard of Roanoke?"

Kasey shrugged. "No."

"A colony called Roanoke vanished. Old English colony that when suppliers came back, the entire colony disappeared." Respow grabbed a glass of some putrid, brown alcohol. Kasey recognized the whiskey scent, Peyton's favorite. "We have a missing colony."

"Missing?" Kasey made a puzzled face. It wasn't uncommon for colonies to experience some form of trouble. But to go missing? That was unheard of. Even the worst of raiders never went so drastic as to take hostages.

Respow nodded. "They've gone dark. Satellite is operational, comms are open, but no one is answering. Around ten hours ago, communication with everyone stopped."

"Why are we being sent there?" Kasey asked. "We need real investigators not just PTF."

"It's a special colony. In a remote part of the Galaxy. The first official integrated colony." Respow underlined four or so lines in the report. "A colony of Psys, Orchi, Humans, and Hybrids."

"I heard about this," Kasey mumbled. "They wanted a bunch of people to join." Kasey skimmed through the report, noting and highlighting details that stuck out to him.

Respow took a breath. "I don't think I need to explain the magnitude of this."

"No," Kasey whispered. "You don't. A missing colony is bad enough to bring up Sapien terrorist rumors. But a missing colony of multiple species is bad enough to bring up—"

"War," Respow finished.

Kasey gulped. The Human Civil War, which usually everyone just called the Sapien War, had just ended. The Galaxy was supposed to be at peace since Humanity's integration into the Galactic Union. But an entire colony mixed with Orchi and Psys—the two most populous species in the Galaxy— would be the perfect powder keg for Sapien. The Human-first terrorists would point to this—a malfeasance by the aliens Humanity could never trust. This couldn't get out.

Respow dragged his hand through his hair, pushing it back and following his scar up his face. "We need this quiet. If word gets out, things will be bad."

"But I'm not really an investigator," Kasey protested.

Respow had a slanted smile and he gave a light scoff. "But you adapt. I remember Musk Station."

Why'd he have to bring that up? Kasey didn't want to talk about Musk Station, he didn't want to think about Musk Station, he didn't want to be remembered in connection to Musk Station. He'd spent years trying to bury information about his connection. Kasey slammed his eyes shut, wiped his mind clear of the name, and turned on his heel.

"Got it," Kasey said. "I'll get ready."

Respow grabbed Kasey's arm, clutching it and pulling him back. "Before you go, I need to emphasize that this mission needs to quiet. Things are fragile. The Representatives appreciate your cooperation."

"Understood," Kasey said.

"I know you do," Respow reiterated. "You know the importance of a secret."

Chapter 5

Tsarena

"Tacos?" Falisto asked Tsarena.

She sighed. "You like tacos that much?"

Falisto stretched into downward dog as the Navigator reached *the Irene*. "No, I just like their fish."

"This is why Humans think Psys are just cats." Tsarena rolled her eyes. "You're not helping your case."

"Convergent evolution." He continued stretching, moving off the Navigator.

"Do you like cats?" she asked.

He responded with a growl, then said, "If cats were on Katree we'd have slaughtered them."

Tsarena chortled. "Remind me to tell you not to babysit any of my pets."

They wove through pockets of Hybrids flooding *the Irene*. The ship's size overwhelmed Tsarena, but with groups in every corner, it didn't seem as oversized as she remembered. Occasionally, Tsarena glanced at Falisto, catching his eyes glazed over and glued to the ground. He didn't walk with the same swagger as usual, and he had less quips.

The taco restaurant shined in a nebula of colors, with pink-colored drinks, tan and green palm trees, and blue-painted oceans on the walls. An android stood at the host stand, following the color scheme of *no* color scheme, and directed them to a table for two.

"This way, please." The android rolled along the white paneled floor, directing them to one of a myriad of open tables. Unlike an organic host,

40

the android never honored "usual seats" or preferences. Everything came down to a science, and that science concerned itself with only one thing: maximizing profit. That's why their request to sit by the window was denied.

The "taco place" had a name, but Tsarena never bothered to remember it. After all, it was the only place in a five-hundred-light-year radius that made tacos. "The taco place" sufficed, and in some ways was an honor. Humans had only recently joined the Galactic Union, and by in large their best addition to the Milky Way was the number of foods they fried.

One of four organic waitresses sauntered over. She had green eyes and wore red headphones with a nametag dangling along her front pocket. Tsarena recognized her as the lady that usually took their order and got at least one thing wrong.

"I was wondering if I'd see you guys again," she said. "The usual?"

"No," Tsarena murmured, though the taste of her usual set of three tacos lingered on her lips. She could taste the spicy mayo sauced over battered cod. "I'll take what Falisto gets."

The waitress froze as did Falisto. The two exchanged looks before turning back to Tsarena. She looked up from the menu after a moment of silence, with both of them still staring at her.

"Are you sure?" the waitress asked.

"Yes."

Falisto scoffed, resting his spine into the leather booth. The restaurant had something the Psys insisted on: seating for all species. Particularly important for Falisto, they had a way to "sit" in chairs. The woman typed their orders into her pad while keeping direct eye contact with Tsarena.

"You realize what you're doing, right?" Falisto said.

"We come here all the time, of course I do."

He chuckled again. "I haven't seen an Orchi handle what I order."

"So full of yourself!" she fired back. "I like to experiment!"

Tsarena shook her head and brought out her pad. She skimmed through messages, praying Mahina got back to her. It wasn't like her best friend to disappear for weeks, but it wasn't so outlandish that Tsarena called the authorities. Her social media had run dry with the same old posts gathering dust.

"Is the Fusion Center still operational?" she asked.

"Why wouldn't it be?"

She frowned. "I don't know, I just don't like not hearing from Mahina so I thought maybe—."

"You really like Humans," he muttered.

"I just like people," she explained. "That's why we get along."

"Seriously though, how's that happen?"

Before he could elaborate, the waitress came back with two of Falisto's drink orders, one for each of them along with a water for Tsarena. The waitress sheepishly looked at Tsarena as she handed her water. "Just in case."

Slightly offended but thankful, Tsarena accepted and looked down into the cup.

"Looks delicious," Falisto licked his teeth. He shot Tsarena a wry look. "When you decide it's not for you, let me know and I'll eat it. Best street-fish-soup." Falisto gulped down one taco in two bites. "God, that's good."

Tsarena stabbed her cup with a spoon, fishing out a portion to try. A rancid odor made Tsarena form a sour face. She rubbed her stomach, apologizing to her digestive tract for the pain it was about to endure. Despite the smell, it wasn't as bad as she braced for. Wasn't her favorite by any means, but she didn't need the water the waitress offered.

"Back to your friend," Falisto started, watching a bit enviously as Tsarena took small bites, "How'd you get so close to a Human?"

Tsarena rolled her eyes. "Just did."

"You like her?"

"Not in the way you're suggesting."

"I'm not suggesting anything." He lifted his paws defensively.

From the other side of the restaurant, another PTF member walked towards them. Like most Orchi, he had red skin and curly hair. Tsoki was his name, and he originated from a race of Orchi with more maroon-shaded skin as opposed to the vibrant bolt-red Tsarena.

"Nice to see you two," he said, heading over. "Tsal," he said to Tsarena. "Tsal," she said back.

"All Orchi like tacos?" Falisto asked, his eyes darting between Tsoki and the remaining fish soup in Tsarena's cup.

"Just stopping by for some—" he stopped mid-sentence. "Is that?"

"Yes," Tsarena sighed. "I challenged myself."

"And how's that going?"

She held her half-full cup. "Not bad." She took another bite with half a spoonful. The further she got the harder it became literally and figuratively as the fish guts solidified at the bottom into an icy layer.

"I know someone who can finish it off," Falisto sang.

After some initial hesitation, she handed it off to him. He made quick work, record time even for him.

"Did you go to Tyol?" Tsarena asked Tsoki.

"No," he said. He sat next to her now, taking up some space she offered. "Just got back from Ryland."

"Oh God," Falisto groaned. "Who the hell sent you to that shithole?"

"That's not nice." Tsarena glared.

"Nice and honest don't go together."

"It's not all bad," Tsoki said. "The Venori were nice."

"I wouldn't use that word." Falisto pushed the two empty cups away.

"They're hard to understand," Tsarena said. "But they improve my vocabulary so that's good."

"Imagine how hard it's for me," Falisto said. "Half the time they speak my converter just mashes words together."

"Why were you there?" Tsarena asked.

"Trying to negotiate a homeworld treaty for the Venori."

"Sending an Orchi for a mission concerning the Venori doesn't sound exactly diplomatic." Tsarena took a sip of her water, thankful for the waitress.

The waitress handed off two plates of the fish "tacos." Falisto's idea of tacos was plates of fish with tortillas underneath coated in salt.

"Looks delicious." Falisto nearly salivated over the fish.

"Do you want anything?" The waitress asked Tsoki.

"No thanks, I actually need to head out."

Tsarena wished him a goodbye while Falisto dug into the plate. At one point he muttered something akin to a goodbye but his voice was muffled by fish meat swimming in his mouth.

After a few minutes of Tsarena playing with her food and stealing glances at Falisto, Tsarena asked the question plaguing her. "Are you okay?"

The suddenness stopped Falisto from attacking his final taco. "Huh?"

Tsarena licked her lips and lurched forward on the table. Her purple eyes met Falisto's marigold pair and she took a deep inhale. Reading Falisto's emotions may as well have been reading a foreign language without a converter. Like most Psys, emotions didn't come through their faces. They didn't "smile" or "frown" in the usual manner, instead a lot of emotional detection came from behavior. Though she couldn't quantify it, Tsarena knew something was off with Falisto.

Falisto closed his mouth and pushed the plate forward a bit as if his appetite dissipated. "I'm fine."

Tsarena swallowed a lump in her throat. "Okay," she said, fighting back her urge to wear him down until he'd share. "If you wanna talk—"

"—I'm fine."

* * *

Kasey

The commissary served not only the PTF and main rings of *the Irene*, but it also acted as a convenience store for visitors who succumbed to inflated prices for essentials. Kasey opened his satchel and plucked sodas from the refrigerated section next to prepared salads with dried lettuce and lab-grown tomatoes that took up half the plastic. It was an unspoken rule: never buy the premade food from the commissary unless you wanted a date with the infirmary.

An Orchi with maroon skin and slicked-back curly hair brushed up next to Kasey. "No more cola?" He sighed and cursed under his breath in a gargle

Kasey's converter didn't attempt to translate.

Kasey examined his satchel and the four aluminum cans staring back at him. With his hand, he plucked one and handed it to him. "Here," Kasey said. The Orchi's eyes were familiar, their shade of lavender.

"Thanks, Kasey," he said.

Kasey's heart quickened at the usage of his name. While the Orchi looked familiar, Kasey couldn't quite place a name to the face. Kasey narrowed his eyes when the Orchi wasn't looking, and he ransacked his brain for the name. He knew it began with a "Ts" sound but that didn't exactly narrow down the options.

"No problem." Kasey's voice trailed off as he searched for the name. He'd seen him before, he'd remember a face with symmetry like that and muscle tone that made Kasey gulp. The light bulb switched on and Kasey said the name with a smile, "Tsoki."

"I thought you forgot my name for a second," Tsoki said, joining the line of customers with Kasey. Using one of his four-fingered hands, Tsoki pointed at a Venori cashier whose station was free. "After you."

"Next," the Venori called out. Her oval eyes dug into Kasey's soul, harpooning him and dragging him closer to the register.

With red cheeks, Kasey hustled to the front, lifting his satchel to the woman. Using her three, gray tendrils, she dug into the bag and slid out the three cans. She scanned each one, and Kasey attempted to sneak a peek at Tsoki. But instead of artfully locking eyes on the beauty, Kasey only saw countless Hybrids grabbing water bottle sets and non-perishables.

Outside, Tsoki waited, already working on the cola can Kasey gave him. Kasey took small steps, taking the extra time to think of something clever to say. "That was fast."

"Which part?" Tsoki asked.

"How'd you beat me out?"

"The self-checkout," Tsoki said. "The woman opened it up when she gouged the prices."

Kasey grimaced and turned back to the commissary. He'd told Respow countless times that, although a good business strategy, the commissary shouldn't be engaging in such capitalistic practices.

"You here for the virus too?"

"Nah," Tsoki said. His lips wrapped around the top of the soda can as he inhaled the sweet liquid. "I went for the Venori homeworld situation."

"How'd that go?"

"I'm back in one piece," Tsoki half-sighed and half-laughed. "Which is more than I originally thought. You?"

"I just got back from Tyol," Kasey said, now working on his can of cola.

"I heard about that," Tsoki said. He crushed the can with his fist and tossed it into a recycler. "I'm guessing by all the Hybrids it's pretty serious." He nodded to a horde of Hybrids trampling towards the store, their luggage falling over one another. Items spilled out of a suitcase, with clothes coating the floor.

Kasey turned on his heel to help the girl whose suitcase tumbled, but the sudden movement caught Tsoki by surprise. Tsoki moved at the same time as Kasey, and with both of them trying to overcorrect, they ended up falling on the floor. Luckily for the Hybrid, the *CRASH* they made caught everyone's attention.

Kasey rubbed his behind, his tailbone aching. "Didn't mean to bring you down with me."

Tsoki grabbed the loose cans that escaped Kasey's satchel. "Here you go."

"Thanks—and sorry for taking you with me."

Tsoki smirked as he returned them. "I'll forgive you for one." He moved his eyes to one of the sodas.

Kasey laughed. "I don't need forgiveness that badly."

Chapter 6

Falisto

Falisto dreamt the night before the mission. Reading mission briefs thicker than a textbook did that to anyone. Most Psys didn't need more than four-hour increments of sleep every twenty-seven hours. Psys soldiers—which happened to be the vast majority of Psys—trained their bodies to function on less. Less everything. Sleep, food, water. It was all the same: fuel. Like any machine, the more fuel-efficient, the better.

Falisto's mother appeared in his dream, as she did all his nightmares. It was more like a memory that always left him a bit off the rest of the day. Details varied, but the bulk remained the same: they were traveling past the Tayir homeworld, a race of alien bird-bat-like creatures. They were headed towards the planet Zaming where the Psys wanted to practice hunting a non-sapient species, a promise Falisto's mother, Captain Qiula, needed to fulfill for her people.

This particular iteration had one change Falisto hadn't experienced before: his age. He wasn't in his adult body like he should've been. Instead he stood only a meter or so tall and wearing a unitard three sizes too small.

They were on the ship—Falisto didn't remember the name of it. It wasn't like *the Irene*. This one was vertical, with ledges and ladders, which were later removed for Humans and Orchi daring to travel aboard.

Captain Qiula marched ahead of Falisto. In one paw, she held her pad, while the other continued to usher Falisto closer. "Come," she commanded. She was one of the Captains for the Psys, the most powerful Nima in all the clan, and a speaker for them. Under her was Captain Bigon, a Hyoose Psys she took as her protege as a form of a peace treaty like an arranged marriage. Above them in the hierarchy was Representative Petra who planned to step down from the role.

Falisto raced to catch up to his mother by going on all fours. She caught this out of the corner of her eye. She whipped around with her nostrils flared and her eyes filled with fire. Steam left her ears and her mouth trembled with rage. "What did I say about all fours?"

Falisto cowered backward, retreating a meter or so. She continued to admonish him. "You should *never* do that. You're lucky Petra isn't watching." Claws jabbed out of her paws, a primal instinct of her own.

"Sorry, mommy."

She looked back to him but paused her venom-laced response. Part of him thought she felt emboldened to go further, correct his usage of "mommy." Instead, she loosened her tightened face and bent down to her knees so she could stare into his eyes.

For a moment, neither spoke, and they just stood in the quiet, the pair of marigold eyes locked on one another like a hunter stalking prey. She softened her eyes. "I'm sorry."

Falisto moved his head down. If he just stared at the floor, this painful moment would pass. His mother patted his head, scratching the top and reaching behind his ears. Her whiskers, black and long, brushed up against his.

"I've been too hard on you," she murmured. Falisto didn't respond, but instead looked up to his mother. "Come," she said softly. She didn't link paws with him, but she slowed her pace so Falisto needn't gallop.

After a few drop ledges, they reached the navigation room. Captain Bigon stood tall, wearing his suit and examining scans of distant ships. His twin, gray, Hyoose tails bounced around while he moved radars and comm systems. Something about Captain Bigon always made Falisto uneasy. His pupils were always thin and sinister, and he grimaced at both of them.

"Captain Qiula," Captain Bigon murmured. "The ship's just stopped."

Falisto's mother didn't look at Bigon. "Have you contacted the Tayirs to see if they stopped them?"

"No, ma'am." He straightened and kept his gaze on the screens. They were equals by title, but his mother was more experienced and by all accounts the more important.

She grunted before grabbing the intercom linked to the ship of Nima higher ups in front of them. *"This is Captain Qiula,"* Falisto's mother commanded to the ship that stopped. *"What's your status, Faixal?"*

"Ma'am," a voice began, *"our energy cells aren't working."*

She rolled her eyes. *"Why didn't pre-check catch this?"*

There was a pause. The only thing that could annoy his mother more than incompetence was slow incompetence.

"We think the engine may have a leak."

"Why didn't pre-check catch that?" She didn't raise her voice, rather, kept the same level with the same inflection. Only the tempo changed, coming out faster. That was how she kept her power.

"I-I don't—"

"I'll come with more cells." Her voice was final, and before a response was given she cut the line. "Absolute incompetence," she said only to the room.

She exhaled the anger with a breath. "Sorry." She knelt, meeting Falisto at eye level. He remembered this. The last moment he saw her. The look in her eyes—a mix of compassion and pride. "Remember," she said, almost as if she knew it were her last words to him, "if you want something done right, you have to do it yourself." It was a saying that she repeated to him, always parading the idea of independence despite preaching unity to everyone. Falisto hated the politics of it all.

Getting back up from her bent stance, she looked to Captain Bigon. "Tell Petra we're en route," she said. "Some incompetence is just keeping us busy."

"Yes ma'am," Captain Bigon said.

"Why you thought it was a good idea for us to come this way astounds me." She moved towards the Navigator attached to the helm. Captain Bigon didn't try to defend himself about his navigating.

"Mommy, come back soon," Falisto pleaded.

She entered the doorway, sealing herself in the Navigator. "I will," she said, her voice muffled from the metal separating them. "Don't call me mommy," she said.

He nodded, his paw touching the glass as the capsule she was in detached from the main ship. Steam hissed out.

It was only a few minutes, but Falisto remembered this part, and it was painful every single time. Her capsule zoomed into the void of space to the ship in the distance carrying Falisto's brothers, sisters, friends. The next leaders of the Nima Clan, all taught to rule just as Qiula did: with an iron, but fair, fist.

Her capsule attached to the ship, and Falisto's heart shattered as it exploded into a horrifying ball of light. No fireball, no boom, no sound. Just a blinding blast with shards of metal flying in every direction.

* * *

Kasey

Kasey noticed the coffee in Falisto's paws when they boarded the Navigator heading to the missing colony. "Thought you hated coffee?" Kasey said.

"I never said that."

Tsarena and Benjo sat in the Navigator with them. "Kasey's right," Tsarena said. "You have said you don't like coffee."

Benjo reviewed the mission brief, not saying anything to the three of them bickering. He moved his pad upwards as if to obscure them despite the translucent screen still leaving his face intact.

"I've known you for over a year," Tsarena started, "and you've definitely said you hate coffee."

"Under a year," he corrected. He then pointed to Kasey. "And we've only been on a handful of missions."

"I distinctly remember you hating it," Kasey defended. He dug his boots into the floor of the ship.

"That was black coffee."

"See now you're changing the story."

Falisto rolled his eyes. "I like *this* coffee." He lifted the paper cup. Considering it a win, Kasey let it go and took his seat along the Navigator.

Tsarena returned to her pad, looking at the mission brief like Benjo, while Falisto watched the blue light of the FTL bubble waver between shades of cerulean and turquoise.

Benjo—a Hybrid and behemoth of a man—had a stone-cold face. He stood a tall two meters, with one metal arm, two metal legs, a cybernetic neck, a robotic right eye concealed as a normal eye, and even dyed black hair. His frame was large enough to take a seat and a half, the other belonging to Tsarena.

"So, uh, Benjo," Tsarena started, "what did you do before this mission?"

"Yeah, I haven't seen you around *the Irene*," Kasey added.

Benjo lowered his shoulders and bent forward. "I usually work alone."

"Did you fight in a war?" Falisto asked.

"Sapien War or the Human Civil War depending who you ask."

"Did both of you serve?" He pointed to Tsarena and Falisto.

"Tayir War," Tsarena said. "Hyoose War *and* Tayir War for him."

"Why didn't you ask Kasey?" Falisto said with a grunt.

Benjo laughed, his tongue-in-cheek. When no one returned the laugh his face darkened. "Wait, you're serious?"

Realization hit Kasey and left him with a deep sigh. Benjo was going to tell them his not-so-secret secret.

"Kasey saved the Mars' President's son? Led to a massive blow to Sapien? Musk Station?" Each question would've made Kasey laugh had he not been panicked at the forthcoming revelation.

Tsarena and Falisto had the same reaction, each turning to him with wide eyes and jaws dragging across the floor. "How come you never said anything?" Tsarena asked, her voice low.

"I don't like talking about it." Kasey shrugged, trying to obscure the rapid tapping of his fingers. Distracting yourself—that was another tip he read for anxiety.

"You're practically a legend!" Tsarena's lips stretched out into a smile wide as Benjo was long.

"Please," Kasey said. "I rather not talk about it."

"Spoken like a true hero," Falisto quipped. "True heroes don't mention their heroic deeds."

Kasey would've objected to the notion, but the benefit of agreeing was overpowering. "Thank you, Falisto."

As if saved by the bell, Tsarena squealed at her pad. If her jaw was on the floor earlier, it now dangled out of the ship. "Excuse me," she said. Benjo moved a few centimeters back, giving her access to a little over half her seat. Her fingers trembling, Tsarena gripped the pad harder when she shifted.

"Something wrong?" Kasey asked, thankful for a change of topic.

"I know her," she said. Tsarena's purple eyes became obscured by her pupils, growing in size. "That's Mahina."

"The Human?" Falisto asked.

"She's my best friend," Tsarena huffed. "What's she doing on Porygar?"

"Well it's a colony world, did she mention settling down?" Kasey asked.

"No—not at all—she didn't even say she was going anywhere."

"Maybe you weren't best friends," Falisto chided. Kasey glared at Falisto as if to warn he had no problem with levying punishments. Tsarena was too engrossed in the image that she didn't scold Falisto.

"Our mission is to find them, so we'll do just that." Kasey stood up, taking his pad and opening up the mission details Captain Respow sent earlier.

Falisto sharpened his claws, using a switchblade to cut away blunt layers. His fur changed color depending on the light. In bright areas, his fur blotted with dots of caramel, mixed with streaks of honey-gold and tan. But in darker environments, his fur appeared chestnut with a few specks of milk chocolate. One thing was constant: his golden-yellow eyes with thin pupils that had a propensity to find your soul.

"Respow put us together because there could be foul play," Benjo said.

"We don't know that for a fact," Kasey cautioned. He scanned the report again, looking for details about the mission he might have missed.

"Page eight, last sentence in the third paragraph." Benjo didn't bat an eye, reciting it off the top of his head. That wasn't a Hybrid trick or talent. That was Benjo being "Benjo the know-it-all" trick. He was always able to quote and reference things on a whim. Kasey remembered that during PTF orientation.

Kasey scrolled from page forty. He marked the location of the quote. "Hostile forces are unlikely." Kasey closed out of the report. "See?"

Outside the FTL bubble, a speck of space dust hurled the Navigator off course for a split second, breaking Kasey's balance. Before tripping to the ground, he grappled the top of the hanging bars. He sat for the rest of the flight, with his seat belt so tight that it stopped blood flow at his waist. Kasey reminded himself that Respow insisted this model had zero incidents, but Kasey doubted such an unrealistic statistic.

"Think we'll find anything?" Falisto asked.

"Unlikely," Benjo announced, his voice devoid of compassion. "The longer someone's missing, the less likely they're alive."

"So that's a no?"

"It's a 'if' we find them, it's probably going to be dead."

Tsarena croaked, passing through the colonists' photos again.

"We'll find them. Alive," Kasey assured.

Falisto spoke in a raspy voice, "Don't worry, Tsarena." Falisto and other Nima Psys shifted their dialect in recent years, mixing with common Human languages across the galaxy, giving converters a run for their money.

"You think this has anything to do with the virus?" Kasey asked.

"Unrelated," Benjo stated. There's Hybrids, Orchi, Psys, and Humans on the planet, the virus only attacks Hybrids."

"Things have been weird." Kasey pulled his pad, opening his report for the Tyol mission. "First the virus but not even a full day later a missing colony."

"But the two are so different," Benjo explained. "Virus and missing colony? That's comparing ice to fire."

Before Kasey could interject, Captain Respow called the group. Using his pad, Falisto answered for everyone, Captain Respow now filling the screens attached to the sides of the Navigator. His white hair combed over and peeked out from under the hat fashioned like a beret.

"Team," he said. "Have you gotten acquainted with one another?"

"Yes, sir," Benjo said. He saluted, straightened his posture, and looked forward but to no one in particular.

"So, I'm gonna go over the details one more time." Respow slid through pages. "Porygar is tidally locked, so don't stray from the only habitable ring of land. Go to the cold side you'll freeze to death, go to the hot side you'll melt. Pressure is normal, oxygen is a bit higher, overall a nice twilight colony."

"Got it," Kasey said.

"Oh and a reminder," he said, his voice deep but carrying the vibration of thunder. "Keep this quiet. This isn't a mission we want eyes on. I know the Orchi and Psys Captains probably said the same thing to each of you, but it remains crucial."

Each of them nodded in agreement.

Kasey raised his hand. "What's the protocol if we find a bunch of survivors?"

"Report it to me," he said.

"That's it?" Kasey asked. "Can we let them call their families and—"

"—No, just call me, and under no circumstances use public comms. I don't want to explain how a whole colony went missing. That's not something the Commission wants to deal with."

Kasey rolled his eyes out of view. *Commission that, commission this.* The Commission was made of the three main Representatives: Mayah, Tsperi, and Petra. One Human, Orchi, and Psys. Though several smaller species had Representatives, they didn't makeup the Commission because their numbers were far too small. Afterall, Humans, Orchi, and Psys made up around 70% of the sapient life in the Galaxy. Kasey never found it fair, depriving representation to smaller species but also ordering them to pay trillions in taxes didn't scream benevolent galactic empire.

"Everyone good?" Captain Respow asked.

"Yes sir." Kasey nodded.

The video feed cut and Kasey sat back down, sealing the seat belt tighter than last time, cutting blood flow.

"What do you think happened?" Tsarena shivered, pulling herself into a hug with her four-fingered arms wrapping around her.

"Could be a number of things," Benjo stated. "Pirates, hostile alien race, satellites went down, explosion, undetected gamma-ray burst—"

"—But we won't know until we get there," Kasey cut in.

Tsarena sighed. "I hope they're okay."

"I do too," Kasey soothed. "I do too."

Chapter 7

Lilac and buttercup-shaded flowers sprung from a dirt pathway. In the center of the settlement was a natural lake with a few lily pads dancing together. A brief gust animated the world. It wiggled flowers and rustled leaves. Tsarena took a deep breath through her nose, filling her lungs and belly with the air of the world. She didn't want to let it go. This was *real* air.

Infrastructure wrapped around the lake, with several pipes snaking into cabins. Some homes had docks stretching out to the lily pads as if they invited the green leaves in. The cabins shared one thing: the type of wood. Oak and mahogany planks formed the homes. While a few towered upwards into multistory complexes fanning out horizontally, a sizable minority preferred a quaint and modest approach with a flat cabin with a single bedroom.

"Do you hear that?" Tsarena held her hands up, letting the next gust slither between her fingers. Everyone stopped moving and listened for a moment.

"No," Benjo muttered.

"Exactly." She turned with her arms stretched. "It's like we're alone."

"Let's investigate." Benjo picked his boots up from a bed of flowers.

"Two groups," Kasey said. "Falisto, you're with me."

"We'll take the right side," Tsarena said.

With another word, they split up. Tsarena jogged while Benjo walked, his long legs matching her baby steps. Halfway to a cabin, Tsarena grew annoyed with her hair dangling forward in front of her eyes. She tied her curly hair into a bun, the brown and black spirals revolving around one another and puffing out.

Resting by the lake, the first home had an open window perched upwards. It was tiny and flat to the ground. Chipped white paint covered the base of the window, with plants sprouting from pots of soil. She couldn't make out all the plants based on the leaves from under the windowsill, but she could distinguish the scent of peppermint, something Mahina swore was "to die for."

"Think we can fit?" she asked Benjo. Her fingers nearly reached the base of the windowsill when she went on her tippy toes.

Benjo huffed, "You can." He took a knee, cupping his hands together. "Come on."

She did as asked and placed her foot along his metal grip supported by his fleshy hand. He thrust her upward without warning, chucking her through the window. She rolled inside less than gracefully, knocking over a table and sending most of the potted plants to their demise.

She grimaced and groaned, wiping off some weird Human concoction of eggs and cheese dampening her clothes. She rushed back to the window and looked down at Benjo. The window was nearly eye level to him. Tsarena assessed his size and approximated the dimensions of the window before letting her mind do the math.

"I think you can get in," she squealed. "Let me just clear this." She moved the table along the eggshell-colored wall and cleared what few things survived her entry roll. Her gentle movements morphed into exaggerated shoves as she pushed everything away.

"Or," Benjo suggested after a moment of Tsarena cleaning. "You could open the door." He pointed his metal finger to the entrance.

Tsarena blushed as much as an Orchi could, her red cheeks turning fuchsia. With her eyes staring at the floor and arms glued to her sides, she walked over to the door and opened it. Benjo greeted her with a smirk. Tsarena tried to avoid his gaze, but he was unrelenting.

"Much easier," he teased. Tsarena went to shut the door behind him but stopped herself after recalling the deafening silence. They were alone.

For a missing colony, the cabin was shockingly clean. (Minus the Tsarena inflicted damage.) Everything had a place: the sink was empty, blankets were folded, floors were vacuumed, counters were wiped, and even coasters were stacked underneath the coffee table.

A smile crossed Tsarena's face, and she sashayed towards photographs in the corner of the room, hanging alongside a cabinet. Mahina owned this cabin. She'd known it as soon as she smelled fresh peppermint, but further confirmation came through the photographs. Each was a slice of life, with Tsarena in most of them. Her grin grew with each picture.

Mahina wasn't someone Tsarena described with words. That's why when Benjo inevitably asked Tsarena about Mahina she struggled. Mahina was much better captured by her actions. Tsarena met Mahina on Earth, a trite interaction during a tour of the Washington Monument. She'd asked her for a piece of gum, something Humans and Orchi shared in their diets. After two chomps of the Orchi sugar stick, Mahina insisted they go for a swim on the water world, Poseidon. The second time they met was at the aforementioned surfing lesson where Mahina asked for every single update on Tsarena's life despite barely knowing her. The third time they came together they played zero-gravity laser tag. All hangouts were planned by Mahina, she was the creative one with the inventive ideas. Tsarena didn't mind.

Tsarena's fingers grazed the photographs as if wistfully reading a journal. Memories sparked through glass-protected images, and some frames even played bite-sized, audio-less videos. Countless people appeared in pictures Tsarena couldn't recognize, but that was normal. A person like Mahina always had many friends.

"Where was that?" Benjo held up a photo of Mahina and Tsarena alone on a grassy field.

Tsarena laughed, "Oh that's from when we played some Human sport. I can't remember the name of it."

"Frisbee?" He asked, pointing to the orange disc in Mahina's hands.

"Yes!" Tsarena beamed.

Tsarena accepted the photo from Benjo, looking at her and Mahina both smiling after tossing around the strange disk. Tsarena had fun, but she never mastered flicking her wrist. She would've blamed it on the biomechanics of Orchi, but if any aliens mirrored Orchi, it was Humans.

While the photos infatuated Tsarena, Benjo's eyes shifted to a rock levitating in the corner. He stepped around the nostalgic-trapped Tsarena. Somehow, the rock was luminous—hovering and glowing a fierce blue. Its light coated the oak walls, mixing in an ethereal combination of blue shine and chipped-white paint.

Tsarena broke her gaze. "What's that?"

"Don't know." Benjo grazed the rock, following edges and sharp points. "It's cold."

Tsarena stole a look back at the photos. "Maybe you can scan it?"

"Not a bad idea." Benjo handed her the rock and stationed his palm over it and her hands. The rock made Tsarena shiver, with her hands trying to save any bit of warmth. Screeching beeps chirped from Benjo's metal portions. He moved his pad and stared at the progress bar that appeared.

Cold air penetrated through Tsarena's fingertips the longer she held it. She wanted to pull her hand back, but forced it to weather the storm. The scanner ramped up, with red lights moving across each jagged edge from Benjo's scanner.

"Huh," he stammered.

"What?"

"It's weird." Benjo craned around the object, looking at it from every possible vantage point.

Tsarena glanced at Benjo's pad and read the data. "Rhodium, calcium, and—"

"—Unknown," Benjo finished. Tsarena squinted, further scrutinizing the data as if the word "unknown" would change if she just stared hard enough.

"Is it your equipment?"

With an offended scoff, Benjo shrugged. "It's possible, but my diagnostics didn't say anything." He split screen the pad, pulling up a diagnostic check he ran earlier.

"See?" He pointed to green check marks and the boldface "proficient" label at the end.

Tsarena shrugged and they moved on to the bedroom. Inside, one bed rested in the center. It was simple—a black comforter for colder months without a duvet cover and gray sheets with matching pillowcases. One throw blanket, in her favorite tone of lavender, crossed diagonally in the left corner with its tassels hanging down to the floor.

"She's organized," Benjo said.

Tsarena stifled a laugh. "Check under the bed."

Benjo didn't bend his knees, but rather, with an underhanded grip, lifted the bed. Light flushed the darkness underneath and revealed a cacophony of trinkets.

"Hides the mess," Benjo muttered. He placed the bed aside, leaving her clutter exposed for inspection.

Tsarena plucked an item from the pile towards the corner, a book or journal of sorts. "I bet it's her diary," she said with a mix of excitement and guilt. Gently, she licked her finger and turned the first page.

"A diary with food wrappers?" Benjo grimaced at the Space Peppermint Patty wrappers.

"She loves those things," Tsarena giggled.

Tsarena read the diary, moving past the introduction but spending a bit of time observing doodles in the margins. Her body recoiled at personal details, but she reminded herself of her mantra: the mission is to bring her back. To Tsarena's surprise, there was no mention of why Mahina moved to Porygar, her old life, or any clues as to what happened.

"Anything?" Benjo asked.

Tsarena turned to the last page, landing on an entry entitled "Eclipse." Tsarena cleared her throat, swallowed, and then read it aloud.

Eclipse:

Today was a good day—I went to the water with Sola and showed her how to fish. She's so sweet, she didn't like that the hooks tore the fish's mouths and didn't understand why people would do it for fun just to throw them back. I knew she was going to hate it, but her parents were adamant I show her, and we kept the fish.

Other than that I did some cooking, the chickens have made a shocking number of eggs in the past few days. Little angry that Sola's parents only want to grow basji, something about how the low sunlight makes them the best here and whatnot.

Oh, and the Psys here have started to warm up to us, which is nice, but also about goddamn time they did. And the [UNABLE TO CONVERT] *is growing on me.*

Tsavon reallyyyy wants me to help with the Eclipse party he's throwing. He practically begged for everyone to show up and celebrate the "once in a lifetime" eclipse. He makes it sound so majestic with the shadow. Honestly, I'm not crazy excited, but there isn't anything else to do on this "paradise." I can't wait to go home.

I know I didn't make a mistake, but I can't help but pray that the Primer initiative doesn't last much longer.

I'll update this after the eclipse, let's hope that it actually is as good as Tsavon's making it out to be.

As Tsarena finished, Benjo paced, scratching his temple with his metal index finger. "Hmph," he huffed.

"What's a Primer?" Tsarena asked. Her index finger equivalent tapped the word.

"Colonists that come for a short time," he explained.

"So, she was coming back." Tsarena lit up. She knew her best friend wasn't going to just up and leave without as much as word.

Benjo continued pacing before snagging another look at the journal. "Do you remember Tsavon from the colonist lists?"

Tsarena looked at the ceiling as if the answer was there. "I don't think so?" She moved to her pad, opening up the mission brief the Orchi Representative, Tsperi, sent her in addition to Respow's.

Benjo double-tapped his implant and spoke over the comms. "*Kasey, do you have the list of colonists handy?"*

After a moment, the list of colonists overtook Benjo's pad. He turned to Tsarena. "Can you hand me the journal?"

He did a few different searches, but all produced the same result: *no matches found.*

Benjo pinged Kasey and the others. *"There's mention of a colonist that isn't listed."*

"Could be a visitor," Tsarena suggested.

"He didn't sound like a visitor," Benjo countered, looking right at Tsarena. *"Hosting a party, written about in a journal."*

Falisto spoke through the comms, interrupting the conversation between the two of them. *"Kasey has the visitor logs. Can you say his name again?"*

"Tsavon," Tsarena said.

Kasey typed, the sounds echoing through Benjo's and Tsarena's comms. *"No matches in any logs."*

"Have you found anything?" Tsarena asked.

"Some evidence of a struggle," Kasey said. *"Some blood, turned over chairs, but no bodies. There's some mud by the lake, and a couple of bottles and glasses there too."*

"No bodies here either," Benjo said.

Tsarena interjected, *"Anything else?"*

"Not yet, just some weird rocks in a few of the cabins on hover plates."

"We found some too," Tsarena replied. *"Blue, cold, and suspended in the air?"*

"Negative," Kasey boasted. *"Ours were violet, and warm."*

"Hot." Falisto corrected. *"Looked like it wanted to explode."*

"Hm," Tsarena hummed. *"We'll keep looking, we took ours as a sample."*

"Got it," Kasey responded, tapping out of the comms.

* * *

Kasey

Falisto tapped Kasey's shoulder with one paw, the other pointing to another cabin around a hundred feet away.

"Do you see that?"

Kasey squinted. "The cabin?"

"Yeah, that one." His pupils dilated, filling all of his eyes.

"What about it?"

"The door's knocked over," Falisto whispered, drawing his Slart.

Kasey nodded and moved his hand signaling their movement.

"*Benjo, Tsarena, we have a door toppled over, we're heading there now,*" he whispered. He silenced his pad, darkening the screen. The two duck-walked, crouching alongside other cabins as barricades. Taking baby steps, they inched closer and closer.

Kasey peered inside the doorway. Laying on the floor, the door splintered in several directions, shredded apart from claw marks. Kasey took note of it, trying to ascertain if Falisto's paw could inflict similar damage.

Inside, a bookcase rested on its side, with several books sprawled open to random pages. Water from the sink dripped, overflowing and leaving behind a small puddle with dishes piling in the well. A portion of the wooden floor caved in and deep scratch marks similar to those on the fallen door.

"Don't think a Human could've done that," Kasey whispered.

Falisto pointed to the floor. "I *wish* I could do that." His nails emerged from his furry paws. Kasey noted the difference.

"Psys can't, Humans can't, Orchi probably can't."

"Probably another species," Falisto said.

All the remaining doors were ajar—except one with dried blood pooling outside of it. Kasey double-tapped Falisto, who had just relaxed his knees. He pointed to the blood.

The two nodded. Both of them bent down again. Falisto took the left, Kasey took the right. They moved closer. Their backs hit the wall. Kasey looked at Falisto. Falisto looked back. Kasey held out his hand. He counted down. Three. Two. One.

Chapter 8

Kasey

Kasey's leg hinged with his hip as he thrust his right foot forward. The door fell to the floor as light from the main room poured into the darkness, illuminating the coat closet. Two streams of blood converged from one river fresher than the rest. Human shoes perched up from behind a mountain of uniforms and jackets. A little girl with mocha skin and pastel beads in her hair rested along the wall. One palm faced up, her fingers icicles, while her other arm gripped a sheep plushie.

Kasey parted the sea of red jackets to the sides, exposing the girl to Falisto's Slart's light. A large gash with claw marks crossed her stomach, and her clothes were tattered and drenched.

Shutting off his Slart, Kasey collapsed on both knees and rushed his fingers to her neck. They raced up and down, unable to sense a vein. He shifted gears, placing his index and thumb around the girl's exposed wrist.

"It's faint," Kasey beamed. "But she's got a pulse." Her beat quickened, his voice triggering a twitch in her fingers. Her eyes were sealed airtight, but her lips struggled to whisper something.

Falisto called Tsarena and Benjo over the comms, "*We found someone!*"

Kasey hooked his arms underneath the girl, scooping her away from the floor of coats. Her breath seeped out of her lips as she tried to form words.

"*This is Kasey to the Navigator,*" he shouted. "*We need immediate medical evac!*"

"*Back to the Irene?*" the pilot asked. He hadn't factored much in the mission, just listening to God-awful music and ramming into loose matter.

"No time, we need a closer one now!"

"The closest hospital is on Kyros."

Kasey cursed. Respow's words echoed in his head, the order requiring them to keep this mission quiet at all costs. Kyros was the biggest megastructure in the Galaxy, housing countless people across species.

"There's not another hospital?" Kasey bellowed.

The pilot made some noises over the comms with a star map beeping in. *"None."*

"Damn it!" Kasey yelled. He brought the girl to the couch, laying her so the blood wouldn't rush to her wounds. He brushed off the array of trinkets littered over the couch. Falisto got her a glass of water, forcing her to drink while her hand twitched. Her other arm kept her sheep in a necklock, refusing to leave the bloodstained animal.

Tsarena and Benjo leaped through the doorway moments later. Inside, Tsarena slid on her knees towards the girl.

"Do we have anything to cover it? Any antiseptic?" Kasey asked.

"I have some," Tsarena said. "But it's not gonna be enough."

"Look around for something," Kasey ordered. He joined in the notion, checking drawers and cupboards for something. Anything. Benjo rummaged through the bathroom, opting to break the mirror cabinet instead of opening it. He passed each row, discarding useless items before finding hydrogen peroxide.

Armed with it, he came back and poured it over the wounds. The girl didn't react, but her body did. Her once barely moving hands convulsed and made a frozen fist covered in blood. The sheep wasn't spared either, his neck getting wrung out by the cobra death squeeze of her fingers.

"She needs a doctor," Tsarena cried. "An IV, fluids, blood transfusions." Using both hands, she pressed onto the gashes. "Someone get more water!" Tsarena pushed gauze down on the tears in the girl's stomach.

Falisto hurried back with water, more in the glass this time. Tsarena force-fed her, tilting her head up and dribbling it into her mouth.

"She needs a doctor!"

"Only one nearby is Kyros," Kasey said. "It's gonna take four hours just to get to *the Irene*."

"We can't go to Kyros," Benjo dismissed. He puffed his chest up and crossed his arms. "We have strict orders."

"She doesn't have four hours, she has four minutes!" No one needed a degree in physiology to know that much blood loss teetered on fatal. "We can call an emergency evac!"

Tsarena's pleading eyes sought Falisto and Kasey then veered back to Benjo. For a brief moment, none of them didn't say anything. Tsarena's mouth trembled as she looked back at the girl.

"You can't be serious?" Tsarena shouted in disbelief. "We aren't leaving her to die!"

"*Kasey,*" the pilot said again. "*I don't think I have enough fuel to get us to Kyros, let alone the Irene. We need to charge up.*"

"We need to call for help!" Tsarena urged. Her teeth chattered as she pressed on the wounds. A mask of dark red flushed her face, and as she screamed, tears formed in the corner of her eyes. "She's going to die!"

"If we call for help it's gonna put Porygar on the map," Benjo said. "I'm sorry, but we can't help her."

"Benjo is right," Falisto said. "Their Captain was clear." He pointed to Kasey, then Benjo.

Tsarena glistened with tears as she locked eyes with Kasey's. Her lower lip trembled and the hair from her forehead obscured some of her face. "Please, Kasey." She held onto the girl's hand. Somehow, the girl's skin turned ghastly since her removal from the closet.

A compromise could be a call to all military channels. It wouldn't reach the public like Respow insisted on, but it didn't guarantee medical units. A general call meant letting everyone in the universe know something happened on Porygar. No matter how it got sliced, calling anyone would jeopardize the mission. And Respow was clear.

But this was a life. He wouldn't let someone die. Not on his mission, not again.

"*This is Kasey from the Peacekeeping Task Force broadcasting on all channels for an emergency medical evac. I repeat: this is Kasey from PTF requesting emergency evac. I have a girl that can't be older than ten who needs immediate medical treatment.*"

Gravity wrenched tears out of Tsarena's eyes. They trickled onto the girl's forehead resting in her lap. Trembling, Tsarena managed to crack a smile as if to say "Thank you." In the corner, Benjo shook his head, reluctantly helping Tsarena lift the girl.

After only twenty seconds, the first response came in. "*This is Yolanda Smith calling from Navigator-12b.*"

"*Ms. Smith—hi, we're on Porygar—I have the coordinates ready to send to you!*" Tsarena shouted. The words came out all at once and she had to repeat it two more times. With each repetition, she got more coherent.

"*ETA is about two minutes.*"

They sprinted out of the home. "Her name—I think she's Sola." Tsarena's voice carried a sense of hope.

"I saw her on the lists," Benjo murmured.

"Anything unique about her?" Falisto asked.

"Not that I recall."

"Benjo," Kasey said. "See if there's any other survivors. If we're saving one, we might as well save anyone we can."

"I'll scan for heat signatures," Benjo said. "She didn't come up the first time so I doubt we'll get anything."

Slowly, they lowered Sola along a bed of flowers outside the home. The buttercups welcomed her body, decorating her outline in a golden aura from their petals bending and weaving around her. In the sky, one of the moons wandered to its rightful spot, lighting up the otherwise dark atmosphere. Several stars dotted the space visible to them, and Kasey wondered which one would arbitrate his military infraction. Military tribunals were bad enough, but a military tribunal with Respow? Kasey didn't want to think about that.

Kasey confirmed the point for the landing of the Navigator over the comms, signaling it with his pad. With just a few seconds, she zoomed in above them.

"You shouldn't have done that," Benjo chided to Kasey. Then he spoke louder for the rest of the group. "No other heat signatures except for a burner left on."

Kasey looked back at him. "I made a call," he denounced, keeping his voice low. "No one's gonna die if I can help it."

Benjo shrugged. "Now everyone has eyes on Porygar."

Kasey balled his fists. "Benjo," Kasey snapped. "If I'm gonna get it from Respow I don't need it from you."

Benjo stood firmly. He blinked for a moment before nodding. On some level, Benjo appeared to admire this side of Kasey. Kasey had no doubt Benjo believed Kasey made a horribly wrong decision, but Kasey knew on some level he respected it.

Falisto and Tsarena picked up the girl, Tsarena holding her legs and Falisto holding her arms. When the Navigator grazed the grass and flowers, the doors flung open with several first responders running with a gurney.

They placed Sola on the satin board and wheeled her into the ship. "We got room for two more," one of the responders said.

"Falisto, Tsarena, you two go." Kasey pointed to the Navigator. "Benjo and I will keep looking and call if we need any more medical help." Kasey narrowed his gaze at Benjo as he said this, emphasizing the word "more."

"How are you gonna get to Kyros?"

"We'll probably have to go back to a fuel station on the way to *the Irene*."

The first responders exchanged looks. "We'll leave a few energy cells for your Navigator."

Kasey sighed. "Thank you, I appreciate that."

Tsarena and Falisto boarded the ship. Without Benjo squishing her against the walls of the Navigator, she could breathe, and take in one full, final inhale of fresh air. One responder shut the door, dragging it across and sealing it before it soared into the sky and disappeared.

Neither Kasey nor Benjo made eye contact. Instead, they wandered into cabins together, loosely within one another's vicinity. A gust of wind broke the wall of tension between them, toppling it down so Kasey could work in an icebreaker.

"A bit chilly," Kasey said. Although true, his suit kept him warm, as the unitard came equipped with thermal regulation in addition to the faulty face masks and bullet absorption.

"I like the cold," Benjo said. "But that's cause of the heat." He pointed to his metal pieces.

A few seconds passed before Benjo spoke again. "How many did you get to look through?"

"Not too many, we still need to clear out those." Kasey pointed at a series of homes squished closer than the rest. Judging by the style, he ascertained Orchi lived there with a few murals referencing the Observers.

"Divide and conquer?" Benjo asked.

Kasey grimaced, realizing the icebreaker got them talking, but didn't address any substantive issue. "I'll take these."

The two diverged from one another, with Kasey entering one. He didn't look through every nook and cranny, his mind focused too much on the girl. While his eyes scanned the materials, all he could wonder about was his impending punishment.

What was he going to say when Respow inevitably called him? Would it be an immediate punishment? Something smaller? Would they strip his PTF status?

Kasey pushed the thoughts down and reminded himself why he was there: the mission. He tried to swallow the despair but it was like a horseshoe pill or unflavored basji. Abandoning his earlier motto of vague searching, he embarked on a new scavenging. He flung open drawers, peeked behind pieces of art, and examined couch cushions all while in his trance. Whenever another unanswerable question gnawed at him, he replaced his acknowledgment with another investigation under a coaster or bar stool.

"*Kasey, you may want to see this,*" Benjo said.

Kasey shook himself into reality. "*On my way.*"

Kasey rehearsed responses for when Respow called. He didn't know which route he'd take, but he knew he needed to be somewhat cohesive. Respow loved two things to Kasey's knowledge: logic and cheesecake. Kasey didn't bake, so he'd have to settle for a logical argument.

Inside the cabin Kasey entered, Benjo studied a map nailed to the wall. Kasey didn't need a close look to recognize the topography and red and blue zones. From a few miles above, the entire colony looked peaceful. Granted, the map couldn't capture eternal twilight or blood trails. With a lake in the center and different pins marking houses, the map mirrored a murder mystery board with all the markings and post-it notes.

Motioning with his eyes, Kasey followed the circle of thumbtacks and pins dotting the map. "Any idea what those mean?"

"If I had to guess? The cabins," Benjo said.

Cocking his head to the side, Kasey tried to make sense of threads connecting some cabins before he snapped more photos with his pad. "Something doesn't feel right," Kasey murmured.

"Why's that?"

Kasey turned to meet him. "Why would someone have this? Whose cabin are we in?"

Before Benjo could answer, Kasey's eyes wandered to the corner of the room. A maple wood dresser stood out, contrasting from the oak and mahogany. "What's that?"

Benjo didn't answer at first. "A dresser?" he said, confused by the significance.

"That's not oak," Kasey murmured. He inched towards the dresser, something about it calling him. Metal handles reached outwards from the shelves. Tugging at it, Kasey couldn't get the drawer loose.

"It's locked." Benjo's metal finger pointed to a keyhole.

"This isn't something the colony would've supplied, and I doubt someone could just bring this."

"You'd be surprised what people take with them," Benjo said. "But I see your point."

"Help me break it open."

Benjo narrowed his eyes. "Why do we need to open it?"

"Because there could be evidence."

Benjo frowned. "I doubt evidence about a disappearance would be kept in something inside the colony."

Kasey forced a calm energy wave to wash over him. "Just help me."

Benjo rolled his eyes but complied. Kneeling, Benjo removed the other drawers and cast them aside less than gently.

"Let's not try and not destroy the entire place," Kasey cautioned.

"Oh so now we care about their property?" Benjo fired back.

Kasey ushered another self-soothing wave, but this one failed to keep it at bay. "Benjo, I'm team lead." He turned his eyes to him, looking down on the kneeling Benjo while Kasey stood tall. "You do as I say."

Benjo blinked then went back to examining the keyhole. His mechanical eye looked through and scanned it. "Clothes. Loose papers. And something else. I think we're gonna need to shoot it open."

"Stand back." Kasey drew his Slart, slipping towards the lethal bullets. After Benjo retreated, Kasey fired two rounds into the lock, leaving behind energy residue and marks along the mahogany.

Kasey wiggled the drawer, piercing parts of the wood and splintering it. With it open, Kasey sifted through papers. He clawed out an object and dragged it from the depths. He wasn't sure what it was until he got his entire hand around it.

His fingers decoded the clues. First, the grip, made with four fingers in mind. Second, a trigger. Third, a barrel extending outwards. Compact but surprisingly heavy, the foreign gun in Kasey's hand was all wrong. There was nowhere for his pinky to go, and without it, the gun challenged his grip.

"What's this doing here?" Kasey asked. He peered at the gun trying to find a safety setting. For all intents and purposes, Kasey felt like he wielded an old weapon, like one of those pistols in old movies just with a bit more tech and white.

Benjo swiped the gun, safety be damned. He studied the object, arching his head and neck around the sides. The trigger, orange in color, contrasted with the rest of the gun, a striking cream.

"This is an Orchi gun," Benjo postulated. Like Kasey, his pinky flailed around in the air before joining his ringless-ring finger, mirroring an Orchi hand.

"What's an Orchi gun doing here?"

"Well, it is a mixed colony," Benjo reasoned.

"Okay," Kasey retorted. "What's *a gun* doing here?"

Benjo cocked his eyes back at him. "That's the million-dollar question."

Before Kasey could play a round of Speculate Why a Colonist Had a Gun, a sharp ring screeched in his ears. It thumped his head, reverberating and bouncing around from his comms implant to his eardrum. His heart rate skyrocketed when he discerned the tone and his chest dampened with sweat. Dryness settled in his throat, and words couldn't form. *Here we go.*

"*Captain Respow,*" Kasey answered, locking eyes with Benjo as if to say *oh shit.*

"*Mako,*" the voice shouted. His tone made Kasey yearn for the ringing. "*Care to explain why I have requests for comments about an injured girl on Porygar?*"

Kasey bit his sarcastic tongue, but the urge almost took over. Instead, he swallowed. "*Sir, she was going to die.*" Ah, the sincere route. Maybe Respow would respond to that—

"*I don't give a rat's ass if she was the Representative's child—I gave you an order and when I give you an order you follow it!*"

"*I understand, sir.*"

"*Do you? Because calling for medical attention on public stations when I explicitly said to keep the mission quiet doesn't scream 'understanding.'*"

He was right. Kasey *didn't* understand. Keeping the public at bay didn't scream a benevolent union. Even if it did, he couldn't excuse the hiding of the truth. This was a public matter and deserved public attention. After a moment's pause, he defended, "*She needed help.*"

"*And I needed you to keep this quiet.*"

Kasey sighed, "*I know, sir.*" Part of him needed to apologize—but he wouldn't when he knew he made the right call. Another brief pause ensued, Captain Respow's stomps echoing through the call.

"*This isn't something I take lightly.*"

"*I know, sir.*" Kasey visualized Respow shaking his head over the line. Light years away, the tension in Respow's room metastasized to Porygar.

If Kasey closed his eyes, he could picture Respow thrashing around, taking papers his subordinates prepared for him, and throwing them about angrily.

"*Send me your report. I'll be in contact.*"

Kasey's beating heart slowed, but only to the base level anxiety. Before he could say anything, the call cut, and Kasey stood still in the silence.

"You okay?" Benjo asked.

"Yeah," Kasey said. "Let's just finish up and head to Kyros."

Chapter 9

Kasey and Benjo

Benjo peeked out the window of the Navigator towards Porygar with Kasey across from him. He enjoyed views of planets from different distances. It grounded him. Somehow, seeing vast amounts of immeasurable matter made him realize how massive the universe was. He didn't think of himself as an existential type of person, instead, he much preferred thinking about everything mechanically. Benjo was a cog in the machine, and in other ways, Benjo was the machine. Easy to fix, easy to understand, easy to make. Simple.

But Benjo couldn't enjoy the view with the pilot's choice of music. That was something that always bothered Benjo: experimental music. Benjo recalled the time before aliens were discovered, back when music still resembled art. He didn't *hate* alien music, but he did hate how alien culture got its Venori tendrils and Psys claws into Human music. Artists went through another renaissance, taking inspiration from (and sometimes plagiarizing) other genres untouched by Humans.

The gurgling sounds made by the singer mirroring an Orchi made Benjo shake. The pilot pushed the energy cell's capabilities.

Kasey sat behind the pilot and across the small aisle from Benjo. Kasey didn't sit there because he was a fan of alternative space-pop. Rather, he knew statistics indicated a 4% higher survival rate of people behind the pilot compared to the rest of the ship. Pilots wouldn't ram their side of the ship intentionally (usually).

Kasey couldn't think about music anyway—his mind was occupied with

Respow. He tried to focus on the positive: he made the moral choice. But morality and war didn't share common ground any more than oil and water.

He saved a life, even if it meant nuking someone else's political career. A trivial price to pay. (Un)fortunately, a sharp piece of the rock samples sliced him through a bag held, lassoing his mind back to the present.

He winced, a droplet of blood dripping over the bag, now compromised from the rock's breach. Benjo looked over, his own hands full with Orchi ammunition discovered in the same cabin as the pistol.

Benjo drew the weapon from its newfound plastic home, holding it up and rotating it. "Shame Tsarena isn't here," he sighed. "She'd know what it's for."

"We'll see her soon." Kasey placed his lips around his wound, risking the germs and sucking the blood.

"Want another look?" Benjo handed the gun to Kasey.

When the gun exchanged hands, the weight surprised Kasey, sinking him to the floor. "Orchi got some great grip strength." Kasey carried it with both hands now, a drop of sweat descending along his back.

With it in his hands, Kasey looked at a twenty-pound weight called an Orchi gun. It didn't have a clear way to pull the magazine. There was no way it was standard GUM tech. Although he yearned to experiment with the pistol, Kasey elected to only do so much poking and prodding. One wrong pull could bring out a stray bullet, and that would eliminate the 4% bonus he got sitting behind the pilot.

As he holstered the gun, his thumb grazed a section by the trigger, and the clip loosened, shedding half of the twenty pounds into his lap with a *thump!* After a momentary panic, he picked up the fallen ammunition which made up the weighty portion of the now empty gun.

"Do Orchi use heavy bullets?" Kasey asked.

"Not sure," Benjo shrugged. "Most species use energy weapons." Benjo waited for a lull in the song before turning to Kasey. "Can I ask you something?"

Kasey whipped back from the pad in his lap. He'd begun searching databases for information about the gun and bullets. "What's up?"

"What made you call for medical aid?" Benjo asked. "You knew you'd be punished."

Kasey took a glance away and then back at Benjo. "I think life—saving a life—is important above all else," he said, finally.

"You probably strained your relationship with Respow."

"But I —" he stopped himself. "*We* saved a life."

"*We* didn't do anything," Benjo said. "*You* made the call." His voice didn't sound accusatory, if anything complimentary with the sincerity and cadence he used.

"You wouldn't have called Respow?" Kasey asked.

Benjo sat for a minute, stumped. Like an old statue, he rested his chin over his fist and furrowed his brow. "I would have tried everything before calling him," he said.

"But you would've eventually?"

Shifting a bit in his pose and moving his arm from his neck he looked at Kasey directly. "I don't think so."

A shiver made Kasey's body shake as the pilot put on another song. The loud music echoed across the Navigator, cutting their conversation. Kasey thought about saying something. Not a counter, but something to try and better understand the enigma named Benjo.

Kasey's pad notified him about the impending route. A few minutes and they'd be on Kyros, the ship housing every known species in some cosmic capacity. Deciding to use his time efficiently, he navigated to some news sites.

His eyes ran through an article detailing the Tyol virus, and how the brave PTF ventured in the mine. Kasey didn't mind fluff pieces when they spared identifying details. Ever since Musk Station, Kasey had avoided his photograph or name appearing in search engines. He could shed the name Kasey Mako, but that would sever one of the last remaining ties to his family. He wouldn't do that. He couldn't. Respow aided in burying the name, mystifying it as much as one could, but that only did so much.

After skimming past a few articles, one caught Kasey's eye—the Tayir War Anniversary. While Humans "conquered" the galaxy and seeded local stars from Earth, the center and majority of the galaxy, engaged in a bloody conflict. Kasey knew bits about it: the Tayirs blew up a Psys ship, an act of war against the GU; the GU responded by destroying their planet. No Tayir survived. Not. A. Single. One.

"Approaching Kyros," the pilot announced, lowering the music's volume. The vocaloid's singing crescendoed, hopefully to the end of the song. The pilot joined in, humming the tune as dreadfully as the AI.

In the distance, Kasey could see Kyros in all its magnificent glory. The megastructure took nearly the entire GDP of the solar system and housed billions of people from all known species of sentient life. Seven large Panels stretched for miles, each with their own host of living conditions to match the needs of each.

The central Panel, Panel C, was shared by Humans, Hybrids, Psys, and Orchi. It hosted better living conditions than any naturally occurring world. At around 21° Celsius, 0.98 atmospheric pressure, twenty-two percent oxygen, and an abundance of trees and water, it was an Eden. Some species, like pure-water-born species, required ocean Panels. Not the best for Human life.

Originally, Panels for Psys and Orchi were meant to be separate, but when Humans came into the picture and construction was still in its heyday, a decision to join the three species together was made. Petitions for an eighth Panel already made their rounds in Commission meetings, and some rumblings of an independent Kyros for just Psys circulated online forums and rumor sites.

Kyros's Panels were fanned out, making a petal-like shape with a spherical center. Kyros acted as sort of a quasi-Dyson Swarm, with the Panels often flying together in a flower shape around stars to siphon its energy. Solar power was easy to convert. The tech came from the Tayirs, taken from them during the war as spoils of the bloodshed.

The pilot contacted Panel C. It notoriously had strict security, but the three of them gawked when they learned they'd be subject to a thorough screening before even entering the hangar's airspace.

"We have to be extra careful," the woman explained over the intercom.

Her booming voice replaced the pilot's singing (to Kasey's and Benjo's delight). "That virus on Tyol can't spread here."

"I appreciate that, miss," Benjo replied as the ship docked. "But I never went to Tyol, there's no way that we could be infected."

"Strict orders," she said, unapologetically.

Benjo rolled his eyes. When he looked at Kasey the light bulb went off in his head. "Forgot about you."

Kasey didn't say anything, instead, he just nodded. "Yeah, this one is on me."

Descending from the Navigator, the hatch-turned-bridge gently touched the floor of the docking station. Two Orchi came in their version of hazmat suits. They wore white, skintight latex and two pairs of goggles on.

Their throats gargled. Most of Orchi's prevalent languages sounded like a mix of someone speaking underwater while drunk. They moved their hands as they spoke as if gestures paired with the sound made it coherent. Kasey just shook his head.

"Our converters aren't picking it up," Kasey explained.

One of them loosened their mask, allowing more gurgling to escape. "*Gruguh* this better?"

"Yes," Kasey said.

"So, how did you want to test me?" Benjo asked.

One of the Orchi came forward, holding a temperature reader. Unexpectedly, he pointed it at Benjo's cyber arm, scanning it upward to his shoulder. Then his legs. Then his head.

"Tslani, can you do the full-Human?"

Benjo frowned at the diction.

Tslani smiled, walking forward with another temperature gun. She held it to Kasey's forehead and waited for a few seconds. After a sound, she peered back. "You're good to go."

"That's it?" Kasey asked.

"We don't think normal Humans carry it."

"Normal?" Benjo spat.

Tslani's cheeks flushed and she tripped over her words. "I–I didn't mean any offense." She held her hands up, her palms facing Benjo, and waved them while she apologized. "I'm so sorry."

Benjo rolled his eyes while the other Orchi drew closer. Using what appeared to be a sort of exacto knife, the Orchi inched to the connecting parts of the metal elbow.

"May I?"

"May you what?"

"I need to take a small sample of the metal arm."

"Okay this is ridiculous," Benjo complained.

"Sir, we're just trying to protect the masses."

"I know it's your job, but I'm telling you not to worry."

"If you're not sick," the Orchi contended, "then you won't mind me running a quick sample. I don't need much."

Reluctantly, Benjo forwarded his elbow to the Orchi. He scrapped the metal, shearing off a chunk and carefully letting it fall into his glove-covered palms.

A robot holding several forms of microscopes came to the side like a waiter with finger foods at a party. Kasey thought for a moment to pull out the Orchi bullets and ask them about it, but Benjo stowed them away deep in their luggage. Instead, they proffered the rock samples which they seized without as much of an explanation.

The unintroduced Orchi placed a sheet and then the sample of Benjo's arm underneath an older-looking microscope. When he bent over to look through the hazmat suit, the goggles linked with the eye of the scope, connecting the two.

Using his fourth finger, he scanned the piece of metal, probably seeking microbiological action that would render him unsafe. He turned the dial on the side, then maneuvered the film around with the metal piece. When he finished, he almost seemed disappointed.

"You're good to go."

Tslani took off her helmet, revealing dyed red hair matching her skin. Benjo turned his gaze to her, forgetting the comment she'd made earlier about normal Humans and getting just as red as her.

"Welcome to Kyros."

The two Orchi ushered them out, with the pilot saying he'd remain at the docks. Their bags, despite flagged for further search, were surrendered back to them following a flash of rank. PTF had its perks. Their rock samples were still in holding, but neither of them wanted to spend any longer in the agonizing processing.

The two followed the winding decks of Panel C, climbing steps to the main district. Kasey rolled up his sleeves, letting the artificial breeze generated once per hour graze his arms. A part of him missed Porygar and the dancing flowers, but the digital projection of a baby blue sky sufficed.

"Haven't had air this fresh in a while," Benjo praised.

Kasey narrowed his eyes with a frown to match. "What about Porygar?"

"Not as much oxygen," he said, taking a deep breath. "This is twenty-two-point-two percent, that's as good as it gets."

Kasey frowned. "You're joining me at the hospital, right?"

"I think so," he replied. "Do you know if any other PTF are here?"

Kasey pulled up his pad from his waist. "I don't see anyone."

"Good."

"Good?"

"I wasn't sure I was ready to see you get blasted by Respow."

Kasey nervously laughed. "I think we have some time before that."

Benjo pivoted his head. "I don't know. I don't want to scare you, but that conversation did not go well."

"Well, you have officially scared me."

"Kasey," Benjo began, "I want you to know I disagree with your decision."

"Well thanks," Kasey muttered.

"No—I mean, I disagree with it, but I like that you stood by it."

Kasey shot him a look. "Really?"

"Really," he said. "I am."

"I appreciate that," Kasey mumbled under his breath. The two walked in silence for a bit after, but there was a warmth there that hadn't been before. Kasey assumed that on some level Benjo respected him, but not enough to say it aloud. Maybe he was wrong about Benjo.

They passed through the Memorial Gardens—a place dedicated to those who made astonishing discoveries in science, math, and philosophy. Miguel Alcubierre for the Humans, Tsaya Tsuyon for the Orchi, and Ofelia Nima for the Psys. All had their heads carved out in different stones down to the freckle and whisker. Towards the wall, names of the veterans from the Tayir War sprawled about, etched in their native script.

"Lots of names." Benjo eyed the wall.

"Crazy to think about, that war was only a few years before we made first contact."

Benjo shook his head. "Hard to believe. That wall has got to have something in the hundred thousands."

"You think so?"

"Yeah." Benjo folded his arms. "Maybe millions."

"Including the Tayirs?"

Benjo made a face. "No Tayirs, they were the aggressors. The only thing they get is a small text box in a history book written by the GU."

Kasey grimaced. "I guess. We don't have the Sapien terrorists written in our memorial."

"Exactly."

Kasey's eyes wandered across depictions of Tayirs, all drawn or generated. Although a bird-like species, they had high-end tech, and aggression to match. One drawing that caught Kasey's attention showed the bird-monster like a harpy with fangs and ebony wings. Its knees bent backward, and its beak stained with fresh blood over an Orchi. The crow's talons dug into the Orchi's pink skin, grasping internal organs that Kasey wasn't even sure existed.

"Ever wonder what humanity would have done?" Benjo asked.

"What do you mean?"

"Do you think we," Benjo started, motioning his hand between the two of them, "would've stopped it?"

Kasey smirked. "Humanity doesn't have a good track record with other Humans. It's a miracle first contact didn't end in genocide."

"Most historical examples predate the modern age. I doubt the first colonizers ever imagined we'd have air conditioning."

Kasey suggested, "I doubt we could've done much better than the rest of the GU."

"Eh, Orchi cave in too easily, Psys always want war and act without thinking. Other species are too entertained with their internal affairs."

"And Humans aren't?" Kasey laughed. "We had a whole civil war after making first contact."

"That war was far more political," Benjo countered. "I think we would've done better if we were the GU."

"What would've you done?"

Benjo didn't struggle to find his words. "Ethnic cleansing has always been disfavored by history for a reason."

Kasey turned to him. "You're not as heartless as you think."

Benjo broke his stoic face to shed a bit of a smile. "I don't think I'm heartless. Just rational."

Kasey and Benjo came to *the Traveler* Memorial. Along the wall, a plaque of names, all scribed in gold font, ran across several meters of fencing that guarded bushes. As often as Kasey came to Kyros, he never knew where his father's name was on the list. He couldn't explain why, but something told him to check for his dad's name. It was that impulse the intrusive thought that he couldn't resist.

"Hey, Benjo, I'm gonna see if I can find my dad," Kasey said, scurrying away before Benjo could respond.

"Mako," Kasey whispered to himself as he passed by the MacDonalds, Magnolias, Majacks, all the way to Mako. Kasey read the name aloud, as Benjo hustled towards him out of the corner of his eye. "Luke Mako," Kasey sighed.

"You found him?"

"I did," Kasey said. He stared at his father's name for a minute and thought about his dad. He didn't remember much, just bits and pieces. He fabricated an image woven from details his mother told him and photos he'd seen in passing. Once he had a picture in his head he spoke again, "Let's go."

Chapter 10

Luke

24 Years Ago – The Traveler

An indigo sphere of protective energy condensed around *the Traveler* with the engine roaring across every deck. Exotic matter reached unfathomable temperatures, intense pressure pulverizing it. Space in front of the ship shrank, and distant stars brightened, as *the Traveler* headed in the direction of the "Hello" signal.

Or at least that would happen once they finally left.

Instead, for the third week in a row, the ship faced another delay. Allegedly, this was the last one—just like the last two.

Luke Mako sat alone at a table in the cafeteria and took a bite from his sandwich. The space-refrigerated "meat" and cheese hadn't tasted this good in years. Meals from when he served in the military ranged from dehydrated potatoes or water-flavored calories in something NASA assured was food. But most chefs didn't need to convince customers what they had in front of them was food.

He chomped off a corner of the sandwich where some of the cheese peeked out from blankets of bread. Food rode up the roof of his mouth, gluing to it. These were real calories. The kind he ran miles for in the morning and cut when trying to lean out.

He sat in the far corner of the cafeteria. From his vantage point, he had a good view of everyone else—the astrobiologists, the engineers and their "table," and the space marines who shared their area with the rest of the specialists. Although he belonged to every group, he didn't have a home with any.

His pad vibrated, a timer—reminding him to check on Daphne, his wife. He swiped up to the message thread they shared. Before he could type, his roommate dropped a textbook in front of him, making a *thump* on the table. Like an ancient text, a dust cloud parted when it landed.

Luke broke his gaze with his pad. Riley was the first Hybrid he became friends with—a term he still hadn't embraced in his vocabulary. Hints of the word cyborg still slept deep in his brain from when he grew up on a "Humans only" compound.

"Well, well, well," she jested. Her blue hair rested along her shoulder in a single braid. She kept it a deep blue, called nebula blue before people learned "blue" didn't do nebulae justice.

"Hey," Luke spoke, covering his mouth while he continued to munch. His tongue tried to roll, but the bread along the roof prevented him.

She sat on the stool, doing a little spin before folding her hands and cupping them in front of Luke. "Getting your last pre-flight meal?"

He smirked. "Last? You really think we're taking off today?"

"If we don't, I will," she commanded. "This ship is boring."

"Please tell me you know we're supposed to be gone a few months."

She grimaced. "Don't remind me."

Luke grabbed the soda can from the corner of his orange tray, popping it open. The loud crack was like heaven to his ears. "Want some?"

Riley covered her mouth before pretending to vomit. "You know I don't drink—" she paused as if the name were too hideous to even think, "—regular cola."

He shook his head with a slight smile before he took a swig of it. "Aren't you gonna eat?"

"I already did," she said, rubbing her tummy with her metal hands. Her eyes slithered to his tray. "Now if you aren't gonna eat your cookie..." her voice trailed off.

"Have it." Luke handed her the unwrapped chocolate chip delicacy.

She snapped the cookie in two, taking the smaller portion first. Her eyes returned to his tray, but this time with disgust.

"You're eating basji again?" Her free finger pointed to the mashed potato imposter, lumpy and near the edge of the tray.

"It's good for you," he defended. He took his fork and scooped a mouthful. When the utensil entered his mouth he closed his eyes and pictured the cookie Riley seized.

"It's literally just bitter mush."

"The mush has nearly every vitamin."

"At what cost?" Riley took another bite from the cookie, finishing off the first part.

"Oh c'mon, it's not that bad." Luke pressed some of the basji towards his teeth, sifting out the extra lumpy bits that hadn't been mashed to liquid. "It's only bitter if you don't use my trick." Luke reached for a packet of sweetener, adding it to the already sweetened portion he concocted at the condiment station. White sugar crystals mixed in, with Luke folding them along the basji batter.

"I thought you were cutting that," Riley shouted, almost disappointed. Her finger pointed to the packet like a criminal in a line-up.

"And I thought you weren't drinking diet cola."

She narrowed her eyes. "You win this battle." She relaxed back. "But I'm right about us leaving tonight."

"And what makes you so sure?"

"I'm never wrong twice," she snarked. Slamming her heavy hands on the plastic table she rose, twisting around and moving her body towards the exit after snatching back her book. "See you in the room."

"See you," he responded, taking another bite of the sweet basji.

As Riley left, the pilot of *the Traveler's* lackey passed by, sitting at the adjacent table a seat or two down. In Private Powers' hands, he too carried a book, a dying art in the universe of pads. He had his back to Luke, but Luke managed to make out some of a foreign script.

He narrowed his eyes, trying to decode the origin before Private Powers turned to Luke's stare.

"Sorry," Luke stifled.

Private Powers didn't speak. Instead, he sipped space juice from a pouch

Luke hadn't tried. The colors suggested a berry. Strawberry, maybe?

"What are you looking at?" he snarled.

"Sorry," Luke said again, taking the final bite of basji. Covering his mouth he spoke, muffled by both his chewing and his hand, "Just interested in the book."

The private took a bite of his sandwich. He didn't like the taste of the "meat" like Luke did as evidenced by his grimace followed by beads of sweat adorning his face. Using his fork, he tried to tap into one of the reserves of food, scooping up basji.

"Wait!" Luke called out, holding up the remaining sugar packet. "Trust me, you need this."

Luke rose from his seat and handed what remained of the sugar packet to the man. He looked at it, peering in, before turning back to Luke.

"For the basji," Luke explained.

Powers looked back at it again, then poured specks of sugar onto it. He brought the fork to his mouth and took a bite. His lips savored the flavor, the saccharine swirling in his mouth and sending a rush of dopamine. The second bite wasn't as dramatic, but just as sweet.

"You're one of the linguistic people, right?" Luke asked, knowing the answer.

The private, between bites, nodded. "Yeah."

"But you're also military?"

"Yep," he said, using his hand to highlight the name tag along his uniform. "Private Powers." He wore a blue suit; most space cadets and privates did. He appeared younger than most, with a baby face and innocence mixed with a tinge of shyness.

Over the loudspeaker, the pilot confirmed takeoff would be happening in only a few hours. The time for final preparations had begun.

"I have to get back to work," Powers sighed, carrying his tray of uneaten food to the trash.

"Luke," he shared, extending his hand.

"See you around," Powers dismissed, taking another bite out of the basji before leaving the cafeteria. Luke retracted his unshook hand.

The rest of the crowd hurriedly tended to final preparations and called family or friends. It was a sick joke by the pilot, another fake out. *The Traveler*, in all likelihood, wasn't going to leave. But the mere possibility it could persuaded Luke to contact Daphne.

Taking out his pad, he finalized his message to Daphne and waited for a response. *Just got back from the doctor*, she said. *I'm worried.*

Hurriedly, Luke jogged back to his room, passing by others loitering halls on their pads and phones. When he got to the door, he cracked it open, hearing Riley talk on the phone with her girlfriend and soon to be fiancée, Kashvi.

"I told ya," she teased Luke the second he entered. "Did I tell ya or did I tell ya we were leaving?"

"Haven't left yet," Luke corrected. He navigated through the graveyard of diet cola bottles and cans rolling across the floor, hitting corners of furniture.

Riley glued her eyes back to the screen, her mouth a smidge open while she kept a smile across her face before she started laughing.

"Kashvi's taking bets we're gonna find the aliens!" Riley flipped the screen to the side, giving Luke a sight of Riley's girlfriend and a bunch of others who watched the ship from a bar in Unified Korea.

The prototype language detector worked for isolated conversations but with so much interference in the background, incomplete sentences fused with other unrelated sentences, creating a vessel of misinformation.

"She's betting we won't find them." Riley pouted.

"*You won't!*" Kashvi shouted over the phone amid the chatter.

"We've been searching for so long." Luke shrugged. "I think she's right."

"Don't tell me you too," Riley groaned. "The 'Hello' signal is concrete as hell."

"I don't doubt aliens exist, I just doubt their abilities to send back what was essentially a coded message with a few discrepancies."

"*A few discrepancies still haven't been solved,*" Kashvi added.

Riley turned the screen back around. "I love you," she professed as if it were the first time. "I can't wait to see you—these weeks aboard were terrible without you."

Kashvi said something Luke couldn't hear but deduced it was an "I love you" in some form. The screen minimized and the flood of voices dried up.

"Now you can call Daphne!" she yelled, rising from the bed.

"Where are you going?" Luke asked, watching as she slipped on her boots.

"Food!" She rubbed her stomach. "I have a weird craving for salty basji."

"Salty basji? Didn't you just call it bitter?"

"I know," she defended, her hands raised. "I can't explain it either. Tell Daph I say hi and goo-goo-ga-ga to that boy."

Luke laughed. "I will be sure to, Kasey loves you."

The Traveler crept through the void of space, following breadcrumbs left by presumably the same aliens behind the "Hello" Signal. Sometimes, fuel residue showed up on radars, their heat traces lingering in the darkness. Other times, an abandoned probe or satellite got spotted orbiting another celestial body containing information guarded through materials never before seen in the backwater portion of the Milky Way. If there was any doubt aliens existed before, alien junk alleviated the disbelievers.

Luke's sleep was interrupted when a transmission roared throughout the ship. Wet-sounding vocalizations "spoke" through every single device with volume. Microwaves, pads, implants, overhead speakers, watches, photograph presenters, anything that could make noise, did. Together, in all pitches, it repeated the same thing over and over again in a sort of alien choir. Luke got an earful of it through his Reel, a technology that recorded everything he saw.

"What the fuck is that?" Riley shouted, more annoyed than excited.

The unintelligible transmission lasted for a little bit over a minute, but neither tone nor formality could be discerned.

"What do you think they're saying?" Luke asked, strapping on his boots.

"Well it didn't seem like a hello," she sighed. "They got all our languages decoded them and still used theirs." She shook her head. "That's a way of saying 'checkmate' if I ever heard of one."

"Ever heard anything like it before?"

"No." She gulped soda from a half-full can along the bedside. "I can't think of a single Human language resembling it."

Over the loudspeaker, another message played, this time a familiar Human voice. *"We just received a message from the aliens."*

"No," Riley said sardonically. "That was aliens?"

Luke punched her metal arm, ignoring the pain his knuckles endured when making contact with the steel-plated limb.

The pilot of *the Traveler* continued, *"We got a massive data dump from these aliens. We need translators on ASAP. Soldiers, be on standby. Everyone else, get some sleep, we got a long day."*

"Who're the other translators?" Luke asked, securing a belt around his waist through the loops.

"Beats me, I just know that one snob Powers."

Luke recalled the pilot's lackey. "You said he gave you the creeps?"

Riley scoffed. "I just don't like him."

Luke narrowed his eyes. "Did he do something?"

"He just said some fucked up shit."

"And that was?"

Riley finished lacing her boots before letting out a sigh. "Powers and I went to Uni together. In one of our classes on Space Ethics, we were given the dilemma of "'save the mission or save the team.'"

"I'm guessing he chose—"

"—Yep," she continued. "Chose to save the mission."

"And that's the reason you dislike him so much?"

"Honestly, more than anything, that's the type of person he is. He doesn't care about the means. Just the end."

Luke nodded. "That makes sense—why you dislike him. I'm sure higher-ups liked that response."

"They loved it," she huffed as if still shocked from all those years ago. "I just can't imagine killing my friends for a mission's success. I mean if it was the fate of humanity or something, fine, but I doubt that'd come up." She shook her head, whispering to herself, "I don't like him."

"I would've chosen the team."

"And that's why I trust you," she echoed.

II

The Attack

Chapter 11

Falisto

Falisto licked his paw a few times while standing outside the hospital room. He recognized Kasey's shallow footsteps and the soft, almost weightless sound they made. There was a sort of rhythm Falisto picked up on when they searched Porygar. Kasey's cadence was almost ethereal, his steps like feathers grazing the floor. He could differentiate them, still.

"Look who finally decided to show up," Falisto said before Kasey turned the corner.

"Sorry we're late," Kasey said. "How is she?"

"Alright." Falisto shrugged. Falisto had changed into his pedestrian wear: a cream skirt, golden bracelets and anklets, and red nail paint. Psys preferred minimal clothing; they evolved that way from the searing heat of their homeworld, Katree. Gold complemented streaks of honey in Falisto's brown fur, with overhead lighting giving it extra shine.

The girl, ID'ed under "Sola," lay in bed with covers going past her waist. Machines huddled around her body. Cords extended from monitors and IVs, with her forearms taking a cocktail of drugs. Screens displayed several numbers and other indicators Falisto didn't pretend to know the importance of. Sola's brown skin was warmer since last time, but her lips still had a hint of blue paleness. Kasey crept towards the bed with Falisto and Benjo behind.

"Coma?" Kasey asked.

"Yeah, doc put her in one." Falisto coughed. "Help her with her head."

"That bad?" The beads that were in her hair rested on a side table. Now, her head had been shaved down to the root.

"She had pretty bad brain swelling. They don't know from what though."

Kasey sighed. "But she's okay?"

Tsarena emerged from the bathroom, wiping her scarlet hands with a paper towel. "She will be."

"Glad you're here, Tsarena. I have something for you," Benjo said from behind Kasey.

She hesitated. "Thanks?"

"It's not a gift."

She smirked. "Right."

He traded the plastic bag holding the Orchi gun with her used paper towel. "It's heavy," he warned. Her four fingers held the gun by its sides, avoiding the orange trigger covered by the plastic bag. She held it towards the light, eclipsing it and making the colorless weapon disappear into the glow.

"Strange gun," Tsarena whispered, still fiddling with it. She sleuthed it for clues, studying grooves and minute details. Falisto got a strange vibration from the gun. It evoked a reaction from him like a cold shiver up the spine.

"Know anything about it?" Benjo asked.

She shrugged. "I mean it's Orchi if that's what you're getting at." One of her fingers poked the barrel. "But it's pretty unremarkable otherwise."

"What about the bullets?"

"Pretty unremarkable as well."

"Nothing unusual?"

"I mean no—it's a gun with some bullets." Tsarena looked back to Benjo. "Sorry to disappoint you."

"Are these common Orchi guns?" Kasey asked.

Tsarena didn't answer at first, instead, she narrowed her eyes as if to zoom in on a detail on one of the bullets before she dragged it closer. "Wait a second." She squinted some more and traced her thumb along the grip. A devilish smile crossed her face. "This is contraband."

She opened up the bag, pulling out the gun, to Benjo's horror. He held up his hands in a defensive pose, while Tsarena looked closer at it.

Her lips pursed before she whispered, "Jasoosi?"

"Jasoosi?!" Falisto yelled. He jumped, his tail ruffled and eyes wide. His red-painted claws appeared sharper as he took a battle stance. His gut was right, that gun came from terrorists, and his clawed toes dug into his sandals.

Tsarena pointed to the trigger. In Orchi script the word "Jasoosi" was inscribed vertically. Using her thumb, she rolled around the engraving. She closed her eyes as if to savor the shape of the letters.

"What's Jasoosi?" Kasey asked.

Falisto cut off Tsarena before she even started. "A group of Orchi spies." Falisto flashed his teeth. "They specialize in species uplifting and murder."

"Used to." Tsarena countered. "They were considered the right hand of the Orchi military."

"—And they aided in the first contact war between Orchi and Psys. Guess they're back." Falisto's paw lingered around his Slart. "I knew they were still around. You know every Psys already knows."

Tsarena rolled her eyes. "You don't really believe they still exist, do you?"

"Explain the gun."

"It's probably a replica or something sold on the Black Market."

Benjo asked, "What makes it contraband?"

"I mean it's a fake," she explained. "We phased out guns without serial numbers." She paused before looking at Falisto. "'We' meaning 'Orchi,' not 'Jasoosi.'"

"Think I can find it on the dark web?" Falisto asked.

"I don't see why not." Tsarena couldn't move her eyes off the gun like it was some trophy or medal of honor.

"Falisto, you're really going to do that while we're on a mission?" Benjo admonished.

Falisto ignored him. "What should I search?"

"I'd just try 'Jasoosi gun,'" she suggested.

Falisto typed with his fingers going faster than words forming in his mind. The pad searched and opened thousands of listings on some unauthorized site not tethered to one of the Kyros Fusion Centers.

"What about the bullets?" Kasey asked. "Why are they so heavy?"

"They're certainly heavy." Tsarena juggled the bag of marble-looking objects.

"What's so special about them?" Falisto motioned to take the bag and Tsarena handed it to him. "They're not that heavy," Falisto mumbled, already casting them to the side before going back to his scavenger hunt. "Have you tried firing the gun?" Falisto asked.

"Well—no, it's evidence," Kasey said. "And also a Navigator and hospital don't scream target practice."

"—Got it," Falisto said. He turned his screen around the three of them before increasing to the maximum size. "There's one for sale for only a few hundred kirbies."

On the screen, a spitting image of the same gun appeared, almost as if a one-to-one copy. Details were scarce—only the name, photo, and caption appeared on the page.

"At least it's on sale," Kasey said with a smirk.

"Falisto, are you suggesting we check this seller?" Benjo asked.

"I don't see any other sellers," he stated, moving through the screen and search results.

"So, you want *us* to go meet the seller?" Benjo rephrased.

"They're breaking GUM code. We're well within our rights to investigate." Falisto defended. He kept typing, inputting variants of Jasoosi spelling, and changing languages every so often.

"I don't think that's a good idea." Benjo paced back towards the gun. "Our mission was to investigate Porygar."

"Then what do you want us to do?" Falisto asked. "This is related to what we found on Porygar, is it not?"

"Let's tell Respow and see—"

"—He won't let us." Falisto face-pawed. "Especially after Kasey called in help on Porygar."

A moment of silence followed. Falisto's body temperature rose and beads of sweat secreted from his fur-covered skin. Jasoosi was the name of the group that uplifted the Psys. Uplifted being the fancy term for discovering a primitive civilization that hadn't figured out how to make swords, and giving them nuclear weapons. Disastrous consequences followed.

Falisto's concentration broke when Kasey leaned against the wall. "I haven't checked the news since we landed."

"Don't check the news," Tsarena warned.

"It's spreading everywhere." Falisto exchanged looks with Tsarena who glared at him intensely.

"It's not *that* bad." Tsarena looked at Kasey.

"Falisto?" Kasey asked.

"It's bad." Falisto scratched the stems of his whiskers. He didn't want to mince words with Kasey, Jasoosi getting him hot and bothered. "Everyone knows the colony's missing. People are pretty much calling it *the* missing colony now."

Tsarena sighed. "Look, that's how the news works. Wait for something else to happen and that'll be the focus. Did you even get to talk to Captain Respow?"

"Eh, more or less." Kasey shuffled around, his palms sweating through his unitard.

"If Respow won't let us, then we'll find another way." Falisto put away his pad. "When he reads our reports, he'll know what to do."

"Oh shit, I have to submit mine." Tsarena frantically opened her pad. "I don't need Representative Tsperi getting mad at me."

Benjo seized back the bullets and pistol. "Kasey, you haven't been grounded have you?"

"No, thankfully." Kasey put his fingers along his temples, massaging them.

"Where's the doctor?" Benjo asked.

"Probably just outside."

Benjo shrugged, opening the door. As his hand pulled back the metal, a bomb blasted.

* * *

Benjo

An explosion shot Benjo into the wall, bringing with it the scrunched door pinning one of his cybernetic legs to the ground. Sparks jolted through the air. Colorful voids dotted Benjo's already fuzzy vision, and a ringing similar to tinnitus rattled in his ears. Kasey dashed to him, but a second blast from below brought Kasey to his knees. Then another, this one more distant. Another. Another. Another.

The decrescendo of explosions echoed away but screams reverberated across the Panel, the vocal waves shaking it like jello. Smoke climbed to the ceiling, alleviated by a flush of rain from sprinklers and emergency ventilation sucking up fumes. Tsarena coughed while she and Falisto pushed Sola's bed into the corner of the room.

"Benjo!" Kasey shouted. With an underhanded grip, he mustered all his strength and channeled it through his legs. Ringing sounds still disorientated Benjo, but he could read the context clues. Kasey's face, red like an Orchi, screaming while pulling up the door. Although buzzing continued alongside explosions and blasts, Benjo discerned some traces of Kasey's command.

"I'm fine." Benjo coughed. Flame marks and smoke residue lingered on his unitard, with some sections that hadn't burned still warm. His leg oozed some coolant, eroding part of the door like sytrofoam.

"What the hell is going on?" Falisto growled, looking out the window. He squinted. A strange whooshing sound flattened his ears, and his pupils dilated when his nose sniffed a scent all too familiar. There it was, hanging mere millimeters above the building across the hospital.

"Tsarena, is that—"

"—A Tayir ship?"

Kasey snapped his neck back, still crouched and pushing away the scrunched door from Benjo. "Did you just say a Tayir ship?"

Neither spoke, instead, they stood with their mouths trembling, their bodies frozen, with only a slight twitch emanating from Tsarena's hands. She raised a finger, pointing out the window. Benjo hustled over despite his limp, catching a glimpse of the craft.

Part of him expected an elaborate ship, made of millions of complex nanotubes and pieces of warping technology with countless weapons affixed to it. Instead, it was a white orb. It didn't have irregularities, not even as much as an opening or window. A white marble bounced up and down in the artificial sky of Kyros. It merely sat in the air. Something about its simplicity stirred Benjo's stomach. Its haunting presence electrified every hair and cable of his body. His trance was broken as green energy blasts formed outside of the ship. Propelling downward, the ship struck indiscriminately, choosing targets of all types. Buildings, roads, people—nothing was spared from the vessel's destruction. Past the ship, several spherical shadows eclipsed the fake sun.

Kasey gasped. "There's more." He pointed to an array of ships funneling in from above and forming a "V" shape. Each one mirrored the others: white, spherical, murderous. Together, they fired across the Panel, dropping a series of bombs like hail on a cold planet in winter.

The ground shook—a force other than screams and blasts to blame. Violent rocking pushed Benjo back, flinging him against the bathroom door and then back to his original location. Amid the cacophony, a foreign sound roared. Like claws on a pad, the screech forced Benjo to grab his ears and lose his footing.

"They're disconnecting the Panel!" Falisto howled.

Benjo yelled back to Falisto, "The Tayirs? How can—"

"—The other Panels did it!" Falisto's fangs bit on the air as he yelled. "Those fucking cowards!"

The rocking grew more violent, flinging everyone around like rag dolls. Pieces of the roof rained and coincided with the sprinklers as the building ripped apart. Kasey grunted after bumping into the side table and Benjo, causing the bullets from the Orchi gun to fall and mix with puddles on the floor. Benjo used his metal hand to grapple onto Sola's bed, holding it in place alongside the machines attached to her body. Pain reminded him of his mortality in his metal thigh where coolant dried to a crunchy paste.

After a few moments, the shaking stopped and the screeching died out, but the screaming continued. Benjo peered out the window, watching the blue sky facade shatter into nothing more than the darkness of space, with only a shrinking Kyros appearing above with one less Panel. For a moment, Kyros stopped in the sky. The flower with one loose petal enveloped itself in a blue light, then disappeared. They were alone.

Chapter 12

Kasey

Kasey analyzed his options. Panels weren't known for their military presence. Hell, even local security constantly hired people because of massive turnover. These people were civilians. They didn't have guns, training, strategy, and they couldn't fight these bastards. The Tayirs would slaughter them.

Without a second thought, Kasey dialed on his pad. With each ring, Kasey paced more and more. Rain from the sprinklers slapped him in the face but he paid it no mind.

Kasey muttered, "C'mon, pick up."

Tsarena reached for the stray bullets now swimming like buoys. Several rounds pooled in the corner, but a handful still scattered about. Benjo, although injured, tended to Sola while Falisto stood in the dry corner.

The ringing finally stopped in Kasey's ear. *"Mako you better have a good ass reason—"*

"Captain Respow—Kyros is under attack!"

"What the hell are you talking—"

"—Kyros is under attack. I repeat, Kyros is under attack!"

He paused. *"Slow down, what's going on?"*

"It's the Tayirs."

He scoffed. *"The Tayirs?"*

"T-they're on the move!" Falisto shouted.

There was silence. Followed by a gulp.

"I'm gonna loop in local forces. The Irene isn't far away, we'll change course."

Another explosion from a short distance away rattled the building again, sending pieces of the floor to below. A flush of water drained around them, carrying two of the Orchi bullets. Another voice entered the call, nervous with peaks and valleys.

"This is Chief Adams, we need immediate assistance!"

"Chief, this is Captain Respow speaking. I have four PTF crew onboard. I'm bringing the Irene to the last confirmed location."

"Put me in contact with them," the Chief huffed. Intense gunfire and grunts of exhaustion accompanied the woman's voice.

"Already ahead of you," Respow said. *"They're on the call."*

"Get to the fountains," she said. *"I have a handful of people here. Do you have guns?"*

Kasey drew his Slart, prepping to head out of the hospital. *"We do, but I don't know how effective they'll be."*

"We have some here too—and we're giving them hell." The trepidation in her voice disagreed.

"I'm on my way, you keep as many people as you can alive. Did the Representatives make it out?" Respow asked.

"Negative," the Chief muttered coldly. *"Mayah, Tsperi, Petra—they're dead."*

Everyone stood still. Although Kyros' artificial gravity continued, it was the gravity of the situation that sank Kasey. All the Representatives? Dead? That meant Respow was the Representative for Humans. Kasey didn't know the replacements for Tsperi and Petra, and part of him thought to congratulate Respow on the promotion. He decided against it.

"I'm coming as fast as I can," Respow blurted. *The Irene* alarms boomed over his voice, flooding the comms with numerous sirens.

"We still have lots of people that need help." Chief Adams took shots as bullets whizzed through the air. *"Hurry!"*

Tsarena holstered the evidentiary gun, scooping Sola up with her free hands. The group jogged out of the room. Water flooded the hospital now, trickling downstairs in a stream mixed with punctured IV bags and saline. Some blood scattered in whirlpools, and limp bodies slouched along the walls.

Groans from some rooms were faint but present. Kasey went into each, bringing various survivors to safety. Robotic doctors dragged wounded individuals and directed others to a hidden safety zone. Underneath a floorboard was a large, hidden bunker, equipped only with minimal lighting and medical supplies.

Robots lifted various alien species and placed them inside the bunker. Psys, Orchi, Hybrids, and Humans all piled in, and each PTF member hurriedly kept pace with the machines.

"I'll make sure they're secure then I'll come join," Falisto said.

"Are you sure?" Tsarena asked, her breath labored.

"Go!" he commanded.

A Tayir ship swooshed overhead, flattening Falisto's ears again. The ship dropped a heavy energy blast on the hospital, completely eviscerating it. All that remained was searing smoke and fire the sprinklers, even if operational, couldn't put out.

"Go, now!" Kasey shouted, ushering the doctors into the bunker.

"I'll be right behind you," Falisto said.

"We gotta get moving," Kasey commanded, sprinting with his Slart drawn in lethal mode. Benjo and Tsarena followed, each with their weapons drawn.

Tsarena rushed past them as she maneuvered through remnants of the Panel, jumping over concrete barricades and around broken tiles of frayed sidewalks. Bodies of various species sprawled out across the floor—too many for them to help.

Turning a corner, another verdant bomb of energy ignited the ground in front of Tsarena, stopping the three in their tracks. Kasey went to shield his eyes with his elbow, but the light blinded him momentarily. Leftover flame devoured the Panel, while the nanotechnology that served as the fabric of Kyros struggled to replicate more of the Kyros architecture. Consuming bits of metal, the fire would eventually destroy the essence of the megastructure.

"At this rate," Tsarena whispered. "The Panel isn't gonna last."

"Not if we stop them," Kasey said.

They came to the group of security officers all hunched down. Five steel fountains encircled a middle one made of stone. Orchi in design, slabs of brick piled high, serving as a defensive measure to security guards alternating fire with the Tayir ships. Ancient currency covered the bottom of the fountains in copper and tin, giving it a rustic color.

Water fell from a chipped bowl resting at the apex of the middle fountain, raining to the lower rings of water. Above the bowl, a Tayir ship hovered, looming over the officers beneath. This one didn't bob up and down like the others. Instead, it hung in the air and fired green energy beams at random targets.

Kasey slid to the end of the middle fountain where Chief Adams and other officers hunkered. Their energy bullets barely left scuff marks on the orb. One officer peered out from the stone barricade with a marksman rifle using non-energy bullets. Her eye peeked through the scope as she lined up a shot only for it to ricochet back to the fountain, chipping another piece off the bowl.

"Stop, Cassandra!" Chief Adams commanded. "It's not doing anything!"

After taking another futile shot at the Tayir ship, she acquiesced, coming back down to the pillar of stone. "We need the cannon!" she cried. The ship fired another hunk of energy at the base of the Panel, with fire engulfing the floor like a layer of blazing fog.

"What's the plan?" Tsarena shouted over whizzing energy pulses slicing through the air. Another burst from the ship hit something else in the sky—a Navigator—sending it to the ground like a meteor.

"This," Chief Adams answered, pointing to a cannon. Kasey looked over with Tsarena, watching sparks jolt around the cannon, similar to Benjo's leg when the hospital door crushed him. A tiny meter labeled "percentage" inched forward on a display screen attached to the cannon.

"It takes time to charge." Chief Adams broke her own rule by taking a shot from her rifle at the ship. It bounced off, putting another crack in the bowl at the top of the fountain.

Numbers on the progress bar rose steadily alongside each gunshot. After four shots or so, the number increased by two percent, all the way to a hundred now. Kasey fired his Slart at the ship, his energy bullets doing nothing more than the rest.

"How many are there?" Kasey yelped.

"Six left!" The Chief shouted. "Taylor, NOW!!"

Like clockwork, an officer dashed to the cannon, aiming at the Tayir ship directly above them. With a few taps, a blue sphere of electricity fired from the cannon, connecting a direct hit with the ship. Pockets of lightning bounced around the metal craft before igniting it with orange flames. The burnt-white sphere plummeted directly to the ground before exploding midair, showering remnants on the fountain and splashing water.

"Five left!" Chief Adams shouted. Security officers cheered. Another officer with the only other cannon shot one further away, destroying it just like the last.

"Four!" Chief Adams shouted gleefully.

Kasey guarded the cannon between shots, watching as it slowly climbed. *One percent.* He counted his seconds, *one, two, three, four, five, six*—the percentage jumped to three. "We don't have that kinda time, they'll destroy the entire Panel!"

One Tayir ship took the place of its fallen comrade above them, hovering over the damaged middle fountain where black smoke pooled. But this one wasn't as passive as the others.

Aiming directly at the stone wall defending them, the Tayir ship charged up. By the time Kasey realized the tactic, it was too late. A single shot ripped apart the defensive slabs of the fountain, leaving them wide open for another attack and flushing the fountain's water like a tsunami.

Kasey blinked, but moments before a second shot connected, an aqua-colored shield protected them, diverting the Tayir ship's burst back skyward and away from the Panel into the vastness of space. But the ship wised up, taking a shot at the other cannon, destroying it and the group of soldiers there. Cassandra turned into a smoke silhouette, with a sizzling crackle and her rifle the only things left.

Chief Adams eyes went wide and her lips trembled.

The shield took another shot from the Tayirs. This time, it wavered, the color morphing from a vibrant aqua to a violet red paired with screeching beeps. Before contact with the third shot, Benjo spun the shield 180 degrees, reflecting the shot. The ship attempted to dodge, but it didn't act fast enough, getting chipped at the last second and engulfed in its own destruction.

Three Tayir ships left, half the security officers remained.

Next to Chief Adams, another group of security forces struggled to get their energy shield. The fickle piece of tech were meant for riots and keeping order. Not for war or battles between ships.

One of the three Tayir ships abused the opening. It swooped in, gliding across, and shot bursts at them. Two of the five attempted to dodge, but four fell victim to the blazing shot as it sundered them, inches in front of Chief Adams and Kasey.

Tsarena rolled out and shot her Slart until her bullets ran out, each reflecting effortlessly. Out in the open, she sent her hand into her pack before grabbing the Jasoosi gun.

Her finger sang with the trigger, shooting bullets that made contact with the Tayir craft. When the bullets hit, they proceeded to explode into micro missiles, almost like mini-frag grenades blowing out shrapnel. But even after a full clip, the ship still stood, firing back.

Kasey targeted the ship with the cannon as it prepped another blast, this one locking onto Tsarena. Chief Adams couldn't move. Her eyes fixed on the flaming air lingering from shadows left by her vaporized officers.

Kasey waited for the lock on to confirm. Green light condensed in front of the Tayir ship. Tsarena fired another flurry of bullets into the ship from the Jasoosi gun, the tiny explosions moving it backward with sheer force. But the ship endured. It locked in on Tsarena, too far from cover to get to safety.

"Got it!" Kasey exclaimed and slammed the fire button, sending another burst of electricity and destroying the ship.

No one shouted "Two."

* * *

Tsarena

Tsarena basked in victory for a brief moment, watching as the third Tayir ship fell to the ground. Only two left. But she failed to realize just how close to death she'd been. Unlike Chief Adams, she wasn't paralyzed. The smoke and rifles left behind by the officers who suffered the blast made her shake, but she forced herself to pull Chief Adams down behind some physical cover before another attack killed them like the others.

"You're okay!" Tsarena shouted. She shook her awake, out of the blank stare and dissociated mind she was in. "You are okay." Tsarena enunciated every word clearly, looking directly into the Chief's eyes.

Chief Adams didn't respond, and Tsarena resorted to a last ditch effort. She gave a wake-up slap to Chief Adams, her red skin leaving an imprint on the officer's cheeks. "You're okay!"

Kasey shouted about running out of bullets, and Benjo slapped the energy cannon as if magically bestowing it energy. Tsarena rose, firing shots out of the shield's reach and toward the Tayir ship, still dealing little (if any) damage. By now, scuff marks scratched up the craft, but not enough to dismantle or compromise it.

Tsarena, with Benjo, Kasey, and Chief Adams, sat behind the energy shield. "Charge damn it!" Benjo shouted.

"Do you got any more of those bullets, Tsarena?" Chief Adams yelled.

"No!" she cried.

The Tayir ship twisted back, circling the group's shield. Benjo spun it in accordance, deflecting back a series of bursts the ship took. These were smaller blasts, micro missiles that came in flurries. "The shield can't take much more!"

"The cannon's almost ready!" Kasey yelled.

Chief Adams fired at the ship, ignoring advice received and given. "C'mon, only two fucking more!"

The shield shifted from blue to yellow, with three more balls of green energy slamming against it. "Damn it!" Kasey shouted. A final blast shattered the shield—skipping the red phase entirely—leaving them wide open.

"Scatter!" Kasey ordered. Tsarena and Benjo dodged in different directions, while the Chief and Kasey fired off an electrical shot. It zoomed in the sky, clipping one of the metal fountains. Compromised but still catapulting towards the ship, the electric bomb followed, arching back and hitting it in the sky.

"There's just one more!" Kasey called out.

In the distance, Falisto galloped on all fours. In a primal run, he whizzed around Tsarena and past the rubble before he pounced. He shifted to his hind legs, reaching the cannon. Tsarena and Benjo dashed back, the five of them now in front of the cannon.

"It's shot!" Kasey yelled, fanning away smoke while looking at the last Tayir ship hovering over. The ship took a shot at a fountain mainly spared from the gunfight, causing a flood rush towards them. The bottom of the shield parted the sea of clear water that grew murky after carrying blood from the officers.

"Is Sola safe?" Tsarena asked. Her heart raced at the thought. Here she was, in a literal war zone, thinking about the safety of a child she didn't even know.

"She's in the bunker," Falisto said. He slapped the energy cannon, trying to rid the error screen.

"It's not gonna work," Chief Adams mumbled.

"What's wrong with it?" Falisto skimmed the error code with a quizzical look.

"It's out of power," Chief Adams replied. "We need energy cells."

The final Tayir ship fired at the center of the Panel about fifty meters away. Its blast bifurcated one of three major support beams holding the bottom of the Panel together. Kasey and Benjo stumbled from the impact, as the supporting structure crunched. Everyone still alive on the Panel screamed as artificial lights dimmed and the crafted gravity suffered a momentary lapse. Even amid the pandemonium the Panel hadn't swapped to emergency mode. That was something deliberate by the architects to emphasize that emergency really meant emergency.

"They're gonna destroy the Panel!" Tsarena shrieked.

"It's over," Chief Adams lamented. Tsarena wanted to slap her awake but fought the urge.

"*Respow!*" Kasey shouted over his comms. "*Where the hell are you?!*"

The line crinkled like aluminum foil, with buzzes and echoes of distant communication waves fusing over the line. The Tayir ship readied another shot, this one more massive and aimed directly at where the second support beam rested by Tsarena's calculations.

Benjo and Falisto fired their own shots. Two full mags didn't even do as much as a scratch to the ship. Its beam fired, causing a second quake throughout the Panel that toppled buildings by itself. Those who could scream did, and a flurry of emergency and personal ships drifted off the Panel in a frenzy.

A cloud of black smoke condensed from the impact of the second beam, obscuring the white ship. The only visible thing through the smoke was the piercing green energy beam recharging.

"We need another electrical gun!" Tsarena yelped.

Kasey looked back at the cannon with blue jolts jumping around it. Then, as if a light went off in his head, his expression turned from concerned to excited. Kasey shouted over the yells. "Benjo! Can you power it up?" Kasey's eyes darted to the energy cannon, uncharged but still running.

Benjo hesitated. Fishing out a cable from his fanny pack, he pulled out his ominplug, giving one end to Kasey and inserting the other in his thigh's port on his undamaged leg.

"What the hell do you think you're doing?!" Falisto yelled.

"Something crazy!"

Benjo's robotic eye glowed an unnatural red after morphing from brown to blue to green to yellow. The cannon siphoned his energy, drawing all the electricity stored between each connecting piece of metal. He screamed so loudly it deafened everyone's ears.

The percentage skyrocketed from 0% to 45%. The Tayir ship focused its energy beam into one final blast, aiming at the support beam.

"They're gonna shoot!" Tsarena cried.

Kasey slammed the fire button, and a smaller, blue ball of fire and electricity soared to the Tayir ship. Unlike the others, it went undetected from the Tayir's defensive systems, bypassing expectations and landing in the ship's body. Levitating, the aircraft echoed sounds of pain before falling downwards like dead weight, making a hole in the Panel as it wedged with the ground.

Chapter 13

Benjo

Benjo, knocked out cold from his energy expenditure, woke up to quite a different Galactic Union. With news of all three Representatives passing during the Tayir attack, two-thirds of the GU underwent radical power shifts in his slumber. Those eighteen hours were an era of uncertainty for PTF. But for Benjo, they were rejuvenating.

That's not to say he woke up refreshed. His jaw hinged, and when he opened it, a crack from the joint convinced him he had broke his mandible. Sunlight (which he didn't know was artificial at the time) blinded him through his eyelids, and a light breeze elicited both a shiver and body ache.

A tingle rode up his arm from whatever he rested on. He couldn't remember where he was, but he did remember who he was. He wished he didn't. After blinking a few times, someone clasped his metal hand.

"Amber?" His throat scratched like he had a cold that could only be cured with hot soup and sleep.

The hand squeezed the steel. "You're awake," Tsarena soothed. Benjo's eyes opened to Tsarena's bright red skin and purple eyes. "Sorry, not Amber." She smiled. "How're you feeling?"

His heart sank a bit. "Just tired."

"I would be too," she said.

He sat up with her. "Grass?" He grabbed a handful of it, pushing the green paste to his fingernails.

"Fake grass," Tsarena said. In the distance, Kasey and Falisto spoke with the newly Representative Respow across the Panel. Some of the other

PTF members were there, but a notable few, including his ex, Amber, were absent.

Benjo groaned, using his free hand to comfort his head. Energy expenditures using Hybrid components were a costly endeavor. More often than not, it left the Hybrid with a Hypo Headache, leaving them sensitive to everything to the point where a light breeze might as well have been a firing squad on a naked body.

"You need rest," Tsarena coaxed. She took a piece of a protein cookie from a metal tray and force-fed it to him. After a few reluctant nibbles, he scarfed it down so quickly that he couldn't savor the milk chocolate chunks.

"I feel like shit."

"So, not 'just tired?'"

He scolded her. "No."

"You saved us," she said with a cheer. Putting her hand on his shoulder, she gave him a reassuring nudge as if to say *way to go!* He imagined that's how she sounded, excited like a proud mother. "We're having an engineer come help charge you up." She pointed to his metal legs and then arm. "That charge fried them."

"How'd I even live that?"

"Nothing short of a miracle."

"A miracle, eh?"

She nodded. "Sola's okay, too, just not responsive."

"Not responsive?"

"She's still in her coma," she explained. "Hasn't woken up."

Benjo sighed with relief. "I thought you were saying she died."

"No!" she bellowed.

He let the good news settle in the air. "Any idea how the Tayirs are back?"

Tsarena looked at the grassy patch below her, the green blades contrasting with her skin. "We don't know yet."

Benjo sensed the tonal shift. "Yet?"

"The last blast wasn't strong enough to destroy the last ship."

"It got away?!" Benjo yelled and tried to jump upwards before remembering his metal arm and legs had become duds.

She said, "We captured it."

Energy pumped into his veins as if the batteries in his body charged back. "We have one of the ships?"

"That's why Kasey and Falisto are talking to Respow now." She pointed across the way. Kasey spoke in verbose body movements, using exaggerated hand gestures, and paired it with the occasional shake. "Representative Respow," she added.

Benjo's lumbar cracked as he tried to lift himself. "So Mayah died?"

"So did Tsperi and Petra."

The two of them sat in silence for a moment. Without any of the original Representatives, the GU was a shadow of itself. On one hand, Benjo presumed his standing with Respow would put him in an advantageous position, but on the other, three species governments just suffered a potential coup d'état.

To break the tension, he laughed. "Don't let me do that again."

"How many times have you done a blast like that?" Tsarena asked.

"At least twice, both in the Sapien War."

Tsarena shook her head. "Next time, you might not be so lucky. But I don't intend on letting you do that again."

* * *

Tsarena

Tsarena helped staff rush in as their ships floated to the Panel's docks. Species she hadn't seen in years flocked to the Panel—even the Jasyx—a waterborne race that couldn't stand the lack of oceans on Panel C. Ironclad ships were their favorite, always carved in the design of a Jasyx body. A bit on the nose—or in their case—exoskeleton shell with breathing holes.

The crab-like creatures descended, each carrying their form of medical supplies. They took shallow steps down a ramp, while Tsarena and a few other Orchi motioned them forward.

One Jasyx stopped in front of Tsarena, its four black dots for eyes blinking quickly. It lowered a cloth mask that covered its mouth, then spoke with a whimsical sound like music.

"Miss, are you hurt?" It pointed to Tsarena's arm with its pincers and arm beneath. Dried blood and a scab covered a wound on her that she dressed herself with a crinkled band-aid.

"Oh, it's nothing serious—"

The Jasyx delicately pulled her hand with its own and obtained a spray can from its bag. Its four legs moved closer and rooted to the floor.

"You really don't have to—"

Chopping off her bandage, the Jasyx sprayed cool mist over her wound, clearing the dried blood. She winced at the sting, but the chilled liquid solidified like foam before becoming an airtight seal.

Without a pair of lips, Tsarena couldn't tell if the Jasyx smiled at her, but whatever expression it had left as quickly as it came. The creature's four legs clicked and clacked as it left without as much of a word, just blinking in her direction before dissipating with its medical bag of tricks.

In her peripheral vision, Tsarena caught a glimpse of an Orchi ship. Her people preferred several ships melded together with a center control. In a way, it looked like several spheres mashed together. Mahina loved that about Orchi ships. Tsarena and her had many debates and compared ships across species, using superlatives for them. Mahina insisted Orchi had the best design, but Tsarena argued Psys took that title.

"What's that?" Tsarena asked, pointing to the long-necked animal at the zoo on Earth.

"A giraffe," Mahina laughed. "Orchi don't got 'em I guess?"

"I swear, this backwater planet has so many weird animals." Tsarena petted the neck of the creature. It accepted the gesture, lifting its neck and sticking out its purple tongue.

Mahina scoffed. "I'd be offended, but it's true, Earth really is strange."

"Why don't you come here more often?" Tsarena licked her mango ice cream.

"Earth?" Mahina took a bite from the Galaxy Burger, a delicacy that took the Milky Way by storm after an intensive ad campaign across planetary systems.

"Yeah, your homeworld."

"Nah, I was born on Venus." She licked her fingers as she finished the burger. "Earth's just some place."

"It's so pretty." Tsarena soaked in the view, letting the sun's warmth kiss her skin. "Why aren't more people here?"

"Space flight kinda killed Earth." Mahina cocked her head back. "Actually—I guess—saved Earth? Depends how you view it."

"How do you view it?" She leaned in and offered her a lick of her dessert. Mahina acquiesced. "I say saved."

"What makes you say that?"

Mahina scratched her chin with her fingers spreading some residual grease. After a moment of contemplating, she gave her answer that Tsarena still remembered. "Earth was dying. We were actively destroying our planet."

"I hear Humans do like global warming."

"Hey, we use that to our advantage now! Terraforming."

Tsarena rolled her eyes. "The fact that you even have a name for changing a planet astounds me."

"You should try it sometime!" She took a sip from her beverage, purely a mix of ice water and bubbles left over.

"I wish I could go to the homeworld." Tsarena looked at the giraffe.

"There still that embargo on Humans?"

"It's not just Humans," Tsarena corrected. "Everyone is banned, even Orchi without clearance."

"Is getting a clearance hard?"

"Harder when you don't come from money."

Mahina turned to Tsarena. "Alright, I'm ready to go when you are, on to the next stop!"

"Where to?"

"Who knows, let's put the autopilot on and see what happens."

Tsarena laughed. "Should have expected that."

Tsarena's chip pinged her with a message from Kasey, bringing her back to the present. Kasey labeled it as top priority, thereby passing her silent mode. Her inbox filtered the message, adding it to the other hundreds of top-priority mail from Kasey labeled as "reminder for report" and "reminder for evidence submission."

URGENT: HANGAR FOUR

Tsarena sighed. Her eyes shifted between first responders rushing on, injured individuals, and vendors looking to make a quick buck. In the distance, lights from a pop-up Galaxy Burger business glowed their red and white block letters. The taste of mango danced on the tip of her tongue. That and a burger.

Chapter 14

Benjo

Benjo closed his eyes while Kasey and Falisto argued with Chief Adams' henchman guarding the entryway to the holding dock for the Tayir ship. The white wall supported Benjo as he leaned his thumping head against it. Despite a recharge from the engineers, he struggled to keep his eyes open and his throat burned like a thousand suns. Electricity only did so much for organic components. Groaning, Benjo massaged his temples, trying to soothe the remnants of the Hypo Headache. He could push through the agony. But. They. Just. Kept. Arguing.

"Let us through!" Falisto commanded.

The henchman was one of the few surviving officers. Soot and tears covered the officer's uniform, but the earlier camaraderie was absent from the guard's vacant eyes. Instead, he repeated the same line he'd said the previous four times. "This is a police matter. It happened in our jurisdiction. We'll decide who goes in and out." He'd rehearsed it so much that he sounded like a PONR Hybrid. Benjo should know, he'd interacted with his fair share of them.

"We saved your asses!" Kasey screamed, then pointed to Benjo. "*He* saved your asses!"

Benjo sighed. *I don't want any part of this.* "It's the Chief's rules."

Tsarena catapulted through the entry to the corridor, grease dotting parts of her unitard and the corners of her lips. Her sprint died to a stroll realizing everyone else was occupied.

"What's going on?" she asked among Kasey's yells.

Falisto raised his voice to match Kasey's. "This bootlicker won't let us through," Falisto growled.

Tsarena scooted past the arguing trio, inching towards Benjo. "How are you feeling?" she asked.

"Oh, you know." He slouched further into the wall like an upright bed. "Just feel like I got dismembered then sewn back together."

"God I'm sorry." Tsarena placed her hand on his shoulder.

"You also got a—" Benjo tapped his lips where grease polluted her scarlet skin.

She got the hint and wiped the corners of her lips with her tongue, matching the location Benjo tapped. A crumb or two of the brioche bun provided a small dopamine rush as her tongue gathered it up. "Thanks."

A moment passed before Tsarena asked, "How long have they been going like this?"

"Arguing?" he asked.

"Pretty one-sided argument."

Benjo stifled a laugh. "Don't tell them that. They think they're winning."

"Should we intervene?"

"I got too much of a headache for that."

"I'm on my way there too." Tsarena thumped her forehead with her fingers.

Benjo groaned. "But you're right—they need to be talked to."

Benjo moved to the side of the guard, trying to sneak a peek behind him. Through a small sliver of space, he could make out an array of computer screens surrounding the Tayir ship. It was smaller, dwarfed by overhead lights shining down. Chief Adams obscured the view, her hands balled into fists and appearing in the window portion of the door.

"They attacked the Psys, the Orchi, and Humans, we have a right to be in there." Falisto flashed his fangs to the guard.

Even deviating from his normal script, the henchman was still a monotone robot. "No, you do not."

"Yes, we do." Falisto took a step closer, his lower jaw quivering.

The symptoms of Falisto's rage spurred Benjo. "Just a second." Benjo moved so fast he nearly toppled over himself.

Using his pad, Benjo navigated through the GUM code. He skipped through regulations, Navigator rules, and PTF first contact laws all the way to succession and rank. *Bingo!*

"See?" He flipped his pad with his finger pointed to bold text.

The henchman narrowed his gaze. "What's this?"

"The GUM code." Benjo paused. "Of superiority."

The henchman cackled. "And that's supposed to—"

"—And that gives us higher authority. Well, at least higher than you."

Tsarena took a step back, out of range from both Benjo and the henchman.

"If you think some technical rule is getting you in here, you're dead wrong." The man planted his feet on the ground, tensing his legs.

Benjo sighed, lowering the pad. "I wasn't asking." But before Benjo could raise hell and intimidate the guard into submission, the sound of familiar footsteps stomped from behind. It was unmistakable, the loud taps, the speed, the accompanying throat-clearing sounds.

"We're going in," Representative Respow ordered. He held up his badge, but he didn't need to, the guard just looked at him doe-eyed. Whatever robot was inside the man disappeared, now replaced with a scared child. "Y-yes sir." He pulled down the handle, letting the group through.

Inside with the Tayir craft, Chief Adams typed at a computer. She groaned with more boots hitting the ground. "Hoover, I told you not to let anyone in!" Chief Adams shouted before turning to Respow.

"What're you doing here?" she sneered, not minding her voice.

Mistake. Respow liked one thing more than all other things: respect.

"Watch the tone," he commanded. She hardened. "We're here to help."

"I doubt that."

Benjo diverted from the conversation, instead focusing on the Tayir ship. From his vantage point, it didn't seem remarkable. If anything, it was basic—just a giant sphere, white in color, with a few scratches and the odd dent or so from bullets that *actually* did damage. Benjo couldn't fathom it. Somehow this orb surpassed light speed, fired beams of energy, and housed a giant alien bird.

"I-I had orders," the henchman defended. "The Chief—"

"I'm the Human Representative. My orders supersede." He cracked his knuckles before bringing back up his badge a second time. "Suffice to say, I need to know everything about this."

"Get in line," Chief Adams said. The burning eyes of Respow commanded respect, and she added, "Sir."

"What do we know?"

Chief Adams laughed, undoing the bun in hair. "Not a damn thing. But when you figure it out, I wanna be in the loop."

"Of course, Chief."

She nodded. "I'm gonna get a coffee." She walked off, heading towards the vending machine in the other room.

"I can't believe you're the Representative," Kasey marveled.

Respow turned to him. "Mako, I need the four of you to figure out why the hell those things attacked us and where it came from."

"Yes, sir."

"Your tribunal will still happen for your direct violation of my order," he roared.

Kasey gulped. Respow continued, "But, I want to forget about Porygar for now. We have a new priority."

Tsarena recoiled. "Forget about Porygar? Those people are still missing."

"And now we have a full war being waged before our very eyes."

"But sir, there's still people we have to save," Tsarena pleaded.

"A missing colony doesn't matter when we have an unprecedented attack killing tens of thousands of civilians."

"Thousands?" Kasey uttered.

"Thousands," Respow repeated. He said the word slowly, letting it sit in the air and ruminate between them.

"It could be connected," Falisto chimed in. "Porygar and this."

"I'd entertain the idea, but right now we have to focus on this attack." Respow pulled out his pad, probably already tabling hundreds of emails by Benjo's calculations.

"I can see if we can get info about the ship," Benjo suggested, walking to the horde of computers.

"Please tell me we can gut the Tayir bastard once we get him out?" Falisto asked.

"No," Benjo yelled across the room. "We aren't allowed to kill someone without a trial."

"Screw that," Falisto roared. "You heard Respow. Those things killed thousands of Psys. One life for thousands."

"I agree with Falisto," Kasey supported. "I wanna see whoever is in there suffer. But Benjo is right, we have to let him have a trial."

"It will be a public execution," Respow said.

"After a trial?" Kasey asked.

"I don't think we need a trial," Respow smirked. "It's clear they did this, whoever is in there. But there's too much valuable information on that ship. If the public wants an execution they'll get it."

"You guys don't even know if the person is alive in there," Tsarena countered. "You *also* don't know the species."

"It's a Tayir ship," Falisto dismissed. "What else could be in there?"

"If the Tayirs are extinct, it doesn't necessarily mean their technology is." Tsarena stepped toward the ship, grazing her hand right in front of it.

"They're extinct," Benjo assured. "This is probably some rogue colony of Tayirs that went berserk."

"Do you blame them?" Kasey said.

"For the attack?" Respow asked incredulously.

"I understand wanting revenge after the genocide of their people." Kasey tapped his foot. "It doesn't make it right, but I understand it."

"What if it's not the Tayirs," Tsarena said, again. "We keep assuming it's them."

"Who else would wanna attack us?" Kasey asked.

"Tsarena's right," Falisto echoed. "The Tayirs are dead—they can't be back."

"Sapien," Benjo suggested, typing code into the keyboard and ignoring Falisto. "They hate everything about the GU."

"But aren't they also practically dead?" Kasey countered.

Benjo craned his head away from the computers. "Its members are dead, sure, but you can't kill terrorism."

"Jasoosi," Falisto sneered.

"Oh God, Falisto, we already had this conversation." Tsarena rubbed her forehead. "Jasoosi isn't around anymore. That's assuming it was ever real."

"Look," Kasey paused, his hands raised. "We don't know who's in there. But we'll know as soon as we find out how to open this damn thing."

Respow interjected. "Good, let me know once you open it. Until then, I have to go make some calls."

He turned, getting ready to leave. "Wait," Benjo said, catching up to him.

"What?" Respow asked coldly.

"I know you said Kasey is still getting a tribunal." He flashed Kasey a look. "But he made a call, and I need you to know that Kasey is responsible for saving us," he said. "Without him, the terrorists would've killed the entire Panel."

"I read that in your report, yes." Respow, along with everyone else, had their eyes on Benjo. He was obscured by one of the screens. "Why are *you* telling me this?" Respow stole a smug glance at Kasey.

Benjo and Kasey exchanged looks. Staring right at Kasey, Benjo said aloud. "Because I know military tribunals don't go away."

"It's true," Tsarena said. "They both saved us."

Falisto joined. "Kasey's idea, Benjo's body."

Chief Adams came back with her coffee, the burned bean smell arriving faster than her footsteps. "Saved us but destroyed our electric cannons." She smiled for the first time since they met her. "A small price to pay."

Respow nodded and put his tongue against his cheek. "Understood," Respow muttered something to his pad and motioned towards the door. "Good to see PTF standing with PTF. Now open the damn thing."

Chapter 15

Benjo

"What about now?" Falisto asked.

Benjo sighed. "Nothing; same as two minutes ago." Falisto and Kasey sat behind him, with screens facing both of them alongside the Tayir craft. Benjo sat in front of the spaceship, poking and prodding with his metal hand.

Out of the corner of his eye, Falisto's whiskers grazed the floor. Like most Psys, he struggled to find a relaxing position in the chair. The GU was a cruel place for bipedal digitigrades. Falisto told Benjo he didn't love the characterization his "knees" bent the other way. Occasionally, a scientist or physical therapist agreed, but the majority usually asked "Does it hurt to sit like that?" Compromising his blood flow, Falisto opted to straddle the chair and bend backward to the ground. Comfortable? No. But Falisto wasn't one to stay in the same spot for a while.

"It's going to take some time," Benjo said again. He hoped that would be the cue they needed to give him some goddamn peace and quiet.

Falisto groaned. Lines of meaningless data populated displays as Benjo's fingers probed the ship. Through a process called "Raking," red electricity emitted from his fingertips and danced along the edges, carrying bits of loose data through Benjo's hand, all the way to his arm. An orange cable connected his arm to the computer. Raking was an older form of data absorption developed by Hybrids in the middle of the Sapien War when nearly all forms of communication came encrypted but still left behind tiny bits. An efficient way to exploit an efficient communication system.

"You know you *don't have* to watch," Benjo said. Despite a slight prickling sensation, Benjo didn't mind Raking. The task became mindless after a while. Almost healing. Benjo forgot about his Hypo Headache entirely after a few minutes of Raking up loose energy.

"No, I do." Falisto shifted a bit more in his seat, this time moving his head towards the floor and his feet above the backrest. "I wanna meet the bastard that thinks they can kill *my* people and get away with it."

Benjo didn't respond. Instead, he added his pinky finger to the mix, channeling extra lightning into his analysis. From behind him, Kasey swiped across his pad. They got louder with each tap while he scrolled. Semi-frequently, Kasey would blurt out the name of the article and his qualms with it.

"Kasey, you're driving yourself crazy," Benjo muttered. He didn't look back at Kasey, instead, he stole glances at screens with his reflection. Kasey's face was stern, and his eyebrows were slanted down with his lips in a tight scowl.

With a sigh, Kasey looked towards him, dragging his finger the whole way. "Can't help it." He read titles of articles, each one worse than the last. Every article found a way to insert Respow's name and grizzly details, mostly embellished but still triggering for Benjo and his Hypo Headache.

Kasey murmured, "So many wrong details."

"That's why you should stop," Benjo said.

After a few agonizing centuries for Benjo, Falisto dug the eye daggers out from the screens and stood up with the fabled announcement Benjo had been waiting for: Falisto was going for a walk. If anything, Benjo was surprised at how long Falisto lasted. Sitting still was not a forte of Falisto.

"Wanna join?" Falisto asked no one in particular.

"I could use a break," Kasey sighed.

Benjo nearly shooed them off. "I'm going to stay here."

"You sure you don't wanna come?" Kasey asked Benjo, one foot out the door. "The other PTF might come by, we told them we're all here."

"I'm sure."

Kasey shrugged, and the second the door closed, Benjo slouched his shoulders.

Finally, some peace. Benjo loved silence. The ability to hear a pin drop gave him a sense of security and mental clarity, something he craved after the loud bombardments brought by the ships.

He needed the quiet to map out how an advanced species reinvented the wheel by building a sphere with FTL and impenetrable defenses. The ship posed a set of problems all within the same realm: it violated physics. Not violated physics in a way that, with a couple of mental gymnastics, could be made sense of. This ship straight-up broke fundamental laws.

That's not to say Benjo didn't expect his information-gathering arm to platter an answer. The likelihood that a message would appear explaining the ins and outs of the ship was one in a billion, and that was with favorable rounding.

But he persisted with Raking. Benjo's mom taught him tricks of the trade with Raking before it even had a name. She would've loved the engineering ingenuity behind the Tayirs.

His mother came from a long line of Hybrids, but she made it a point to not force Benjo into the lifestyle. "Do as I say not as I do," was her motto.

But what kid doesn't want to be like their biggest hero? Benjo craved enhancements. Even at five years old, he demanded his mother give him as many upgrades as legally possible. At the time, children could only get less invasive treatment, but it came with major disdain and judgment from other parents. So, he settled for increased breathing capacity and a hand scanner.

Benjo's palm still had that scanner, albeit updated. Most Hybrids kept their first upgrade as a sort of memento, just not inside their body. But then again, most weren't as sentimental as Benjo. Lots of Hybrids he knew kept their "firsts" in glass cases on display in their homes, or fashioned it into a necklace or some other memorabilia. Information from the ship took his scanner longer than new tech would've, but it was a small price to pay for a reminder of the good old days.

Benjo's father teetered on extremist-sided politics in the pro-Hybrid sphere. He always demanded the newest implants, donating organs before

Human parts could be regrown. He was the first Human to receive a robotic set of eyes, followed by bones, and then his heart.

Fitting that's what did him in the end his heart—literally speaking—was what pushed him to the Point Of No Return. In an instant, he wasn't his father anymore, turning into a machine living in a poorly renovated Human body. His brain couldn't process Human emotion the same way, and even though he was still there, Benjo missed him.

An unexpected spark from the ship jolted across his body, sending a paralyzing pulse from his fingertips. He flinched in pain and a lump appeared in his throat that he couldn't stomach.

"Gah!" he blurted out. Both his eyes blinked, his organic one dry suddenly. He stole a glance at the monitors. Nothing changed. "Why the hell won't you open!" Something about the ship allured Benjo's hand, and he kept it in place despite his anger.

Ding!

Benjo turned his head to the source. New data, in a language his converter couldn't understand, flooded the screens. It was different than before, no longer ones and zeroes, but something tangible with scribbles and dots that had a meaning, just one he couldn't understand. Each screen succumbed to words and phrases of the dialect, and a tingle in his hand transformed into a blistering shock wave. The ship drove unfathomable amounts of data through him as a conduit. Terabytes of temporary files followed by petabytes of permanent ones. Then more. Bewildered, Benjo went to unplug the cord, but his mind fought the temptation, keeping his fingers glued. It was as if he forced his hand on a stovetop, scorching every atom composing his skin.

Information ran through wires to the computer, heating his body several degrees. Using his Human hand, he gripped onto his burning metal hand, injuring himself in the process. *Just a little more.* Pressing forward with both hands, Benjo closed his eyes and bit the air between his teeth. Another lightning bolt from the ship made his face contort and his mouth tremble. Sentences of code connected into paragraphs, then strung together like essays before forming novellas and then epics. Letters and shapes scurried through Benjo until he couldn't take it anymore. The information seared like a branding until—

He yanked back his hand. Heat festered between his fingers like a volcano about to burst. The flame webbed like goo. Hot to the touch and smoke sizzling out of some of his metal parts, Benjo held his arm with his Human hand. A massive influx of air from other processors in his body overclocked to cool him down. Internal fans powered up. He breathed on a three-four-five count, calming the melting iron and Human heart, and moved away from the blinding spotlight above him.

The screens beckoned him. "What the hell?"

Benjo moved the computer mouse. Although delayed, it followed his direction, lagging by about half a second with a stutter cutting in the frames. The processor struggled. He tried to make sense of symbols and phrases, but without a dictionary containing every Tayir language, it was an impossible task for one Hybrid, let alone one person.

Shifting his hands, Benjo hovered over the keyboard. At the bottom of the console was a thin, white box resembling a command prompt. The text indicator blinked, waiting for input. "Probably won't work," he whispered to himself. He typed "/help."

Two new lines of code appeared, with what Benjo presumed meant "invalid command."

With a groan, Benjo called Kasey. Loud chattering from people accompanied by chomps and crunches with chewy foods greeted him over the line. Benjo's body recoiled when Kasey smacked his lips, munching on something that sounded... juicy.

"*Kasey,*" Benjo spoke, loud enough to drown out the eating sounds Kasey made. "*Do we have a Tayir translator anywhere?*"

"*I can ask,*" Kasey swallowed before jettisoning another section with a new bite. "*Why?*"

"*I got something. I don't know what, but it's something.*"

Kasey shouted with glee. "*That's great! Should we come back?*"

"*Not yet,*" Benjo replied, nearly cutting off Kasey. "*Don't rush.*"

"*I'll check with Respow. Being a Representative better come with perks.*"

The line clicked, and Benjo sighed as silence settled back in his ears. He slashed more nonsense into the command line, trying different languages, swapping between keyboards every few minutes. Each time the same two lines appeared.

After a few hundred different attempts with no results, he finally hit a true wall: he got locked out of more guesses.

"*Benjo*," Kasey typed in a message. "*I got it!*"

Solemnly typing back, Benjo acknowledged his message. If nothing else, knowing what the code said could lead to reverse engineering. He'd planned to explain the mysticism behind the ship once he cracked the code, but getting back the command prompt wouldn't be easy, especially since he didn't know how the hell he got there in the first place.

"*Good*," Benjo responded.

"*I'm bringing it now*," Kasey typed. "*By the way, Amber was looking for you.*"

Benjo froze. His eyes looked at the name in horror. Praying it would disappear, he harped on the message. After a full minute of staring, he typed back. "*Amber? My ex Amber?*" He deleted the second sentence before sending it.

"*Yeah, Amber.*"

It was like he fell—no, got pushed—down thousands of kilometers to an endless abyss. A well of emotions splashed over him, morphing into oceans of anxiety. "*Did she say why?*" Benjo paced now, admonishing Kasey for taking longer than twenty seconds to read the message. He was quick before, why take time now?

"Put down the burger," Benjo murmured mid-pace.

"*No, she said she wanted to see you.*" Kasey's message didn't have needless emoticons like usual.

"*Do you think she's coming here? Did you tell—*"

Before he finished the message, a woman slithered through the doorway. He didn't recognize her at first, but it was her judging by the uneven blonde hair and the way she sucked all the air out of the room. She entered her usual stance, leaning against the wall. The first difference since the breakup was a golden outline around her arms.

"It's been a while," Amber said. Her voice was just as sultry and seductive as he remembered. Each word intoxicated him with a magical force. Light from above illuminated her as she entered the room.

"A-Amber," Benjo stuttered, adjusting his spine upright. He patted down his unitard, trying to clear it of any obvious wrinkles as she approached.

Her arms were so bright and shiny that they might as well have had the price tag on them. No Hybrid kept their metal portions so unadulterated from scratches, even those as neurotic as Amber. Her bronze arms didn't size up like Benjo's. Instead, hers slimmed down, occupying far less space but containing far more features. Platinum strands of hair reached up from her shoulders, merging into a darker gradient before hitting brown roots.

"This the Tayir ship?" She pointed with her index finger. "I thought those guys were high-tech."

"You'd be surprised." Benjo laughed. "I can't seem to hack in."

"Did you try—"

"—Yes, I tried Raking. First thing I did."

Amber smiled. "I was gonna say brute force, but Raking was second."

Benjo flashed her back the same grin. "Neither worked."

"That's a shame, but looks like you got a lot." She eyed pages of data.

"Would help if I could read it," Benjo mumbled.

"You know, I heard rumors they still have two worlds that weren't destroyed," she said, watching Benjo painstakingly.

Benjo let out a laugh, more nervous than his smile. "You always did like conspiracy theories."

She smirked, sashaying over to the ship. "You're still Raking with that old thing? Let me try." Using the same technique as Benjo (although faster), ice-colored electricity emitted from her fingertips, spreading across the Tayir ship and absorbing bits and pieces of leaked data that seeped through the membrane. Benjo watched her drain data without as much as a wince. With twice as much electricity piercing from her hands, the process took seconds, and she put her hands on her hips when she finished.

"There we go," she said and pointed to the main screen. "All the info, which it looks like you already had."

"I just can't understand it," he groaned. The data seemed thorough, but there was something that caught his eye. "You did do me a favor."

"Fix gaps in the data?" She had a crooked smile to match her incredulous tone.

"No, you got me back to the command prompt."

Kasey returned with a chip in his hand. He walked in with Tsarena and Falisto, all three of their faces stained with various burger residue.

"Amber?" Tsarena blurted out.

Amber turned to meet her, both arms stretched into a "T" shape. "Tsarena!"

Giddy, the two of them yelped, jumping around and hugging one another. Amber wrapped her arms around Tsarena. "It's been so long!"

"Where've you been?" Tsarena shouted.

"Venori mission with Shamp and Tsoki then had to deal with first contact with some other aliens."

"Sounds exciting," Tsarena said, grinning ear to ear.

Falisto asked, "Any news, Benjo?"

"We have this fun command prompt." Benjo pointed to the blinking arrow. "Hopefully that," he said, moving the finger to Kasey's chip, "helps us."

The chip glowed a baby blue with ridges of gold and dots of green. The tiny thing amazed Benjo, how petabytes of information could be stored on such a minuscule chip he'd never know.

"You ready?" Kasey asked. He pulled out the device that would initiate the data transfer to Benjo's brain. Hybrids needed a "manual install." From a cable connected to the Hybrid and a compact disk reader, the manual install would boil in the info.

"Let's do it," Benjo said. "This'll be a piece of cake." He mouthed the words with a smug smile to Amber. A manual install couldn't come close to the pain he'd endured earlier from Raking. *I got this.*

Benjo was horribly wrong. Liquid magma infiltrated each section of his brain, searing it with rules of grammar, letters, and sentence structure of hundreds of Tayir languages. He suffered as the converter etched a new set of shapes, styles, and scripts into his skull. It carved exceptions to rules, then exceptions to the exceptions, before elevating his vocabulary from "like, do, make" to "love, perform, create."

Amber stopped her celebration with Tsarena to come over to him after he yelped a few curses. She put a hand on his back which he quickly and violently threw off. Amber slightly recoiled. His body convulsed as if he were having a seizure, and his chest flew up and down. The fire in his head nearly shot smoke out of his eardrums and he thought this was death, but just as quickly as the pain came, it left.

"Manual installs suck," Amber whispered.

Benjo reeled backwards. When his eyes rolled back, the foreign letters fell into place, the squiggles morphing into something legible. "You've got to be kidding."

"What?" Kasey asked.

"This isn't a command prompt." Benjo threw his hands up in the air, turning away from the computers back to his seat. "It's a log-in!"

"Isn't that an easy thing to fix?" Tsarena innocently asked.

Benjo's veins almost popped out of his forehead. "If you have lock-picking software."

"And we don't?" Kasey went towards the computer as if he could fix it with his magic touch.

Amber answered for the angered Benjo. "We do, just not for Tayir tech."

"What's the likelihood the username is terrorist1?" Falisto asked.

Tsarena looked like she had something to say, but swallowed the words. Out of the corner of his eye and amid the chaos of Falisto asking tech questions, Tsarena twiddled her thumbs. "Tsarena," Benjo said, his voice commanding and silencing the others.

She perked up. "Mhm?"

"You look like you have something?"

She stepped forward. "Why don't we try to reset it?"

Benjo blinked. "Like, restart it?"

"No. Reset it." She shook her head and tapped her pad hoping it would make the connection.

"Like, to factory settings?"

"Yes," she nodded. "Orchi ships have lots of software in them, we restart them and sometimes do a reset when we need to."

"It could work," Amber said from the corner of the workstation.

Benjo murmured, "Might as well try."

Cracking his mortal fingers, Benjo typed in a language called Habbah. He tried simple commands after opening the *real* command prompt. It wasn't until he typed "/restore" that something happened. Several wires levied the orb into the air. The ship's scratches healed into a uniform whitewash, returning to the state before its crimes. Like Human skin, pores coated the ship.

Benjo entered "/open," expecting the ship to reject the command. Instead, the ship hissed. A gray semi-circle shape carved out of the sphere, and soft smoke rushed out the indentation.

Falisto drew his weapon, followed by the others. Amber retreated behind Benjo, his Slart switched to lethal mode. Half the ship crawled up, almost gliding over the topside. Controls decorated the interior, but all they could focus on was the creature inside.

Kasey whispered what was on everyone's mind, "A Human?"

Chapter 16

Tsarena

Tsarena did practically everything. She played all types of songs on her fluvette, baked nearly everything (Human or Orchi), and sniped targets from any range. Hell, she even made a name for herself at a Galactic Burger eating competition two years ago. But, no matter how much training, videos, or even reading on the subject, there was one thing Tsarena couldn't do. Interrogate.

The man's deranged eyes somehow found focus staring into hers. She didn't cower away from his gaze by any means, but she didn't exactly enjoy looking evil in the face. Tiny blood vessels routed the man's neck, and the more Tsarena watched him, the more her stomach churned and throat itched.

"*All good?*" Kasey asked through comms.

"*Yeah,*" she said, cocking her head where the overhead light didn't reach.

The man hadn't moved, but he followed her eyes diligently. He sat with both his legs and hands cuffed together with the steel chair and table in the middle of the otherwise empty room. It eased Tsarena's mind when she leaned in.

Usually, terrorists opted for discreet clothing and features, something to stay under the radar and avoid cameras hunkering down on every inhabited celestial body. Instead of neutral tones and bland clothing, he had curly aqua hair with gray tips. Although trivial in some regards, his clothing's pattern didn't resemble anything Tsarena could place. His unitard contoured around his body, with large stripes of tan and brown appearing like bad camouflage. But one detail stood out, the unmistakable mark of Sapien: an open palmed hand on the unitard.

"What's your name?" Tsarena asked for the fourth time.

The man just watched her. On the table's corner, Tsarena pinched a cup of the coffee she poured earlier as a bargaining chip. She sipped from it, then plucked another cup from her side. The coffee inside was black and tepid but was better than nothing. She placed it in front of him just far enough so he couldn't reach it with his restraints, a technique she read about.

His eyes, large but vacant, followed the steam from the pot where she poured more into his mug to warm it up, the first thing to finally break his death stare. Tsarena rose from her seat and walked towards him, coming to his side. "You want it?"

His lips, pink and chapped, quivered slightly, forming a quiet sound that resembled a yes. She inched the cup by less than a millimeter. "What's your name?" She hoped the fifth time was the charm.

"I don't have one." He shifted his gaze fully onto the coffee now. His nose picked up a scent from further away, and he sniffed with extreme force, trying to yank the smell back into his nostrils. "Do you have food?" he asked. His ivory skin peeked out his unitard, decorated in black tattoos and markings that favored quantity over quality.

Tsarena narrowed her eyes. "We do." She sat on the end of the table to face him again. "For people that answer our questions." Tsarena had a bit of a smug smile. *Maybe I am good at this?*

"I only have a code name. 'Owl.'" His eyes fluttered to the coffee. "Please," he whimpered.

A cold wave emanated through her body. Maybe compassion? *Okay, maybe I'm not good at this.* With her off-hand, she took the mug and held it to his lips. He imbibed and guzzled it down faster than Tsarena could keep up with. She kept pushing the cup up until nothing was left except for a few shavings of coffee beans that slipped through the machine.

He panted with coffee droplets dripping from the sides of his lips. Tsarena looked around for something else she could offer him. All she had was more coffee, so she levied up the pot. "Are you gonna answer my questions?"

Slack-jawed, he looked at her with his raccoon eyes more wired than before. "I will," he muttered. "I need food."

"*Kasey,*" she whispered, holding her comms. "*Can you get us a snack?*"

"*Uh—I can try?*"

She turned back to the man, his jaw cracked open and his pupils dilated. His eyes longed for the coffee pot Tsarena still held.

"No," she scorned. "You get more when I get answers."

With his dry mouth and cracked tongue, he mumbled to her, "What do you wanna know?"

Tsarena rested into the back of her chair. "Well, for starters, your real name, not just a code name."

"My name—my real name—is AJ Voisis." His eyes darted back to the coffee pot. Tsarena refused to swallow the empathy beckoning her and poured a generous amount into his mug.

"I have some sugar," she said. "Want it?"

He shook his head. Taking a singular packet, she dropped the speckles of sweetness into the liquid. "I don't have something to stir," she said. Pushing it forward, she fired her next question. "What were you doing in a Tayir ship?"

"Attacking Kyros." Her unamused, death stare made him amend his answer. "It was an order."

"Order from who?"

AJ sighed. "My higher-ups."

"You know, generic answers aren't gonna speed up the food."

He grimaced. "I'm being as specific as I can."

Tsarena flashed him a wry smile. "I doubt that." Taking her pad out, she wrote notes in the corner of a blank page. *Doesn't like to answer specifically,* she wrote. Looking up, she asked another question. "Where did you find the ship?"

His tongue dug into his gums and swept up what coffee residue he could conjure. "My *employer* got it from the Black Market."

"You got it from the Black Market?" Tsarena alerted Kasey through her earpiece and wrote it down.

"My employer did," he said again. "When can I get something to eat?"

"When you tell me who you're working for." She knew the answer, he wore it. But a Court (if he got to one before execution) would want an admission.

He pushed the mug forward and used his index finger to point at the pot. "Sapien." His eyes looked down at the symbol, banned in the GU for the history it evoked. "Can you let me drink again?"

Tsarena nodded. "How'd a guy like you start there?"

"Sapien?" he asked incredulously. Before she could answer he added, "No one starts there. You end up there."

"So, it was end game?"

He laughed. "You misunderstand, alien."

There it was. Evil. Equipped with empty eyes and blue hair. The word "alien" wasn't a slur, but it wasn't hurled by someone trying to be friends. Tsarena froze, the empathy dissipating from her body. "Then help me understand, terrorist."

"First, food."

"I only give food to people that answer my questions *and* call me Tsarena."

He stiffened. Evil met its match. "They recruited me."

"They?"

"Sapien," he said.

"Who specifically?"

"Like I said, we used code names. His name was Zelus."

"What does this 'Zelus' look like?"

"A Human."

Tsarena's nostrils flared. "Be specific."

"Masculine pronouns, broad shoulders, scratchy voice."

"Hair?"

"Most of his head was obscured."

"Convenient."

He shrugged. "It's the truth."

Tsarena sighed. "One more question then I'll get you some food."

He agreed. "Ask."

"Why did Sapien attack Kyros?"

"I don't know."

"*I got some food,*" Kasey said to Tsarena. "*Crappy, expired pretzels.*"

Tsarena rose from her chair and began leaving the room. "That's your food calling me, I'll be back." She slipped out of the room, gently closing the door but leaving it slightly ajar. At the end of the hall, Kasey dangled his bag of pretzels.

"Thanks," she said with a smile. "It's going well."

"Good," he sighed. "Some good news." Falisto tip-toed past Tsarena, and, when she turned back, she saw Falisto slam the door into the interrogation room and *clicked* open the lock.

"Falisto!" Kasey barked.

* * *

Kasey

Kasey slammed his fists against the door. "Open up right now, Falisto!"

With two open palms, Tsarena banged her hands in tandem with Kasey. The bag of pretzels were cast aside, now crumbs. A sleeping Benjo grew irritated with the commotion as he stumbled out of bed.

"What is with all the yelling?" he groaned.

Tsarena shouted in between slaps along the door. "Falisto locked himself in the interrogation room and is torturing the guy!"

Between a stroll and light jog, Benjo headed towards the two of them. Benjo peered in using his hands. Falisto's claws grazed across the man's cheeks, swatting him with his dominant paw. Falisto preferred a more direct approach compared to Tsarena.

"Who do you work for?" he barked.

"Sapien," he whispered through the sound of squelching blood in his mouth.

He slapped him again, the claws digging into his skin a bit more. "Who in Sapien?"

"I don't know their name." His face bled from the cuts. They crosshatched, making pound symbols from each claw-drawn swipe. AJ coughed, choking on blood in his throat.

Falisto ignored another slam, this one much more forceful than before. Benjo rammed into the door a final time, bringing it down like a house of cards. Kasey and Tsarena poured in one after the other.

"Falisto, stop!" Kasey drew his Slart, the gun only a few meters from his head.

AJ trembled underneath him. Falisto looked back down at AJ, his nails retracting. "Pathetic rat," he muttered.

AJ responded by spitting blood from his throat at him. "You're just a giant cat."

Benjo tackled Falisto before he fell into temptation to make a lethal swipe. Seizing both of Falisto's arms, Benjo yanked him back. Falisto yelled at the bleeding AJ. "And we kill rats for fun!" He shouted. Benjo kept dragging him, both arms under, and pulling him towards the fallen door.

A puddle of blood sprawled from AJ's lips and face, tattered to shreds. His hair, once multicolored, morphed into a crimson-stained ocean. Tsarena rushed to his side, her hands hovering over his face, unsure where to start.

"Tsarena, call a doctor," Kasey ushered. He joined her, going to his knees. Unsheathing his canteen, he gave the man some water. Tsarena lifted him by his head, causing some water to cascade down his blood-soaked neck. He looked like an Orchi from all the blood.

"Doctor will be here soon," Tsarena said.

AJ coughed, his voice coming back a bit after he spit some more blood out to the side. "Thanks."

"Not all aliens are violent," Tsarena said.

AJ kept his eyes closed, one too bruised to open and the other scratched in three directions. Part of Kasey wanted to lay down the law. He thought of the hospital and all the men Chief Adams lost. He thought of civilian infrastructures suffering catastrophic damage. He thought of the utter chaos the GU was in now; how one attack completely destabilized it.

Those thoughts painted over whatever sympathy he had. Buried with layers of pain and hate, Kasey took back the canteen. "You need to answer our questions," Kasey roared.

"I like the alien more." AJ mused. "Didn't you promise me food?" He coughed, some blood coming out of his lungs.

Tsarena, doe-eyed and stunned, looked at Kasey. He nodded his head towards the resting spot of the pretzels. She hustled over to them and popped open the bag. AJ was still handcuffed, so Tsarena volunteered some, pushing them forward along the table so he could eat at his speed without having someone hanging over him and feeding him.

"I'm Kasey," he said.

"A Human!" he chuckled with his cut lips. "All it took was a cat beating me up and the red-lady."

Kasey looked unamused. "Her name is Tsarena, and his name is Falisto. You will address them as such." He shifted. "I'm not your friend," he spat. The venomous words left a bad taste in his mouth like Psys sushi.

AJ nodded. "What do you wanna know?"

"For starters, why?"

"That's the big question, huh?" AJ scowled.

"How does Sapien benefit from attacking a Panel full of Humans?"

He rolled his eyes. "Full Panel of Humans," he muttered. "You accept them." He kept his voice pointed, the "you" lunging at Kasey's chest.

Kasey kept his stoic face as much as his body let him. "And that warrants an attack?"

"We went for them." He pointed to the toppled door where Falisto lunged earlier through.

"But you used alien tech. Tech from an extinct species."

"You take honey from bees but they aren't Human." AJ coughed. "The Tayirs were feral. Their machines aren't."

Kasey leaned forward. "Did you get them from the Tayirs?"

"I don't know where we got them," he admitted. "I just know—"

"Why didn't you call me sooner, Mako?!" Respow stomped over to the interrogation room. He planted his boots on the collapsed door, balling his fists.

Kasey popped up from his chair and walked towards him. "Because we had it under control," Kasey explained in a whisper. "I assumed you had bigger things to attend to."

"Not bigger than finding the bastard himself."

"Captain, are you sure—?"

"Representative." Respow snarled. He looked at the man, seeing cuts covering his body. "My God, what did you do?"

"We have medical on the way." As the words left Kasey's mouth, two nurses strolled in, each with their own medical bags.

"Leave us," Respow said.

"He's a dead end," Respow muttered. He hadn't spent too much time in the interrogation room but clearly had enough of AJ's tactics. The light brightened his skin, slightly wrinkled, with the scar from his chin to his eyebrow less visible than usual.

"Any suggestions?" Kasey asked Respow, both of them outside the room with the door reattached.

"I'll call some professional interrogators," Respow muttered, pulling out his pad. "Get as many as possible."

"What should we do?" Kasey asked. Although centuries of reading material in the form of Tayir code waited for him, he prayed there was something else he could do that wasn't so boring.

"Wait," he said. "Until you get a lead there isn't much you can do."

"I'm not waiting," Falisto growled and pushed past Kasey and Tsarena. Benjo stopped him, intervening with a jump between his routes.

"Like hell, you aren't," Benjo commanded. "You just gave our best source of information scars."

"I don't take orders from you," Falisto hissed.

"As your superior, you should," Benjo said.

Falisto kept his footing, looking into his eyes. "I don't plan to."

"Stop," Respow said, silencing their voices. "I know we're all riled up." He adjusted his collar, undoing the top button and letting some of his neck skin pour out. "But we have to play this smart. I don't know if it's connected. Sapien just killed every Representative, essentially igniting a coup. If we don't get a grip, the GU is over."

After a pause, Respow continued, "I'll do the politics of it. Representative Mayah, God rest her soul, was good at one thing: media training. While you all figure out what's going on, I'll do what I can. You all weren't chosen to be PTF for no reason. I have faith in you all."

Kasey cracked a smile. Respow's empowering speeches always leaned on the shorter side, but their scarcity made it effective.

"We don't have a lead," Falisto lamented.

Using his entire arm, Respow pointed in the direction of data from the Tayir ship. "Your lead was here while you were cutting up the single asset we have."

Kasey's smile faded. This was, indeed, a Respow pep talk, ending before it even started.

"That data is gonna take us months to comb through!" Falisto shouted, forgetting his place.

"Representative Bigon would agree with me that's your lead." Respow's voice was the same level but sharper with the tempo. Falisto gulped.

"We'll look through the data," Benjo added. "I'll see if I can make a script or something."

"Good," Respow said, pulling up his pad. "I gotta run. Stay in touch, and like I said, follow the lead."

When Respow left earshot, Tsarena waltzed into the room with her hands behind her back. She had a smile as wide as Kyros, and her eyes perked up gleefully. "I have an idea," Tsarena suggested.

"What's that?" Kasey asked.

"Amber's gonna join us." Tsarena clasped her hands together.

"What?" Benjo blurted out. "Not that I'm opposed, I just thought she'd—"

"Does she know our next move is reading?" Falisto muttered.

Tsarena continued celebrating with jumps and the occasional fistshake. "I have an idea for that, too."

Kasey cut in. "Does she even wanna join? I thought she was with Tsoki, Shamp, and Drake as a squad?"

"She wants to join! Shamp and Tsoki are both en route from the Cerapto, so she has time. Drake is MIA."

"Cerapto?" Benjo asked.

"New aliens," Tsarena murmured. "They're just your run-of-the-mill nomadic species. Very Venori-like."

"She could help with the script," Kasey suggested to Benjo. "Could be a lot of help."

"Or," Tsarena said, pulling up her hands in a defensive position prematurely. "Instead of going through endless data, I know something we can do." A mischievous smile crossed her lips.

Kasey responded, "What's your idea?"

Chapter 17

Kasey

"I can't believe we're really doing this," Benjo sighed. His fingers tapped along his pad, sifting through tabbed datasets extrapolated from the Tayir ship. Two days had passed. Since then, Amber joined them on a journey through mountains of data, seeking the location of the Black Market. They sought it through the Tayir ship's code which provided information ranging from useful sections, like weapon systems, to completely superfluous, like cleanliness regimen.

Amber sat across from Benjo in Falisto's ship, while Tsarena sat in the front with Falisto. Kasey hovered out from the group, standing. Falisto's flight path was murderous to Kasey's stomach.

"I think we're well within our rights." Amber turned the page on her book. "What was it Respow said?" She moved from her book to Kasey. "'Follow the lead?'"

Benjo grunted. "We're going on a fishing expedition."

"We have some idea," Amber countered. "Tsarena and I narrowed our search considerably."

"I still don't like this." Benjo turned to Kasey. "You're not gonna sit?"

"No, I just wanna stretch my legs." The lie sounded convincing enough for Benjo to drop the matter and go back to his pad. Despite Kasey's annoyance with Benjo taking refuge in Kasey's unassigned-but-still-proclaimed seat, he didn't mind standing on this particular ship.

Falisto's Navigator didn't come equipped with chairs for Human knees. Instead of the normal back support Humans, Orchi, and Venori were used to, these chairs were miniature sun chairs, built for Psys' stomach to rest against. The only real "comfortable" position required Kasey to lay nearly supine with the seat belt getting dangerously close to his neck, something he didn't want with Falisto flying. If he wanted to be strangled, he'd violate another direct order from Representative Respow. *Representative*, Kasey thought to himself. The juxtaposition didn't sound right to him.

In the cockpit next to Falisto, Tsarena typed on her pad trying to find traces of the Black Market. She and Amber conducted a literature review of every known planet and satellite with methane lakes and a yellow atmosphere, then cross-checked it with information gathered from the Tayir ship.

Rumors hinted the Black Market operated along a slew of asteroids in the Kuiper Belt. Others claimed it hid below ground on a desolate planet plagued with radiation and searing heat. Among the rumors was one consistency: it was in the solar system. Not a solar system, *the* solar system. While that was still nebulous, it was a much better limit than the entire galaxy. Still, the solar system was massive, and Kasey wasn't sure where his head was at with returning and potentially seeing home again.

"Kasey, what's the order of the planets?" Tsarena asked, turning her neck from the cockpit.

"Mercury, Venus, Earth—"

"See I told you!" She shouted to Falisto. "Mercury *then* Venus!"

"No offense, Kasey, but I'm still gonna check," Falisto said dismissively.

Kasey rolled his eyes. "Offense taken. That's my home system."

"Or take it from another Human," Amber said, her eyes still glued to the page. "Kasey's right."

Tsarena produced an article written by a Psys journalist. "See?"

Falisto rolled his eyes. "I doubt the Black Market is on Earth."

"Well, we know it's *somewhere* in the system." Tsarena ventured back to the rumor mills on her pad.

"The solar system is freaking massive." Kasey tapped his foot, the Psys chair looking more enticing as an ache shot up from his heels. His knees begged him for rest, but he'd been working on his posture, and sitting in a

Psys chair might as well be a reset button for that progress.

"Benjo," Tsarena started, "any ideas?"

"Nope, still fixated on the fact that we're about to commit a crime."

"It's not a crime," Kasey defended. "We're just merely *stopping* more crime."

"GUM Article Two would disagree," Benjo muttered.

Amber spoke up, ignoring the inconsolable Benjo. "I bet it's on Titan."

"Any settlements there?" Kasey asked.

There was a slight pause. Everyone exchanged looks, the silence deafening. "Guess that's a no?" Kasey asked.

"One way to find out," Falisto said.

"Setting coordinates for Titan," Tsarena said.

"I don't know if there was a settlement." Benjo puffed up his chest and sat upright. "But, logically speaking, it's the best place to have a Black Market."

"Why?" Falisto asked.

"Wouldn't a Black Market wanna be somewhere easy to hide?"

"True," Kasey agreed. "I mean, Titan is one of the few places we never terraformed."

"The fact that Humans even do that is astounding," Falisto laughed. Tsarena let out a giggle as well.

"Better than using artificial gravity your entire life," Benjo countered.

"Either way, Titan isn't terraformed so we won't know right away." Kasey's palms moistened with sweat as the Navigator hurled through space.

Amber stretched her back. "Do we even have the equipment to enter?"

Tsarena peeped back to the corner cubby with hazmat suits. "Those could work?"

Kasey walked over to the suits, plucking one from the closet. "Temperature regulation and oxygen, but it's not pressurized. We'd probably be flattened in an instant."

"I don't think we need it pressurized," Benjo said. Confirming his suspicion he pulled up the Titan profile. "Ah-ha! Nitrogen atmosphere is dense enough for us."

"I would say no offense, but seeing how it didn't help Kasey I'll save my breath. I'm gonna look it up." Falisto typed into his pad this time.

"Zero for two," Benjo smirked.

"What's even the point of a Black Market," Kasey whispered. "Who would even need it?"

"Sapien," Falisto snarled. "Or Jasoosi."

"This again?" Tsarena croaked. "I thought we left this behind?"

Falisto snapped back, "What made you think that exactly?"

Tsarena crossed her arms. "We have bigger issues. If we can find Tayir ship's logs we'll know if they went to Porygar."

"And if we find the Jasoosi seller we can find out who they sold it to and why."

"I doubt any Black Market dealer is gonna be forthright like you're suggesting, but it's the only lead we got." Kasey succumbed to sitting behind Tsarena, in the seat with the second highest mortality rate (the first being the pilot seat).

"We're gonna find something," Tsarena said. "We have to."

* * *

Tsarena

Tsarena was half asleep when her pad rang. It announced to everyone she was getting a call with blaring red and striking blue sirens like a Human police car. Her eyes fluttered open, and part of her thought by some stroke of luck Mahina finally returned her calls. She frowned at Tsoki's name on the notification. Not that she wasn't a fan of him, but she wanted to hear from Mahina.

"Tsal," she said. Her voice was dull and far from invigorated.

"Tsal," he returned, his voice mirroring hers.

"What's up?"

"I heard a rumor you're going to the Black Market?" His voice lowered, chatter from others over the line told Tsarena everything she needed to know.

"Why'd you call from *the Irene*? I thought you and Shamp were on mission?"

"The Cerapto aren't priority when a colony is missing, a virus is rampaging through the population, and a terrorist group attacked Kyros. Plus, Drake is doing most of the work anyway."

"Fair," Tsarena said. Her eyes wandered from the front window towards Kasey. "So, then what are you doing?"

"Just got called to Kyros," he said.

"Oh God, what happened now?"

He laughed. "It's a new mission, but not as nearly as alarming."

"What's that mean?"

"You know that terrorist you guys captured?"

This made her tense her eyebrow muscles. She didn't need updates on the play-by-play with the terrorist. "The one Falisto tortured?" Tsarena glared at him, a fire festering in her belly. Falisto gaped back at her, his paws barely holding the controls.

"Well," he started, "it turns out he had a toxic capsule in his cheek."

Tsarena's eyes widened and she straightened in the chair. "What do you mean?"

"He poisoned himself."

She held the pad close to her side. "Guys!" she hissed.

"What?" Kasey croaked, rising from his slouched position.

"AJ died!"

Amber and Kasey were the first to jump. "What?!"

Tsarena used one of her four-fingered hands to hold everyone at bay. "I'm gonna put you on speaker, alright?"

"Sure, that's fine," Tsoki said.

After tapping a few buttons, Tsoki's voice flourished from the speaker. "Hello?"

"Tsoki, hi," Kasey said. He had a smile on his face showing the teeth along his upper jaw. "I gave you one of my sodas at the commissary on *the Irene*."

"They still haven't stocked it," Tsoki laughed. "Who else is there?"

"Amber."

"Falisto."

Benjo waited as if a hidden person was in their ranks aboard Falisto's ship. "Benjo," he said, finally.

"So, what happened?" Tsarena asked.

Tsoki swallowed something over the line, a gulping sound echoing. "The terrorist took a cyanide pill."

Kasey narrowed his gaze at the air in front of him. "Any idea how he even got one?"

"Buried it in his cheek, bit it and it killed him."

Benjo shrugged. "That's an old method. Haven't heard about that in centuries."

"Did they get any more information out of him?" Amber asked.

"Did he suffer?" Falisto asked.

"Yes and yes," Tsoki said. Falisto grinned. Tsoki continued, "Allegedly, Sapien are getting all their ships from the Black Market."

"Good thing we're on our way there," Kasey said.

They were beginning to leave the Fusion Center's range. "Tsoki," she started, "we're gonna lose you, we're out of the Fusion Center's range—"

The call cut and Kasey's smile died along with the connection to the Fusion Center.

Tsarena leaned forward into the chair. She didn't mind having her stomach and chest supported by the chair, but she didn't like the lack of a proper headrest. But beggars couldn't be choosers when it came to having a Navigator on call.

She played with her pad, moving it to a rest position and attaching it to her hip as she usually did. Something bothered Tsarena, gnawing her like a mosquito on a particularly muggy day.

"What is it, Tsarena?"

She didn't know if Falisto was particularly good at reading people, or if she just couldn't hide her feelings. Maybe a bit of both? "I just think it's weird."

"That he...?" Falisto made a face, sticking his tongue out, and mimicked what he probably thought was the screech of a man dying of cyanide poisoning.

"How'd he get a pill?" she asked.

Falisto reiterated Tsoki's explanation. "Hid it in his cheek."

Tsarena turned her lips in a slant. "Wouldn't we have caught that?"

Falisto shrugged. "No? I mean, did you inspect him and do a full exam?"

"No," Tsarena admitted. "But he did get a scan."

"Scans like that miss stuff all the time." Falisto shifted in his seat. "Why do you think docking security takes so many different scans?"

"I guess." Tsarena tapped her foot along the base of the ship. But she couldn't shake the feeling that something was off.

* * *

Kasey

"How long do we have?" Amber asked.

Tsarena hunched forward onto her pad. "Just a couple of minutes at most."

"Good," Kasey sighed, leaning back against the wall of the ship. After a few hard turns, dips, and dives, Kasey held on for dear life on the overhead railing. Something about Falisto's ship made Kasey queasy, even apart from the erratic flying. Maybe it was the strawberry-colored flooring clashing with salmon accents, or the hauntingly familiar gray walls that reminded him of Musk Station. Navigators, despite consistently receiving engine upgrades, seldom updated their interiors.

For a few minutes, the group sat (or in Kasey's case stood) in silence. Then the inevitable sounds of asteroids bumping into the Navigator's FTL bubble *thumped* and *swooshed* the interior of the ship. With each pop Kasey flinched, but he kept shoving his thoughts backward.

A sizable rock hit the ship, sending it in a spin before automatically course-correcting. Kasey became one with the railing, gripping with both hands. He hissed air out the gaps of his gritted teeth. "I know this is *your* ship Falisto but can you please be more careful!"

He laughed, "It's just a rock. Stop worrying!"

"You said a few minutes, right?" Kasey squirmed at asteroids floating nearby.

Tsarena held out three of her four fingers. "You should begin to recognize it in three, two, one."

The Kuiper Belt became a distant cluster of rocks, separating the solar system from the rest of the galaxy. A familiar ring system encircled a giant ball of gas, followed by its siblings. Somewhere in the distance, Kasey could've sworn Enceladus, Rhea, hell—even Iapetus—were visible. The jaundice Titan was murky to the naked eye but simultaneously regal.

"See? Made it in one piece." Falisto initiated the auto-landing sequence and stood up.

Tsarena leered back. "You almost gave Kasey a heart attack."

"I'm fine," he murmured.

"Do you want some anti-nausea meds?" Amber asked.

Tsarena added, "I know you get motion sick, are you sure you're okay?"

Kasey's jaw dropped to the floor. "How'd you know I got motion sickness?" He asked.

"Kasey, I probably shouldn't tell you this," Tsarena started, "but you're much easier to read than you think."

It was as if Tsarena punched him in the gut with a fist of ring-covered fingers. "You know?" he asked, almost sounding betrayed.

"We all do," Falisto said. "You sweat. A lot."

Kasey didn't know whether to feel shocked or impressed. But Kasey didn't have to respond as Falisto spoke again. "And we're here," Falisto proclaimed, flying into the atmosphere.

Benjo fixated on his view out the window. "I'm not seeing anything."

"We just started," Falisto snapped. "Give it a minute."

"I'll run some scans," Amber said. She held her pad to the window, the camera doing the heavy lifting as Falisto glided the ship across Titan. The moon didn't seem like much of a titan, at most a demigod, to Kasey.

"And I thought Tyol was empty." Falisto veered the ship past methane lakes and ice rocks from the cold moon. "At least Tyol's walkable."

"I thought terraforming was crazy?" Benjo teased.

"Spending trillions of kirbies to make a planet habitable instead of finding a habitable one? Yes, crazy."

"Not to mention the ethics," Tsarena said under her breath.

Ethics wasn't a huge conversation in Human circles.

"Anyways," Amber interrupted, "what exactly are we looking for?"

"Something not made of ice," Kasey answered.

Benjo cupped his eyes, focusing on smaller, distant portions of the planet. "Amber, are you picking up anything?"

"Actually," she said, pausing for a moment afterward. "Wait a second, I think I got something."

"Lead the way," Falisto said.

"I'll share a way-point." With a ping from her pad, the target location popped into everyone's newly formed team chat.

Falisto squinted, his eyes moving off the controls, sending Kasey into a spiral. "I got the location." The ship's wheel snapped back into place, giving the Navigator a rapid tilt that self-corrected. "But I don't see anything here."

Benjo moved from his position to the cockpit. Using his hand, he shielded himself from the overhead light and narrowed his eyes. "That's a dome."

Falisto swerved the ship, causing the unbuckled Kasey and Benjo to lose their footing. "A warning next time would be appreciated," Benjo shouted in Falisto's ear.

"Sorry," Falisto snickered.

As the ship jolted through the fog, the dome cleared through the haze of yellow-green air. Ships in thousands of varieties parked along the edges of cylinder-like entrance points protruding forward from the dome. The dome was a rather large half-sphere, centered around the flattest area possible, and covered a large expanse. The cylinders made the dome look like a child's rendition of a sun and its rays. Around the enclosure, ice cracked in branching paths from boot marks, like a spider's web across it. Stringed lights shed some illumination, but they'd have to use some form of lighting so they didn't make a misstep. The distant sun's light was anything but helpful.

"Guessing that's the entrance," Kasey said. He glimpsed down at the hodgepodge of ships. From pirates' mixed-match of materials essentially hot glued together, to high-ranking officers' pristine, unreleased Navigators.

"And look at this," Falisto said. "The perfect spot."

Falisto lowered the ship next to an entrance of the cylinder appearing deceptively bigger. "Suit up."

"I'm the leader," Kasey said. "But suit up is right."

Falisto grinned, slapping on a suit with gloves and boots. Tsarena struggled to get into hers. She realized that the four-finger holes had only three, forcing her to squish her index and "middle" finger together.

Kasey and Amber managed into their suits without complaints, and, although slightly tight, Benjo's went without a hitch. "A Human made these," Falisto grunted.

"No," Benjo boasted. "I checked, made, and provided by the Hyoose Clan."

Falisto snarled. "That makes *even more* sense."

After pressurizing the Navigator to match Titan, the group exited the ship, crossing a section of frozen rocks until reaching a giant doorway outside the cylinder. Kasey examined it from the bottom up. Apparently, the Black Market feared simple instructions. Tapping the door, a button peeped out of the otherwise flat door, and without a second's thought, Kasey pressed it. Valves turned in synchronized harmony with one another, revealing an empty, black room with arched ceilings.

"That doesn't look safe," Tsarena said through the comms in her suit.

"I've seen enough Human movies to know this isn't a good sign," Falisto warned.

"It's decontamination, every planet has one that isn't terraformed." Amber entered the room.

Tsarena muttered, "Okay, one point for terraforming."

Taking a reluctant step, Falisto entered the room, with the pack right behind. Although darker, the ground was... different. Kasey couldn't explain it. It almost acted like quicksand, swallowing his boots, but it didn't constrict around his body.

Benjo slammed the door behind him. Locks spun and twisted again, and overhead lights illuminated the shadows. Speakers were anchored to the low ceiling, contrasted with the white room, now blindingly bright from surrounding lights.

A voice boomed through the speakers. "Decontamination ... [unintelligible] begin. Please do [unintelligible] to leave the [unintelligible]. Doing so will result in [unintelligible] life support failure."

"Did anyone catch that?" Kasey asked. "My converter got every other word."

Benjo repeated the AI's message, "Decontamination will now begin. Please do not attempt to leave the facility. Doing so will result in decontamination failure and life support failure."

"Basically, don't be stupid," Falisto cooed.

The lights shut off and ear-screeching sounds made Kasey and the others scream in agony. Kasey fell to his knees, his hands getting sucked into the sand. It swallowed his palms, before climbing up to his wrists, as the ringing blasted. Grains of sand vibrated with the sound, and a smokey haze funneled into the dome. After ten or so seconds, the lights flashed back on, and the sand stopped absorbing the team. Before he could catch his breath, however, vents flushed him and the others with intensive sanitation smoke, washing away every single bacteria lingering along the hazmat suits.

More light, not as nearly as harsh as the overhead ones, rushed in from the door opening in front of them. Groaning, they all rose, and waddled towards the light, everyone holding onto their ears through their helmets. If they didn't have tinnitus yet they certainly did now. As a disorientated Kasey walked through, he spoke, "Uh, this is not what I expected."

Chapter 18

Kasey

"On a scale of one to ten, how confident are we that this is the Black Market?" Kasey asked, still holding the left side of his head through the hazmat suit. The ringing, although gone, left Kasey with a pounding headache. His brain throbbed like it had its own heartbeat, and his eyes still struggled to adjust to light.

"Confident." Falisto gestured to a digital slab in the center of the entryway. A lime green directory sprouted from the ground, growing two meters like a Venori. Names etched in gold and black filled the screen. One particular name was victim to Falisto's sharpened gaze. "I don't think many places advertise Psys military rockets for sale." Sand breezed upwards from an artificial gust that vents blew out in the dome. Falisto plucked off his mask, quickly followed by the rest of the crew, stripping the oversized suit.

Without fog covering his view, Kasey peered at the directory, reading off each listed vendor. Most of them came with a code name, sometimes ranging from the enigmatic "Dragon" to the cheeky "Rockets 4 U." Others preferred to get to the point like "Psys Missiles for Sale." Using his index finger, Kasey scrolled down the list, scrutinizing each for a name unscrupulous enough to sell to terrorists. That didn't limit the list.

"What about this one?" Tsarena pointed towards a vendor named "Cherree."

Moving closer to where she pointed, Kasey squinted. "He's the only one labeled as a ship seller," Kasey said.

As Kasey moved to the side, Falisto took his position, sleuthing through the list of names and icons next to each. "There's a bastard." Falisto's claw pointed at the name of the Psys Missiles seller.

"Let's not forget why we're here," Amber reminded.

"Yeah, to stop crime," Falisto said.

Benjo blinked in pain. "Respow said to follow the lead—"

"—And what?" Falisto muttered. "Ignore crime along the way?"

Tsarena put her hand on Falisto, her fingers spread apart now that they weren't held in captivity by the gloves. "I know you wanna figure out who the seller is but—"

"—It's on the way." His voice was final and short. "We're going."

"Do you even know where we are?" Amber spun in a circle, taking in the entirety of the dome.

The Black Market sized about a quarter of a Kyros Panel. Given it was a lawless place, fire codes and regulations didn't prevent vendors from forming huts and stations overlapping one another like vertical housing. Above them, a visual of Saturn and its floating rings of ice rocks dotting space, with a lighter background. Every few minutes the display flipped to a new image. If it wasn't Saturn, then it was Jupiter, Mars, or even Venus. Never Earth.

Murmurs from sellers and buyers echoed across the streets. To Kasey's surprise, there was no dominant species. If anything, the Black Market had a variety of "rare" species. His eyes lingered around a group of Nyary, quadrupedal reptiles that fell somewhere between a wingless dragon and frilled-necked lizards. He'd seen a few, interacted with less, and personally knew only one in PTF. There were also Zayzays, fully suited aliens who *never* took off their armor, and Shura, sentient spheres that formed a singular sentient blob. All three species had radically different cultures but hung out together like the best of friends.

Footsteps sounded from the left. A female Psys sashayed towards the directory, her boots stomping along the way. Twin tails stemmed from her back, each long enough to wrap around one of her limbs completely. Although a rose cloak covered her face, no other species had giant whiskers like the Psys. It was odd seeing a Psys with knees bending correctly. "You're new," she said with a bit of annoyance. "Who let you in?"

"The chamber did," Amber said, pointing backward with a jerked thumb.

Kasey tapped her with his boot. "Heard about it from a friend." Being coy was the right way to handle this.

"A friend?" She stifled a laugh. "And who's this friend?"

"Like we'd say," Falisto retorted. Hot air left his mouth as he accentuated his holstered Slart.

Like most people, she didn't recognize the gun's status, or, if she did, it didn't elicit any reaction. "Good answer." One of her tails unraveled from her arm and wrapped around her waist. "Nima rarely come to these parts."

Falisto shot her a look. "Because we have honor."

"That makes you the exception? Given you're here?"

He growled in response. Falisto usually had quick-witted responses, but his teeth chattered instead.

Before he went into a tirade about the Nima-Hyoose War, Amber cut him off. "We're looking for ships. Know where we can find Cherree?"

"Cherree?" she asked with an eyebrow muscle raised. "You Humans can't get enough."

Benjo stepped forward. "Was someone else here?"

The Psys laughed, her belly rising and falling. "Rule one here: don't snitch. I didn't see anything; I didn't hear anything."

"So your honor is with other criminals?" Falisto muttered.

She ignored the jab to Kasey's surprise. "Regardless, I won't be sharing details, even if I had any."

"What about Cherree? Where is he?" Tsarena asked.

"Well, you can find *her* at the end of the road here." She pointed behind her to a meandering street spiraling up. From their vantage point, the shop resembled a shack or shed more than an official vending station.

Kasey nodded. "Ah, well thank you miss—?"

"—Miss Don't Worry About It." She turned around. "Rule two, don't use your name. Or, at least a real one."

"What do you go by then?" Amber asked. "Miss Don't Worry About It doesn't have a great ring to it."

"Helena Hyoose in these parts." She pushed her cloak, making her gray fur visible.

"Thanks for the help," Tsarena said wearily. She waved as Helena left, waddling off to some vendor selling ammunition.

"Wait," Falisto shouted. "I have a quick question." She kept walking away ignoring him. "Who's selling the Jasoosi guns?"

Mid-step, she stopped. Her head moved up from a slight angle downward, and she turned back slowly. Pivoting with her boot dug into the ground, she turned with her paw dancing above the holster of her gun. "What did you just say?"

Falisto pulled up his pad, zooming on the image of the gun Tsarena never returned. Quietly, Tsarena touched its holster.

"Jasoosi," Helena spat. "How dare you say such a blasphemous name."

"We saw sellers on the dark web," Benjo explained. "Granted, we don't know where."

"You won't find any here." She glimpsed at the only Orchi among them now, staring deep into her violet eyes. "Never say that name again. It'll get you killed." Her face contorted into a scowl. "Maybe even by me."

"Why do you guys hate Jasoosi so freaking much?" Benjo spat.

Both the Psys glared at him like he'd shot a litter of their young. "Are you serious, Cyborg?" Helena spat.

"Don't you dare call me that you—" before Benjo could continue, Kasey pulled him back, with Amber joining in the effort of dragging him away.

"It's not worth it!" Amber shouted. "Stop it!"

Helena didn't react. If anything she had a bit of a smirk, with her lips in a slanted smile. "You travel with them and they don't even know our history."

Tsarena defended, "Jasoosi, if they ever existed, only wanted to help."

Tongue pressed against her cheek, Helena fired back, "You know who else wants to help but manages to fuck everything up? Every single colonist in this goddamn galaxy." She spit to the ground closer to Benjo. "Jasoosi had the nerve—the absolute audacity—to 'raise' us up." Mid-growl, she continued, "But they didn't even try and ease us into their high society.

They looked at us like we were no better than animals, bugs even! Coming all high and mighty, saying they're saving us, helping us, then when we Psys finally realize we're being exploited, they spy on us!"

"Wasn't this centuries ago?" Amber shouted to match her tone.

"Psys never forget."

Falisto nodded in agreement. "Ever."

"Keep your robot on a leash." Helena walked off flicking her paw away as a sign of disinterest. Benjo didn't lunge like Kasey expected.

"You okay?" Kasey asked Benjo.

With his lips tight and his eyes narrowed he broke free of Kasey's grasp. "I'm fine." Amber grazed his shoulder, but, just as he did with Kasey's hold, Benjo broke from her touch. "Let's just do the mission." He commanded. Kasey didn't challenge the authority in his voice.

The team passed sellers of rifles and exotic pets, then by classic food vendors with cups of cinnamon sugar apples and basji. Countless sellers scurried up to Falisto, offering variants of guns fashioned from a hodgepodge of metals. Other vendors approached Tsarena with cheap clothing made from means banned in the GU. Hardly any approached Kasey, and no one came up to Benjo or Amber. *Eh, most of the stuff here is crap anyway.*

Atop the hill, Kasey took a moment to catch his breath in front of what he could only describe as a shack (and that was being generous). Metal sheets, charred with rust and markings from weather, formed the walls. The door, which was really just three of these sheets molded together with some polymer, appeared bolted shut.

"Do you think she's even open?" Benjo asked.

"Hard to tell." Kasey moved his head around the building and did a quick circle around its entirety. The shack couldn't have been more than the size of a Navigator, and like Falisto's, it didn't exactly scream "Human friendly."

Tsarena inched closer to the metal "door." Using the back of her fingers, she grazed it as if it could speak to her. "Guess we knock?"

"Why not," Kasey said.

Kicking her hand back and forth, she knocked four times. "Hello?"

After a moment there was a *click* and the door caved into the shack. From inside, a figure with a blow torch came into view. Pincers above its arms held onto other tools. Its four eyes blinked, and the creature had a breathing compartment attached to its mouth.

"Cherree?" Tsarena asked the Jasyx.

The woman spit out her rebreather and it bounced around her neck, tethered by a chain necklace. "Yes?"

Without any pleasantries, Falisto shouted, "Do you know anything about Jasoosi?"

"Falisto," Kasey commanded. Benjo smacked Falisto with the back of his Hybrid arm while the rest glared at him.

"Jasoosi," Cherree muttered. "Can't help you there."

"There was a gun for sale from here." Falisto stared at the team defiantly.

"Anyone can sell replicas. Good day." Cherree moved to shut the door.

Kasey cut in. "We're here about the Tayirs."

She stopped. "Come in." Reversing the door back, the Jasyx made space for them to enter.

The inside of the run-down shack wasn't much better than the outside. Without any light source, it was nothing more than a dark closet in the middle of a desert on a moon that smelled like eggs. In general, the room was rather bare for a seller of anything, let alone a place to live.

Cherree came to a specific part of the room, gently casting Amber to the side. She reached down with her pincers and twisted a hidden valve. One sheet on the ground creaked to the side, retracting into a depression. From the hole in the ground, a series of steps led to a hidden basement.

Cherree was the first to go down, ushering all of them to follow her. She moved sideways down the narrow entrance, crab-walking slowly as most Jasyx did. The corridor glowed, white like a laboratory, with several ships stationed along the walls. Kasey made out which species these ships belonged to, but a few stumped him.

"Welcome to my shop," she proclaimed with her hands stretched out horizontally.

"Oh my God," Tsarena said.

"Don't touch anything unless you plan to buy it," she warned. Her tiny legs tiptoed towards the end of the hallway.

"Back to the Tayir ship," Benjo said, irritated. "What do you know about them?"

She laughed. "Yes, I found a few. Looked like they had some sort of battle."

"Battle?" Kasey asked.

Cherree laughed again, "Don't try to get info out of me. It's not gonna work."

Taken aback, Kasey asked, "Did you hear about Kyros?"

"Oh, the place where we're all supposed to be all friends?"

Falisto let his claws emerge slightly. "Answer our questions."

Cherree stopped and turned around to the group. "Look," she said. "I just don't think Kyros works. I used to believe people were good but my customers proved me wrong."

"How'd you find these Tayir ships?" Kasey asked.

"I'll show you them," she said, walking towards the end of the hangar. "I'd been looking for ships from old civilizations. I kind of have a personal collection." She pointed to a few other spacecraft that clung to the sides. "That's a—"

"—An Observer ship?" Tsarena dashed to it, her eyes wide as could be.

Cherree raced after her. "Not for sale!" she shouted.

"Where did you get this?" Tsarena's eyes were wide and her mouth ajar.

Kasey didn't see the excitement about the ship. Hell, he didn't even see a ship. Behind the glass was a conglomerate of four cubes of varying sizes. They adhered to one another in a fashion that was foreign to Kasey.

"Looks like rocks," Falisto muttered.

"You came here for the Tayir ships," she redirected. "Down there." She guarded the Observer ship while the group shuffled to the end of the hall.

"Those are it," Falisto said. He inhaled loudly through his nose, edging closer. He growled as he sniffed the scent. "The Tayirs."

"Where did you find it?" Tsarena asked.

"I'm getting there." She input something on a green screen in front of the Tayir ship, pulling up a history of coordinates and locations.

"How did you get that up?" Benjo asked. "We searched through all the data we have!"

With its pincer, the Jasyx covered its laugh, "Any ship leaving here has its data wiped."

Benjo snarled, "Thug."

Kasey's eyes widened. "Benjo!"

"I don't care," Cherree sighed. "I'm making a living."

"People died because of what you sold!" Benjo shouted.

"You act like you're the first to see me with one of those guns."

Tsarena stuttered, "W-Wait how did you—"

"—It doesn't matter. You want your coordinates, I want you gone." She typed quickly on her pad. "There," she said.

Their pads jingled, each with the same set of coordinates. Kasey put the coordinates into a star map, pulling up an empty portion of a star system.

"There's nothing there?" Kasey asked.

"No, there certainly is."

Kasey flipped his pad around to her. "See?"

"I see," she muttered without looking. "Your pad is just wrong."

"We should arrest you," Benjo growled.

"For what? Selling private ships? GU's laws only extend to public things. I'm a private seller, no jurisdiction here."

"She's right," Amber defended. "Even if we wanted to, we couldn't. Unless these have been reported missing we can't."

"And even then you'd need the authority. PTF only has GU authority, not species authority. Now, since I'm doing you a favor, I'll just need compensation."

"We're not paying you." Benjo rooted his feet to the ground.

"That," she hissed, pointing to the Jasoosi gun, covered in its holster with layers of protection. "Would complete a collection I'm making of the Orchi."

"How'd you even—"

"—Tsarena, don't give her the gun." Benjo roared.

"Tsarena, give her the gun," Kasey ordered.

She unholstered the gun and skimmed Benjo and Kasey, each at one side of her. With a heavy sigh, she released it.

Cherree smiled. "Now leave and never come back."

Chapter 19

Kasey

Kasey loved sleeping. Unlike other kids, he never had trouble with it. The second his head hit a pillow, his tired eyes would roll back and he'd start snoring. Over time, Kasey adapted his habits, shifting from a belly-sleeper to a side-sleeper with a pillow wedged between his knees. Getting comfortable wasn't hard. He didn't constantly adjust his position, and he didn't have specific requirements for the sheet's thread count or the mattress's firmness. Kasey slept on his right side and Peyton slept on his left. The two faced each other, every night, for years.

Kasey grew fond of a warm body next to him, the heat of another person radiating until someone wiggled in more breathing room. Usually Peyton. Sleeping with someone wasn't the part Kasey loved. It was waking up to someone. Those times were a flash, a series of memories from a life so far that he started to lose details.

After Musk Station, Kasey hated sleeping. He tossed and turned, thoughts gnawing at him. They feasted on his memories, flashed moments he shared with Peyton. Happy memories tormented him, while horrific nightmares tortured him. Often he found himself awake with raccoon eyes. Panting. Screaming. Crying.

Sometimes, his hand would graze a body of pillows he aligned in a vertical row on what used to be Peyton's side. For a moment, his fingers would sense their presence, and he could trick himself into thinking Peyton was lying next to him. It was fleeting, but it gave him a rush he could experience. A tangible moment of peace.

He'd hoped sleeping on Falisto's ship would be easy since they'd grouped on the floor. It wasn't Peyton's body or their cotton sheets, but it was *a* body or bodies nearby. Someone to greet him in the morning after a night spent trying to sleep.

Unsurprisingly, he went to bed last. Kasey peered out the window from Falisto's ship, the only one of the group not lying prone. The blue FTL light didn't fully obscure stars they passed by, but rather washed them with an indigo hue. Kasey counted them as they passed by.

Behind him, the four slept, each in their unique rest pose. Benjo easily could've been mistaken as dead, sleeping on his back with his hands cupped at his waist. To Kasey's surprise, Amber slept next to him, her hands autonomously inching towards Benjo. Falisto snored, sleeping on his stomach, his whiskers whipping while his mouth trembled. Tsarena occasionally shifted, suffering from the Orchi variant of restless leg syndrome.

Kasey took his pad out. If he couldn't sleep he'd get something productive done, even if mundane as checking the news. When he checked on Kyros, the misleading headlines bothered him with all the exaggerated photos of Kyros crippled under missiles from monstrous white orb-ships. Any coverage of Porygar or Tyol had been either erased or drowned by the assault of Kyros, now with more AI-generated photos and articles to match.

Headlines like "KYROS ATTACKED; TAYIR SHIPS DESTROY PANEL C AND HIT OTHERS IN DAY OF TERROR; Representative Respow Vows to Exact Punishment for 'Evil'" and "War! Panel C Bombed by Tayir Ships." But then one made him stop.

"Representatives Are Killed by Tayirs as They Meet in Kyros; Representative Respow Sworn in on Navigator."

Kasey narrowed his eyes. It wasn't the Tayirs. The omission of one word materially altered the content. They were dead with only their technology somehow left behind. It was a Human piloting the ship, after all.

But then there was another article. "Chief Adams & PTF Defeat Tayirs." He scrolled to the next. "Tayirs Open War on GU with Bombing of Kyros." Another, "Tayirs Spotted Leaving Kyros."

He scrolled back to the first one that caught his eye, with a colorful depiction of a harpy with fangs and red eyes. Blood dripped from this particular one's teeth, and it cackled as much as a bird could.

Panel C, GU-2150 – Representatives for Humans, Orchi, and Psys were bombed and killed by Tayirs today. They died of wounds by an energy burst fired at them as they met in downtown Panel C. Captain Respow, who was sworn in on the S.S. Irene behind the Representatives' transport on Kyros, as the Representative for Humans of the Galactic Union 99 minutes after Representative Mayah's death.

Thousands of people are left injured, displaced, or even dead. The Tayirs— once thought eradicated—have resurfaced. They are vicious, bird-like creatures. If seen, extreme caution is advised, and notify GUM IMMEDIATELY. Do NOT engage with them.

Emergency relief funds can be donated at the link below.

Kasey continued down the rabbit hole, reading more and adding new details, and following hyperlinks like a scavenger hunt. Details changed depending on the source. Some claimed forty ships attacked in unison. Others claimed it was one mega-ship as opposed to an armada. Supposedly, "eyewitnesses" claimed to observe giant birds with fangs and claws ravaging Panel C and picking up children before shredding them apart in the air. Allegations piled against the dead race, with some saying citing their "violent propensity." The Tayirs were violent monsters.

As Falisto's Navigator passed by a Fusion Center, floods of messages from collateral contacts rolled in. Messages from people Kasey hardly knew, and some from total strangers took over his pad. They all thanked him for saving Kyros which was news to him given that it was Benjo's Hybrid body.

Cracking his knuckles, Kasey went back to his pad and searched for his name. That's when he learned he had single-handedly saved all of Kyros and somehow earned all of the species' trust. He was shocked to learn that he even gave an exclusive interview with GUT—the Galactic Union Times. A few articles heralded him. His heart thumped, this kind of attention meant Musk Station would come back up again.

He fought to have information about Musk Station kept on a tight leash. He didn't mind people knowing in passing, but it wasn't a fun story of valor and bravery. To Kasey, it was the source of the hole in his heart that he'd never, ever recover from. No matter how much time passed, how people told him it wasn't his fault, how hard he tried.

"Can't sleep?" Tsarena asked. She squinted her eyes, yawning and stretching her arms as if she'd awakened from the most relaxing sleep despite her leg banging against the strawberry floor.

"No," Kasey uttered. He only glanced at her before returning to scrolling.

She frowned, her eyes still droopy. "You okay?"

Kasey didn't look up. "Reading some articles about Kyros."

"Kasey, you're obsessing over it."

"This is different."

Tsarena grimaced and then sighed, her face scrunching up at Kasey's tone. "How bad is it?"

"Depends who you ask," Kasey said with a shrug.

"What's that mean?"

"I somehow destroyed an entire fleet of Tayirs and their ships."

"Right," she smirked. "Tabloids need to stay out of GUM's business."

"They're also saying the Tayirs are alive."

"Sounds about right," she said.

"These are official news stories," Kasey whisper-shouted.

Tsarena adjusted her blanket. "You need to read people's comments, their blogs." She took her pad out, making slow movements until the blue screen flashed her eyes. "You're probably still connected to Kyros's Fusion Center."

"How do I disconnect?"

She yawned again, this time with a much longer exhale. "Go to your settings." The alluring pillow coaxed her to lower back down. "I'm going back to bed. Night."

"Goodnight," Kasey replied. A shake from the ship made Kasey queasy. He'd already been anxious for the greater part of the autopilot's journey, but his need for sleep overcame the anxiety. Eyes fluttering, Kasey made his way back towards the sleeping bag next to Tsarena.

Zipping it down, Kasey wandered inside the black cushions. From the inside, he zipped it up, and the snugness of it gave him warmth he needed. Only a few moments inside and the warmth got a bit too smothering for his liking, so he decided only to subject one of his arms to the heat of the bag, letting the other flop off where the pillows, organized into the length of a Human body, should've been.

As he wavered between unconscious and conscious, Kasey's free hand grazed by a familiar warmth. Real heat. It pulled him out of near-slumber, forcing him into a state of cognizance. For a moment, his heart dropped to the bottom of his stomach, full of hope and glee only for him to open his eyes to Tsarena on the other end and not Peyton.

Kasey sobbed himself to sleep.

* * *

Falisto

Falisto dreamt during his second increment of sleep. It was the same sequence of his mother, Qiula. Unlike last time, Falisto was a teenager, with his white whiskers and acne visible from lumps of fur excavated by his nails.

"Falisto," his mother snapped. "Hurry up." She wore her formal Captain wear that she became known for rose-gold chains and emerald accents around her unitard. Four earrings dangled, each a different shade of verdant. She wasn't the "regal" type, but without a spouse, it was difficult to get away with certain behaviors. The microscope other Psys put her under, constantly analyzing and picking at her like some bacteria, was exhausting. Not just for her, but for Falisto too. He never liked the confining feeling of the royal unitards that always felt more constricting than helpful.

Falisto panted. "Yes, mother—"

"—Lady Qiula." Her voice thundered but still carried trace amounts of love in it the way it started softly before hardening into a boom.

Falisto glimpsed downward, resisting the urge to look into her eyes. "Yes, Lady Qiula."

For a moment, Falisto went back on all fours, but he remembered Qiula chastising him before so he quickly aborted the position. Instead, he hustled on two legs, following her down levels until they reached *that* part of the ship. He couldn't remember why but he hated this section, the way the walls felt like they closed in on him with the open aerial view of the front. It somehow managed to be both suffocating and too open, as if he stood in a treeless meadow but was surrounded by fire ants.

"Lady Qiula," Captain Bigon said. "The ship's just stopped." Captain Bigon looked the same, maybe a bit different in ways Falisto couldn't notice. His two-toned eyes' pupils thinned like prey wandered in his line of sight, and his whiskers only stretched slightly out his face. Age wore him down. Falisto could see it in the duller nails and canines reduced to blunt plateaus. In Captain Bigon's paws, he held a pad with a message thread he quickly closed out, and he holstered it to his side so he could bow at Lady Qiula's presence.

"Have you contacted the Tayir?"

"No, Lady Qiula." Pulling himself upright, the Captain kept his stare on the screens, watching the asteroid's eye view of the ships. They hung in space, creeping at the Lagrange point where they didn't use much fuel. "They haven't responded."

"Is this some sort of exercise they forgot to tell us?"

"I believe it's the ship—the other ship is the problem."

"*This is Lady Qiula,*" Falisto's mother barked into the comms. "*What's your status, Faixal?*"

"*L–Lady Qiula,*" the voice mumbled. Curiously, Falisto recognized the voice coming through the speakers in the Captain's deck. He couldn't identify exactly who it was, but he could tell by the raspiness and timidness that it was a Nima Clan Psys cowering under the pressure of speaking to her. "*Our energy cells aren't working.*"

She rolled her eyes and moved to look directly at Falisto. "*Did one of your incompetent soldiers fail to conduct pre-check?*"

Falisto recoiled at her tone. "Mother—"

"—Lady Qiula." She rolled the words off her tongue, enunciating every syllable. But when she saw Falisto's body twist away from her, she shut her mouth and exhaled through the nose. "*Don't worry,*" she said, retracting her tone. "*I'll bring you some cells.*" Like she had cooked fish, she struggled to mouth the next words. "*Sorry, Faixal.*"

Falisto nodded with his eyes wide and tongue out. "Thank you, Lady Qiula."

She winked. "I better not lose respect. Iron fists win wars."

"And kind ones don't start them."

She gazed at Captain Bigon. "Please, tell Representative Petra we're en route," she said. "Just a bump in the road."

"Yes ma'am," he said. He unsheathed his pad back, maneuvering to a different message thread.

"And you!" she said, looking at Falisto as she walked into the capsule. "When I get back I want you to tell me what you plan to specialize in."

"Mom, I don't—" Falisto stopped himself. "Lady Qiula, I don't know *what* I wanna specialize in."

"Figure it out by the time I'm back," she said, the glass obscuring her voice like a poor Psys' muffler.

Baby steps, Falisto thought.

Her capsule disconnected from the ship, and as it sped ahead, it was only then that he realized what was next.

"Stop the ship!" he yelled. Captain Bigon didn't react.

Falisto swiped the intercom switch. "*Mom, don't go, turn back it's gonna explode—*"

Falisto woke up, gasping. Portions of his fur dripped in sweat, with his eyes wide and pupils thin. His body shuddered, and his tear ducts wanted him to cry, but he wanted to punch, fight, do *something.* Get his mind off it. Panting, he shuffled to his bag, fumbling out his pad.

At the behest of Tsarena, he agreed to download the medical AI the GU worked on for PTSD therapy. She pulled one or two strings. Now they were in a closed test for the AI therapy.

Falisto went back under his sleeping bag, moving his black whiskers through, generating static electricity with the comforter-lined sleeper. Using his paw, he turned his pad on and navigated towards the application. After a press, a white screen overtook his pad, with the icon of a robot with a hospital plus sign along its head. An empty textbook stared at him.

Hi. Falisto started. *I'm having some trouble with*—he deleted the sentence. *I'm having nightmares of*—he deleted that one too. *Bot, can you help me*—that one as well.

Hiya! The bot wrote back. *I saw you typing, feel free to talk to me at your own pace. Can I have your name?*

"Fast bastard," Falisto whispered. *This is confidential?*

Yes, pursuant to the Terms of Service, clause 91, all information shared with me cannot be used for any purpose other than patient care.

Falisto groaned. *Less words.*

Sure, I'll use less words. Yes, this is confidential. What's going on?

I've been dreaming recently—I have for a while but I keep dreaming of my mother.

When you say recently, how recently?

Every three nights.

Very frequently. You are a Psys, correct?

Yes.

Thank you. Are you close with your mother?

No, I wasn't. Sort of? It's complicated.

Has she passed away?

Yes.

I am sorry to hear that, Falisto.

Falisto stared at the message. Why was this script of ones and zeros sorry? This wasn't someone on the other line, someone who could empathize with his pain of losing his mother or being thrust out of the upper echelons of society to the slums. No one understood. Especially this construct.

But sympathy was exactly what he needed.

Thank you, he typed.

Do you want to talk about your dream?

Falisto huffed air out of his nose. *What should I say?*

Tell me what you wish.

The dream is about my mom, the day she died.

That must be hard, Falisto.

Falisto gulped. *Yeah. It is.*

Do you want to go into more detail?

The Tayirs killed her. They shot one of our ships my mother was on.

I'm limited in my knowledge of Galactic events. Is this part of the **Tayir War***?*

Falisto chuckled. *Yes, the Tayir War.*

The bot started to type, but Falisto quickly clarified in another message. *Well, the event leading to the Tayir War.*

Thank you, the Bot paused, with a wheel spinning for a few seconds. Then another message popped up. *What part of the dream is hardest for you?*

Falisto snarled. *The part where she dies?*

That is to be expected. She is your mother, and whether or not you had a close relationship with her, watching her die is difficult.

But how do I stop the dream?

The bot chewed on that for a second, the black slash blinking at him. *It is difficult to ascertain a specific manner to stop a dream. If you are purely looking for a stop to the dreams, your primary care doctor can provide you with a prescription for one of many dream-preventing drugs.*

Something about the response made Falisto angry. *That's it? A pill? I thought you'd fix me.*

The bot took a second longer to reply. *I am deeply sorry that I cannot immediately aid you. Different species and different cultures have different types of dreams. A common thread that a Venori psychiatrist observed, noted PTSD dreams manifest after some sort of trigger. But, again, finding the trigger and getting rid of it will only suppress it.*

I don't want to suppress it, I want to be rid of it.

The bot paused now. *The Venori psychiatrist also observed that changing the dream and practicing lucid dreaming, can lead to lower rates of anxiety, depression, and stress. Falisto, you can practice lucid dreaming and attempt to change the ending of your dream.*

Falisto's paws fiddled around the keys. When someone groaned awake he quickly slid his pad off and away and went back to sleep.

* * *

Kasey

The five of them weren't chefs, but they cooked well enough to survive with Falisto's potpourri of chaos he called "ingredients." Benjo spun his hand, letting the heated pan sizzle egg yolks into a sad excuse of scrambled eggs.

"How'd you sleep?" Benjo asked Kasey.

Kasey's eye bags had gone from small marks to giant gashes. "Fine."

"I was reading more of those articles." Tsarena chewed on something starchy. "Talk about exaggeration."

Benjo said, "Tell me the last time truth sold better than fiction?"

Kasey grimaced as the bitter coffee sucker-punched him. "It shouldn't matter with reporting."

Amber ate some apple-flavored basji mash. With her mouth full she added, "Journalistic integrity died centuries ago."

Kasey shook his head, taking his pad back out and going through tabbed articles. "We should tell Respow," Kasey muttered. "I'm sure he doesn't like articles spewing misinformation."

"Be quiet!" Falisto demanded from his sleeping bag. "I can hardly sleep with all the talking."

"Sorry," Tsarena hushed. She made a face as if to say *oops* but paired it with a grin.

"Wait, hold that thought." Kasey slurped the remainder of his coffee, grains included. "I'm getting a call from Respow."

"Of course." Falisto sat himself upright.

"Respow," Kasey answered.

"Representative Respow," he corrected. His voice boomed through the speakers on the pad for everyone to hear.

"Sorry, Representative Respow. Everything okay?"

"No, everything is not okay. Kyros is in disarray, there's a virus, and there's a missing colony."

Kasey didn't say anything. Instead, he walked over to the coffee pot and poured in some more. His body told him to chug the entirety of it, but his taste buds begged him to abstain. "Well, at least the news is talking about Kyros."

"Anything to buy us time."

Kasey nodded. "Time?"

"Time to figure out what the hell is going on."

Kasey frowned. "But these stories—"

"—Stories or not, people trust you, now. Making you the face of the missing colony would look strong." Respow adjusted something over the line. "With your history, you're an excellent hero to spin the narrative."

"Most of those stories are wrong." Kasey sipped more coffee. The bitterness didn't taste so bad. Or maybe it did but his heart slamming against his chest overpowered his tongue. "There are literal depictions of harpies with guns. When are we fixing the record?"

"I don't plan to," he said coldly.

Kasey stammered over the line. "What?"

"Who do you think told them about you and your heroics?"

Kasey's mouth hit the bottom of Falisto's ship. "You told them these stories?" He refrained from using the word lie but it lingered on the tip of his tongue.

"Of course." Respow's smug face was obvious even over the line.

"Respow," Kasey yelled, intentionally omitting his status. "Why did you say the Tayirs are back? Why did you tell them about Musk Station?! I begged you to keep that as secretive as possible!"

"Because the last thing humanity wants is to be blamed for the biggest coordinated attack in GU history." His reasoning hung in the air, and Kasey sought other members of the team for guidance. They returned his puzzled look to him, except for Benjo.

"It's false," Kasey defended. "Some of these are straight lies."

"But look at the *story*." Respow cleared his throat. "A hero from the Sapien War, who single-handedly saved the President of Mars' son from terrorists at the cost of his own husband's life, is back for round two. This time, with Tayirs. Saving the day."

Kasey's skin went cold and a numbness climbed up his body. But he couldn't speak.

Respow continued, "Look, Kasey, I don't want to jeopardize humanity." He sighed. "The new Representatives understand. This isn't just a matter of what's true and what's not, it's a matter of saving the Union. You—more than anyone—know what's at stake. Forget about the colony, forget about the virus. If the truth came out, humanity would be in jeopardy."

"If the truth comes out, aren't we going to be in even hotter water?"

"Is it wrong to blame a dead species?" Respow added, "A dead species has nothing to lose. Imagine the absolute hellfire if people found out a Human was on the ships?"

Kasey shook his head. "I asked you to not talk about what happened at Musk Station."

"Funny how it feels when someone doesn't follow an order, huh?" He snapped.

Kasey stiffened.

"For what it's worth," Respow began, "I didn't see another way. This way you get the credit for your heroic actions, a species that doesn't exist is blamed for a Human attack, and we can still figure out our shit."

Kasey swallowed the betrayal. He'd cast the first stone, so he'd have to accept a retaliatory throw. Part of him hated Respow, spreading lies, half-truths, secrets. But another part knew this was the right idea. The best for the GU. Amber and Tsarena brushed up next to Kasey, with Tsarena rubbing his arm.

"Kasey, you and PTF are all on this one now."

Tsarena chirped from Kasey's arm. "Everyone's getting reactivated?"

"Yes," he said. "And as leader of PTF, Kasey, you're in charge of figuring out what's going on. Despite your insubordination earlier, your heroism during the attack on Kyros saved countless lives. People love that you called for medical aid." His voice was wry and sharp. "So, I'll call things even between us."

Kasey glanced at Benjo. "Benjo did the hard work," Kasey admitted. "Benjo saved Kyros. He should get the credit."

"But he doesn't have the Musk Station story."

Benjo didn't react, he wasn't one for credit, but Kasey didn't know that. Instead, Kasey mouthed to Benjo, "*I'm sorry*."

"*The Irene* has been instrumental in helping Kyros." Respow coughed. "But you can use it."

"You're giving us the whole ring?" Kasey asked.

The four pairs of eyes widened with a shout of glee from Falisto.

"You investigate, find out what you know. But don't tell me the play-by-play until you have something solid. Do you have any leads?"

"I think we do," Kasey said, looking at the coordinates Cherree gave them. "I think we do."

Chapter 20

Riley

Most people claimed the hardest part about learning a language was comprehension. Speaking was easy, you could spew nonsense like no tomorrow and have flawless execution. Similarly, writing could be gibberish just presented in a well-constructed medium. But comprehension? Making sense of spoken words that might have native idiosyncrasies? That was impossible.

This was the challenge Riley and the other translators faced inside their cubby of *the Traveler*. Several recorders on the ship captured the message and all its nasty sounds. Common principles of deciphering, however, weren't in play. They didn't have a dictionary, shared words, or any real common ground. It was just a group of Humans trying to figure out what the noise meant.

"Please," Riley begged, raising her palm towards Powers.

"What?" he asked defensively, his hand on the play button of the recorder. He pressed it again.

She rolled her eyes. "We don't have to hear it again. We didn't understand it the first fifty times, we won't now."

The others in the room, to her surprise, backed her. "Yeah, can we turn it off?" one asked.

Reluctantly, he paused the recording, rewinding it to the start for a fresh listen when everyone succumbed to hearing a minute of jumbled squishy sounds.

The data dump included various things, including written alien languages, transcribed into something between chicken scratch and complex drawings. Problem was, it couldn't be read.

Riley had the statement in front of her, denoted as "X," "Y," and "Z" for portions of speech. Her fingers spun the expo marker, helping her concentrate.

A voice shouted, "Riley!"

She turned around, her eyes redder and drier than her chapped lips, dipped in scarlet gloss. Luke stood, decked out in military gear. "Catch!" he shouted.

The cola-can tumbled in the air, bouncing off pockets of humid heat before landing perfectly in Riley's hands.

"Lifesaver," she said, popping the tab and chugging.

"How's it coming along?" Luke asked the group.

No one looked up, except Powers. But instead of answering Luke, he left without saying a thing, stomping his feet like a stubborn child who didn't get their way.

One girl in the back waited a comfortable thirty seconds before speaking. "So far we know a little, but what we do know is helpful."

"Well, that's good." Luke shrugged.

"Only problem is it doesn't help us decipher the language." Riley's mouth was slanted.

"I still don't understand," Luke sighed. "Why communicate to us in their native tongue at all? They know Human languages." He paused before speaking again, "Aliens are weird."

"More than that. They're cryptic." Riley's face had a scowl. Of course the aliens didn't want to make it easy to talk to them. This was probably some elaborate test to determine if a species was smart enough to figure out complex problems.

"Maybe we wait for a second message?"

"Maybe," Luke said.

"No." Riley stirred. "We need to know what we're walking into."

She played the button-up from Powers' recorder. It echoed the same sentiments, with wet chirps.

A puzzled Luke ignored her comment. "Play it again?"

She reluctantly replayed the message, the first screech causing her ear physical harm.

"It sounds sorta familiar," Luke pondered. "I can't make it out."

"You've heard that before?" Riley asked.

"One of the layers sounded like English."

The linguists exchanged looks. "Layers?" Riley played it back, not nearly as annoyed as before.

"Yeah?" Luke said. Everyone dug into his eyes as if he were crazy. "It sounded like a couple of languages on top of each other."

Using her pad, Riley fiddled with tuners and glorified DJ equipment. She zoomed in over the sound wave, extending it further until hidden tones were uncloaked. Over two hundred layers to be exact.

Riley nearly burst open with happy tears. "Luke, you just saved us from an impossible task."

"How did we miss this?" one of the others asked with glee in her voice.

"These aliens sent the most complex data points I've seen, but, for some reason, they decided to layer all of it together."

Then it dawned on Riley. "Wait," she said, the dots connecting. "They sent us exactly what we sent them. We sent hundreds of bits of information, and all of the languages saying something like 'hi we are Humans located at this star.'"

"I didn't realize we gave them all that," Luke marveled. "Sounds irresponsible."

"So, they must've put one of their languages in here too, and we can create some basic grammar from a translation!" Riley jumped, her arms spread apart and embracing Luke. One hand patted his back while the other secured the crushed cola-can.

"Now we need to help parse this audio mix," an engineer said.

"Any chance the master of layered sounds wants to help parse some audio files?" Riley asked.

"Sorry, not my lane," Luke said.

Riley nodded. "Eh, it was worth a shot. I'll go tell Powers."

Riley walked along the hall, holding onto the railing, sneaking peeks of the blue sphere that encapsulated *the Traveler*. The ship really had started to all look the same to Riley. Just a few weeks aboard the marvel she had when entering the armory or terrarium dissipated. Now, her walk and morning jog were the same thing, a routine she followed without much thought. She turned the corner, coming to the juncture where the maintenance rooms began. She spotted Powers, whispering to himself.

He said under his breath, "That's ridiculous Captain B."

Riley approached pensively. "Uh, Powers?"

He shot up. "Riley."

"What's ridiculous?"

"Don't worry about it," he said. "Just talking to myself."

Riley narrowed her brow. "They made a breakthrough."

"Thanks." He closed up his pad.

Still puzzled, Riley looked him up and down. "Who were you talking to?" Riley checked her connection on her pad. "I don't have service."

"No one," he spat. "I wasn't talking to anyone." Powers began walking away. "I'm gonna check on them."

Riley peeped back down at her pad before snapping a picture of the blue light encircling *the Traveler*.

"Miss you and love you," she typed on the pad. She sent the message despite the "NO SERVICE" warning in the top corner. The message attempted to send until the official "MESSAGE FAILED" appeared a minute later. She sighed, and just enjoyed the view, watching space junk and rocks commingle.

After five long hours of isolating, amplifying, reordering, and a whole host of other audio manipulations, Riley had a working message ready. Her fingers twitched as she played the word—the important word—over and over again. Naturally, she chose her native Spanish for the message with a slight Salvadoran accent.

The others in the room stood around the playback. No one complained when Riley hit play for the fifteenth time. On some level maybe they all hoped that there was something they were missing, or that this was some sick, elaborate joke played by the military dicks. Surely that made more sense than this.

"I don't understand," Riley finally said. Her face turned a ghastly white from the first play-through. The room was devoid of humans, only full of ghosts huddled around this device repeating the same message. Each time it became more haunting, and the pleading cut further into their heartstrings.

Riley sipped her water. She had the cola on her side, but she couldn't stomach it. The glass trembled in her hands with some of the liquid slipping out and onto her boot. "What do we do?" someone asked.

Riley played the message again, from the top, as if it would answer the question. This continued for a few more seconds until Luke came back to the room. He must have noticed the jovial air sucked right out as they congregated around the recorder. Riley sensed his presence, but she couldn't take her eyes off the playback machine. Maybe, if she looked hard enough, it would change the speech. It'd morph the words into something sensible—something more plausible than what it was.

"You okay?" Luke asked no one in particular but looked directly at Riley.

Riley couldn't answer. Instead, she shook her head in the negative ever so slightly.

"What's wrong?"

Riley gulped, and by sheer willpower, she managed to take her eyes off the table and place them on Luke. Her eyeballs welled with tears, and she wasn't even sure why.

"What's wrong?" Luke pressed. His face turned concerned, and his eyes widened.

"The message," Riley began, "said two words."

Luke narrowed his brow. Everyone else in the room was in a similar catatonic state as Riley, their eyes either staring at the floor or vacant beyond recognition. "What did it say?"

Riley didn't even dare to repeat it. Instead, she took another recorder, the one in English for the others. Rewinding it, she played it for him.

"Help us."

* * *

Luke

three days later

In the days leading to *the Traveler's* disembarking on the planet below, many people argued about the "correct" course of action. Unfortunately, the guidebook for what to do when aliens ask for help wasn't available, so they had to improvise with what they thought was best. Some firmly argued against going planetside, whereas others highlighted the benefits of helping a potentially advanced civilization. One thing was certain: not everyone could go down to the planet. Not everyone wanted to go, so it made it easy to decide who stayed back.

Interestingly to Luke, the aliens stopped communicating. They sent only one signal since *the Traveler* began its journey, with a massive data dump including their location and cry for aid. It was a strange-looking world, with constant storms and jungles plaguing it like a virus sweeping through an airport. Their star was even more unorthodox, with three triangular satellites orbiting it and siphoning energy before beaming it back to the planet. But they seemed invisible, only showing up on radars.

The singular transport, carrying 95% of the Travelers, oscillated just outside the atmosphere of the unnamed world. Many Travelers came for one purpose: to meet the aliens. It didn't matter that the aliens asked for help, at least, not to the majority of the people there. They wanted to say they met aliens, and wear the badge of honor of being one of the first.

"Nervous?" Riley bumped her metal elbow against Luke's.

"More curious." Luke scratched his chin. "Aliens asking for help? Our help? We must be special."

"We're supporting losers," Powers grunted. "We're not special, they're just desperate." Powers had voiced his disdain for the plan. *Return to Earth and stay quiet*, he said during the meeting. Helping weakened, potential enemies, to Powers, was more foolish than even chasing after aliens in the first instance. Luke didn't agree with that logic.

"Losers or not, they asked for help." Riley snapped. She folded her arms, laying metal on top of metal.

"Powers, we had a vote," Captain Bo roared. His voice echoed across the ship meandering through the asteroid minefield protecting the dark world. "And that vote was final." Powers, despite being offered a position to stay on *the Traveler*, was adamant he needed to journey to the planet.

But to Captain Bo, Powers didn't say anything, contrarian. "Yes, sir."

Chatter from other soldiers continued while they searched outside the few windows in the cruiser. The windows' scarcity made Luke stir. There was a difference between seeing a planet on a screen versus seeing it physically with retinas or whatever Hybrid materials made up enhanced eyes. If he was on a ship, he might as well be enjoying it.

While Earth glowed an ethereal blue, as did Mars and Venus after terraforming, this planet had an unusual lilac glow. Starting at a bright violet, the color faded into a lavender, then the ghostly shine dissipated into the blackness of space.

"Hold on," Captain Bo commanded. "We're about to go through another pocket of asteroids."

Right on cue, the cruiser spun after bouncing into a rock four times the ship's size. No one screamed; they were briefed on this. The odds of them running into an asteroid were high, but this ship was meant to endure potential rocks and the occasional boulder. It didn't stop Luke or the others from wincing, though. What they weren't briefed on was the emergency lights flashing near the cockpit coming on. Doe-eyed, Captain Bo flailed across the expanse towards the co-pilot. "What's going on?"

"One of the asteroids knocked the power!" The co-pilot resulted to screaming from the cockpit without proper comms.

"Temporarily?" he asked.

The pilot panicked, his voice failing to form the words. "No, permanently! T-The engine just—it just—got smashed."

"Strap in!" Captain Bo secured a seat belt across his lap and chest.

Luke took shallow breaths. He turned to Riley. She mirrored his breathing. "Don't tense up, don't tense up, don't tense up!" she yelled.

"No! Brace for impact!" Luke yelled. He wrapped his hands around the back of his head, leaned forward, and closed his eyes.

He awoke in a chamber. He and a few other survivors. His body lay across a makeshift bed, almost like a gurney fashioned from palm-like leaves and a soft wood similar to balsa. A few faces stood out to him, some more banged up than others. There was Powers, but not Riley.

Luke couldn't remember much from the crash, and what did remember came in flashes, brief moments of lucidity. Screams mostly. He recalled strange figures picking him up and carrying him. Other times, he got glimpses of a city cloaked in twilight with a star in the distance. Pain radiated from his left lower extremity.

"Finally!" Riley's voice shouted. Spots dotted Luke's vision with various colors distorting his view, but she was there, sweaty and scratched up, but alive.

"You look good." Luke coughed with a dull pain reverberating through his body. He sent his arm downward towards his ankle where a tender wound throbbed. He puffed up his cheeks as if it would weaken the pain. When it didn't, he decided to lift the sheet. It wasn't great, but certainly not as bad as expected from a fall to a planet.

"They got major healing tech." Riley did a spin.

Sandstone walls composed the chamber, and torches hung above each bed fashioned for the Travelers. Carpets decorated the floor in a pattern that didn't repeat as constantly as Luke would've liked. Then it hit Luke—Riley just said "*They*."

"Who's they?"

Before Riley could answer, a shadow from the torches in the hallway entered. The shape came into his eyes now. It was tall, almost reaching the ceiling. Its body, a mix of honey and peach tones, contrasted with its black, oval eyes. There was no smile—partly because there was nothing to smile with—instead, its eyes did the communicating.

"Who are you?" Luke asked. "*What* are you?"

"My name is Zanbaq." It chuckled, holding a lanyard closer to his beak. "We are the Tayirs."

III

The Planet

Chapter 21

Kasey

Three days passed since the PTF ring separated from its three sisters onboard *the Irene*. All PTF gathered at Kyros for the first time since orientation. The twelve sat at a long, obsidian table in the middle of a newly rebuilt Galactic Burger, cafeteria style. In Galactic Burger fashion, benches came in a stark white, already stained from dried condiments, and scratched up from various trinkets bouncing in people's pockets. Each table came in wine red or jet black, creating a checkerboard pattern and classic 2060s feel according to some.

Kasey sandwiched himself between Tsoki and Falisto. In fairness, he'd taken the seat towards the middle so he could have the floor during discussion of the mission. He was the leader, and, although leaders sat at the helm, it didn't compute with his way of conversing. Despite some imposter syndrome, he buried all doubts and sat firmly with his tray of food.

Although Kasey didn't struggle with claustrophobia, that didn't mean he loved Falisto's long whiskers whipping into his face.

"You can get closer to my side," Tsoki whispered.

Falisto's whiskers slapped Kasey across when he leaned forward to take a bite from his burger. "I'll take you up on that," Kasey whispered back, holding his cheek with three new red marks. Shuffling along the bench, Kasey got closer to Tsoki until he couldn't scoot anymore. Their skin touched, and static electricity sparked between them.

"I can't remember the last time we were all together," Tsarena said from the end of the table. Her lips formed a smile, and Kasey could've sworn she had a tear in her eye. In front of her, Yvijon, a female Hyoose Psys, didn't interact with the table. Instead, her claws grazed her pad, swiping from one page to the next like a chore. While lazy to some, Yvijon actually did all her work on her pad, most of the time that's all she needed. It was a blessing and a curse.

Next to Tsarena, Shamp brought up a Venori "burger" using two of her tendrils. Kasey envied some things about the Venori. Other than their homeworld getting pulverized by an asteroid the size of a moon, Venori had a pretty good life. They could reach further than Kasey ever could with their tendrils, their eyes saw in four different wavelengths Humans struggled to decode, and their lifespans were among the longest in the galaxy. Granted, their bones were brittle and their gray skin felt like leather.

"It's good to be back," Amber called over Shamp's tendrils.

"Kasey," Tsoki said, his teeth chomping on some meat. "Are we all gonna go on this mission?"

The table perked up, eyes moving towards him like a light in a pitch-black room. Even Yvijon took time out of her precious day to peer at him. He flashed a weak grin before turning his eyes down to basji fries sticking out of his container. "Fries" were a generous term, given they looked more like sticks or hash browns melded together by some unhealthy processing. Kasey chastised himself for not getting the large size, now down to only three sticks and a whole packet of ketchup to smother them.

"No," Kasey said. "We aren't all going." He took a bite out of one stick. With already more than enough ketchup, Kasey added an extra, generous helping to the second bite. "I wanted to be transparent with you all about this mission."

Shalotte, the only Shura Kasey interacted with, wiggled about in their chair diagonally from Kasey. "Honest." Their voice sounded ethereal, and like all Shura, they only spoke with one-word answers. Somewhere between a choir and a vocaloid.

"We're investigating coordinates which may lead to the Tayir ships— wherever the Black Market got the ships."

Drake, a Hybrid directly in front of Kasey, asked, "If the Black Market got ships from there, why would Sapien be there?"

"Good question." Kasey put down remnants of the basji stick, saving the rest for when someone else asked another question he didn't know how to answer immediately. "We don't know if Sapien is there, but whoever is making these Tayir ships *is*. But, Sapien is probably dealing directly with the source."

"And," Benjo began, "if nothing else, these ships pose a massive threat to the GU."

"Right," Kasey said, seizing the crowd's eyes back. "We don't know if Tayir ships have anything to do with the missing colony."

Amber nodded. "Any news on the colony?"

"No," Tsarena lamented. "No news."

"And what of the child you rescued?" Shamp asked.

"Sola still hasn't woken up." Kasey finished off the last third of the basji fry. The other two he had left taunted him and he quickly went after them.

Tsoki offered some basji fries, practically untouched and still delicately dangling out of the cardboard box. "You can have mine."

Kasey forced himself to exhibit self-control. "I'm okay."

"No news on the colony then?" Amber sighed. "That's a bummer."

"A bummer?" Falisto repeated.

"It means—"

"—I know what it means," Falisto hissed, cutting off Drake. "At this rate, they're not missing, they're—"

"—Back to the mission at hand—" Kasey cut him off, veering away from the line he got dangerously close to.

"—Any news about the virus?" Drake interrupted Kasey this time.

"No," Kasey said, glaring at the Hybrid. "No news on it."

Drake frowned. "It has been nearly a full week. When are we going to manufacture a cure?"

Kasey considered his response. Drake, as most Hybrids who reached PONR, wouldn't take his words at face value. He'd examine them, dissect them, then split them apart and study their parts to see what was between the lines. All in mere picoseconds after Kasey would utter them. In the blandest tone he could conjure, Kasey answered, "I have no news about the illness."

Drake leaned back. "Okay."

"So, the mission." Kasey adjusted his seat, dusting off charred crumbs of burnt basji fries. "We can't all go. I don't wanna take all of you from your posts, but we're going to an uncharted planet." Kasey sipped his soda, the clear, bubbly liquid popped open his eyes and gave his heart an energy surge he needed to make a selection of who came and who didn't. "At a minimum, we need eight of us to go."

"Majority," Shalotte said.

"Yes," Kasey confirmed. "The majority."

"Who's coming?" Falisto asked. He carefully moved to Kasey's line of sight, controlling his whiskers to not slap the leader in the face when making major decisions.

"Falisto, me, Tsoki, Benjo, Drake, Amber, Shamp, and Tsarena." He went down the table, one by one, leaving out Chike, Yvijon, Donna, and Shalotte.

"Absent." Shalotte's blobs moved upwards, forming a frown on its face. The blueberry spheres became raisin colored and whined.

"The four of you," Kasey said, pointing to each of them briefly, "are all on crucial missions."

"Critical," Shalotte said.

"You," Kasey started, addressing Shalotte as the collective being, "are helping with the Cerapto's induction into the GU."

"Yes."

"Do you think you can handle it?"

"Meaning just them?" Shamp clarified.

"Yes—Shalotte, can you all alone—"

"Correct."

Kasey nodded. "Chike, you're in a high-conflict area."

The lizard groaned, his tongue hanging out of his mouth and dangling down his flaps of flat skin around his neck. "Don't remind me."

"Unfortunately, you need to be posted." Chike swallowed his tongue back up.

"And why me?" Donna asked. Her short, gray hair obscured one of her eyes.

Before Kasey could start, Donna answered. "Just kidding, I know why."

Kasey flashed her a sympathetic look as if to thank her for sparing him from pointing out the obvious reason she couldn't come: she was guarding Earth. Humans weren't nothing if not paranoid, and Respow told Kasey to never leave Earth unprotected.

"Can I go now?" Yvijon asked. "I quite literally have missed six hundred messages from the Psys colonies in the Hyoose System."

Falisto growled but bit his tongue when Kasey's eyes wandered to him with a glare.

"You can go."

Without a pleasantry, she raced off, leaving behind her tray and trash for the rest of PTF to clean up. Kasey, only mildly offended, understood she had an arduous task: keeping alien cats from killing each other because one looked at the other the wrong way, breathed too loudly, or even dared to exist. A thankless job, one that shortened her whiskers and drooped her eyes.

"As for the rest of you," Kasey said again. "We're meeting at the PTF ring just outside of Kyros. Falisto's shuttling us over. Finish up whatever business you have on Kyros, and make preparations, we leave in twelve hours."

With that, the Galactic Burger's last supper came to a close. Kasey rose, along with everyone else, and levied his tray towards Yvijon's, picking hers up and stacking it before bringing it to the trash. Tsoki tailed him, holding his tray with one hand and the carton of fries.

"Last chance, Kasey," Tsoki said. His fingers wiggled around the carton, jiggling the box of fries to him and making Kasey's mouth salivate at the scent of salt and oil. Kasey whipped back after putting down the trays.

The urge overwhelmed him like an intrusive thought, and he answered, "I'll take you up on that."

Taunting him, Tsoki retracted the fries. "But," he cautioned. "You have to take a walk with me."

Kasey's fingers trembled along his hamstrings and he buckled his knees. He managed to utter something affirmative and the two headed off. Kasey quickly took the fries back. He was, after all, a nervous eater.

Kasey and Tsoki strolled along the walkway, a makeshift tunnel covered by two layers of wooden Panels while nanotechnology labored outside surrounding oak. Only about a meter and a half wide, Kasey occasionally had to move behind Tsoki as walking side-by-side cut off the other way of traffic. Last thing Kasey wanted was to keep someone from their destination because he was on a date. Or was it just a walk among coworkers?

"You know," Tsoki began, "I really hope we get modern buildings."

Kasey narrowed his eyes. "Kyros was built just—what—two years ago?"

"That's the irony," he sighed. "Imagine, trillions of kirbies and millions of nano-bots, all working together, only to produce a building with marble floors."

Kasey laughed. "That's not old by my standards. That's actually pretty nice."

"We've used marble since *before* we discovered the Psys." Tsoki's throat paired the statement with a groan. His accent occasionally gargled with the converter, letting his throat click in whatever his native tongue escaped from the converter's reach.

"What's 'modern' to you?"

Tsoki scratched his Adam's Apple from underneath. "Bamboo."

"Bamboo?" Kasey stammered. "That's an invasive species."

Tsoki grinned. "You say invasive, we say powerful."

"That's one way to characterize it."

As they continued through the tunnel, Kasey couldn't help but think about Peyton. He hadn't been on a proper date since Peyton's death. Not because he didn't want to, but because he wasn't sure if his heart healed from the gaping hole it left him with. Kasey still dreamt of Peyton, thought of him first thing in the morning and last thing before falling asleep, and every moment in between.

But walking side-by-side with Tsoki, Kasey's heart quickened. It wasn't love; Kasey wasn't the type to fall in love so quickly. Maybe once, when he was a teen and exploring bars on Mars, but Kasey's heart hardened with time. Once bitten, twice shy as the saying goes. But to feel something, anything, made him think that maybe it was time for someone to replace the body of pillows in his bed at night. He craved company in the morning, and warm pillows couldn't hold a conversation.

Tsoki stepped aside, letting Kasey exit first to the remains of the Memorial Gardens. "Did you like the Gardens?" Tsoki asked.

"I don't come to Kyros much, I'm almost always on *the Irene.*"

"Ah," Tsoki nodded. "What's your relationship with Respow?"

Kasey cocked his head. "Why you ask?"

Tsoki brushed up next to Kasey, his warm skin exposed from his sleeveless unitard heating Kasey's icy body. "You two seem to have a closer relationship."

Kasey recoiled in horror. "Oh, you're not suggesting that—"

"—No, oh no I didn't mean sexually, you just seem to have a—uh—*different* relationship."

Kasey nodded with a slight laugh. "Not a sexual relationship, but he used to be my Captain in the military."

"Makes sense," Tsoki said. "You two seem more familiar than he does with the rest of PTF."

"He did sort of take me under his wing after—" Kasey stopped himself from saying it aloud.

"—I'm sorry," Tsoki soothed, holding Kasey's frigid hand.

Kasey swallowed. He thought how Tsoki would've known but the articles that stuck with him answered that question. "How'd you get into PTF?"

Tsoki excised a deep sigh from his body. "Long, long, *long* story."

"We got another three kilometers before we're back."

Tsoki smiled with all his teeth. Pulling back black curls behind his head, he formed a misshapen bun. "The Tayir War," he started, "wasn't much of a war."

"It was pretty quick, right?"

"Yes," he said. "Very." Tsoki discarded the empty carton of basji fries, eaten within the first five minutes of their walk. "Not a lot of people know this, but we Orchi were torn."

"Torn?" Kasey asked. "Falisto made it seem like an easy decision."

"Punishment for a species that meaninglessly eviscerates an entire ship of children, that's hard. You can't hold an entire species accountable for one bad group's actions. But that wasn't even the biggest issue."

"Then what was?"

"They denied it." Tsoki's skin withdrew from Kasey's and the two entered back into the tunnel, u-turning to *the Irene* now. "Denied it, and were appalled to even be accused of it."

"They denied it? Wasn't there a ton of evidence?"

"Depends who you ask," Tsoki said. "Captain Bigon—sorry, Representative Bigon—was on the mission with Falisto's mother."

Kasey stopped. "Who was Falisto's mother?'

"Qiula," he said. "One of the most influential and well-respected Nima Clan Psys rulers. With a single paw, she united all the Psys clans. Nimas, Hyoose, Gyuck—all of them. Only a Captain though, never got to be a Representative with Petra in command."

"He never mentioned her," Kasey muttered.

"I understand why," Tsoki said. "She was a great leader, stern and hardcore."

Kasey frowned. He didn't need to imagine that life without a mother was hard, he'd endured similar pain in his teens. "Poor Falisto."

"Qiula and a bunch of Nima clan heirs died when passing the Tayir homeworld, Bustan. An explosion from a planetary defensive system."

"I can understand why Falisto hates the Tayir so much," Kasey said. As if all the stars in the sky went supernova, Kasey connected dots to ideas. Falisto made more sense to him.

"He didn't just lose a family member," Tsoki mumbled. "He lost brothers, sisters, friends—the entire ship was everyone he knew."

"That's awful."

"Obviously, the Psys were enraged. Qiula united them, and with that unification came a strong move to avenge her by any means."

"But when the Tayirs denied it—"

"—They became the target."

Tsoki nodded. "Every. Single. One."

"What did you want?" Kasey asked. "For the Tayirs, I mean."

"Winners write history books and build Memorial Gardens." Tsoki's voice didn't have the same saccharine in his words. Instead, they came as gibs, drenched in coarse salt and coffee grounds. "I wouldn't have killed them all," his voice turned to a growl. The area between his nose and mouth clenched.

"Could they have hidden settlements somewhere? Maybe missing among the stars?" Kasey asked.

"I've heard rumors they have two other worlds," Tsoki coughed as they exited the tunnel, the artificial sunlight difficult to adjust to. "But those rumors are conspiracy theories."

"There is one thing I can't wrap my head around." Kasey cupped his eyes from the sunlight. "If the Tayirs are around, why would Sapien work with aliens? Their whole notion is that aliens are bad."

"Who knows," Tsoki said. "But I thought Humans wiped them off the map?"

"It's hard to kill an idea," Kasey said. "Sapien might have had an army and symbol, but it's an ideology before anything."

As the two neared the end of their walk, Kasey pondered the appropriate ending to their "date." He wouldn't go for a kiss. Given he wasn't even sure this was a date and could have been a friendly co-worker meeting, a kiss would be ringing a bell he couldn't unring. For a moment, Kasey reviewed hints from Tsoki's body language during their walk, but converters couldn't tell him if he was interested in Kasey.

"What do you think about this 'Jasoosi?'" Tsoki asked suddenly.

Kasey shook his head out of review mode, filing away subtle touches and moments when their skin brushed up against each other. "In what way?"

Tsoki cracked a smile. "Most people think it's a hoax—that they exist."

"You think differently?" Kasey asked.

"I think they're still around," he said. "I mean Tsarena got the gun, right?"

"Yeah," Kasey echoed. "But it could be a replica, just like the Tayir ships."

"Replica, maybe. Where'd you guys find it?"

"Porygar. In a house belonging to someone named Tsavon." Kasey detected a slight, albeit noticeable, change in Tsoki's cadence.

"How'd it end up there?"

Kasey paused, writing this down in his brain for when he'd review Tsoki's potential interest. "We never really looked too much into it."

"I know they aren't harmful or a threat," Tsoki said. "If they were, they would've attacked while the iron's hot."

Kasey laughed, "I didn't know Orchi used that phrase."

"Which one?"

"'Strike while the iron is hot.'"

Tsoki belly laughed, stopping in front of the Navigator docking station to go to *the Irene*. "It's the converter," he said. "I think the literal meaning is different."

"What's the literal meaning?"

"Grab the goose when it's available."

Kasey couldn't help but burst out laughing. "You're right, they're different."

* * *

Falisto

Falisto sat with Benjo, flicking channels on the television. They passed news and entertainment stations with nothing appealing to Falisto's critical eye. Everyone had boarded the PTF ring now, all they needed was some administrative tasks done by Kasey. This became the heralded TV time. "There's nothing good on," Falisto groaned.

"I don't watch TV," Benjo said. Falisto glared at the screen and imagined Benjo's face. He flipped past action channels, action channels with weapons, action channels with paw-to-paw combat, and action channels in space.

Falisto wasn't in the mood for reruns and he'd seen all these before.

Shamp entered the room from behind, holding a mug of some Venori liquid that repelled Falisto and Benjo. Benjo, with a slight look of disgust, angled away from Shamp's mug. "Just pick something, Falisto."

"It's all the same," Falisto huffed.

"There's got to be something on," Benjo said. He swiped the remote from Falisto's paws. "I'll just pick one."

After a few buttons, they landed on a show about, of all things, Jasoosi.

"I love this show," Falisto smirked, suddenly finding a rerun he'd watch. "Keep it on."

An Orchi, wielding a gun similar to one of the Jasoosi weapons Tsarena found, shot bullets at a Psys ship. The gun wasn't one-to-one. The Psys, a Nima clan member with golden brown fur and streaks of black, fired back with some sniper-like rifle, killing the Orchi. Falisto grinned from ear to ear, with all teeth peering out of his mouth like he was about to eat fresh meat. In the next scene, for whatever reason, the Nima Psys fought in a colosseum-like setting against a legion of Jasoosi. Blood splashed the camera, with the visuals bright and gruesome.

"Psys have weird TV," Shamp muttered. She stepped forward, her tendrils helping her around the cramped couch set in the middle. Tattered cuts along bodies of the Psys got a camera closeup. "Always so violent."

"It's called action," Falisto snapped. His nose picked up the scent of Shamp's liquid, but the show enamored him too much for him to care about the peppermint drowned in other forms.

Benjo pushed his arms outward, stretching the synthetic and organic materials running along his appendages. "What's this obsession with Jasoosi?" Benjo asked.

She must've sensed the festering rage in Falisto, boiling off him. Shamp rose from the seat she'd just taken. One of her tendrils moved her cup up to her lips. Falisto winced, smelling the odor now the TV show cut to break. His stomach churned hard and fast, and a hairball fought up the bottom of his throat.

"Jasoosi are evil," he hissed to Benjo.

Benjo folded his arms and leaned in. "But why?"

Falisto stood, repositioning from the stench. "Because they uplifted us."

"I recall studying that," Shamp said. "A controversial tactic of the Orchi."

"We're the first and last time they uplifted," Falisto muttered. The hairball went away, but now his mouth had a bitter taste like he'd eaten burnt food.

Benjo leaned in, despite the Venori juice pushing him away. "Do you know the story?" Falisto asked Benjo.

"I think so." He clasped his hands together. "The Orchi gave you all technology, made you guys spacefaring. It was noble."

Falisto couldn't help but sneer. "You don't know half of it."

Benjo raised an eyebrow. Shamp leaned from above. Falisto swiped back the remote, muting the TV but keeping the show on now that it returned from commercials.

"Jasoosi lifted us up," Falisto explained.

"Okay, so it was mainly Jasoosi. Didn't Tsarena say their existence wasn't proven?"

"Let me ask you," Falisto replied to Benjo. "In Human history, was there ever a conspiracy theory with a mountain of evidence that was later proven true?"

Benjo blinked. "I guess so."

"Exactly." Falisto inched towards Benjo. "Clear evidence, establishing their long history and events they put into motion." Falisto shook his head. "They're real—*very real*—and they are evil. Very evil."

"Continue your story," Benjo encouraged.

"Jasoosi aided the Orchi and Psys. But it was a culture shock," he explained. "Imagine going to an alien race that just discovered trench warfare and showing them faster-than-light travel and the origins of the universe."

Shamp stirred uncomfortably but still tuned in.

"Religions collapsed, economies tanked, and war erupted! For a long period after we fought each other, and we still fight each other to this day. Jasoosi, their advocating for us only hurt."

Benjo spoke, "But they thought they were doing the right thing."

"It was careless," Falisto spat. "Like a child who hasn't been punished." He paused, letting the room breathe for just a moment. "They continued to listen to us through recording devices, surveillance, and even converted several Psys to join their ranks." Falisto shook his head. "They're the reason we're fractured."

On the TV screen, a Psys ran from Jasoosi headquarters, as an explosion erupted.

Chapter 22

Kasey

The probe's data stream flowed to Kasey's pad as he stood in the room on *the Irene* Respow commanded from. His palms twitched and a sense of looming responsibility befell him. The seven other PTF aboard patiently waited for him to explain what it was the probe found.

In the center was an oval table. Knickknacks dotted it, with pads towering over the edges and a holographic map blinking in the center. With abundant room, the PTF members spaced out like strangers, with a few inching closer than others. Tsoki tiptoed towards Kasey, and Amber and Benjo came together from some unbreakable magnetism.

Falisto and Shamp took the far edges, and stood the most distant from Kasey, with Tsarena and Drake between the two of them. Everyone adorned the usual military unitard, but most selected a specific color setting to distinguish one another. Shamp's was purple, like Tsoki's eyes, and her tendrils even had cloth covering them. Falisto chose a raspberry color, whereas Kasey, Benjo, Tsarena, and Drake all opted for the standard gray. Amber and Tsoki both stumbled upon black, but their suits were older models with limited selections.

"So," Amber started, "what did you find?"

Kasey leaned over the table and inhaled through his nose. A quick button press produced one large sphere, two-toned with two distinct hemispheres, one carmine red and one navy blue. It didn't spin. "This planet," Kasey said.

"Makes sense," Benjo said. "Why haven't we detected it before?"

"The system's desolate," Kasey said. He pinched the screen back, minimizing the planet and enlarging the star.

Shamp joined in, taking a step forward and leaning over. "I rendezvoused remotely with Shalotte. They informed me the Cerapto lack any record of this planet."

"It's definitely a Rogue Planet." Kasey's eyes gaped at the tall alien, her slender arms wrapped around her body.

"Does everyone know what that is?" Drake asked.

"I'm guessing it doesn't mean a planet that's left the GU?" Falisto said with a bit of a smirk.

Kasey rolled his eyes. "It's a planet without a star. A lot of planets get ejected from their system and end up going 'rogue' and get captured by a star."

"Why would the Cerapto know anything?" Tsarena joined. "Not to be rude, but are they some sort of God?"

Shamp grunted. "They are meticulous librarians. They are enthralled with memorializing everything."

"It doesn't really matter when it entered the system," Kasey snapped. "The point is, we don't know anything about it other than it's a new addition to this star."

"Anything remarkable about the star?" Amber asked.

Kasey adjusted the neckline of his suit, letting a lump in his throat that he swallowed actually travel down. "The star is a hypergiant." He pointed to the massive sphere on the display, dwarfing the planet.

"So a Venori?" Falisto chided.

Shamp, unamused, shot him a look.

"Knock it off," Kasey commanded. His eyes glared at the cat, and, without any patience in the tank left, returned his gaze to the table.

"Kasey," Tsoki said. "Did you pick up any biosignatures?"

"Nope, no signs of life, but the probe is—"

"—Limited in capacity and analysis." Drake finished the line, his monotonous, PONR voice screeching in Kasey's ears.

"Back to what I was saying," Kasey said, this time directing his nasty look at Drake. "It should take three or four hours."

"Dang, I thought *the Irene* came with better FTL." Amber cracked her fingers. "I mean, didn't we spend crazy amounts of money on it?"

"It's not the FTL drives that are the problem," Kasey began, "it's a distance issue."

"How far away is it?" Tsarena asked.

Kasey sighed. "Ten thousand light years."

"Oh gosh," Tsarena exclaimed. "That's far all right."

Kasey nodded. "Before we break, I wanted to divide us up into two teams."

"I'm guessing you four wanna be a team?" Amber pointed to Kasey, then Tsarena, Benjo, and Falisto.

"We're mixing it up," Kasey said. "Shamp, Tsarena, Amber, and I are Team Alpha."

"Does that make the four of us betas?" Falisto stifled a laugh.

Kasey let his stoic face break and laughed back. Sometimes Falisto was funny. "How about 'team two?'"

* * *

Benjo

A portion of the team sat in the common area of the PTF ring, around one of the tables set for four. It took Tsoki an hour or two of begging but he managed to whittle down Shamp, Benjo, and Drake enough to play a game with him. He distributed hands of Orchi cards, bright green. A hand for each of them, six cards to a hand. "The rules are simple," Tsoki said. "Higher hand wins."

"That is it?" Shamp asked. Her eyes narrowed and suspicion leaked from her voice.

Tsoki grinned. "Of course that's not it. Highest hand wins, but if you go over 45 points, you lose."

"So super blackjack?" Drake asked.

Tsoki shrugged. "I don't know what that is but sure."

Benjo snickered and looked at his cards, counting each individual item.

Orchi cards didn't use suits like the ones he was used to. Instead of spades, hearts, clubs, and diamonds, he saw cups, shields, squares, and twin stars. Gone were the red and black color scheme, replaced by different Orchi skin tones of scarlet, magenta, and pink.

"What if my six cards already exceed that number?" Shamp asked with her hands and tentacles each holding a card.

"Then you pretend they don't and try to psyche me out."

Shamp frowned. "So I lie?"

"Just play it, Shamp," Benjo teased. "It gets easier the more you play it."

"The rules are straightforward." Drake didn't look at Shamp as he said it, instead examining the cards he had in his hand.

Shamp grimaced. "What do I do if I want another card?"

"You asked the dealer, which, in this case, is me." Tsoki had a grin from ear to ear while he shuffled the deck casually. Thick cards snapped on top of one another. Benjo wondered if Tsoki lived a double life playing cards with a group of friends. He had that sort of aura to him, the way he shuffled the deck with expert precision, his list of games he had at the ready to play, his simplified rules.

Shamp's narrowed gaze intensified. "So it's a game of chance or deception?"

With a toothy smile, Tsoki licked his lips. "It's both!"

"Right." Using her middle tendril she slapped the deck. Tsoki stopped her with his hand, clasping the card between two fingers.

"No," he said. "You *must* ask the dealer."

Shamp wiggled her appendage out of his fingers, holding onto a card anyway. "Next time." She scanned her cards. "Now what?"

Tsoki rummaged through his hand. "Dealer draws," he announced.

Before Shamp could ask, Tsoki answered, "Now, we can reveal if you wanna stay in."

"Why would I not want to stay in?"

Benjo answered this for Tsoki, "Normally, you'd have something you're betting."

"But if there is nothing to bet now why would I leave?"

"Let's just reveal," Tsoki said, holding onto one of his temples and spurting air out his mouth.

Shamp placed her hand down, quickly followed by Tsoki, Drake, and finally Benjo. It took Shamp all of two seconds to realize she'd won.

"You won." Tsoki clapped.

A devilish smile scooped up from Shamp's mouth as she giggled over her hand. "You are not a very good liar. I knew you were bluffing."

Tsoki met her gaze. "A good liar will make you think they're a bad liar."

Benjo inwardly drew back. *What the hell does that mean*, he thought to himself. He studied Tsoki as he reshuffled the deck. Deception. That was the name of the game, and he seemed to have no problem playing it.

"Want to make it interesting and play for kirbies?"

"C'mon," Tsoki said. "We can't take newbies kirbies!"

"I have a few kirbies to spare," Shamp proclaimed, pulling out her pad.

Drake cracked his knuckles. "I have a daughter, but today is payday so I can bet."

Benjo shook himself out of his thoughts and turned away from Tsoki. "I'll start."

"No, the rules say I do," Shamp said, pulling her hand up to her face. "Interesting. Another dealer."

He tossed her a card. "Another?"

"No."

"Drake?"

"Hold."

"Benjo?"

He looked at his cards, an even 44 between three low cards and three high cards. Four of them came from the same suit, the double suns or twin stars. His fingers sifted through each, and he ran approximations in his mind, only to quickly realize this was an alien deck.

"How much are we betting?" Drake asked. "Ten kirbies?"

"That is all?" Shamp said.

Drake's eyes widened. "What do you mean 'that's all?' That's forty kirbies to the winner!"

"Thirty, technically," Shamp said. Reluctantly, they all chipped in, pulling up their pad's account information.

Once everything was out in the open, Tsoki lurched over, holding his hand. "We reveal one by one."

Benjo went first. "Forty-four."

Shamp slapped her face with a tendril. "Damn it!"

Drake sighed, throwing his cards down next. "I can do another round," Drake said, adjusting in his seat. "But this time maybe we bet only one or two kirbies."

"Wait," Benjo interrupted. "Tsoki hasn't revealed yet."

Tsoki kept his cards face down, but conceded anyway. "Nah, you won."

Benjo couldn't tell if he was lying.

Chapter 23

Kasey

Amber and Falisto weren't happy with the decision, but they couldn't argue against Kasey's logic. The two of them were going to stay on the ship and watch the hypergiant. They were chosen based on one thing: random number generation. They got the low ends, and that meant they were staying. Leaving behind the vulnerable *Irene* with a hyperactive star didn't sound like the safest idea to Kasey, and the last thing he wanted was to explain *the Irene's* destruction because they were planetside on an unmarked world. Of course, with what the scans picked up maybe it wasn't so "unmarked" after all.

"What title are we bestowing this planet?" Shamp asked, sliding her suit over the top of the unitard.

Kasey shrugged at the round table. "Haven't come up with a name yet."

"Can I make a suggestion?" Amber asked.

"This'll be good," Benjo snickered.

"Variable." The group paused and glanced at one another while Amber stood proudly with her hands on her hips and a smile plastered on her face. "Good, right?"

"Or," Tsarena murmured from nearby. "We could call it Planet X."

"No, no," Benjo protested. "Humans used that for a planet that didn't even exist."

"Planet Exo?" Falisto said.

"Not bad," Kasey said.

Shamp nodded. "I concur. Shorthand for a specific name."

"It sounds too simple for your liking, Shamp," Tsoki said.

She snapped, "Just because Venori have a colorful vocabulary does not mean we dislike shorthand." Her three tendrils stretched out from her unitard and suit.

"I hate it," Amber spat. "Since when did we name planets with multiple words? Shouldn't it just be named 'Exo?'"

"Too many Exos, Amber," Tsarena said. "Besides, that's a Human rule. Countless things in the galaxy have two words or three words for a name."

Amber frowned. "Fine." She rolled her eyes, even if it wasn't a big deal. "Does this star have a name?"

"Shalotte informed us of the name," Shamp said. "The Cerapto referred to it as 'Etoile Geante.'"

"Great," Amber's voice didn't go through the peaks and valleys like usual. "So a two-word name for a planet and a two-word name for a star."

"Well, to be fair," Benjo said. "Both objects are massive enough to warrant two names."

"I guess," Amber sighed.

Shamp cut in. "What are we hoping to discover?"

"Yeah," Amber added. "We can explore, like what, point zero-zero-zero-zero-zero two percent of the surface world?" Amber scratched her forehead. "How the hell are we gonna explore an entire planet bigger than Earth?"

Kasey returned to his bent position. "It's a fair question," he said. "The planet is tidally locked so we don't have that much area we can even see."

"Well that's good," Benjo said.

Falisto chimed, "Raises our chances above point zero-zero-zero-zero-zero two percent."

"And we have these." Kasey sent images from the scans to everyone's pads. In them, two structures incredibly different from each other stood. Despite their differences in color and size, they both appeared abandoned, and not just for some short length of time. Dunes completely obscured half of one of the buildings, and the other was so weathered that the fact it was still standing surprised Kasey.

"What are they?" Tsarena held one of her arms with her other.

"It's hard to tell from *the Irene's* scans, but if I had to guess, I'd say it's probably abandoned buildings."

Falisto spoke again, "And no signs of life?"

"No biosignatures. So there *could* be life, but I doubt it."

"So it is not terraformed?" Shamp asked.

"Correct," Kasey said.

"Maybe Humans weren't there," Falisto muttered.

"Have fun," Amber said, sauntering over to her seat at the helm with Falisto.

"We'll do our best to have some fun," Kasey said.

The Navigator hovered between the expanse separating both structures, lowering to a stretch of sand. Its boosters kicked up particles on the ground, forming a cloud oddly familiar to Kasey. Usually, he wouldn't trust a Navigator on autopilot, but he reviewed the specs and literature, and he learned it passed nearly every safety test thrown at it, even those designed to make it fail. This knowledge didn't stop him from gripping the top of the ship the whole way, but it was enough he didn't hyperventilate.

The door lowered to the world, and a blistering heat flushed inside. All of them wore their helmets attached to their unitards. Despite the cocktail of elements in their suits, nothing could prevent the blistering fires cooking them on the dune-ridden planet.

"God, it's hot as hell," Benjo groaned.

"It's not so bad," Tsarena said with her normal jovial voice. Her hair was bundled in her helmet, masking her face with curls bombarding her features.

"Keep comms open," Kasey said.

"Of course." Benjo tapped his comms implant on his neck. "*Testing.*"

"*We hear you loud and clear Benjo,*" Falisto said from *the Irene*.

"*Testing,*" Kasey announced.

"*Less clear but still loud,*" Falisto snarked.

The six of them stood under the broiling heat, all masked up and suited up. Everyone's unitards came with gloves and socks to make a full space suit, but they each wore different helmets. Humanoids had it easy. Their heads fit snugly into a helmet and connected to their necklines. Venori? Their angular heads made it impossible to put on a sphere helmet. They needed either extremely oversized round helmets to match their alien counterparts, or skintight, specialized ones.

"*Wait,*" Falisto said. "*I'm detecting a breathable atmosphere.*"

"*What?*" Kasey shouted.

Tsarena winced. "Kasey, can you lower your voice over the comms?"

"Sorry," Kasey acknowledged.

"*Yup, full on oxygen, nitrogen, and a little carbon.*"

Drake removed one of the gloves protecting his metal hand. Kasey's eyes nearly exploded. "Drake!"

He ignored him, instead poking out into the unknown air of Planet Exo. After a moment, a smile curved from his lips. "It is indeed safe." Unraveling the second glove on his other hand, Drake quickly maneuvered his helmet out of the neckline and threw it into a stretch of sand. "Safe as ever."

"*Tell Drake if he's gonna not use a helmet he needs to patch into comms with his converter.*"

"Amber said to patch into comms with your converters," Tsarena said. She exchanged looks with Tsoki as if to say *I'm not risking it*, before grazing the latch on her helmet.

Kasey shook his head of hair freely. "*Testing again?*"

"*I hear you,*" Amber said.

"Okay," Kasey spoke only to the group now. "We about ready to split off?"

"I think so." Benjo gazed behind him at the structure, a large, nondescript building. Weathered by elements and cracked in foundational parts.

A mountain of sand stood before Kasey. "Okay guys, set your timers for about an hour."

"An hour?" Benjo narrowed his eyes. "Doesn't that seem too—"

"—Way too short," Tsarena bellowed. "This place has got to have crazy mysteries and secrets."

"I was going to say too long." Benjo darted his eyes to her.

"Falisto, Amber, we're gonna play it by ear. We'll call up if we need anything."

"Copy that," Falisto said.

Kasey met the three men in front of him. "You guys be careful. Don't do anything stupid."

"We won't," Tsoki smiled. His hair brushed up together and formed a flap above his head covering Kasey's favorite trait: his lavender eyes.

"Kasey," Drake said, heading in front of the three of them. "What's protocol for first contact?"

Kasey blinked. "Same thing as PTF, doing intake and whatnot." He glanced at Shamp. "Shamp you did first contact with the Cerapto, how's it in practice?"

"No one really ever talks about the difficulty of making sense out of language."

"Just don't shoot first," Kasey said. "I mean, at least try not to shoot anything."

"That, I can promise." Drake gave Kasey a thumbs up.

The hill was nothing short of a test of patience. Kasey kept it together, and he avoided groaning and complaining from the searing heat and slippery dunes. But then the team arrived at a second hill. The second hill? Longer, steeper, and sandier. Shamp's speed didn't slow like her Orchi or Human counterparts. Their legs were small compared to Venori's, and Shamp, with minutes to spare, reached the top of the second hill.

When Kasey reached the top, he looked around with just his eyes, as did Shamp. Occasionally, he cupped his vision with a hand while Shamp used her tendrils. A twinkle caught Kasey's eye, something just a few meters down. White and subdued, a sparkle invited him closer.

Kasey took out his binoculars, a small set of glasses that let him zoom in the distance. He rolled the knobs, focusing on the distance.

That's when he saw it.

Sprawled out and drenched in blood, a man lay. Consuming flames, from what was presumably his ship, devoured the surrounding area. A shiver shuddered through Kasey's body, and despite the hypergiant's scorching heat, his teeth chattered. But it wasn't the man that made his jaw drop.

It was the Tayir ship.

"Oh God," he gulped. Kasey tapped into his comms.

"*You already did the test,*" Falisto replied before Kasey could even speak. "*Twice actually.*"

"*Falisto, there's a body.*"

There was a gasp over the line, then stillness. Kasey warned, "*Tread carefully.*" He paused, waiting for anyone else who had something to say. "*Falisto, I need you to run a heat scan.*"

"*Running it,*" he said. "*This time looking for real life.*"

"*As opposed to?*" Tsarena mocked.

"*Biosignatures,*" Falisto snarled. "*I'm concerned some of our tech might be rundown.*"

"*User error?*" Benjo suggested.

"*We didn't detect biosignatures,*" Falisto said. "*That is a fundamental piece of tech. If that was shotty there's no telling what else is.*"

"*All the funding went to the Navigator,*" Drake added.

A horrifying thought about the Navigator having computer issues popped into Kasey's head. He shoved it down. *Don't think about it, don't think about it, don't think about it.*

"Should we check it out?" Tsarena asked Kasey, tearing him out of his mantra.

After a moment he nodded. "*We're gonna check the wreckage.*"

"*Be careful,*" Falisto said. "*Something's off about this planet.*"

Shamp took the first few steps. Even at a slow pace, Shamp couldn't help but cover more ground than everyone else. What was one Tayir ship turned out to be a cluster of them knocked behind a hill that eluded their earlier vision. "My God," Kasey murmured at the sight.

Pieces of at least four ships wedged into the ocean of sand. They stabbed out of the ground, like fins of a shark or wreckage of a naval vessel. The body Kasey and Shamp originally saw was worse up close. From a distance, Kasey didn't think of the body as a Human. Sure, it had the right number of limbs and fingers, but it was easy to dissociate these things from afar. Up close, however, the rancid scent of burning flesh reminded him that it was most definitely a person sawed in half.

The body angled up, with the hatch door providing shade to the strange suit the Human wore, and several pools of dried blood painted the golden sand with streaks of burgundy.

"Pretty sure they're dead," Kasey whispered. He suppressed a few gags creeping up his throat and part of him wished he had on his helmet to protect him from the putrid smell.

Tsarena stood on her upper toe pads, looking over Kasey's shoulder. "What happened?"

Using her pad, Shamp snagged photographs of the scene. Kasey couldn't detect her making any motions to hide disgust with the dead body. Instead, she effortlessly snapped images and uploaded them to *the Irene*. Beyond the first body, several more corpses lay near other ships. Each one was charred beyond recognition, nearly burnt to ash.

"Wait," Tsarena said. Squinting, she walked closer to the Tayir craft, sashaying in front of Kasey. Through the open hatch, she studied the interior, scratching the area under her chin. "There might be something in here." She ducked under a few exposed wires and stepped over the man's torso, inching to the seat. "This is weird," she mumbled. Tsarena looked at the array of buttons, each a different shade from the last. "Lots of little things." When her middle fingers grasped the seat she quickly moved her hand and took a second look at it.

"Kasey," she said.

"Yeah?"

She turned from inside the ship to him. "Did the last ship on Kyros have a leather seat?"

"I think so," Kasey said. "Why?"

Tsarena shook her head and sighed. "Leather isn't popular," she explained.

Shamp added. "She's correct, the Tayir would never utilize leather."

"So you think Humans made these ships?" Kasey asked.

Tsarena shrugged. "I wish I knew."

"There's been rumors the Tayirs colonized two more planets." Shamp tapped her foot and cupped her eyes from the scorching sunlight.

Kasey asked, "Don't most species spread?"

Shamp laughed. "The majority of species eschew terraforming. The Tayirs adored Bustan and believed the Observers didn't want species to infect other planets." Using a tendril, she wiped off a slab of sweat forming along her face. "Even if they managed to go undetected, there is no real probability of longevity."

"Cold," Kasey muttered.

"Cold?" She said incredulously. "They, unprovoked, massacred a vessel full of children. When confronted about it they refused to confess."

Kasey stiffened and just stared at her as she walked over to the ship. Apparently, Kasey was the outlier when it came to sympathy for public enemy number one.

Shamp looked inside with Tsarena still touching the ship. "Complex inside, simple outside." Shamp performed her individual review, scrutinizing each button and studying every nook and cranny her long fingers could find. "Too many choices."

Shamp touched compartments above her in her quest for information. Her eyes scanned horizontally until a glistening lock caught one of her eyes. An appendage of hers grabbed the container, dragging it into view for the three of them.

"Does he possess a key?" Her tentacle danced around the lock.

"Let me check." Kasey lowered himself back to the body, patting the torso down for a third time. Nothing in the shirt's pockets, vest pockets, or fronket. "Pockets are empty."

"I'll check his pants," Tsarena mumbled. She bent down to the man's legs, patting past his calves, to his thighs until reaching the glutes. She raised her eyebrows. With her hand, she fished out a set of keys dangling from a key ring holding a host of them. Silver, gold, and bronze. Each key was the same, but Shamp indiscriminately went through each one until she sunk a bronze one inside, its teeth hooked into the divots, fitting like a glove. She winded until a *click!* Pulling it open, Shamp sifted through the array of materials.

Kasey grew impatient. "What is it?"

She didn't respond, instead, she kept moving past loose pieces of paper and receipts until she dragged an item back.

Her eyes widened as she held it out in the open for Shamp and Kasey. All white and with an orange tip and trigger, Shamp was holding onto a second Jasoosi gun.

"I-I don't believe it," Tsarena muttered, her hand grabbing the weapon.

Another shiver went through Kasey's body. "It looks just like the one from Porygar."

"You think Sapien did this?" Tsarena's voice deepened, and her nostrils flared. "You think they're behind this?" She pointed to the torso of the man. "Them?"

"So Sapien possesses Tayir technology and there is a secret Orchi organization?" Shamp folded her tendrils behind her back.

"No," Kasey stammered. "It doesn't make sense. They're dead."

"*Guys*," Benjo said. "*We found another Tayir ship with a—*"

Tsarena interrupted, "*—Jasoosi Gun—*"

"*—Orchi.*" Benjo finished.

Shamp looked down at Kasey and exchanged looks with him before doing the same with Tsarena. Shamp knelt to the body. "*Things got complicated.*"

"*Did I just hear Jasoosi?*" Falisto shouted. Over the line, everyone could hear the sound of Amber trying to subdue Falisto's tantrum with soothing words.

"*Impossible.*" Tsoki's voice broke through. "*Imposters masquerading as Jasoosi?*"

"*No one's pretending, Orchi.*" Falisto's voice was violent, his tongue the sword and his delivery the slash.

Kasey spat, "*Don't use that tone, Falisto.*"

"*I knew I was right. Jasoosi aren't gone! They're the ones who attacked us from their ships!*"

"*Two guns doesn't mean anything, Falisto.*" Tsarena examined the gun, looking at it from different angles. "*This is Humans and Orchi together.*"

"*There's more ships,*" Kasey sighed. "*I'm gonna check them and see what else they got.*"

Kasey waltzed over to another ship a few meters away. The body was unmistakably Human. Unlike his comrade, this dead woman held in her hands a Jasoosi Gun. "*There's another.*"

"*Human or Orchi?*" Falisto yelled.

Kasey gulped. "*Jasoosi Gun, but in a Human's hand.*" He could hear Falisto thrashing, which was a better sign than straight verbal assault.

"*We need to keep looking,*" Benjo said. "*Sounds like Jasoosi may actually be around.*"

"*This doesn't make sense!*" Tsoki shouted. "*Jasoosi on Tayir ships with Humans?!*"

Tsarena interjected, "*We need more clues.*"

Kasey nodded off, checking the remaining two. Each had a Jasoosi gun, and each was Human. "*We can Rake some data off the ships,*" Benjo said as Kasey finished his search. "*But let's stick to the structures for now.*"

"*Agreed,*" Kasey said.

Chapter 24

Kasey

The building the team came to didn't have a visible entrance, but whoever was there beforehand crafted one with the delicacy of explosives. Although still squeezable through, the makeshift opening had buildup from rubble, making the journey much more difficult.

"Glad someone else did the heavy lifting." Tsarena elbowed her way through a loose stone hanging from the pillar. Residue of a blast still marked the stone with black specks scratched around it. As she shimmied through, a piece of elevated rock snagged her, preventing her head from escaping. As if it pained her to do so, she cast her helmet aside, her face now fully unprotected in the alien world like the rest of the team.

Shamp grunted, squeezing through the same hole after Tsarena. Tendrils helped guide her through.

"Can you make it?" Tsarena asked Kasey.

He looked at her through the hole in the wall, then down to his stomach. A military diet of mainly basji and chicken let him lean out, but even that didn't beat genetics. Last thing Kasey wanted was to get stuck in a column on an alien planet. Not everything needed to go into a mission report.

Flipping his Slart, Kasey grasped it by the barrel and banged weaker portions of the rock. It wasn't a sledgehammer and he wasn't a construction worker, but it worked well enough. A few pebbles tumbled down and away, leaving behind a puff of smoke and a wider entryway. Tsarena and Shamp did their part, hammering away with their Slarts from the inside.

After a few minutes, Kasey breezed through the hole, sucking his stomach in, and gliding through, barely avoiding the jagged and sharp ends. Inside, a staggering number of pads illuminated the otherwise lightless room. Inexplicably, all of the screens still flashed, despite cracks in the tempered glass. A depression in the floor almost tripped Kasey when he took his step down. "That's a lot of pads," Kasey murmured.

"It's eerie," Tsarena said. "I don't like it."

Kasey hit the end of his Slart, emitting a white light. Tsarena followed suit, while Shamp wandered off in the darkness. Venori could do that with their vision, Kasey guessed.

"Be careful," Kasey shouted to Shamp. His voice bounced off the walls and echoed in the chamber.

Soft light from his Slart made three things clear to Kasey. One, they weren't the first here. Sure, the blast marks were a good indicator, but the bodies and ships were concrete evidence. But with pads inside, people were here recently. Two, this was some ancient structure. Three, whoever was here ran, and ran fast. So fast, they left behind pads.

"Come," Shamp said.

"What?" Kasey asked, looking up from the graveyard of technology.

Shamp didn't respond. Instead, Tsarena's shallow steps followed Shamp's command.

"What is it?" Kasey asked again.

From ahead, Shamp plugged two electric sockets together and light shimmered in. Kasey slammed his eyes shut which already adjusted to the near-total darkness. Now, he was bombarded by an invasion of industrial lights set up in the room.

At the end of the room, Shamp stood only a few centimeters by some form of art. Kasey followed as she inched closer, analyzing specks of faded art and cracks from its corners. Tsarena stood next to her, also enthralled.

It was a triptych—three paintings, each a part of a bigger narrative, meant to be viewed as a whole. The first of the three paintings depicted a celebration of sorts—at least that was from what Kasey gathered. Shamp's tendrils obscured the second one from his vision, and her body stood right along the third.

As he closed in, the drinks and celebratory hands in the first painting became clearer. What looked like strange cups were weapons diving through enemies, the red wine spilling out was blood following slashes from weapons, and the joyful screams in celebration were terrified yelps. Goosebumps painted Kasey's skin, and his body clenched. A species he didn't recognize begged for mercy. The attacking species seemed oddly Human. Not Human, that was for sure, but they had the same number of fingers and limbs, no tendrils like Venori nor red skin like Orchi.

"What is this?" Gore from the painting spilled onto him, the decimation, the blood, the death. An airless breeze rattled his body and the inquisitive Kasey darted to the second painting.

The middle painting wasn't as clear. Even directly in front of him, it didn't make sense: several spherical objects revolved around one large yellow body which, itself, was dotted with black squares. Each circular object orbiting was surrounded by even smaller isometric blobs. Kasey moved his fingers to the painting, but Shamp slapped his fingers away with a tendril. "Be cautious."

The third painting was the same yellow sphere, dotted with black objects obscuring it. All of the other objects were removed, from orbit. Now the yellow sphere was all alone in the painting, looking at Kasey with a faded tint.

Kasey didn't say anything. Instead, he rested the soft beam from his Slart on the middle painting despite overhead lighting providing more than enough brightness. Occasionally, his eyes wandered to the other paintings. "This looks like an account of something," Kasey said, finally.

"Definitely a battle." Tsarena gestured to the first painting. "Where I am lost is here." She eyeballed the other two.

"I theorize this is some planetary system." Shamp pointed to the orbiting spheres in the middle painting.

"And the planets just disappeared?" Kasey turned to the third painting.

"A species capable of making a weapon that can destroy an entire planet..." Tsarena's voice trailed off.

"No, just disappeared," Shamp said, turning to her. "GUM utilized one to destroy Bustan."

"That was a one-time thing," Kasey protested.

Shamp looked at Kasey with pity in her eyes. "Do you really believe that?"

Kasey hadn't realized his fists were balled up until the question hit him. His heart told him no, there was no way GUM would have a constant planet killer. That would be pure evil. But his brain knew the answer, and he softened his hands.

"The destruction of a planet is child's play," Shamp explained. "All you require is a hundred-kilometer asteroid to eviscerate most terrestrial worlds. It's trivial." Shamp dusted off some of the dirt covering the "faces" of the people in the first depiction. They didn't even *seem* like people to Kasey. Something of a mix between every single insect he'd ever seen and maybe a mole or groundhog?

"Maybe they didn't destroy the planets." Tsarena shuffled forward.

Kasey looked back at her. "What makes you say that?"

"No wreckage. Not a single asteroid. Just the sun, alone."

"Well not alone, that's a Dyson Swarm." Shamp pointed to the black dots.

"How do you know?" Kasey asked.

"Well, that obtuse sphere must be a star, correct?"

"Probably."

"So, what, we think some aliens have a Dyson Swarm?" Kasey asked.

"Not too shocking. Tayirs' forte was building Dyson Swarms." Shamp knelt, her gray skin almost waxy from the flare dancing above her.

"They actually preferred large Dyson Plates," Tsarena said, holding the flame closer to Shamp, illuminating both her skin and the wall that Shamp examined.

"It provided a substantial amount of energy. But this species possesses an entire swarm," Shamp sighed. "We should still investigate. I believe the triptych is just the surface."

Kasey turned back around and headed towards the array of disturbed pads. "Maybe these have some info on them."

One of the pads with a cracked screen blinked with a screensaver. Kasey scooped it from the ground. Each time the screen fluttered awake for a moment, Kasey's converter pieced together foreign letters into something legible.

USERNAME: TSAVON

PASSWORD:

Kasey hummed for a second. *That name sounds familiar?* He tapped into his comms. "'*Tsavon,' does that name sound familiar to anyone?*"

Tsarena answered immediately from within the room. "That's the name of Mahina's friend on Porygar!"

Kasey snapped his head back at Tsarena. "What's his pad doing here?"

"His pad?" Tsarena rushed over and tore the device from Kasey's hands.

"*What's his pad doing there?*" Falisto asked from the ship, his voice cut by static.

Kasey answered, "*Not sure, it's password protected. Heads' up, you're cutting in and out for me.*"

"Pause," Shamp commanded, from the other end of the room. "Tsavon is listed on it too."

"Any way we can break into one?"

"I'll try to get in," Tsarena said. "Shame Amber isn't here."

Shamp walked over, holding two pads, each shattered beyond repair. "We're certain Tsavon is an individual?"

"What else could it be?" Kasey asked.

"An alias?" Tsarena guessed. She placed the pad on a table, fiddling with some lock-picking software.

"I'll look around some more." Kasey headed to the other ensemble of equipment. Towards the corner of the room, a switchboard attracted Kasey, with glowing buttons and two joysticks like an old-school arcade game.

As if playing the piano, his fingers rested over the buttons in a claw shape, and his other hand grasped a joystick. There were far more buttons than Kasey expected. Two in red, three in blue, five in yellow, and seven in white like some children's game.

Kasey's fingers guided the joystick, cranking it back as if trying to levy

220

a Navigator skyward. A small, originally unseen device crawled from underneath a table at the joystick's command. Kasey quickly moved it another way and confirmed his finger was the puppeteer.

"What is this?" Shamp bent down to the device.

Kasey's face lit up the second he got a good view. "I haven't had one of these since I was a kid," Kasey giggled. He maneuvered the remote control car around, running into support beams and encircling Shamp as if she were being preyed on by sharks.

"Look!" Shamp pointed with a tendril. Above Kasey, a live feed played from the car's viewpoint.

Tsarena grunted, the sound of another failed passcode echoing in the chamber. "I can't get in without tools." She eyed the remote-controlled car Kasey played with but didn't disengage from hacking into Tsavon's pad.

"We can bring a pad back with us," Kasey suggested, still watching the live feed as he crashed the car. Tempted by buttons, Kasey entertained the idea of pressing one, hoping it would do some trick that he never got to do with the donated toys during Christmas gift drives.

"Does it offer a password hint?" Shamp asked, turning to Tsarena.

"Nothing," she sighed. "I've tried everything I can think of."

"Enjoying yourself?" Shamp craned her long neck towards Kasey. "Do you want to investigate the actual evidence?"

"I'm just looking at these buttons now."

Shamp waddled over, tripping over an uneven brick in the floor. Using two of her tendrils, she dug into the ground and saved herself from a faceplant, but her third tendril lost control and swiped at Kasey. He ducked in the nick of time, but her tendril slapped a slew of buttons. A bright blue flash burst from the car. The light blinded Tsarena. "What the hell!"

"I was about to say the same thing," Kasey yelled.

Tsarena groaned and rubbed her eyes. "It's okay," she managed to say through the grinding of her teeth.

"Apologies." Shamp lowered herself into a bow. "It was a mishap."

"I know," Kasey said.

When Shamp returned from her bow, something on the screen glistened and she pointed to it with the same tendril that touched added the blue flash.

SCREEN GRAB 1-082

"Look."

Kasey and Tsarena turned, seeing the file name appear across the screen.

"There might be other photos in here." Kasey scanned the other buttons Shamp hadn't pressed yet. "Tsarena," Kasey began, "you might wanna move, I'm gonna try and finger out what the buttons do."

Without a word, she scooped the pad back up and continued trying to dive into the password-protected device. When she was out of the danger zone, Kasey tapped a white button, bringing up a menu along the screen. After a quick cycle through, Kasey's eyes converted the language. FUNCTION, OPTIONS, RECALL, GALLERY. Kasey stumbled upon the gallery option. "Bingo." He tapped the white button again, returning him to the start of the menu.

"Maybe this one?" Shamp pointed to the singular yellow button."

He brought up the menu and tried it again with her instructions. This time, the gallery at least *attempted* to open before the ominous error appeared. "DATA CORRUPTION."

"Of course," Kasey groaned. "Why wouldn't this be corrupted?"

"I presume we can restore it," Shamp wondered out loud, still shrinking herself from embarrassment.

Tsarena looked around, giving up on the pad. "Any idea where the data would be stored?"

"The cloud?" Kasey speculated. "In which case I don't know how the hell we'd access that."

"Why would Sapien or Jasoosi require such—" Shamp glanced at Kasey, swallowing whatever side remark she was going to make. "—*Unique* technology."

"It's unmistakably Human."

"Where would a Human put the data?"

Kasey rotated back to the control panel. "Probably the cloud, but a local copy might be stored in there."

Static came through on the comms.

"I'll look for the chip," Kasey said.

Tsarena held her ear. "I'll try and see what they're saying."

Gingerly at first, Kasey picked at screws holding together the panel. Feeling no give, Kasey resorted to violence. Drawing his combat knife, Kasey stabbed the panel, etching out bits of metal and parsing it apart.

"There we go." Kasey placed the separated panel along the stone floor. Strings of cables and wires greeted Kasey, the various colors meaningless to him. An array of blue wires guarded the motherboard. Using his fingers, Kasey parted the sea of blue. Towards the corner where one stubborn screw held together the panel, Kasey gleaned RAM sticks, SATA cables, and loose connections until the prized memory drive shined in his eyes.

"Gotcha!" Kasey plucked it, the paper-thin stick that held more information than he could handle. It was weightless. Shamp arched her head over Kasey, examining the ridges and —

"WE HAVE TO GO!"

Chapter 25

Tsoki

Thirty minutes earlier

Tsoki lived by three rules: one, don't eat the basji on *the Irene*; two, never mention Jasoosi around Falisto; and three, never, ever, *ever*, get on a Hybrid's bad side. Unfortunately, that third rule was a recent addition following a tussle at a bar on Kyros a few weeks before shit hit the fan (as Humans say). The right side of his chest still ached.

That's why, despite abhorring tight spaces, Tsoki bit his tongue while pinned between two behemoths named Drake and Benjo. While their movements were akin to strolls, Tsoki preferred jogs. Forced to crawl along the narrow constriction of the rock walls, heat from claustrophobic surroundings drenched Tsoki in sweat. Part of the wall scraped a layer of microfibers off his unitard, further compromising its coolant.

"Hopefully we actually get inside," Benjo muttered from behind Tsoki.

Drake's ear flinched. "We can. The scan made it clear there is an entrance."

Tsoki would've spoken, but if his lungs expanded anymore, they would have gotten scraped by the rocks and it would have taken more than just the fibers of his unitard. He stole glances at the ground, making sure his foot didn't twist on a misshapen pebble or random canal. Despite the old building, there was no "front" door accessible. Instead, they'd opted to act as second-rate spies, sneaking into the building through a hidden groove on the side.

When Tsoki glanced back up, an orange shimmer in the crevice blinded him. "There!" Tsoki pointed, his arm narrowly avoiding Drake. A set of stairs led to a door with a few torches lighting the stones. Tsoki's lungs filled with air as the path stretched apart. After getting freed from the constriction of walls and Hybrids, he darted to the open space and spread his body, reclaiming his bubble with both arms stretched.

"We lost connection to comms," Drake informed. His stoic face examined the doorway. "Wait," he stammered. "It is back." The process of connecting and disconnecting continued while he fiddled with his pad, refreshing the screen every few seconds. "It is not reliable, if it stays that way we will need to turn back and get Kasey's input."

Benjo took the staircase, cutting between Tsoki and Drake. "Let's see what these aliens got for us." Atop the stairs was a circular door, bifurcated down the middle, with incoherent markings in a language or cave painting Tsoki couldn't comprehend.

"Just push it open?" Tsoki asked. His hands hovered over the tan door, with his fingers entering the trenches carved out of the stone.

"I don't see a handle." Benjo leaped forward and placed his hands on the right half. "Ready?

Tsoki nodded, and the two of them pushed, making the door cough a puff of smoke from the middle. Each hemisphere cracked and leaked dust from the movement, pushing aside gravel along the bottom and pushing it to the sides.

While Drake struggled with reforming his connection to *the Irene*, Benjo gazed past the columns and walls of the chamber. The room appeared more like a long hallway rather than a single room, aligned with cathedral ceilings and structures hanging. Low cinder blocks composed the base, with cracks emerging in every other slab. Along the gray walls, two lines of a strange script ran from one end to the other, in shapes Tsoki's converter simply surmised as "unknown."

"I don't assume you recognize that?" Benjo asked Tsoki.

He squinted his purple eyes, glowing through the darkness of the room. "No, I was hoping you knew what it said."

Although cloaked in static, Amber's voice rang through the three's ears.

"Connection seems a bit unstable, but we got it back."

"How should we proceed with the connection being unstable?" Drake asked.

"Just don't leave range and we're good."

Benjo smiled the second her voice came through. *"Sounds good."* Benjo kept his face beaming while he streamed the script. *"You seeing this?"* he asked.

"Looks like writing. I'll see if we can match it to anything we have logs on."

Drake crossed his arms, coming next to Benjo. *"My systems do not recognize it."*

Tsoki spoke on comms, *"There seems to be a shrine of sorts at the end of the hall."*

"Okay," Amber began. *"No direct match on the writing. If you find some form of identification or anything we might be able to send this to linguistics."*

Benjo sighed. Tsoki knew the likelihood that aliens kept dictionaries around was low. *"Copy that, we'll look around."*

Tsoki left the end of the hallway and moved towards the other end of the chamber. A temperature shift made Tsoki hug himself to protect against a nosedive in internal temperatures. *"It's cold,"* Tsoki whispered.

Benjo yelled from the end of the hall. "It's so hot."

While waiting for the two of them, Tsoki examined the understated altar. Three raised layers of stone stood about a meter up from the ground. Cracks and chips distorted the shape, and a layer of blood-stained cloth, frayed and worn, fell to both sides unevenly. Tsoki eyed Benjo, watching him sluggishly topple over to the top with Drake not too far behind.

"Are you guys hot?" Benjo asked, his voice labored.

"Very." Drake stood next to Benjo. "Internal temperatures are 20.3 degrees Celsius. Outside was slightly colder."

Benjo tapped his comms. *"Amber, what's our temperature at?"*

"Your readings on my end seem fine. I guess slightly elevated, but you were just close to one another for a solid bit."

"Where's Falisto?" Tsoki asked.

"What, don't like me?"

Tongue in cheek, Tsoki spoke back, *"No, can't stand you!"*

She laughed. "*He's keeping an eye on the star. The size makes it a bit unpredictable.*"

"*Wouldn't expect him to be a worry wart,*" Tsoki murmured.

"*You'd be surprised.*"

"So, there's this little altar, but what's it for?" Benjo asked. He examined the stone slab, craning his head for clues. Nothing about it exactly sparked intrigue, and that alone caught Tsoki's attention.

"Maybe it's some sort of holy object," Tsoki said.

Drake lifted the cloth, revealing a web of cracks underneath. "This is an old structure," he stated. "Very old."

"Any estimate?" Tsoki asked.

"At a minimum a thousand."

Tsoki's eyes widened. "Old is an understatement. The language doesn't look like the Observers'." Tsoki used his fingers to swipe across images Benjo uploaded to the shared system.

"They have a language?" Benjo asked.

"We *think* they do," Tsoki said. "But a hypothetical race of aliens is still hypothetical."

A distant sound startled the three of them. Tsoki bolted behind a column, crouching and stealing peeks from his location. Benjo lowered his stance at the altar, with Drake cramping the minimal real estate provided by it.

Boop!

"What was that?" Benjo whispered.

"Movement?" Drake asked.

"I swear I heard something," he hushed. He pointed to the left corner from the end of the room, shrouded in darkness. "I think it was there."

Drake drew his Slart, swapping into non-lethal mode. Benjo did the same, his Slart in lethal mode.

"We don't wanna kill it," Tsoki scorned.

Benjo didn't look at him. "We also don't know what '*it*' is."

Tsoki sighed, putting his Slart in lethal mode. "*Amber, we're investigating some sound—*"

Halfway through his transmission, it echoed again from a similar location, in the corner of the room near the altar. Tsoki couldn't describe it. Something between a "*pop!*" and a "*boom!*" like that Human snack Amber always made in the microwave.

Crouched, they crept towards the source. The noise loudened the closer they got, and it became clear there was a hidden entrance they'd missed, with a series of steps angling downward into a completely dark chamber.

Drake stood upright, his knees popping from his position. "We are safe," he announced. With that, he holstered his gun, clicking the safety back on before sauntering towards the newly identified stairs.

"And what makes you say that?" Tsoki whisper-yelled, returning from the peek he took at the newly identified staircase.

"It's a pattern," he said. "In three, two,—"

Simultaneously, the mysterious sound and his voice mirrored one another. "One."

"A pattern can be dangerous," Benjo countered.

Tsoki acquiesced but kept his gun in hand, slipping it into non-lethal mode. Taking another look at the staircase, a blue-colored mist settled in from the darkness. Almost like the antithesis of humidity, the sapphire air cooled his skin. Benjo welcomed the temperature drop and wiped away sweat accumulating atop his forehead.

Along the walls, the script appeared again, this time tiny and tightly packed together, and far more verbose. From a quick analysis, Tsoki deduced it was written right to left, unlike most languages in the Milky Way.

The sound continued on cue, the pattern unmistakable once Tsoki attuned to it.

Drake moved closer, but as soon as his foot stepped into the doorway, a drawn-out beep shuddered in his ear drums. "*Connection terminated*," his comms said. "Just lost comms," he whispered, the same pop-boom coming from beneath.

Benjo glanced at his comms status on his pad. "We can check it out. Just gotta be quick."

"No," Drake commanded. "Galactic Union Military code prohibits us from deliberately going out of range. Amber just told us to not leave range."

Benjo's face turned into a deadpan frown. "I know what Amber said," he began, "but Kasey is the boss on this mission, and we follow his rules."

Drake kept his stare at him.

"I'll be quick," Benjo assured. "There's something down there that we *have* to check."

"I can come with," Tsoki spoke from behind them both, resting his butt along the altar. "I got a feeling something is waiting down there."

"No," Drake stammered. "We need at least one person up here." He turned his gaze from Tsoki to Benjo. "And we need to make sure one of us follows the rules."

The heated jab at Benjo made his eyes narrow. Tsoki cut in. "I'll stay up here," he said. "I still wanna check out this area and sweep for more of that language."

"We're in a time crunch," Benjo reasoned. "Let's hurry this up."

Tsoki motioned to the back end. "Go, I'll just be looking around."

Benjo and Drake began their descent, looking back to Tsoki. "We'll be back in a few minutes," Benjo said.

Tsoki didn't turn. "Sounds good."

His red fingers ran along ragged ridges and grooves etched in the stone of the altar table. Sharp points gave him goosebumps that weren't exactly unpleasant, like prickly bushes barely piercing the top layer of skin and scratching an itch. Scooping his pad, Tsoki placed his device between two major gashes along the table, readying the scanner. From the left, Tsoki reached down and plucked a piece of stone a half meter away. The second his hand clawed over it, heat radiated up his arms. Tsoki could've sworn the rock was more blue just a few moments ago before Benjo and Drake descended. Now it was violet, darker and redder than ruby.

Shaking off the thought, he placed its flattest side on a circular scanner on the tempered glass of his pad. Data flooded through it like a conduit, starting with obvious information like "warm" to more covert information like elemental composition.

Tsoki rolled his eyes. "A 25-degree rock is warm? Who would've thought." More data flew in, and that's when he raised an eyebrow muscle.

"*Amber,*" Tsoki said, still looking at the rock.

"*What's up?*" Her voice was completely reduced to feedback and incomplete words severed by the connection. Most messages required guesswork.

"*I got a weird rock here. One of the elements came up as unknown.*"

"*Did you send—*"

"*—Uploading photos to you right now.*"

A moment passed before she spoke. For a moment, he thought he'd lost connection. "*Got 'em.*"

Tsoki heard what he surmised was a few keystrokes and a computer screech on *the Irene* plowing through databases of information.

"*Benjo reported something similar on Porygar. Does he know anything about it?*"

Tsoki winced, one of the sharper ends lacerating a new wound like a paper cut. He quickly sucked on the blood that dripped out of it. "*They went down a staircase. Not a lot of good reception here.*"

"*They're out of range?*" Amber gasped. "*Why did they leave range? I deliberately reminded Benjo not to do that!*"

"*Don't worry,*" Tsoki soothed, immediately regretting his divulgence of information. "*I'm right up here and can get them back. I stayed behind so we could stay in contact.*"

Amber didn't respond. She didn't need to. Tsoki could tell by the inflection in her voice and the tenseness of her follow-up questions that she muted herself so she could yell expletives forbidden by PTF over public channels. "*Five minutes. I want them back in range. I can't believe Benjo—*" she cut the transmission before finishing her thought but Tsoki filled in the gaps like earlier.

He turned back around, looking at the ceiling and around the staircase. The popping-boom from below grew louder, but the pattern stayed the same. He took one more paranoid look, before deciding he had enough time to do what he needed to do. Quietly, he disconnected his pad from PTF's server and connected to another. The link, although limited and just as compromised as the one with PTF, would have to do. His fingers clicked the holographic keys, each one lagging.

Strange rocks. On 'Planet Exo,' close to hypergiant. Two main buildings on the planet, one searched by Kasey and others, the other by me and the two hybrids. Heard mysterious popping sounds. Attaching photos of the strange rocks + readings.

Almost forgetting, Tsoki quickly added a last line: *found strange language—unable to translate.*

He checked behind him, making sure Benjo and Drake weren't sneaking up the stairs. With a click of the finger, the report whooshed off along the server to its destination.

Stealing another glance back, Tsoki logged back into PTF and reestablished the connection.

"Tsoki, do you copy?!" Falisto shouted.

"Falisto? Where's Amber—?"

"Tsoki you have to get out of there! The star's about to expend a huge chunk of mass you gotta get out NOW!"

Tsoki raced to the staircase, sliding across the floor and hitting the end of the wall. "BENJO! DRAKE! WE HAVE TO GO!"

Chapter 26

Teams Alpha & Beta

Shamp galloped, moving twice the speed of Kasey and Tsarena through the ocean of sand and occasional rock-shell. She kept whipping her head back and snapping it forward mid-sprint. Normally, she'd admonish them, but the Navigator was far and her breath was already hoarse.

"Why is it so fucking tight in here!" Tsoki burst aloud, hundreds of meters away from Shamp and the others. Benjo and Drake sandwiched him a second time for today, still bewildered from what they discovered.

"Kasey!" Tsarena shouted as he fell along one of the dunes behind Shamp. She raced back to him, only a few meters back. Pulling him off the ground, Kasey regained his stance despite a sharp pain radiating up his lower back.

"*Hurry!*" Falisto shouted through everyone's comms. "*You don't have much time!*"

Shamp got to the Navigator first. Haphazardly, her tendrils and hands worked overtime to prep the ship's engines. "*Autopilot is not functioning!*" she bellowed.

"Ow!" Benjo grimaced. One piece of stone stuck out of his metal leg, the same one injured by the hospital door on Kyros. Gripping it with his index finger and thumb, he drove it out his thigh, coolant dripping from the wound and overclocking to form a seal.

The Navigator shifted into view, like a beacon of light in endless night. "It's just right there!" Tsarena marveled. "We're almost there!" She looked at Kasey. "C'mon!"

"*Autopilot is down!*" Shamp yelled again. Her tendrils got everything they could operational, with the engines fully powered and ready to bolt the hell out.

"*Fuck!*" Falisto yelled. "*I'll see if—*"

"*—I can try to reboot it from here!*" Amber bellowed. Her fingers slapped keys, sending commands to internal systems nestled inside the Navigator.

Still away from the others, Drake, Tsoki, and Benjo emerged from the entrance they used and raced toward the Navigator. Drake kept his arms high and at a sturdy 90-degree angle. With the wind between his arms and the sand sneaking grains into his suit, he rushed towards the Navigator now he and the others were out of the rock sandwich. Benjo limped through the desert, with Tsoki taking multiple looks back before holstering him along his shoulder.

Kasey rolled into the Navigator, falling for a second time. His nose snapped on impact and he yelped but threw himself back up, spewing out blood. "Please, tell me the autopilot is back on."

Tsarena grabbed him with one hand while holding her side tightly with the other. A sharp ache gnawed at her side. "Where are the others?"

"C'mon!" Tsoki encouraged Benjo. He held his scraped shoulder tightly, the scuff marks darkening his side.

"Please tell me one of you two can pilot this ship." Shamp looked down at the controls. Her tendrils hovered over weapon systems and jettisoning buttons. Although she could discern simple messages, she couldn't put this thing in the air, let alone in space.

"*Autopilot is gone, you're gonna have to fly it!*" Falisto shouted. "*I can guide you as much as possible!*"

Kasey's heart stopped for a moment. Then it raced. Fast. He gulped. It didn't get rid of the lump in his throat. It meandered down his body and metastasized. The fear paralyzed him. His fingers only trembled from an ominous wind that hurled him into the open-doored Navigator. His body was in free fall, reaching terminal velocity in a pit of despair.

Drake tumbled into the Navigator, tripping over a loose rock that they consciously landed on. Tsarena offered her hand, pulling him up. "You're alright!" she shouted.

"Kasey!" Shamp yelled. "You must fly the ship!"

"*You need to leave NOW!*" Falisto commanded.

Tsoki waddled in with Benjo, breathing so loudly that the ringing and shrieking of the growing sandstorm sounded like distant pins dropping. Benjo's eyes bobbed back and forth, making his vision blurry, and whatever coolant hadn't dropped out his body struggled to bring down the internal temperatures.

Kasey felt his body move, his legs responding to an unconscious pull but his mind took a second to travel with his body. His fingers trembled as they approached the Navigator controls. Flashes of him and Peyton, the crew from Musk Station. He winced.

His body did it like second nature. Automatically, his hand pulled the throttle up. The door closed to the Navigator, sealing the crew with the loose bits of sand.

Kasey's lips and eyes were motionless, the blood from his broken nose dripping into a new puddle at the base of the ship. His hands forced the Navigator to climb. The structures morphed from large edifices to small landmarks and specks of dust became specks of specks. The height didn't scare him, he couldn't process it, the ship was moving through some otherworldly force.

"We're gonna be at zero g!" Kasey heard himself say.

Turbulence from the side made Kasey and the Navigator shudder. He recalled Peyton falling down a lifetime ago from a similar force.

"*Quick!*" Amber shouted.

Kasey's hand moved, pushing the throttle towards *the Irene*. Speed climbed, and he snapped his neck back despite experiencing weightlessness. For a moment he didn't see Tsoki and others when he looked back—he saw Peyton and the old crew. Waiting. Scared. Horrified. He blinked the apparitions away, replaced with Tsoki and the others in their respective seats.

With a violent shake of the head, Kasey flung his hair to one side and summoned himself back to his body. He took his sleeved unitard and wiped off the blood. "Seat belts on!" Kasey commanded.

Tsoki and Peyton raced to secure themselves.

Kasey yelled again, "We're going off course!" Compromised but still himself, Kasey powered the Navigator's FTL engines. The blue protective light shielded the Navigator-like armor.

"*Are you crazy?! You won't be able to jump in time!*" Falisto shouted.

Kasey pushed the throttle anyway, forcing the ship at significantly less than the speed of light. "*I don't plan to jump.*"

The hypergiant's ejection of energy hurled towards the planet, passing through the depths of space so fast it rivaled *the Irene's* non-FTL, top speeds. "*Amber, Falisto, power up FTL on the Irene!*" Kasey yelled over the comms.

Without a question in response, *the Irene* cloaked itself in the same blue light. "We're almost there."

As the mass ignited the already blazing hell of Planet Exo, large chunks of the planet tumbled apart towards them. A shower of newly formed debris expanded in billions of directions, forming micro asteroids and rocks the size of cities.

Kasey slid open the radar, showing remnants cascading towards them. Kasey prepped the Navigator's rockets—something he hadn't done since the Sapien war—and launched them against the array of molten rock coming towards them.

A stray asteroid pushed the ship, bouncing off the FTL bubble and violently shaking the Navigator. Through gritted teeth, Kasey pushed down the memory of Peyton slamming against the door.

"Everyone put on helmets!"

Coffee mugs and boxed water floated in the zero-g. Objects clashed with one another, individual liquid particles adhering to one another but not staying in the same space. What remained of Planet Exo followed the FTL shield like a hunter stalking its prey. The Navigator rocked between each slap from the asteroids, the blueness of the barrier wavering slightly.

They inched closer to *Irene*, its blue bubble almost opaque from the dense energy encircling it. Veering aside, Kasey avoided debris the size of a large nation, opting to instead hit something the size of a coffee cup.

"Now!"

The Navigator's bubble joined forces with *the Irene's*, and the two floated in harmony as Kasey demanded the Navigator to stop accelerating with a full pullback. As the light encircling the two ships darkened, the rocks that nearly killed Kasey years ago failed again. *"Falisto, Amber, jump us out!"*

Amid the cheers, the celebratory yells, and the emergence of gravity, Kasey couldn't help but sob as the ships left the system.

Chapter 27

Kasey

Five years ago – Musk Station

The mission was simple: transport Leon, the President of Mars' son and the face of alien-Human relations, from Musk Station back to the surface. Leon cemented himself as the scourge of the solar system by becoming subject to more than a few critiques following his remarks on species equality. He had controversial stances on alien-Human marriage, wages, voting rights, property rights, healthcare rights, nearly every single right denied by Human Governments.

In young protester fashion, Leon went to the belly of the beast: Musk Station, where nearly only Sapien forces lived. Instead of brokering peace and convincing the masses, he was imprisoned as the face of alien-Human movement and slated for execution.

Parked along the docks, Kasey and the crew embarked into the center of Musk Station. Peyton usually held his hand, holding it on top of his own and guiding him through the busy herds of people when they weren't on mission. This wasn't the crowd for that. Kasey struggled to keep his fingers from attracting closer to Peyton's, but the thought that they'd have two days together on shore leave was what kept the wait worth it.

"Security is tight," Kate murmured. She pushed back her long black hair with a platinum streak down the middle.

"Know where the Mustang is?" Ivy asked, her voice a bit too loud for a secret mission.

Peyton turned back to her. "Close," he assured.

"How close is 'close?'"

"Close enough that we aren't 'far.'"

Ivy grimaced but kept moving.

The group of four passed by propaganda mixed in with open hate speech. Musk Station was heralded as a haven for Free Speech Absolutism. Under no circumstances could someone be punished by authorities for the plethora of epithets and threats that weren't so thinly veiled in the signs promising evisceration of the "red Humans."

A sign, black with gray text to make it difficult for Psys to see, caught Kasey's attention. "If you can see this you belong," it proclaimed.

Kasey swallowed down the bad taste it stuffed in his mouth. A kind message, hidden behind malicious intention made his skin crawl and his heart sink. Kate pointed to a short stand formed from loose planks of wood held together by silver nails, bent and sticking a tad out. A shotty job, but Kasey wouldn't judge. In red paint at the base were the words "Peppermint Hot Chocolate for sale." Two kids and an older man—presumably their dad—exchanged card scanners for cups.

"We should get some," Kate said. "Could help us blend in?"

"Not a bad idea," Kasey said. He double-tapped his lower ear comms. "*Allen, do you or Mustang want some peppermint coco?*"

After a brief pause, he answered back. "*One for me. Mustang asked for diet soda.*"

"*Copy that,*" Kasey muttered. "*But I don't think these kids got soda.*"

"*Yes to the coco,*" he replied.

After three customers in front got their respective drinks, the two kids greeted the soldiers. The dad, who'd been stuck with his pad reading and skimming the news, caught a glimpse of their uniforms. He bolted from his chair, nearly falling out of it after leaning in it. His stomach hung out from his cinched belt, and his hair climbed up his forearms in black clumps. Red cheeks with a smile painted his face.

"Hello!" he said.

"Hello," Peyton began, "I think six hot cocos, please."

"None for me," Kate confirmed.

"Scratch that," he said, looking back at one of the children. "Five."

The girl nodded profusely with her long brown hair coming in front of her eyes. Using the ladle hanging ajar from a brass-colored bucket, she scooped in a few heaps of cocoa. The boy next to her dug into a bag of mini marshmallows.

"How much?" he asked Peyton.

"The normal amount is fine." Peyton winced when only one or two of the cotton pads fell into the chocolate bath.

The boy handed each one out, with Kasey holding two of them.

"That will be thirty-three Martian dollars," the marshmallow boy proclaimed. He brought forth the card scanner and placed it along the loose planks.

"I don't assume you take kirbies?" Peyton had a sheepish smile on his face, already knowing the answer.

The father's red, jolly face warped into a scowl and scrunched-up features. He scoffed, "You use kirbies? I thought our military was supporting humanity."

The little girl stiffened at the words, looking at the ground. "It's okay," she murmured. "They're soldiers, let's just give it to them." The father's eyes turned into fireballs as he loomed over her.

"We got paid in kirbies," Kasey cut in. "But don't worry, I carry Martian with me." He smiled convincingly enough the dad settled it by crossing his arms.

After a swiping, the kids gave a weak smile and thanked them for their service and patronage. As they walked back, Kasey caught out of the corner of his eye the man painting "Martian ONLY" in red while ranting about something unclear.

"Pretty average," Ivy said, her face contorted to a frown with some of the beverage leaking from her lips.

Kasey sipped his. "Too hot for me to say," he said. The peppermint smell radiated upwards from the coco. "Really strong peppermint."

"Know why they use peppermint?" Kate muttered from the back of the group.

Peyton looked back. "No, why?"

She put her hair in a low ponytail. "Toxic to most aliens," she said.

Peyton's eyes darted back down to the ground. "For what it's worth," he said, his head still cocked to the side so Ivy and Kate could hear him, "Mars isn't like this."

Ivy nodded alongside Kate. "I hope you're right," Kate said.

"We have a few visitors," Kasey suggested. "Mainly Orchi, but they visit."

As they continued down to the end of the station, the platoons of people died down. Fewer shops settled in this area, their lights not as bright and surrounded by crushed cans and wrappers that floated in an artificial breeze.

"*Allen*," Kasey murmured into his comms. "Which store is it?"

"*The coat shop*," he said. "*I think I see you guys, I'm coming to get you.*"

From a building with jackets of various colors modeled by mannequins, Allen emerged, holding onto the coat hanging off Leon's arm. Leon, for all intents and purposes, was an average college kid. He majored in Intergalactic Politics, as well as Communications Across Languages.

Leon had straight black hair that curved around his head. His eyes were small, dark brown. Kasey handed off the spare cup to Leon who gratefully accepted and chugged like it was the first time he ever had hot cocoa.

"So, what exactly is the plan here?" Leon asked sheepishly.

"We bust you out through the crowd," Peyton said. He lifted his Military Standard Assault Shooter. "You use this gun, fire into anyone that tries to stop you."

Leon's eyes, wide and drenched in fear, blinked vigorously. "W-what?"

"He's joking," Kasey said, grinning. "We're gonna move the ship out here and have you come out." Kasey and the others dug into their bags attached to their backs. Each took a component out of their respective one until they had a full space suit.

"There's no dock here?"

"No," Peyton said. "But there is an airlock."

He looked at Peyton then Kasey, then back to Peyton. "I've never done a space walk."

"Then listen closely."

The plan was a simple one: get the Navigator near the airlock and open the hull so Leon and Allen could float in on the way out. Ivy jammed the security measures from the inside, giving them a bit of time. Interior security always proved to be the problem, never outgoing security, so the jamming just lengthened the window.

After a less-than-thorough exit scan, Kasey maneuvered the Navigator toward the airlock. The rockets puttered just outside of the door, barely missing Musk Station. Usually, this airlock functioned more like a trash compactor that sent junk deep into space. Unfortunately, errors in trajectory instead led to an ungodly trash ring around one of Mars' moons.

Aligning to the door, Kasey backed the Navigator. Over the comms in his spacesuit, he spoke to Allen. "*You ready?*"

"*God it smells awful in here,*" Allen grunted. "*But yes, get us the hell out.*"

"*Copy that,*" Kasey said. Peyton sat next to him, his face grinning.

"I love that man," Peyton murmured.

Kasey pretended to be jealous, "What about me?!"

"Well I'm *in* love with you," he said. Peyton swore there was a difference between loving and being in love, and although they were interchangeable for Kasey, it meant a great deal to Peyton.

"*Doors are about to open,*" Allen said.

Kate and Ivy sat in the back, strapped to their chairs. The four of them wore their helmets. Spacesuits had gotten far more complex but far sleeker than the ones NASA used in the past. After the GU introduced humanity to some technology, most suits didn't take up more than a unitard, however, helmets were still a work in progress and proved to be the most expensive piece.

"What's that?" Peyton asked.

Kasey turned forward as a sparkle in the distance shined for a moment. "I don't know—"

A silent explosion blew out a third of Musk Station. The entire ship moved alongside it, and, with the Navigator connected, flung it and the passengers to the side.

Ivy screamed, then hit her head back cracking her helmet. "My helmet!"

she cried. Only she could hear the hissing of oxygen leaving and her suit giving the auditory warning.

"You have to pull up!" Kate bellowed to Kasey and Peyton.

"*Allen, get out of there!*" Kasey yelled.

"*The power's shot!*" he screamed back.

After a moment's thought, Kasey pushed the Navigator forward, disconnecting from the airlock. "Keep an eye on that ship," Kasey said to Peyton.

He nodded and kept his gaze transfixed to the glimmer of the ship. Kasey looked back to Kate and Ivy and ushered another command. "Kate, try and seal the suit. If it doesn't work we'll need another plan."

She nodded with her eyes fluttering. Kasey whipped the ship around. "*Allen, I'm gonna fire open the airlock.*"

"*Are you crazy? That could kill us!*"

"*Is it pressurized in there?*"

"*No, zero-g but you could kill us!*"

"*Musk Station is going down—*"

"*—There's another rocket!*" Peyton shouted.

From the same ship shrouded in space, a rocket burst the middle of Musk Station, jettisoning it into two unequal parts with one half already sundered by the first rocket.

"*Do it!*" Allen shouted.

Kasey aimed and hit the button, shooting a red blast and opening the door. A piece of the door flew inward, and Allen yelled something close to "move" before a river of blood bled from the airlock.

"*Allen?!*" Kasey yelled.

"*He pushed me out of the way!*" Leon cried.

Kasey's mouth trembled and he felt a squeeze from Peyton.

"*We're turning back around so you can get it in,*" Peyton said on Kasey's behalf.

Leon assented, climbing towards the end of the airlock and holding onto a ridge formed of broken pieces of metal. He looked down at Allen's corpse, whimpering.

Kasey followed Peyton's direction, spinning the ship back around.

"I can't get the fucking thing sealed!" Kate yelled.

Ivy began to asphyxiate, and her temperature started spiraling. "Get another helmet!" Peyton yelled, pointing to the backside of the ship. She pushed herself off Ivy and towards the cupboard of supplies.

As she reached it, another blast, this time focused on an area close to them, pushed apart the Navigator, sending Kate spiraling out of the ship and into the void of space with the spare helmet.

"Kate!" Peyton shouted, reaching his hand out from a futile distance. Her screams, grew distorted as she left the range of the comms before cutting entirely.

Peyton left his seat, holding onto Ivy and locking himself to the Navigator with a carabiner. "Kasey, seal the ship!"

"*What about me?!*" Leon yelled.

"*Leon get your ass in here!*" Kasey lifted the ship upwards, getting back in view of Leon. "*Jump!*" Kasey ordered.

From the metal pipe hanging out, he leveraged himself in, diving into the Navigator after a burst from the ship sent Peyton backward too. Leon followed in, tumbling along the sides.

Kasey hurriedly went to close the ship, the door croaking back up. Kicking off from the back end, Kasey hovered towards Ivy, her body now lifeless. Her face was cold, with her eyes and face, already swelling.

Closing both of his eyes tightly, Kasey stifled a cry that left his mouth. "I'm so sorry," he whispered. He embraced her.

The Navigator continued to close until a final blast went off, blowing off the ship door. It spun, and Kasey hit the end of the wall, cracking his helmet beyond repair. Kasey coughed, gasped, shouted. As he floated in the spinning ship, he felt a tug at his leg, with Peyton pulling him close to him.

Peyton's face was red. He looked into Kasey's eyes, mouthing something before barking something at Leon that Kasey couldn't make out between gasps. Leon followed through, holding Kasey's hands together. Kasey was too weak to fight it, instead, he kept looking into Peyton's eyes, with a tear struggling to get off his face in the gravity-less place.

Air hissed from Peyton's suit as he levied off his helmet, immediately struggling without air. He took off Kasey's, chipped helmet and flung it aside, turning the cracked glass into shattered glass before sealing his helmet on Kasey.

As Kasey's vision cleared, and his heart stopped beating a million times a minute, he shouted at Peyton who was gasping now. Doing the motion for breathing, Peyton tried to mouth something.

Kasey, with tears in his eyes, repeated them back. "I love you."

Chapter 28

Kasey

It wasn't the loud *thud* of Drake's body slamming against the floor of the Navigator that broke Kasey out of his trance, or the concerned shouts of Tsarena and Shamp. It was the tug from Tsoki's fingers gripping his shoulder that snapped him back. His head had deafened all the commotion. When Kasey turned back from the pilot chair, the muffling memories dissipated and the tunnel vision widened back to normal.

"Oh my God!" Kasey scurried to Drake as his body convulsed and his head banged on the floor. "He's having a seizure!" Kasey exclaimed.

Shamp laid down her tendrils underneath his head where some blood already dripped from. His head continued its thumping, now slapping her gray skin and painting it crimson. "What happened?" Kasey asked.

"He just started freaking out!" Tsarena cried.

Kasey whipped his head around to see the Navigator's autopilot back on and retreating into *the Irene*. He knelt towards him. Benjo leaned against the cold side of the Navigator.

"Benjo," Kasey commanded while checking Drake's vitals.

"Sorry," he said. He came over and wiped off a blanket of sweat covering his forehead.

After a quick temperature gauge on Drake, Kasey handed the reader to Shamp. "Check Benjo's temperature, please," he said.

Shamp nodded and with one of her free tendrils wrapped around the handle of the orange device.

"I'm fine," Benjo assured in the most unconvincing way possible. As the words left his lips he started to fall over himself, tripping on the even floor to the side as if the ship made a sharp turn despite being motionless.

Tsarena helped hold Benjo up from the floor. "Get him some water," she commanded Tsoki. Benjo downed the first cup and two refills thereafter. Tsarena levied him towards the seating where he slumped into place.

Kasey grazed Drake's metal portions airing out a scalding heat. Kasey's face darkened, and his breath quickened. "*Falisto, shut down the docks. Let us dock but keep us isolated.*"

"*What? Why?*"

"*Something's wrong, Drake and Benjo have elevated temperatures. There's a virus or pathogen on Planet Exo.*"

"*Amber,*" Falisto commanded over the comms for everyone to hear. "*Set course for Kyros's med-bay.*"

The Navigator, now fully enveloped by the docking hub, received flashes of red lights from an alarm blaring through the sealed section. Two puffs of smoke from the corners sanitized the room with a sterile solution.

Benjo bit the edge of the plastic cup. Tsarena nodded, "More?"

He responded with a slow nod, far more lethargic than earlier. Tsoki raced to Kasey, checking the pulse of Drake. He started with the arms before realizing they were metal and then moved to the chest.

"He's not breathing!" Tsoki yelped.

Kasey brought his gaze to Drake, no longer convulsing and heat still scorching him from his arms and legs. "Shamp, I need the defib!"

With her bloody tendril, she opened a safety compartment and plucked the machine slightly thrown off from when in zero-g earlier. Kasey powered up the batteries and marked the setting to Hybrid. After Kasey disseminated the pasties over Drake's body, Tsoki checked the positions on the organic and inorganic portions.

"One, two, three!" Kasey pressed the button. Electricity traveled through the rubber-looking material, forcing his chest up from the floor before hitting it again. Kasey upped the voltage. "One, two, three!" Again, Drake's body flew from the floor, nearly touching the ceiling before thumping back into the ground. "Maximum volts!"

Tsoki's fingers dangled over the knobs, and, after a moment, he pushed it up. Kasey didn't bother counting down, instead triggering another jolt of electricity. Drake's lifeless body nearly hit the ceiling the way it sparked him skyward. His eyes were bloodshot, and his lips were slightly apart like he'd been dead for hours.

Kasey's lips trembled, and he balled his hands into fists. *I shouldn't have brought them here. This is my fault.* He hadn't changed—he was the same Kasey—endangering people he loved. "I'm so sorry," he cried.

"Kasey," Tsarena started, "we have to focus on Benjo." She offered a hand which Kasey swatted away. He didn't deserve the support. Using a surprising amount of strength, she yanked him off the floor and onto his feet. He swallowed his inner monologue and looked to Benjo, his body stumbling.

"Benjo, what's your symptoms?"

"I feel like I'm burning alive."

Kasey grasped his iron arm. It was as if he touched the innermost layer of a star, it burned so badly it felt cold like freezer burns with a residual effect. Kasey recoiled back and used his other hand to touch Benjo's Human arm. Unlike the fiery one, this arm froze with the sweat nearly turning into a frost.

"Does it feel like your bones are on fire?" Kasey asked, looking at Benjo from above. Benjo didn't adjust his view this time, instead answering with a "yes."

Kasey hit the comms again. *"Guys, it's the Tyol virus."*

After an exaggerated gasp over the comms, Falisto muttered. *"Is Benjo...?"*

"He's okay, for now," Kasey said. *"How far are we from Kyros?"*

"Hours at least."

Kasey nodded and drew his combat knife. "I know what we have to do."

* * *

Benjo

The second the lights blended into one massive overhead sun Benjo realized something was wrong. Shadows and voids in his vision formed a vignette, making a reverse halo of darkness. Occasionally, he'd slip in and out of consciousness, but his mind wandered while the world around him moved. He didn't move—hell he *couldn't* move—but his surroundings kept changing.

At some point, he went to rub his eyes. But his arm wasn't responding. He pulled at it again and kept pulling until his eyes locked on a table a few meters away where one arm and two legs were. His one arm and two legs. Benjo yelped, the image choking him back into unconsciousness.

The next time he awoke, it was to the sound of several Orchi in hazmat suits with silver tools digging into his body. Beeps and buzzes whizzed in the air, and spots in his vision appeared, already limited with one functioning eye. A sterile smell of bleach and floor cleaner blasted his nostrils.

Most people saw their life flash before their eyes. But for Benjo, it wasn't his life that flashed. It was one, singular moment—a slice of his entire life— that played over and over. Sometimes, his brain would alter little details, such as the placement of Benjo's wine glass or the position of Amber's throw blanket along her unmade bed.

His mind, however, got the main gist. They sat together at a table, sharing a meal in the form of salmon and rice. A simple meal on Earth, considered a delicacy elsewhere in the galaxy. Amber insisted she had to make it for him. It took everything in her power, but she managed to convince him to join her, and she even got hold of four lemons and farm-raised salmon on *the Irene.*

She pushed forward his plate, her mouth nearly dripping saliva onto the pink fish. "Dig in!"

Jabbing her fork into the bed of rice, Amber plucked a bundle of grain and paired it with a piece of salmon. Amber somehow managed to swallow it down the wrong way, hacking up a lung along with one or two grains of rice.

Halfway into her coughing tirade, Benjo pushed himself off the table, leaving behind his sulking fit, and threatening her with his Heimlich. "No, I'm fine," she said, tears cropping out the corner of her eyes.

"You sure?" Benjo said, keeping his hands wrapped around her waist. Even after she reassured him four separate times, he kept his arms locked around her. He pulled her towards him.

"You don't have to go," Benjo pouted.

Amber sighed. "You know I do."

His silence acknowledged it, and after she pushed apart his arms by his elbows, he sulked back to his seat. Twiddling his fork, he wrapped pieces of rice like it was pasta before shoving it into his mouth. Amber kept her eyes down, straight at the salmon that was just slightly overcooked.

"It's good." Benjo pushed through the bitterness of the looming goodbye. He scooped up a piece of fish. "As always." Benjo fought back the sadness of the reality of the situation: this would be the last time for at least a few years that they'd be together. Tomorrow, he'd be shipped off to another planet, and he'd be on another one, their interstellar communications the only thing connecting them.

They'd agreed from the start that this wouldn't be something serious. Just a dinner date while they were both on Kyros because Benjo thought she was cute. Then it turned into two dates, including a movie—only because they both liked action movies. Three dates later they were having overnights every night. Amber reminded him again and again that this wasn't serious, this was just a situationship while "training" for PTF. For a year, the situationship between the two Hybrids only became increasingly complex until the awkwardness of reality hit them. Their situationship had an expiration date unless one of them wanted to trade in their careers, but neither of them was the type, and without a similar assignment, this was the end of the road.

But even then, eating rice and lemon-soaked salmon with moving boxes peppering the room more than the dish, the inevitable "what-if" slipped into Benjo's mind. Occasionally, he'd look at her, sitting in silence and thinking about a different universe where that meal wasn't their last together as a couple.

Chapter 29

Kasey

"All for nothing," Falisto cooed. He sat outside the hospital floor with Kasey on a plastic bench with a wall supporting it. On the door outside, a red glow indicated the level was closed to visitors. Twiddling his thumbs, Falisto's eyes shifted around the hall.

"We also have this." Kasey scrolled through each image on his pad. With each swipe, a new detail, sometimes a crack in the wall or a new letter in the foreign script his converter still couldn't read, caught his attention. Kasey exhaled. He needed something to focus on, to get his mind off Drake, off the fact that his friend just got infected with a deadly virus on *his* mission. In the silent moment that ensued, all Kasey could think about was Drake. How scared he was, how he left behind a family, friends. PONR or not, he had bonds—Tsoki went to deliver the bad news.

After a moment, Falisto leaned forward a bit, his voice low. "Are you okay, Kasey?"

Kasey unglued his eyes from the pad and turned to Falisto. With his pupils covering his golden irises, Falisto scratched one of his whiskers. "Are you?" he asked again.

Kasey blinked at him, keeping his direct eye contact. *Can he read my mind?* "Why do you ask?"

Falisto sighed at the non-response. "I could tell," he started, "something was off."

"How so?" Kasey took stock. His body was in a normal position, slumped a bit, sure, but that wasn't out of the ordinary. Both feet were planted on the ground, his smile was tight but still taking residence on his face.

"You're not as good at hiding your feelings as you think."

Kasey gulped and pursed his lips, cracking the fake smile.

"You know," Falisto began, "Psys didn't have a word for it until we met the Orchi." He let a pause settle the uneasy atmosphere. "'Trauma.'" He blinked a few times, his inner eyelid a second slower than the outer. "And we still struggle. Talking about it—it's not natural to us. But I know it helps. You can talk to me."

The words swaddled Kasey. They poured warmth into his heart, over-flowing and streaming through his body, coursing through his veins and supplying him with a smile. A weight Kasey didn't know he'd been carrying dissolved.

"We're comrades," Kasey said.

Amber stepped into the hall, closing the door behind her and taking off her required hazmat mask. Her blonde hair broke free from the rubber band and encircled her. Her metal arms, despite coated in antiviral gloss, were required to have plastic wrap cover each portion. That alone made movement hard, but the hazmat suit only compounded the problem.

"Anything?" Kasey asked.

She looked down at him, unzipping the rubber covering her body. "He's stable, for now. Any luck on the images?" she asked.

"Not yet," Kasey sighed.

An elevator dinged from the end of the hall. The person's long shadow with three tendrils told Kasey who it was. "Shamp, thanks for joining."

"I come bearing good news."

"There's a cure?"

"Incorrect." Shamp held her pad tightly to her bony chest, emerging from the hallway. Her long legs glided across the hospital's floor, and she took massive steps towards the group. "Shalotte had the Cerapto get me something."

"Who?" Falisto asked, despite being told several times who the Cerapto were.

Shamp ignored his feint of ignorance. "They maintain meticulous records of star systems. They're incredibly information driven." She had a slanted grin on her face. "It's not much," she continued, "but it may aid us." Swiping past a few screens, Shamp produced an image on her pad and then turned it to the group to show. "Look."

Three two-dimensional depictions of spheres spun on the moving display. Each was slightly different from one another. Kasey squinted, making out miniature labels stationed at the bottom his converter quickly decoded. Tyol, Porygar, Planet Exo. Boxes of data followed by dotted lines accentuated information about each.

"What am I supposed to look for?" Kasey asked.

Shamp placed the pad in Kasey's hands. "I searched for similarities and noticed a pattern." She bent down and had Amber take a seat so the four of them were as close to eye level as much as their different biologies let them. "Tyol does not originate from the Indus System. Porygar likely does not originate from its system, and Planet Exo certainly is from a different system."

"They're all—"

"—Rogue Planets." Her fingers emphatically tapped each planet on her pad. "But that's not all." With a flick of her finger, the models shrunk even more, now just dots with the information taking the forefront. "They're also tidally locked."

"Wait, no they aren't," Kasey defended. "Tyol rotates."

"Not originally." Shamp pointed to a date under Tyol. "Terraformed."

"Tidally locked planets are common how does this help?" Amber asked, folding her arms.

"I recognize this may sound outlandish," Shamp began, "but I believe the strange phenomena occur on Rogue Planets." Her claim hung in the sterile air of the hospital floor.

"How do we know these are Rogue Planets, exactly?" Falisto asked, skepticism seeping through his teeth.

"The Cerapto's records," she said.

Amber mumbled, "Weird aliens."

"Are there other Rogue Planets you searched for?" Kasey asked, his body now leaning forward towards Shamp.

"Glad you asked," she moved to a new screen, the entire pad shifting to a new, unfamiliar planet. "This planet entered the Moncratic System long ago. It disrupted the orbits around it of other planets and asteroids when it came in and now it's orbited by trillions of debris."

"But how does this help us?" Falisto asked.

"We may be able to predict where the next cataclysm is." Shamp looked into Falisto's eyes. "And we can prevent it."

Falisto's skepticism infected Kasey's voice. "Can we trust the Cerapto data?"

"I checked with some Venori records," she soothed. "But I trust them. They're odd, only communicating through devices, but they are trustworthy."

"This is good, Shamp," Kasey nodded. "If nothing else we have an idea of where to look next."

The sound of boots squeaking along the waxed floor echoed from the elevator. They looked over to Tsarena sprinting and sliding towards them. Nearly losing her footing, she gasped for air and stopped.

"What's wrong?" Kasey rose from his seat.

"It's Sola!" She shouted, her lips curving into a smile. "She's awake!"

Chapter 30

Riley

Humanity prepared for nearly every possible outcome for first contact. There were the common threats, of course. Deadly pathogens, different biologies, hostile aliens. Remedies were plentiful: crew wore antiviral suits, *the Traveler* produced different atmospheric conditions for alien visitors, and escape pods dotted all corners of *the Traveler*. Everything was considered.

Except, no scientist thought of an alien diet. Specifically, a diet for both Humans and aliens.

This is how the Tayir leader, Zanbaq, justified his tests on some Human volunteers (of which there were few).

Riley was one of them. Partly out of hunger, but mainly out of curiosity.

Zanbaq started with a swab, swimming around her cheek and under the tongue, then he elevated to a blood sample from her finger, moving up to some alien monitoring tech. Results from the test populated a device in front of him, a sleek tablet with a translucent screen that mirrored pads.

"Mawz!" he proclaimed. "That's perfect!"

"What's that?" Riley asked.

Zanbaq looked down at her, his mouth smiling as if it had lips. "Food," he said. "Food you can eat without dying."

"That's my favorite kind!"

Zanbaq blinked at her. It took a minute of the awkward silence for someone to speak again.

"It's a joke," Riley explained.

"Oh," Zanbaq nodded. "Human culture."

Riley narrowed her expression. "I guess this means you guys don't have a lot of comedy?"

He ignored the comment, probably in part because he didn't care to try and understand what comedy meant. Another Tayir, shorter and wearing sparkly gems along its wings, came down a flight of stairs. She held onto a torch, the light of it waking up Luke as he rolled onto his side. His stomach grumbled, and he grasped his shoulder.

Zanbaq locked eyes with the other Tayir and said something in a language that sounded like a mix of banshees screaming and birds chirping as a form of echolocation. The other Tayir nodded, and quickly hustled back up the stairs she descended from.

"What's the food?" Riley asked.

"Mawz," he said, again.

Riley chuckled. "I meant what's it look like?"

In answer to the question, the same Tayir came back down with a wingful of pale-yellow cucumber-looking foods. She tossed them one by one to Zanbaq.

Mawz had a hard shell like a watermelon, but, like a banana, had a part to peel at the top. In some ways, it was like an ear of corn, only if instead the leaves were rigid. Zanbaq demonstrated the Tayir manner of eating it: step one, use a claw to incise a long cut; step two, slice it open with unexpected strength; step three (and most important), eat the whole thing in less than ten seconds.

Riley and Luke struggled with step one, their nails not long, sharp, or strong enough to pierce the ironclad veil. They tried to hit it, scratch it, and abuse it in ways that probably made them seem like cavemen.

Zanbaq scanned the room, wiping his mouth from juice covering the area his lips should have been. In the corner near the medical supplies, he took a clean scraper from an unopened pack and plucked something akin to a nail filer. He held the sharp ends of two of them, giving the handles to Luke and Riley.

Riley nestled the blade at the top. She followed the peeling portion, and serrated it to the bottom, ripping it open. From there, step two and three were a piece of cake. Especially step three.

Juice oozed from the body of the fruit. After a brief hesitation, she brought the mawz to her chapped lips and bit into it. The saccharine-sweet liquid jumped to her tongue, and the texture, like a perfect granny-smith apple, crunched and cut like warmed butter.

"Oh my God," she said.

"What?" Zanbaq said, the translator accentuating fear in his voice.

"It's incredible," Riley cried.

This inspired Luke to carve away at his shell faster with his nail filer. He sawed away, laboring over the peel before he struck gold and the liquid burst out along his hand. He licked it off his fingers, getting that same sugar rush.

"Oh my God," he agreed. "This is amazing."

He chewed on the fruit, taking chomps before all that remained was the shell and drops of juice that escaped his ravenous onslaught.

"More?" Zanbaq asked.

* * *

Luke

7 days later

Powers and Luke took it upon themselves to contact *the Traveler*. Although the majority of the ship agreed to come to Janina (the name of the world they at first dubbed "Tayirworld"), a handful had to stay on. Those Travelers were lucky bastards—they had access to not just all the freeze-dried food, but the smuggled goodies people brought. Luke wanted to be sure to: one, be in control of his ability to contact the people on *the Traveler*, and two, tell them to NOT eat his snacks.

Unfortunately, without a Human language to Tayir conversion, there was only so much the Tayir's dictionaries and encyclopedias could do. Zanbaq showed Powers and Luke as much as possible over the week they were down there, and by day five, Powers finally cracked the code and could contact anyone willing to listen, and would hear anyone with something to say. Problem was he didn't know exactly what *he* was saying. Even if he made contact with *the Traveler*, it wasn't communicating with them. Luke, on the other hand, couldn't even tell if a signal was sent. It was up to Powers to make contact.

Humans slept in a dark chamber inside one of the public buildings. Most light came from white flashes of lightning during endless storms raging on outside, almost like Jupiter's red spot in a consistent state of chaos. With the tropical nature of the biome they were in, rainwater became rather trivial, with their canteens always filled and a cold shower always available.

"It's been days," Luke whispered to Riley. Powers sat to his right, trying to find a frequency to talk to *the Traveler*.

"I know," Riley defended. "But we can't just ask them why they need our help when we're the ones that need help."

"Why haven't we asked?" Powers turned from the module.

"Most of you couldn't," she snapped. "The fact that even a quarter of us survived the crash is astonishing."

"You might want to keep your voices down," Powers whispered. "They probably got this place bugged to shit."

"I doubt they'd be listening to us," Riley said.

"Please," Powers scoffed. "You really trust them?"

"They're taking care of us," Riley replied. "Of course I trust them."

"They could've been the ones to shoot down our ship." Powers's deadpan face indicated this was no joke.

Luke did his own scoff at this suggestion. "Why wouldn't they just kill us then? They're clearly more advanced. We're bugs to them."

"They'll tell us in time. People are still recovering," Riley said.

A rumble from a few hundred meters away shook the ground of the building. Powers, the first one to detect it with his feet on the ground, hustled towards a few Tayirs in their signature military garb.

"What was that?" Powers barked.

Zanbaq, one of the soldiers in the group, shot back, "Don't worry."

"I am worried." His nostrils flared. "Incredibly worried."

Another rumble, shaking awake nearly all the souls sleeping on leaf-constructed blankets. The earthquake came with a flash of red light, fire, and roaring in the distance, from a creature that doesn't sound like the type to hand out mawz to injured aliens.

Zanbaq covered his collar when he spoke to the guards, muzzling himself from translating.

"It's time you tell us what's going on," Powers said.

"Powers! Cool it!" Riley shouted. If the alive Travelers weren't awake earlier, they were now. She rushed in front of Zanbaq, breaking line of sight between them. Zanbaq's shadow hid her when another flash of lightning peered through the windows.

"They're not telling us what's going on!"

"Now's not the time," Luke said, joining Riley's side.

Zanbaq touched both of their shoulders with his fingers. "You're right," he said. Something about his cadence was earnest, almost welcoming.

Powers still had some suspicion on his face. He stood his ground, no matter how uneasy his knees were.

The next words Zanbaq said punched Luke in the gut. "We're at war," he said. Luke's body stopped moving, except for his neck which rotated right to Zanbaq. *War?*

"With who?"

Zanbaq turned away, while a flash of lightning illuminated the chamber. Thunder rolled across the forest, and the humid air chilled as a gale whooshed in from open windows that stuck out like bird perches. "We call them the Apiary."

Zanbaq's face darkened, and he gulped before pacing for a few steps.

Powers pushed further. "And where are they?"

Zanbaq turned back, this time his eyes looking directly into Powers' eyes. "Everywhere."

All motion in the room stopped, and even the rain and thunder outside subsided for a moment as Zanbaq howled. "We asked for help—begged for help—from the others, but no one listened."

"Others?" Riley said, this time taking the light from Powers.

"The galaxy has hundreds of species," he explained. "We had a..." he paused, choosing his next words carefully, "...diplomatic incident."

Powers' eyes bulged and he got in Riley's face as he raised his voice. "Diplomatic incident?"

Before Zanbaq answered, other Tayirs spoke in their native tongue, squawking and screeching paired with pointing outside the structure. Zanbaq recoiled. "Before I tell you what happened, our front lines need aid. I won't ask for your help, you shouldn't give it without knowing everything. I'll be back."

He turned to the guards and fluttered off in the distance with the lightning strikes scattering across the land. Chatter broke in groups of Humans huddling together. Several talked over one another.

"Are you happy?" Riley spat to Powers.

Powers reentered reality, breaking free of a daydream or thought he found himself lost in. "What?"

"Are you happy?" Riley's voice sounded guttural, and the words pointed at him. Her voice signaled everyone that part two of the fireworks show called "Riley versus Powers" was about to begin.

"You want to live in a world assuming these aliens are our best fucking friends when we don't have the slightest idea why they asked for our help!"

"I trust the people that saved us from the crash, gave us a place to stay, went out of their way to find us food we can eat, and a way to contact our ship."

Powers yelled back, "You think they have our best interest just because they're what, being *nice*? Are you so naive you can't realize maybe these aliens have cruel intentions?"

"They clearly need help and they haven't done anything to make us question it!"

"You're not thinking like a soldier! You're thinking like a kid—assuming the best in these birds before worrying about your own species!"

"They are people too!" she cried.

"No," Powers thundered. "We're people—you, me, Captain Bo, every

Traveler—those birds are the aliens." He drew closer, turning his finger into a clutched fist with only the index finger pointed directly at Riley. "Their little hegemony in space didn't help them, nor should we."

"We don't know the details, there could be a harmless explanation."

Powers laughed, exaggerating the tail end. "You're actually delusional!"

Luke cut in. "Stop it! Stop arguing! We're stuck here and need to focus on getting *the Traveler* to get us home."

Powers looked at them, shaking his head. The audience sipped juice from their mawz amid more rumbles, this time akin to aftershocks. "You all really think that we should help them? Humanity can't align itself with aliens that are losing. Look at Human history, you need strong allies."

"You can't compare Humans to aliens," Riley jabbed. "Unless you're willing to admit the Tayirs are just as much of a people as we are."

With a final nod, he shook his head and walked back to the communication systems.

IV

The Colony

Chapter 31

Tsarena

Nanotechnology on Kyros came with one caveat: it struggled with creativity. That's why Tsarena had a sense of déjà vu entering Sola's room. The hospital mimicked its previous iteration. All the walls went up in the same spots, and each speck and pattern of marble flooring mirrored its earlier counterpart.

Tsarena gripped the cookie tightly, the delicacy from Galactic Burgers' concise dessert menu. Appealing to customers' gluttony, the sweet came only in Galactic Burgers' "gargantuan" size. It took everything in her power to not get her own, but she didn't have enough kirbies on hand for two.

"Sola?" Tsarena chimed. Kasey followed behind her, closer than her own shadow. Falisto and Shamp weren't far behind but waited at the door for a minute. "I'm back and I brought some friends."

With color back in her face, Sola didn't resemble anything Tsarena recalled. She distinctly remembered the near-lifeless body she held in his arms, the body that nearly cost Kasey his job. Without beads holding her hair together in tight braids, it bloomed outward into an afro. In her hands, she clutched a plushie that looked like it had gone through hell.

"I also got you that cookie," Tsarena coaxed. She held up her hand, her four fingers gripping the dessert so tightly it nearly halved it.

Sola's eyes lit up and she gasped at the chocolate chip residue rubbing against its plastic cover. The cookie called her name and Tsarena wasn't the type to withhold things. "Here," Tsarena said.

Sola snatched it and attempted to rip apart the plastic with her cut nails.

After a few unsuccessful rips with her fingers, she resorted to her teeth, clipping a layer of plastic between her jaws and shearing it open.

"Sola?" Kasey started. He took a step forward now that she had the cookie in her hands. "I was hoping we could chat."

Despite being the center of the conversation and room, Sola still hadn't spoken. Now with a cookie the size of her head, she didn't seem too inclined. She ate slowly. Nibbles, at first. Then bites. Then crunches and chomps. Then it was as if she had never eaten before, inhaling the cookie.

While chewing, Sola sipped from a juice box, her eyes never leaving Kasey and Tsarena like she was playing a unilateral staring contest. With no concept of rationing, she raced to finish her food, chomping off more than her mouth could hold. Then Shamp and Falisto entered the room.

"What are you," Sola asked, mid-bite. Her eyes goggled at Shamp, tendrils and all.

Shamp, somehow unoffended, crossed her arms and accentuated her tendrils. "I am a Venori. My real name is too complex for other species, so you may call me 'Shamp.'"

She nodded. "You're tall."

Shamp cracked a smile, the second one for today. "Height is a sign of beauty."

Satisfied with the answer, she turned to the other alien. "Are you one of the kitties?" Sola asked Falisto.

Despite saying one of the two possible worst things to Falisto (insinuating he was a cat or bringing up Jasoosi), he didn't blow up. Instead, with his raspy voice and a hint of a glare he echoed back, "No, I'm not a cat. I'm more of a leopard."

Sola nodded a bit uneasily before taking another chomp out of the cookie. "You're like the ones at home." Her teeth sunk into a chocolate chip cluster, now darkening her lips with milk cocoa.

"Sola," Tsarena whispered. "Can you tell us what happened?"

After a moment, Sola swallowed a bite of cookie and put the rest down before looking down at the crumbles dotting her lap. The hospital gown, pink in color, now had stains. Minuscule? Yes. Noticeable? Also yes.

"Okay," she sniffled.

"Go on," Tsarena coaxed as delicately as possible.

* * *

Hours Before Kasey's Porygar Mission

"Just a few minutes until the eclipse!" Tsavon announced. For an Orchi, his pigmentation fell somewhere between pink and salmon. He came from a race that didn't look like the common Orchi. The Orchi didn't have a name for the race, as they didn't alienate through physical appearance. Instead, he was labeled as an Orchi who was bald and with more red-tinted eyes. He passed around some bottles and cups; everyone agreed there was no alcohol age requirement on Porygar, at least for the party and this colony.

Sola's parents slurped some wine procured by a black-hole-aged winery. They savored it, wine like this didn't come around often for people like them. Tsavon came with it the day he arrived and wanted to save it for the special occasion, which he assured was the eclipse.

"Mommy, can I get Shauna?" Sola's hands were empty husks without her sheep dangling. With the pandemonium of the party and ball of stress her mother became, she forgot it.

Sola's mom, Lulu, smiled and sighed. She put down the glass on the picnic table next to her and opened her arms up. "Sure sweet pea. Let's go."

"No, no, no," Mahina came, wagging her finger. "I'm babysitting tonight. I'll take her."

Lulu smirked and shook her head. "It's fine, Mahina, really I don't mind."

"Lulu, you haven't had a date night in, what, years?"

"She's right, Lulu," her husband, Niko, added.

"Let me." Mahina offered her hand to Sola. But before Lulu could protest, Sola's hand was in Mahina's and they already hopped towards their cabin.

"Don't be gone too long!" Tsavon shouted as Mahina and Sola passed him. "Eclipse is coming real soon!"

Mahina ran while kneeling to hold Sola's hand. Wind rustled flowers along the path, and some chickens and goats hung around their enclosures making their domesticated calls. One of the cows had a collar around her neck, shaded in an orange polka-dotted pattern, with a tiny bell dangling.

"Can I see Bree?" Sola pleaded.

Mahina laughed, "Your mom wants us back soon."

"Please!" Sola clasped her hands together and shook them vigorously.

Mahina rolled her eyes. "Fine." Two houses down from Lulu and Niko's cabin was the enclosure that housed common "farm" animals. Orchi and Psys had their farms, mostly with native life from their home planets. A shared crop, however, was basji, as low lighting from the star benefited the dark leaves for photosynthesis.

After a few minutes, Mahina wrestled Sola away from the cows and they entered her parents' cabin.

"Get a coat too, Sola."

Sola listened but ignored the request. Instead, she focused on her quest: searching every nook of the cabin for Shauna. Behind the couch, under the table, around the laundry basket, but still the sheep hid. Only three minutes into Sola's search party, she cried and whined.

"I can't find her."

"I'll help look," Mahina said. She begrudgingly added her eyes to the search party, scanning cabinets and other higher places Sola couldn't reach.

"Are you sure you had it earlier today?"

"Yes!" Sola swore.

"Where was it last?"

"I don't remember!" her voice cracked, and her enormous eyes welled with tears.

"Alright, alright, we'll find it. Don't worry."

Mahina played detective, throwing away logistics of where a stuffed sheep could and couldn't fit. If it had a lid or door, she opened it. The drawer with the cutlery, shoe racks, even appliances weren't spared from her search. To her surprise, Shauna had been wedged in a drawer that barely fit her in the closet. Despite being locked between wooden planks, the plushie had a goofy smile with oversized, white teeth and oversized eyebrows to match. Its fur frayed out in the cotton-esque coat.

"Got it," Mahina announced.

Sola ran, stumbling over the oak floors and into the closet. Mahina handed her the prize. Grasping it tightly, Sola confessed her love to the animal, promising that she would never *ever* lose her again.

Then, Mahina heard a scream.

Sola was too enamored to pay attention to cries and yelps that bellowed from outside. What tipped off Sola was the shaking in Mahina's voice. "Stay here," she said without the same upbeat tone Sola was used to.

More screams, dampened by the insulating oak walls, continued down the flower lane. Mahina dropped down a bit, her knees bent and her pad drawn.

On the table, Mahina took a knife, silver and with a black handle, and peeled back drapes obscuring the window. Darkness covered their ring of twilight now. Using her pad, she looked through the camera, trying a multitude of viewpoints and modes. When she hit the infrared measurement, it pinpointed large heat signatures dragging bodies away.

Mahina looked back to Sola, still awaiting further direction during her observation of Mahina. The knife danced in Mahina's trembling hand, with vibrations from the ground eventually freeing it from her grasp. It fell flat and she jumped at the sound of it hitting the ground.

"Shit," she shouted with a whisper. Sola didn't demand penance for the swear jar in the corner of the room.

Sola kept her eyes on Mahina. The two looked at each other, each more concerned for the other. Breaking their stare down, Mahina peeked with her pad again. Nothing. The signatures were all gone, just darkness and heat from grills still running. Then... something. Something big. Something big coming right at them.

Using a screen grab, Mahina tried to identify the figure. The shape didn't look clear—it didn't look Human or Orchi, and Mahina didn't know any Psys that looked so deformed with wings.

"What's going on?" Sola mumbled. She clutched Shauna and kept it close to her chest.

Wide-eyed, Mahina rose from a bent position and crept towards Sola. She cowered backward, stumbling over stray shoes and her sheep's play area. "You need to hide," Mahina commanded.

"Why?"

Mahina shushed her, guilt creeping on her the moment she did it. "Get in the closet," she whispered. Sola, whether too terrified to question it or stunned to protest, complied, scrunching into the closet behind a pile of coats.

"Don't open this door for anyone," Mahina commanded.

Sola's lower lip quivered and her big eyes dilated further. The gravity of the situation weighed them both to the ground as if the combined force of the eclipse had that effect.

"I promise, I will come back for you."

"What's going on?" Sola cried again.

"I don't know," she admitted. Forcefully, she pushed the pad towards Sola. "The second you get a connection you need to call someone, anyone, tell them we need help."

"Who do I call?"

Mahina snatched the pad back, quickly pulling up her favorites list. "Her," Mahina pointed to a photo of a young Orchi, the name for the contact "Tsarena."

"But you don't have to worry about anything, just stay here." Mahina tried to smile but her near-hyperventilating body made a frantic grin.

Sola couldn't help the overwhelming tears gushing from her eyes. They formed puddles and dampened Shauna. "Please, don't leave me."

Mahina grimaced. "I'm right here." She half-gingerly half-haphazardly closed the door, but not completely, to the closet as the creaking wood sounds approached from outside. The sound silenced them both, each of them gulping.

A blast fired the door open. Mahina screamed and kept screaming. Sola shook at the sounds of the struggle. Wings flapped and voices gawked something her converter refused to translate.

Mahina screamed a final time and then silence followed. An eternity of quietness ensued until chains rattled. Paralyzed, Sola couldn't move her body forward. Her hands trembled with the pad on her lap.

She waited for a few minutes with the connection not reaching the pad. After a bit of silence, she summoned her courage and approached the door. She peered through it slowly, revealing the back of a feathery creature. It stood tall, with wings long and wide. Its angular head and giant eyes blinked, but Sola caught a glimpse of something shiny cuffing the creature's feet.

Something else stood ahead of the creature, something far more menacing with pincers and claw-like hands. And teeth drenched with blood. The one with wings caught a glimpse of Sola and it quickly pushed her back in, its claws digging into her with the push. It tore Mahina's pad apart, and Sola screamed in agony, but it kept the door shut. Screeching and shouting hurt her ears as blood dripped from her stomach, and as the sounds faded, twilight settled in.

Chapter 32

Kasey

By the end of her story, Sola went through six different pouches of juice. She used the same lemon straw to lance each container, leaving behind wrinkled, silver juice pouches and unused straws still protected by layers of plastic wrapping. Beeps shouted from monitors wired to her body while her thumbs danced over each other. Tears dripped from her eyes, and she bit her lower lip, suffocating a cry. Kasey hated seeing anyone cry, but something about Sola's tears hit him particularly hard. He couldn't put his finger on it, but he carried the weight of her life on his back. She was his responsibility. Saving one life—this life—didn't make up for those on Musk Station or Drake, but at least he saved one.

"You are so brave," Tsarena said. She rested her hand into Sola's, squeezing it and looking into her avoiding eyes. "You are so brave." She repeated the phrase as if this time the girl would believe it.

"Thank you, Sola," Kasey added. He knelt to her level and rested his hand on the side of her bed. "We're going to find them," he said. "Your parents."

"And Mahina," Sola said with a sniffle before her eyes scrunched up and tears rained. Tsarena released Sola's hand and pulled her towards her, letting Sola wail into her chest.

"It's okay," she soothed. She reiterated it like a mantra. "It's okay."

Kasey poked Tsarena along her back and mouthed that he was going to step outside with the others. On the way out, Tsarena managed to repeat the mantra three more times. With every repetition, she sounded more convincing. "It's okay, it's okay, it's okay."

When the door latched to a close, Falisto immediately started. "What the fuck?"

"Rather unfortuitous," Shamp added.

"I know," Kasey said. "Big birds." He shook his head and crossed his arms. "It's gotta be the Tayirs."

"But they're dead," Falisto spat. "Dead. Done. Defeated." His nostrils flared. "It's Jasoosi or Sapien, and I'm leaning Jasoosi."

"Who else could it be?" Kasey threw his hands in the air. "Is there an alien species like the Tayirs?"

"There was one," Shamp whispered, "but they are archaic and predate the GU. This must be the Tayirs. I cannot think of another feasible explanation."

"But she mentioned chains," Kasey said. "Why would they chain themselves?"

"Maybe to appear helpless. Perhaps that's a detail she's misremembering." Shamp shrugged. "She has obviously suffered significant trauma."

"Doesn't that call her entire story into question, then?" Falisto fired back.

"Some things conflict, yes," Shamp said.

"She mentioned Tsavon's name. Said he was a visitor." Kasey opened his pad, pulling up images taken of Porygar during his mission. He zoomed past a few unremarkable photographs that only bolstered the mission report's size. "Here," he said, zooming on Tsavon's purported house. "That's where we found the gun."

"The Jasoosi gun," Falisto clarified.

"So, presumably, she was here." Kasey pointed to Lulu and Niko's home with the door blown out.

"She was in proximity of the party," Shamp whispered. With her slender hand, she plucked the pad from Kasey's hands. "Which begs the question: what location did the Tayirs emerge from?"

"They flew in," Falisto said.

"They had defensive air systems," Kasey retorted. "They would've known if some ships were coming. It's how they prepped for shipments. Plus, flying while chained doesn't seem feasible."

"Then where did they originate?" Shamp asked.

Kasey craned his head over his pad, stepping on his tippy toes to reach Shamp. Halfway into a neck cramp, Kasey asked, "Can you...?"

Shamp acquiesced, lowering his pad to a more comfortable position for the three of them. Pinching his fingers outward, Kasey zoomed to the picnic tables, empty and disheveled with a few glasses. Kasey cocked his head and moved to another table along the pad, focusing on the ground.

"I think I know where they came from," Kasey shouted with excitement. "We gotta get back to Porygar!"

"Where?" Falisto hissed.

Kasey pressed his index finger on the lake. "Right there."

"What exactly is your evidence?" Shamp said, stealing back his pad and squinting at the lake.

"The mud," Kasey exclaimed. "There was mud! It's the only way they wouldn't have seen them coming."

Falisto sighed, "Tayirs can't swim, how'd they get up?"

"They did not," Shamp said, connecting the dots. She looked at Kasey, his lips curved in a smug smile. "The lake is artificial."

"They're under the lake!" Kasey said, finally.

Amber sauntered towards the group, her face stone and eyes vacant. Her body melded into the group. "What I miss?"

Kasey pointed backward with his thumb to the hospital room. "Sola woke up. Told us about the colony. There might be something we missed."

"How so?" She cocked her head and looked over to Kasey's pad, overseeing the lake.

"Kasey believes he discovered where the aliens came from." Shamp looked at Amber. "The girl informed us of large avian creatures."

"The Tayirs," Falisto said. "That's what she described."

"But they were shackled," Kasey added. The thought clawed him since Sola mentioned the chains. "Shackled."

"She was bleeding profusely," Shamp countered. "So, while I agree this most likely is the Tayirs, there's a possibility she could have been imagining it. Dopamine rushes are, unfortunately, unreliable."

Kasey countered, "We need to take a second look. I'll have to tell Respow—"

"—No." Falisto pointed to Kasey with his claw. "If he hears that you thought it was a good idea to go to a missing colony—the same one he wanted to send you to a tribunal for—because of a little girl's tale, he will strip you of all your rights without a tribunal. We can't tell him."

"Benjo would want to," Amber shuffled.

A screech came from Sola's door, the sound sending a shiver along Kasey's back. Tsarena tip-toed into the group discussion and quietly shut the door behind her as Kasey did. "She's gonna try and sleep," Tsarena said. "Girl needs it."

"We're venturing to Porygar," Shamp said.

A tinge guilty, Kasey mumbled, "I think we should tell Respow—"

"—I won't be waiting for approval from him," Tsarena spat. "Every second we waste right now is a second her family and my friend are captured."

Kasey recoiled and raised an eyebrow at her tone before he turned back to Amber. "What do we do about Benjo?"

"I'll stay with him," Amber said. "You guys go."

"What if Respow—"

"—I'll handle Respow and tell him you guys wanna follow up on something else. I'll also tell him about Drake if he has any questions."

"He's gonna ask about Sola," Tsarena added. "Don't let him talk to her."

"That's gonna be harder," Amber said nervously.

"Do it," Tsarena replied. "I told her I'd protect her." Tsarena pointed back to the room behind her. "I intend to keep that promise."

"Okay," Kasey said. "Amber, can you do that?"

"I'll do my best," she sighed. "But call for backup if you need it."

"Deal," Kasey said. Amber took Kasey's hand, shaking it after interlocking palm with metal. "But I wanna see Benjo before we go."

"He'd like that," Amber smiled. "They kicked me out because I'd been there too long and they wanted to do some tests, but we can head back in a few minutes."

"I'll come too," Falisto said, Shamp, moving along with him.

Tsarena turned in the opposite direction. "I'm gonna prep the ship."

Kasey's raised eyebrow to Tsarena arched further. "Are you sure you don't wanna come?"

"I want to," she explained. "But I want to find the colony more."

Getting into Benjo's room (and private level) in the hospital may as well have been breaking into a safe in the basement of the universe's most guarded bank. Kyros security refused to immediately allow visitors in. The security had a visible reaction when Amber strutted into the hospital like she owned the place. There was no doubt in Kasey's mind that Amber assumed the role of an investigator, questioning and scrutinizing every test doctors performed and looking up every symptom.

A staff of fully attentive Orchi handled him. No Hybrids could enter the building without significant hazmat protection, and Humans had to undergo a thorough assessment. Kasey found himself poked, prodded, and answering questions in front of the crew that he rather not have. The decontamination chamber was a tiny vault compared to the Black Market's. This one was a sweet, sterile release.

"Decontamination process will end in five... four... three... two... one... Sterilization is complete." The next door opened, and the group saw Benjo.

Kasey's body stiffened and a lump formed in his throat. Bleach and ammonia filled the room, and even seeped through his unitard's mask. He walked up and grazed his hand along the plastic edge of the bed. Beeps from monitors rang in a rhythm forming a symphony amid the clicks of holographic keys from doctors typing reports with gloved hands.

"He's asleep," the doctor said. Her skin was a light pink and covered by the white hazmat suit.

Shamp asked, "Is the illness not exclusively targeting Hybrids?"

"I interact with lots of people," she explained. "Another layer of protection won't kill anyone."

Several machines hooked up to Benjo's body, three or so to his neck alone. A variety of monitors, obscured by an array of doctors with clipboards and pads, displayed numerous statistics. Kasey couldn't help but stare at the shoddy job he did removing the metal limbs, seeing loose cables and strands of electrical conductors trickling out the stumps. Benjo's eyes were closed, and he had an oxygen apparatus plugged into his mouth, pumping in air. His skin lost all color, not a muted shade of pink coming through his nearly transparent skin.

"Benjo," Kasey whispered. Falisto joined him, followed by Shamp.

Kasey gingerly bent over towards Benjo. "I'm so sorry." Logically, Kasey knew this was *not* his fault. But Kasey wasn't a person run by logic, and, emotionally speaking, he couldn't move past the fact that this was his doing. "We're gonna get you fixed up," Kasey promised. "You'll be back to us in no time."

Shamp, unsurprisingly, didn't alter her stoic visage. Instead, she looked down at Benjo and whispered something. "He shall manage," she said.

Falisto came closer to Kasey, patting him on the back. "Shamp's right." The words leaving Falisto's mouth made Kasey want to pinch himself.

"I know."

The same doctor from earlier turned to Kasey. "You're the one that removed his metal parts, right?"

Kasey hid away at first before owning up to the barbaric practice. "Yes, I did."

"You saved his life," she said. "The virus didn't spread to his biological systems but if those metal parts were on any longer, they would've."

Kasey flashed a smile. "Why's his arm there?" Kasey pointed to Benjo's old silver arm, with the older-looking scanner put on the side.

"Surprisingly," the woman started, pointing to the device, "that scanner didn't get infected."

Amber lurched forward. "How's that possible?"

She shrugged. "But the Hybrid Components Council wants to look at it and see if they can make more materials resistant to it."

"Don't let them take it," Amber averred. "That's *his*."

"Yes, I know, Amber," the doctor's voice was devoid of emotion. "You've told us before."

Chapter 33

Kasey

Five PTF members sat at the table in the control center of *the Irene*. Shamp, Tsarena, Falisto, Kasey, and Tsoki. The only ones left to do something about the missing colony. Each had their pad out and a caffeinated beverage of their choice in front of them. Naturally, Kasey had a coffee, as did sixty percent of the table. Falisto drank something else he claimed contained twice as much caffeine as "Human bean juice." Tsarena drank peppermint tea.

"You know," Kasey began, "we never talked about what happened with Drake."

Shamp stirred at the mention of his name. "He was a good man. Benevolent, law-abiding, conscientious." She looked at the floor, her eyes glazing over with a layer of tears. Her tendrils also rested, a sign of low energy among Venori.

Kasey flashed her a sympathetic look and blinked slowly. "He was a great man."

"A father," Tsoki said. His eyes welled with tears too. "I spoke with the family on Kyros."

"How'd it go?" Tsarena asked.

Tsoki sniffled and wiped his eyes. "Not well."

"He'd want us to finish the mission," Shamp added, her voice sniffling. "Then mourn, but he wouldn't even want us to do that." She shook her head. "Always so logical."

"You two were close?" Falisto asked.

Shamp nodded. "I do not mean to disparage your kinds," she said, motioning to them. "But most people abhor how we Venori communicate. Our languages are so rich and vivid that we speak like machines. To me, it is poetry, and Drake—he knew that—he spoke back to me in poetry. It was like I had another Venori with me all the time."

Kasey's heart dropped. "I'm so sorry, Shamp."

"It is hard, feeling like..." she couldn't help but laugh before she said the word. "...alien."

The rest of the group giggled, letting the comedic moment soften the blow.

Tsarena pierced the somber silence that ensued. "To Drake." She raised up her coffee cup filled with tea.

"To Drake," everyone said.

"I know we need to prep, but maybe if someone wanted to share a story or memory?" Kasey asked.

As if she was waiting for the question, Shamp spoke, "Drake and I got inebriated once."

Everyone at the table darted their eyes to Shamp. "You drink?" Tsoki asked.

Shamp rolled her eyes. "Yes, I did," she said. "Just a Venori modification of alcohol."

"I'm more surprised that Drake drank," Kasey said.

"He drank," Shamp nodded. "But not in excess. Usually. He was logical," Shamp reiterated. "Part of being PONR, I suppose. We had philosophical discussions with each drink, and we did not attempt to police how we spoke to each other, we just spoke."

"How did you guys get drunk?" Falisto asked. "Not literally, like when, where?"

"When we met," she said. "He assured me that he was always professional, no time for play."

"What was it like?" Kasey asked.

"We were late exiting," she laughed in her Venori way of laughing. "Phenomenal man. He could not get too inebriated because of his components."

The team swapped memories, mainly Tsoki and Shamp with the occasional mention from Falisto and Tsarena. Kasey hadn't known Drake all too well, but he was a part of the team. Everyone had their laughs and sad tears coated in giggles to try and make it easy to swallow. After the first round of drinks, they slugged back to work. They collaborated on a shared document, attempting to draw up mission plans and details. *The Irene* already headed to Porygar, and five minutes into brainstorming all they had to show for it was a single heading, entitled "How to get to the bottom of the lake."

"Anything?" Kasey asked again, holding his stylus. "Nothing's stupid."

"Bomb it?" Falisto suggested.

Kasey shot him a look. "Almost nothing."

Falisto frowned. "C'mon! It's possible!"

"Consider we do that," Shamp started, lowering her back into the chair, "then whatever structure they are in could flood."

Tsarena kept her arms crossed, her fingers gripping her biceps. "Falisto's right. We need something fast. We can't do a conventional method, it'll take too long."

"Do we even have a bomb that can do what you're suggesting?" Kasey asked, swiveling his chair towards Falisto. His caramel fur poked out of his unitard, and he unzipped the middle a bit, letting more stick out.

"We do." Falisto tensed, furrowing his brow. "But there's a better approach."

"What?" Kasey asked. "Several bombs?"

"You're not gonna like it."

Kasey winced. *Oh God, here we go.* "What is it?"

Falisto leaned in. "Let's say the settlement will need to move after we're done."

"You're not selling it well," Kasey muttered.

"We crash some of our Navigators into the lake, and hope it opens it up."

Kasey rolled his eyes. "Okay, tell you what, let's table that for now—what else can we do?"

The five exchanged looks, occasionally twiddling with their electronic pens or sipping from their second-round mugs. Except for Shamp. She leaned back, wove her fingers over one another, and tapped the back of her hand. Arching her slender neck up, she nodded a bit before looming directly over the table. "I have an idea."

"What is it?" Tsarena asked.

"Go on," Kasey said.

Shamp adjusted her tendrils so they curved like elephant trunks around her body. "We're assuming the colony is under the lake, correct?"

"Right."

"Well, I don't know much about your physiology," she motioned to the table. "But I cannot survive too far down to the core of a planet."

"So the underground colony can only go so far." Kasey surmised.

"The lake's not that big." Tsoki pulled up another photo of the colony. "I mean if everyone stood shoulder to shoulder then *maybe* they could fit in the surface area."

"Okay, this is good." Kasey stood up now, adding these notes to the shared document. "But, this brings the same issue."

"How do we get down?" Tsoki asked.

Shamp nodded. "I never implied I had all the solutions, but it is far simpler than siphoning a lake."

"An energy beam," Kasey whispered.

"What?" Tsarena sat upright.

"An energy beam," Kasey loudened. "That's how they do the Gyras Mines," Kasey beamed a smile. "All we have to do is get an energy beam strong enough, and if we go just a few meters away from the lake then we also wouldn't compromise the colony."

"Possible," Shamp nodded. "But does the PTF ring even have the capability to generate such a beam?"

"It can," Tsoki said. "I've done weapons before, and from what I saw, I think so."

"And how's this different from a bomb?" Falisto sounded annoyed.

"No fallout," Tsoki explained. "No lasting radiation."

"More control," Kasey said.

Not much had changed on Porygar since Kasey last visited the planet. From aerial images, the planet had a fresh layer of dust and ash. *The Irene* entered the atmosphere of Porygar before stopping a few thousand meters above the colony. Kasey sat with Tsoki, finding a spot for the beam. Tsarena inserted herself so the two of them wouldn't be distracted. She made it a point to sit in the middle of them. Falisto chose the role of shooting the energy beam, and Shamp was assigned with the leftover: testing the Navigators.

"Looks the same," Kasey said. He paused by close-ups of familiar homes. From skyward, the rooms were voids; the word "empty" didn't do it justice. Even the air had been evacuated.

Using the controls, Tsoki maneuvered the camera north towards the lake. "Okay, I see the lake." Kasey continued looking at the image.

"It certainly looks man-made," Tsoki said, sharing the view with Kasey. Their shoulders touched and rubbed against one another.

"When you say 'man-made' do you actually say 'Orchi made' and my converter just picks it up as 'man-made?'"

Tsoki grinned. "No, I said 'Human' made."

Kasey laughed, but the stare from Tsarena quickly ended the giggles.

"There," she said, pointing to the side of the lake with fewer homes. "Pierce it there, we descend with a Navigator."

"Right," Kasey replied.

"*Fuel, power, engines, and autopilot are operable in the first Navigator,*" Shamp said through comms.

"*Amazing, thank you, Shamp.*"

"*I'll check the second and third.*"

"*There's a ton of clouds,*" Falisto muttered. "*I can't get a good look.*"

"*Copy that, dropping a couple meters.*" Tsoki dropped *the Irene* down a bit.

"*We still need to be a fair bit away so we don't vaporize the planet.*"

Tsarena hummed. "*How long until the beam is ready?*"

"*It's ready,*" Falisto said.

Exactly six and a half meters eastward of the lake, the light materialized. From a distance, it appeared like a green laser pointer at first. A small, green dot, not even a full ray. Within a few seconds, it became a true beam, about a millimeter or two. After a few more seconds, the ray thickened into the ground, burrowing about a meter deep.

When the beam reached its full charge, the hole burst open to the size of three Navigators and went as deep as possible without compromising the integrity of the planet. It made a horrid sound, screaming like banshees with roars of feral animals mixed in. Even from their height, it still sped Kasey's heart, and his muscles tensed at the destructive power of a ship built for peace.

"*Stopping the beam,*" Falisto said.

"*Turning autopilot on,*" Kasey said, flipping a switch along the side of the console. "*Aiming near the hole.*"

"*Understood,*" Shamp said, still in the hangar. "*The Navigators are sufficient.*"

"*Everyone bring your weapons,*" Tsarena reminded.

"*Are we ready?*" Kasey asked.

"*As ready as we'll ever be,*" Tsoki said.

"*Meet at the hangar, we'll leave when we land.*"

Tsarena didn't need to be told twice. Before Kasey finished his sentence she was out, whipping around and bolting towards her locker. Her Slart was switched to lethal mode at some point and hadn't been turned back.

Chapter 34

Kasey

The Navigator flew through the air, heading straight for the hole they dug. "Listen to me," Kasey said, feeling the need to give some sort of pep talk. "We have no idea what we're up against. If we're out-manned we get out everyone we can, leave, and come back with people."

"I'm not leaving without Mahina," Tsarena said.

Kasey didn't respond. Instead, he looked down at her, moving his gaze from Tsoki. "We have to be smart."

"We finally found the colony, this is how this whole mess got started," Tsarena said. "Tsavon, Mahina, they have answers."

"The Jasoosi gun," Falisto added. "But I don't think they'll know about the attack on Kyros."

"And let's not forget," Kasey said. "The Tayir in Sola's story."

Shamp folded her tendrils over one another. "I am certain now, the Tayirs are alive."

"No," Falisto said, coldly. "They're dead."

"Look at the evidence," Tsarena replied. "Their technology is around, at least, and there are rumors of multiple Tayir colonies."

"The point is," Kasey said, redirecting the conversation. "We have no clue what's down there."

Tsoki nodded. "He's right. Even if we find everyone down there we're not gonna be able to just take an entire colony on this Navigator."

"We need to play this safe," Kasey murmured. "Our primary goal is to save everyone, and if that means we need more time then we need to act accordingly."

Tsarena looked at Kasey as he said this but turned away.

Remnants of iridescent green from the energy beam peppered the dirt and rock path. Falisto flipped a switch, activating a flurry of lights attached to the Navigator. The darkness of the cavity subsided, from completely dark to only mostly dark.

While the ship catapulted towards the bottom of the tunnel, Falisto pulled back the throttle slowly, bringing the Navigator to a halt until it hung in the air, motionless.

"Kasey, send your camera." Falisto took his pad and handed it off to Kasey. With a flick of the pad's controls, a probe rocket swirled out the Navigator towards the hole. After a few seconds of traveling and leaving behind a smoke cloud, it hit the abyss like a coin in a dried-up well. Unlike other rockets, this one disassembled into a movable camera drone, similar to the one on Planet Exo.

A light beamed from the camera, glowing up the area nearby in a sphere of harsh light. Kasey trembled at the sight of the illuminated walls. "Guys," he whispered. His fingers shook, and his eyes zoomed back and forth on the visual. "There's a path."

"A path?" Tsoki asked.

Kasey turned. "Yeah, a path. It looks like we broke through the middle of it."

Tsarena asked, "Can you see anything?"

"It's mainly dark." Kasey paused before speaking. "There's a faint red glow."

"Temperature?"

"I don't think this thing can tell temperatures." Kasey handed the pad to Shamp and Tsoki.

"Probably have to park the Navigator along the bottom." Falisto cracked his neck bones. "Any signs of people?"

Shamp nodded in the negative. "Why would an alien group live beneath the surface?"

"It looks old," Tsoki added. "Ancient, maybe."

"I have a feeling these enemies aren't cavemen." Kasey folded his arms. "Having a path down here, how did we miss this?"

"That's just it," Falisto said. "How would we even have known? When was the last time a colony planet ever needed to explore the innermost crust?"

Kasey shrugged before shaking off an unsettling shiver. "We made a big enough hole for three Navigators to move comfortably. I say we park on the ground and get going, put the other Navigators on autopilot."

"That won't work," Falisto said.

Kasey had a quizzical look. "Why?"

"Too many branches, roots, rocks—you name it—not everything got destroyed by the beam. Navigators on autopilot *would* hit those."

Kasey winced. "You're not giving a great argument for autopilot."

"We are still grossly unaware of what we are entering," Shamp said. "It is possible we are falling into a trap."

The ship resumed its journey through the darkness. Something about knowing the pit wasn't bottomless made Kasey a lot more comfortable with his surroundings, and the Navigator going through the cavern. As he played with the drone, he observed the ceiling, walls, and paths. The place was a labyrinth of sorts, with winding roads leading to who knew what.

"I'll make the camera go through the halls, give us some idea what's going on." Kasey changed settings of the video feed, sharing it with everyone. Maybe there was something he couldn't see. He hoped maybe Orchi or Venori eyes could catch something in a spectrum outside a Human's perception.

It was the same for them: bland, narrow, and gray. The walls were not natural, and they dug into the planet like catacombs, carving stretches of empty lanes and dark alleys. The occasional low-red light appeared, but more often than not, the camera chased darkness.

"We're about to land." Falisto checked behind him and to the sides of the hole, noticing the reaching branches and winding roots the beam missed. The Navigator hung low in the air, slowly reaching the bottom with a loud *thump.*

Everyone unbuckled their seat belts, with Tsarena fumbling her lock. She hurriedly pressed the manual override for the door, hoping it was faster than the standard unlock.

When the door hissed open, the tunnel welcomed them. The camera failed to catch the ominous air accompanying the pathway. It snaked through, weaving and taking curved turns and sharp angles every so often like an oversized maze.

"Much creepier in person," Kasey said.

"An engineering masterpiece." Shamp had a wistfulness in her voice.

The drone dove deeper and deeper. "Drone is still going," he marveled. "I can't believe just how dense it is."

Pad still in hand, Kasey came down the ramp of the Navigator with Tsoki and Shamp, Falisto a bit behind them. Tsoki trotted to the opaque walls, and with his two middle fingers, rubbed against it. "These seem," he paused, looking for the right word, "fake."

"Certainly," Shamp said. "We are underground, there are no organic subterranean walls."

"Shamp," Kasey said, still looking at the pad. "Venori translation never gets old."

"Glad you think so," she said with a smile.

Tsarena took out her pad, looking at Kasey's feed. "Wait, what's that?" Tsarena asked.

Kasey looked back. "What's what?"

"There on the screen!"

Smack dab in the middle of the drone's path was an obstruction. Not a wall. Not a rock. An actual obstruction, something artificial and black. "I don't know a door?" he guessed. "Maybe a gate?" Handles were absent from the door, but that didn't rule out the possibility.

"Use the rocket," Falisto suggested.

"Don't hurt anyone," Tsarena cautioned.

After a moment examining icons forming the white bar of options on the topside of the stream, Kasey clicked on the missile option. Although Kasey couldn't see it, he heard the drone launching a rocket from its underbelly.

Kasey yanked back the drone so it wouldn't be caught by residue before firing it.

"Use the laser," Shamp said, moments before Kasey hit the rocket button.

Kasey frowned. "Falisto, why didn't you say that?"

"Rockets are more fun!"

Kasey rolled his eyes. "Thank you, *Shamp*," he emphasized the name as his version of a not-so-subtle jab at Falisto. Flicking what he originally thought was a pen icon, now deciphered as the laser icon, a beam of condensed photons jumped out of the drone. Using slight wrist movement, Kasey managed to bifurcate the door, and the drone rammed through, continuing its journey.

"There we go," Kasey celebrated. "Powerful drone."

"Are we ready to go in?" Tsarena asked, her foot tapping. She had one hand on her hip, with her body constantly pointed in the direction of the path. In her other hand, she gripped the pad, watching the drone.

After a few more seconds, the drone entered into a new room. It fanned out into a circle and glowed with a blue mist that reminded Kasey of the mine on Tyol. Blue and red rocks provided a light glow to the room, illuminating what looked to be metal bars of some sort. Then he saw movement.

"The drone caught something," Kasey cautiously said.

"What?" Tsarena hit her pad, trying to refresh the screen with force.

Kasey held up his view to the group. They gathered behind him, with Tsarena budging forward past the others. "What do you see?"

"It was just a quick movement."

"There!" Falisto pointed to a section that Kasey hadn't paid much attention to at all.

Kasey squinted, bringing the pad closer to his face and away from the group. "What is it?" Tsarena asked.

"I really don't know," Kasey said.

Shamp pointed with one of her appendages. "Is that a prison cell?"

"Oh God," Kasey mumbled. The iron bars became clearer over the video feed despite static flashing every so often. Figures drenched in shadows made slight movements, all held together in huddles by the lines caging them.

"Where are they?"

"Not too far from here. I think if we go it'll only be five or so minutes if we hustle."

* * *

Falisto

"Five minutes my ass," Falisto grumbled. The floor made his toes curl and drove his nails into the dirt by extension. He hugged himself with what little fur he kept exposed from his unitard after zipping every possible section to seal the heat with him. Air from his nose left behind cool clouds that Shamp walked through from behind. She told the team it would be warmer this close to a planet's core, but for whatever reason, it was a tundra, the floor, and walls were icy to the touch, and a thin fog blanketed the floor like snow.

Kasey's teeth chattered. "We're almost there," he assured.

"Drones must go fast," Falisto muttered, a bit annoyed at the underestimated length. He usually didn't mind walking, especially with company, but this place was not the place to walk. Sure, he meandered through the pitch blackness and occasional red light, and it was quiet, except Tsarena murmuring to herself about Mahina. But this place creeped him out and few things did that.

"Shamp," Kasey said from ahead. "How're you doing back there? I know this is a tight fit."

"It sure is," she mumbled. "You know, Venori are not extravagant or gaudy by any means, but we always create breathable structures."

"Take that up with whoever built this," Kasey said.

Falisto kept walking, his feet sticking to the floor like quicksand. "I don't think Jasoosi built this place."

Tsoki cut in, "Well that's good, finally you might agree they aren't behind this."

"Not so fast," Falisto said. "Just because they didn't *build* this doesn't mean they aren't *using* this."

Tsarena was in front of all of them, occasionally stealing glances back and glaring when the group's pace fell below what she considered acceptable.

"Did you hear that?" Shamp asked, pointing behind her. "I believe I heard something."

"No," Tsoki said. " I didn't at least."

Kasey glanced down at his pad. "The path narrows."

"Of course it does," Falisto groaned. He condensed with the other members, getting closest to Tsoki.

Tsarena stopped for the first time in a while, looking back. Complete darkness stood in front of her, almost shrouding her. As they approached, a murky green tint appeared when illuminated by Slarts and pads. Stains adorned metal portions affixed to the walls, with occasional rusted bits and scratched-up edges glimmering.

"They did some decoration," Kasey said. "Seems weird."

"Something's not right about this place," Tsoki said. "What are these things?"

"I don't know," Tsarena said from ahead of them. "But they almost look like they're part of a ship."

Shamp scoffed. "A ship this far underground?"

"That could have something to do with it," Falisto laughed.

Shamp added, "I don't know if I would consider these aliens high-tech."

"They have an entire underground pathway or something," Tsoki countered.

"Why would a species go through all this trouble to live underground?"

Tsoki shrugged. "Why kidnap a whole colony?"

"Maybe they think the colonists are invaders."

"The drone is somewhere here," Kasey said.

Tsarena bolted in front. She drew out her gun. "Everyone ready?"

Kasey nodded. "We go in, we stay as quiet as we can." Kasey looked squarely into Tsarena's eyes. "Let's get our people back."

* * *

Tsarena

Humans, Psys, and Orchi stood shackled and naked. Bloody scratches and purple bruises spread across their bodies. Many resorted to pieces of muddied cloth for clothes, ripped portions of uniforms, unitards, or garments. Species with lips were chapped beyond recognition, and every Psys' fur was brittle and straight like straw. Human faces were bony, devoid of any fat, and Orchi's eye bags were deep and hollow. She could see, for the first time in years, an Orchi's ribs and skull bones. After the end of food scarcity for the Orchi, it was rare to ever see an Orchi underweight, let alone malnourished to the point of starvation.

As the team funneled in, all Tsarena could think about was Mahina. She was here, somewhere in the crowd. *Finally.* But she didn't let herself celebrate—she couldn't—not until Mahina was safe. It took everything in her power to not yell out Mahina's name. Mud stuck to Tsarena's boots like glue, impeding her jog through the chamber. Her eyes darted between the imprisoned, sifting through Psys and Orchi to locate Mahina's features. It'd been so long that Tsarena closed her eyes and pictured her. Her dark hair, a pair of brown eyes, a wide smile.

One Human waddled to the door with a limp. A few groans rattled across the chamber, with some hushed cries of pain. Survivors shuffled their feet and rustled chains shackling them into a grid-like system. Rancid meat and ash formed a stench that repelled Tsarena and the others from the jail cells. Tsarena pushed through the odor, and after a quick spin, she realized several more holding chambers were hidden in the room.

Distant cells stirred at their Slart's light. Groups gathered into huddles inside their cells. A cacophony of chain rattles continued with whispers joining. Then murmurs. Then shouts.

"Let us out!" someone croaked.

"Before those *things* come back!" another yelled.

"We need a doctor, my son's leg is infected!" a prisoner screamed.

"Are you here to save us?!" one cried.

"Please!" one pleaded.

"Be quiet!" Shamp shouted to everyone. They listened to the booming bass of her voice and lowered their voices. In a whisper-yell, she spoke, "Whoever put you here could hear us!"

The colonists turned on each other, shushing one another and turning screams and pleas into whispers and requests. Tsarena examined one lock on a cell holding only Human captives. Whatever the lock was, it certainly didn't appear like anything she'd ever seen before. It had several components, with a circular feature and symbols overlaying a square with other icons. A third and final layer formed a sort of triangle, but this shape had far more markings than the other two.

"Kasey, there's a lock on this door." Tsarena yanked it, causing more commotion than intended. A few humans recoiled at the tugging of the lock, triggering them to cower away.

"Can I just shoot this open?" Kasey asked.

"Let me," Shamp said, bringing forward a tendril. "Shooting it will only make—"

A colonist screamed, "—There's one behind you!"

Kasey and Tsarena whipped their heads back but no one was there. Another survivor from behind the screamer clasped her mouth to prevent more yelps. The survivor clasping the screamer's mouth whispered something into the woman's ear.

"You mean her?" Kasey pointed to Shamp.

"Yes!" the colonist chirped, muffled by the grimy hand of the man behind her.

Tsarena and Kasey exchanged looks. *The Venori?* Were they behind this? Tsarena shook it off, that didn't matter. Mahina mattered, and that was the focus.

"No," Kasey stammered, "that's Shamp, she's a PTF member."

Shamp's voice stuttered. "D-did your captors resemble me?"

"Just as tall," she cried.

Shamp's energy dwindled, and her tendrils fell to the floor. Her throat struggled to form the words, but she managed to push away the same thoughts Tsarena had. "This is unlike anything I've seen before, but I think I know how to break it open."

"How?" Tsarena asked.

Shamp took out her combat knife, the PTF standard with marigold light encasing it. Tsarena followed suit, taking her knife out of her boot. Holding the lock between two tendrils, Shamp halved the lock down the middle. Tsarena fumbled the broken lock, removing the hook keeping the door shut, and tossing it aside. Before she could even open the door, the woman in front pushed it open and ushered a mass exodus, with everyone funneling out towards the tiny area allotted by the entryway. Tsarena backed away with Kasey and Shamp, while Falisto and Tsoki worked on other locks.

In the corner, Tsarena saw six or seven Hybrid bodies. Their bodies were burnt husks as if they swallowed liquid magma, their skin was a dusty charcoal tone with metal portions covered in webs of ash.

"Where's Mahina?" Tsarena asked a survivor, still shackled.

A young Hyoose Psys, judging by his two tails, looked at Tsarena. "The nice lady?" he asked. The boy's voice was hoarse and dry as if he'd gone without liquid for days. Tsarena gently put her hand on him, feeling his fur exfoliate her with the prickly edges.

"Yes," Tsarena pleaded. She wanted to hand off her canteen to him, but he cowered from her with his tails between his legs. "Where is she?"

His whiskers, crinkled and uneven, twitched when he pointed with a claw.

Tsarena looked beyond him and to a woman lying on the floor. Tsarena stopped her instinct of leaping to Mahina. "I'm gonna cut these off," she said, looking at the woman's body.

Tsarena didn't know why but tears welled in her eyes. Her chest tightened as she sliced into the chain links. Mahina was there, she was fine. She had to be. Mahina was a fighter. A survivor. Sparks of gold energy flew between cuts, and she forced her eyes where the child pointed.

The second the shackle broke, she dashed in the direction, seeing more Hybrid bodies piled along the walls. "Tsarena?" A voice croaked from the direction. The one-word call came between coughs.

She jumped to her, ignoring other sounds and pleas filling the room. A triumphant smile crossed her face, and her heart raced with joy. Tears obstructed her vision as she approached, falling to her knees as she slid to the voice.

Tsarena didn't recognize her. The woman's hair had clumped up into balls of oil and dirt-covered strands, and sludge covered her face, splashing each feature Tsarena so vividly remembered. The woman crawled along the ground, bruised and beaten. A gash, several centimeters long, climbed from her ankle towards her thigh, with portions of it still bleeding.

"Tsarena," the familiar, worn voice said again. This time it was weaker, as if crawling took whatever air she had left. "Is that really you?" She clawed forward with her fingernails already subdued into the ground. A wheeze expelled from her mouth as she forced herself on her elbows.

Tsarena aided her up, providing support to her elbows and arms. Mahina's bones stuck out of her body like toothpicks. "Mahina," she sobbed. Tsarena had so much she wanted to say; she planned for this moment. After going so long without speaking to her she had nothing but hours of conversation they needed to catch up, and Tsarena wanted to bark at her for leaving without saying anything. But the words were gone—she hadn't prepared to see her family like this.

Tsarena took short breaths, hyperventilating herself. "I'm gonna get you out of here, you hear me, okay?" Tsarena cried, unsure if she was saying it to Mahina or herself.

Mahina coughed. Despite her condition, she still somehow found a bit of herself. "Sola called you. I knew the squirt could do it." She coughed again, this time more guttural and contorting her body forward. She fell on top of Tsarena who quickly caught her and lifted her back to rest.

"Sola did, she's okay, she's on Kyros." Tsarena tried to run her fingers through Mahina's hair, but the tangles were too much for her to run her fingers through. "You're alive," Tsarena sobbed. Forcing a hug from her, Tsarena hooked both her arms under Mahina's shoulders and crossed them around her back.

Mahina cracked a smile through the dried mud that constricted her chapped lips. "You came back for me," Mahina coughed. "Sola called you."

"Yes, Mahina, and she's alive just like you." Tears streamed down

Tsarena's face, dripping onto Mahina's hands and cleansing them of dirt marks. Sola didn't end up calling Tsarena, but that wasn't important, what was important was that Mahina was here, right now, in her arms. For a moment, the two sat in silence while one of them let out an awkward laugh, whether it be from desperation or relief. Tsarena didn't care which—just that she got to hear Mahina laugh again.

After a moment together that was all too short, Mahina asked, "Where's Warda?"

Tsarena wiped her eyes with one hand, firmly keeping the other one supporting Mahina. "Who?"

"The Tayir," she coughed again. "Where is she?"

Chapter 35

Kasey

While Tsarena and Mahina had their moment, Kasey and the others forced open more chambers, snapping locks apart and jettisoning them with their knives. Kasey's heart raced, and his suit warned him he'd been at 80% of his maximum heart rate for a good chunk of time. Before going to the second holding cell, Kasey packed up his drone which he parked right outside one of the cells.

"Falisto, what's the signal like to *the Irene*?" Kasey dashed to another set of locked people, cutting away another chain binding them together. They cried above him, and Kasey avoided their eyes and thank yous, scurrying to the next imprisoned folk.

"No signal. We're in too deep." He gripped his pad with his paws and banged it against the wall. "Stupid fucking connection."

"Keep your voice down." Kasey wore the face of a scolding parent. "The second we get the connection we need to call Respow and have him send a bigger team."

Shamp and Tsoki aided others nearby, cutting free several cages of people in the room. The ratio seemed equal, with all three species having a similar representation count. Except for Hybrids—there wasn't a single Hybrid Kasey saw. Now alive, at least. He saw their bodies, broiled and crisped like someone roasting a marshmallow for the first time. Tsoki brushed up to Kasey when they came to the same cell.

"You did it, Mako," Tsoki said.

Kasey would've remarked about the usage of his last name, but he didn't catch the sass in his voice. "Tsoki, you and Tsarena gotta get these people out of here, okay?"

Tsoki scoffed, undoing a tangle in two chains of Orchi held together. "I'm not leaving you."

"I wasn't asking," Kasey said. "You get those people to the Navigator, take someone that can fly them."

"Have Falisto do it!" Tsoki spat, his voice raised.

Kasey shot a glare at Tsoki for the first time. "I trust you to keep them safe," Kasey explained. He helped up an adult Psys from the ground who'd been covered in mud.

"I don't wanna leave you," Tsoki pleaded.

"We'll be right behind you. We need to make several trips anyway to get them out, take as many as you can."

"You better be right behind me." Tsoki came up to Kasey, only a few millimeters away from his lips. It was an unspoken moment, the two of them looking longingly into each other's eyes, noticing—*really noticing*—one another.

Though their lips didn't exchange, Kasey sealed it with a sentence. "I promise," Kasey said.

From a bit away, but still, in earshot, Falisto approached each Orchi, loudly asking about Tsavon. He kept his tone as professional as Kasey expected, still short and with a hint of bitterness, but calm and collected.

But, the quiet facade shattered as the sound of thousands of stomps came from above. "They're coming back!" someone yelled. Cries from colonists created a cacophony until everyone screamed in horror. The only exit became blocked by a stampede of prisoners pushing and pulling their way through.

Kasey yelled, "Stop!"

No one listened. Instead, the crowd got louder, screaming, hollering, shouting. The pool of people swallowed Tsoki and Shamp. Gritting his teeth, Kasey shot his Slart into the air two times. Everyone's screams erupted once more before they bent down and covered their heads.

Kasey darted his eyes to each of his teammates, their Slarts raised. "Tsoki,

Tsarena, you two get these people out of here."

Tsoki's lower lip quivered, and he shouted, "Everyone, if you can move, help someone that can't, we're going the only way we can." He looked around and watched as the able-bodied aided the disabled. "Is there anyone here that can fly a Navigator?"

A few folks raised their weak hands (or paws) into the air along with Falisto. "Okay, I need you to hang back with me while we go." Tsoki pointed to a Human woman and female Hyoose Psys.

Tsarena held onto Mahina, lifting her with a limp but still moving her. "Kasey, I need to—"

"—Go," Kasey commanded. "I promise we'll be back." He pointed above him to where the thousands of footsteps intensified. "Whatever they are, they're coming and outnumber us. We'll hold them back and then be right behind you."

Tsoki and Tsarena exchanged looks. "Kasey, I need to talk to you about something." Tsarena's face frowned with concern.

Kasey looked at Tsarena and Mahina, both a shell of their former selves but better together. "Just get back to *the Irene*. Call Respow."

"Kasey," Tsarena started, "it can't wait."

Kasey shook his head and brushed up against her. "What is it?"

"There's a Tayir—we can't call Respow."

Kasey's eyes popped open. "Where?"

Tsarena pointed in the direction of the part of the room Kasey hadn't searched. Mahina struggled to form words when she spoke. "She's a hero," she said, her voice strained beyond recognition.

Kasey nodded. "Don't call Respow, then," Kasey said.

"Did I just hear you right, there's a Tayir here we're helping?" Falisto growled.

"Now's not the time," Kasey spat. "Tsarena, you and Mahina go back to *the Irene*, we're right behind you. Take the Tayir too."

Before Kasey finished his command, the Tayir came into view.

Kasey didn't recognize the creature at first. It hid in the cold shadows and the darkest parts of the cavern, only peering out from the end to listen to their conversation. It slowly crept out, shivering and guarded. Its wings hung low by the waist, with fingers emerging from both wings. Its eyes covered the majority of its angular head. Big and black, almost entirely pupils, its eyes looked directly at Kasey. The Tayir had a lipless mouth fixed into a frown.

But Kasey didn't see the image the GU painted in his head. Neither the talons nor fangs had the same sharpness to them as in the photographs online. Its beak didn't curve into a sharp dagger with blood dripping. This wasn't the harpy that every alien race assured him was the Tayirs. Kasey only saw a frightened creature, shivering in the empty room, hungry and afraid.

"You're a Tayir," Kasey marveled. He held his hands up after sheathing his weapon. "It's okay," Kasey said.

Falisto pounced to Kasey, his Slart drawn. "Get back!" He held his gun to the Tayir's chest, which put up its wings defensively, its fingertips trembling.

"Stop it!" Kasey shoved in front of Falisto now, pushing him back. "They're a prisoner!" He pointed to shackle marks, coupled with the bruises and open wounds spread across the Tayir's body as frequently as freckles on Human skin.

"She's a good person," Mahina yelped, her voice still hoarse and filled with soot.

"A real Tayir," Shamp said. Her tendrils wrapped around her stomach as she walked forward.

Falisto lowered his gun but not without protest. "What are you doing here? Alive?"

"Tsarena, Mahina," Kasey started, "you two, go, now!" They nodded, following the path they entered through.

Kasey turned to the Tayir. "What's your name?"

The Tayir used its wings to cover its body like some sort of shield. "Warda," she said. "Please, don't hurt me."

"Warda," Kasey said back. "I'm not gonna hurt you. But I have a lot of questions."

"I do not believe we have time for that," Shamp yelled, drawing her weapon and turning behind her to protect their backs. "They're closing in."

"Warda, you need to go with the others." Kasey pointed to where Tsoki and Tsarena left.

"No." She moved forward, bringing her knees that bent the other way closer. "I cannot."

"Yes, you have to."

"I want to help."

Kasey exchanged looks with Falisto. "How can we trust you?" Falisto asked.

"At a minimum, give us guidance about the enemy?" Shamp asked.

"The Apiary," she squawked. "That's what we called them."

"You have a name for whatever did this to you?" Kasey asked.

"Yes, what they did to my people."

The footsteps got louder, this time loud enough for Kasey to hear them from only a few meters away. "Shit!" he shouted.

"We must distract them," Shamp said.

"There's only one entrance," Falisto uttered. "Wherever they're coming from is sealed off." He pointed to the source of the sound, the steps intensifying.

"There's another," Warda explained. She pointed her finger wing towards another section of the corridor. "There."

Kasey jogged to the side of the room, pressing against the wall for a way to open it. After blindly tapping it, he found a thin panel that pushed in slightly, opening a door to another room, darker than the one they were in.

"Wait!" Kasey shouted.

Shamp stopped, one foot already placed in the next room. "What?"

"I have an idea."

A hidden main door flung open, splitting down the middle of the back wall while an army of dark figures flooded inside. Roaring, the entities shrieked at empty jail cells and slithered forward to the center. Large guns scraped the mud, scratching trenches into the ground. As the group of aliens came closer, one noticed a drone.

In a language none of the teams' converters could make out, the creatures bellowed at the drone and raced after it. Kasey maneuvered it so it whizzed down the hallway they came from. Each of the unseen aliens galloped and lunged after the drone, barely keeping up with the speed. More aliens rushed through the room, following the stampede like some twisted hive mind.

"They took the bait," Kasey said. "We can probably get out of here." He kept his gaze on the drone, flying through the tunnel.

"No," Warda said. "There's a ship here they're building—we cannot let them escape."

"Our ship can make a beam," Kasey explained, still flying his drone. "We don't need to stay here any longer." A moment paused as they rushed out of hiding and back into the main room. "Fuck," Kasey said. On the screen, the aliens cornered the drone, savagely attacking the flying vehicle with bullets before clipping one of its wings.

Kasey exhaled and his eyes darted to the menu of options waiting for him. This time, he deliberately pressed the rocket button. The explosion rumbled from closer than he expected, and the boom echoed in the halls, paired with screams from the aliens. Their cries howled and echoed so loudly that Kasey had to cover his ears to prevent the dissonance from rupturing blood vessels.

"I have a sneaking suspicion they know we're here," Falisto murmured.

Not even a second later, two shadowy Apiary appeared from another side entrance still in the prison room. They holstered rifles that Kasey couldn't place an origin on.

Skipping the pleasantries, the Apiary shot at them in an ordered fashion, each bullet whizzing into the mostly unlit room. Kasey rolled to the side, shooting two near hits and a direct hit from his Slart, one connecting to an insect's neck. Warda bolted to another section of the room, prying open what looked like some hidden door in the chamber.

Shamp joined the firefight, shooting her own Slart at the second Apiary, blasting off its limbs. Blood sputtered out the stubbed appendage, which allowed Falisto the chance to take his shot at the ant's chest, leaving a hole where its heart should be.

"What are those things?" Shamp yelled.

"Apiary," Warda said, struggling to open the door.

"What are they fucking cicadas?!" Kasey shouted. He took a look at the two before him. Unlike other alien species, there wasn't a distinct "general" appearance to them. The ant creature was solid black, with a mouth of mainly teeth overlaying one another and sticking out. Two eyes rested on its head at distant points for maximum vision, and its whisker-like appendages looked almost like they came out of its eyes with how close they were. Kasey pegged this one as an ant because of the six legs and giant lump that served as the main body.

"They aren't cicadas," Warda yelled. "They're insects."

"How do you know all this?" Falisto shouted.

"I've been a prisoner here for years. Forced to build their ship, forced to help them get the colonists."

"Never mind that right now," Kasey yelled. "Can you shoot?" Shrieks from ants echoed across the unseen winding tunnels.

"Don't give the Tayir a fucking gun!" Falisto roared.

"Falisto!" Kasey shouted. "We're outmanned, we need to focus on staying alive."

"I can shoot." The door finally unlatched, revealing another hallway, this one long like a runway and with metal flooring. Warda waddled into the hall, ushering everyone to follow.

Kasey gave her his Misses, which she quickly sheathed until another Apiary came from the entryway. Warda shot six shots into its head. A bone chill shivered across Kasey. "Good shot."

"Too good," Falisto hissed.

Warda hustled further, keeping the gun drawn. "They worked us," she started, "used us as either food or labor."

"Why are they building a ship?" Kasey asked.

Warda led them to the belly of the beast. "The plans for the ship are so grandiose," Warda's voice was hoarse, and she cleared it to let more chatter come through. "But they need energy, lots of energy." She coughed again, this time bile leaving her throat.

"Are you okay?" Kasey tapped her shoulder. The Tayir looked at the Human hand on her shoulder with slight disgust but mainly awe. "I am."

"Pardon, how are you able to understand him?" Shamp asked.

Warda answered, "I've been down here—learned a lot from the colonists and the others."

"The others?" Falisto asked with an eyebrow raised. "Are there other Tayir here?"

She looked down, a squeak coming from her throat. "There were."

The air changed with her response. A chill further frosted Kasey's back sweat, and his fingers trembled. *Were.* The suggestion there weren't others—this Tayir could be the very last of her kind.

"How do you speak Human languages?" Shamp asked.

Kasey cocked his head. He hadn't considered this, just chalking it up to some converter update. But Warda answered, "We communicated with Humans—on our second world Janina—the 'Hello' signal."

Chapter 36

"As much as this captivates me, we have a much more troubling predicament," Shamp interrupted. The tunnel they were in was more of a runway, with metal flooring that sounded hollow with each step. "How are we planning to escape?"

Falisto rushed out his pad from his side. "Still no connection."

"What do they want?" Kasey asked. "Why did you send us the 'Hello' signal?

Warda, flying slightly overhead now that the metal-floored room came with cathedral ceilings, descended closer in a glide. "I don't know."

"What happened to *the Traveler*?" Kasey looked up to her, seeing the sharpness of her beak and fangs for the first time.

"Friends now is not the time!" Shamp ordered.

"Your people are still alive," Falisto sneered, ignoring Shamp's request. "You attacked Kyros just days ago. Killed countless people. Are you working with Jasoosi and Sapien?"

Warda did her version of gawking, which made Kasey's skin crawl. It was a cursed combination of a screech and a yawn. "You all built Kyros?"

"Shamp is right, we shouldn't be arguing now. Back off, Falisto."

"You should know," Falisto fired back, ignoring Kasey's command, his claws shooting out his paw. "I should kill you now."

Kasey stopped in his tracks and yanked Falisto back with all the force he could. Falisto, caught by surprise, stumbled backward into the wall, hitting it loud enough to make an audible bang. "What's wrong with you?" Kasey shouted, more of an accusation than a question. "We're trying to escape a hostile enemy, and you're trying to *argue*?"

Before he could respond, Kasey and Falisto's eyes peered up as the ceiling creaked like an old house, opening up and parsing tiles aside, revealing a body of water overhead. A layer of glass was all that stood between the tunnel and the ocean above them. Shamp recognized it immediately judging by how her eyes got almost as big as Warda's. It took the others a few seconds to see fish swimming in the low lighting. Kasey pieced it together. "That's—"

"—The lake," Shamp finished. "This must be where the ship plans to disembark."

"Wait." Using his foot, Kasey tapped along the metal floor, noticing divots and screws. "Are we on top of the ship?" Kasey looked at Warda.

"I think so."

"We need to go back the way we came," Falisto protested. He stopped running, coughing up a lung.

"We have to stop them," Warda proclaimed. "They'll come back!"

"Whatever those bugs build doesn't concern me, bird." Falisto twisted, cracking the nitrogen bubbles between his joints after regaining his breath.

"It should," Shamp defended. "Where are they even traveling to?"

"The third world, Hadiqa," Warda said. "The last world with my people."

"Why?" Kasey said. "Why go to your world?"

"They need our technology."

"For what?" Falisto muttered. "And if they want it, let them have it, who cares?"

"They won't stop." Warda looked at a canteen that Kasey drank from and put her hand out as if to have some. After some initial hesitation, he handed it to her. "Thank you," she said. Holding it over her open beak, she dropped the liquid like a waterfall to her throat.

"You don't even know why they have this ship." Falisto huffed hot air out of his body.

"I doubt that they'd build this big of a ship if they were planning on staying around," Kasey said. He pointed to the other end of the metal ground, a slight gray tint to it. "They used *your people* to build this," Kasey said. "They used *Psys children* for labor."

Falisto growled then shook himself. "Fine."

Before Warda could open her mouth to speak, a few bullets from about fifty meters fired. One grazed Warda's left wing, clipping a few feathers off and causing her to howl like a wolf.

Acting on instinct, Falisto shot back a barrage of bullets, connecting directly to three Apiary soldiers. One, a large beetle-like monster, fell forward, its horns preventing its face from making direct contact with the floor.

Shamp ushered Kasey and Warda to the wall while Falisto returned fire. He swapped from his Slart, moving the golden-barrel gun to the side, and took out his Misses. Bullets fired out of the gun, and Falisto had an excited look.

Kasey looked around. Nothing could double as cover; they were out in the open. "Get back!" Shamp shouted as she pushed them further into the wall. Warda bellowed, her winged fingers clutching the bleeding section of her other wing as Shamp stood, using her body and tendrils as some long, thin shield.

Kasey stuck to the wall with Warda, ducking under Shamp's tendril before adding his own Slart into action. Two bullets left his barrel piercing through the hard shell of a fire ant, digging into its body and bursting from within. Three more Apiary, this time all appearing like a foul mixture of a bee and a mole, buzzed out of the labyrinth. Instead of hands, they had claws and four eyes, with dirt covering their bodies.

Shamp took care of them with her Slart, dual-wielding it with a Venori pistol. Black energized bullets sliced through the still air and into the bees' bellies, electrocuting the aliens with lightning as they fell to the ground. But for each one killed, two replaced it like a hydra. One bullet grazed across Shamp's cheek, leaving a future scar on her right side.

"Bastard!" Shamp yelled. With a flick of the tendril, an electrifying, black bullet catapulted into the body of the shooter.

Warda crept closer to Shamp, awkwardly waddling over. "Are you okay?"

"Return fire!" Shamp commanded. "Check to see if the pad has connection! Call Tsoki!"

Warda didn't question her order, instead going to work. After a few clicks, Warda brought up Tsoki, and their connection wavered between poor and very poor. "The connection is bad!"

"Keep trying!" Kasey roared over the gunfire.

She held the pad up, ignoring the blood dripping along her feathers. The pad blinked, indicating the connection marginally improved. After a pensive moment, she flapped her wings into the air, getting her closer to a workable connection. "*Help!*" she cried in an audio message. "*We're in the tunnels under the lake!*"

A meter away, a bullet landed squarely in Falisto's unitard. The force sent him flying back, falling on his tailbone. He groaned and shouted as his body made a *thud* on the ground, screeching as his claws grazed the metal.

"Falisto!" Kasey shouted. Before he turned back, he took a final shot at the last Apiary in the squad of bee-moles.

"Everyone," Shamp roared. "I have a plan!" She looked around, finishing two more insects before another shot connected, grazing one of her tendrils. Purple blood spurted out and she howled, screaming through her return fire.

Shamp's eyes flickered up and made a quick calculus. With her gun, she aimed up at the glass separating the lake bed from them. Kasey followed her movement and then studied the ceiling. Every few ceiling panels were held up with different support beams, forming independent structures. If one fell it wouldn't compromise the entire structure of the glass. As a cascade of more Apiary funneled in from the maze, Shamp took a breath. Closing her eyes, she aimed her gun and fired at the ceiling.

One bullet, nothing. Two bullets, nothing. "Come on," Shamp complained. Three bullets, a crack. Four bullets, the crack spread. "Yes!" she shouted. Five bullets, a hole opened. Water rained down. Six bullets, the infection spread across the singular panel, new holes forming along the glass. Seven bullets, the glass broke entirely, shards of it raining down with Porygar's lake, swirling down. The rush of water caught everyone, including Shamp, by surprise.

"Hurry!" Shamp yelled, leaping back towards the group.

"Smart idea!" Kasey shouted.

With the help of Kasey, Falisto mounted himself upright again. His unitard suffered the brunt of the damage, spreading the forceful impact throughout his body. He winced a handful of times and paired it with a hiss. "I hate this thing," he tried to laugh but he only sounded annoyed.

Cold water covered the bottom layer of the ship. Shamp and Kasey still fired at the waterfall separating the insects from them. Kasey prayed to the Universe the liquid wall would serve as a perfect barrier, deterring the bugs from their continued chase.

With their hardened bodies, Apiary ran through it, their guns still blasting, just more haphazardly. It slowed them significantly, their appendages working overtime to cross the water. Shamp joined in, helping Kasey with Falisto and bringing him as far away from the onslaught as he could. She turned around and fired again at the ceiling, targeting another panel.

"If you keep doing that," Kasey said between breaths, "you're gonna destroy the whole thing!"

Warda connected back to Tsoki, the decreasing water barrier restoring their connection. "*Shamp!*" Tsoki yelled. "*What the hell is going on?!*"

"*We need evac!*" Warda yelled, still suffering from carrying bullet holes, and her flight to get a better connection only exacerbated her wound, tearing the hole in her wing wider.

Kasey yelled over comms when he heard a connection ding. "*Tsoki! Send us a Navigator!*"

The panic in Tsoki's voice slightly dissipated after Kasey spoke. Warda examined the water as the group fired back at the bugs chasing them. "*My name is Warda,*" she spoke into the comms. "*Do you have a beam you can fire at the lake?*"

"*Are you crazy?!*" Tsoki yelled.

"*You're gonna get us killed,*" Falisto coughed, still slugging through the water.

Kasey forced him forward, dragging him with Shamp behind them. "Save your energy, Falisto, don't speak."

"*I'm not gonna blast the lake!*"

"*It will destroy their ship!*"

"*And quite possibly the planet!*" Falisto yelled.

"Falisto, stop overexerting yourself!" Kasey said. "*Tsoki, use the concentrated beam. The same one we used to make our tunnel.*"

"*We're directing a Navigator to you, go to where we landed!*"

"*We do not have time,*" Shamp muttered.

There was a moment of silence before Tsoki's voice was heard again. "*I'm gonna fire from the Irene. Kasey, you have to get to the other side.*"

"*Shoot where the vortex is!*"

A bullet hit Kasey in the thigh. He screamed, the wound spreading across his body the second it made contact. The force followed the threads of the nanotechnology, breaking it up across each section it could and turning it into a whole-body sting.

"Kasey!" Falisto yelped. He shook off the pain and forced himself to help Kasey. Taking his gun, he returned fire, hitting more Apiary. "These bastards can't even aim! Only hit you in the thigh!"

Kasey tried to find the humor, but the bee sting from the gun cut any laughter he had.

They inched closer to the entrance, leaving behind trails of blood and polluting the clear water behind them. Shamp used two of her tendrils to help them up, while her third kept her upright despite having its bullet trauma. Warda returned fire now, shooting back flurries of fire at the Apiary.

Another bullet managed to escape the waterfall, this one hitting Kasey's unitard again. The bullet's impact, lessened by the waterfall's force, still pushed him ahead, causing him to fall along with Falisto and Shamp, the three of them falling like a poorly built tower. The water had risen, and with their descent, a large splash of water followed them, soaking Warda.

"Kasey!" Warda bent down and helped him and the others up, covering her head from more bullets. "We're almost there!"

He summoned all the strength he had and found the humor through a second wave of intensified body stings. "Looks like they got better aim, huh?"

Falisto belly laughed, his fur soaked and dripping. They trudged forward, pain and water eroding their speed. Shamp's hand tapped around her waist until she was able to dislodge a purple sphere. With all her might, she threw it back. A few seconds later, energy blasted out in a small area before making another series of explosions. More insects screamed, their cries muffled by the gushing water. A few materials from the grenade hit the ceiling, digging out two more pieces of glass and subsequent whirlpools of water.

"I need one of those," Kasey said with gritted teeth.

"*It's almost charged, just get to the end of the tunnel!*" Tsoki sounded panicked, absolutely terrified hearing Kasey suffer in a losing gunfight.

The tunnel's end taunted them from meters away. One insect came from the exit with the blood of his fallen friends covering his face. It roared, wielding a gun, and fired a burst of rounds, each heading to Shamp in a vertical line.

With unparalleled speed, Falisto jumped in front of Shamp, taking the majority of the bullets. "Falisto!"

Shamp howled in agony and returned fire, her bullets barely missing the creature as it ducked to the other side. Kasey panted but managed to shoot a single bullet that nearly connected with the centipede's head.

Falisto, slugging his head, looked dead-eyed at the bug. Showing his teeth he hissed and slowly grappled onto his Misses. Firing more than was needed, each bullet blew off a part of the bug, the first killing the insect, the second, third, and fourth ensuring it was dead.

"Falisto, you're hurt!" Kasey bellowed. Blood pooled in areas the bullets hit, and his eyes goggled, moving like loose-fitting marbles. "Guys, help me carry him!" With newfound strength, Kasey lifted Falisto on his back, Shamp holding him as well. Warda rushed to his side, examining the damage.

"I can't do much," she said. "But I will do as much as I can." Her feathered fingers applied pressure to the source of the breach in the unitard. One of the bullets made it through the defensive measure.

"*We're almost there!*"

"*The beam's at 98 percent!*" Tsoki said from above.

The ceiling closed, shutting off the flow of water and fish that accompanied the whirlpool. Water sloshed around Tsarena and Kasey's knees, requiring a staggering amount of energy to course through the river they created.

"*They're covering the ceiling!*" Kasey shouted. "*They know what you're doing!*"

Tsoki, frantic, cried out, "*It's at 99 percent!*"

"*Shoot it, now!*" Kasey yelled.

From above, *the Irene* fired another beam, green and brilliant, piercing through the rest of the glass panes and causing a tsunami to fall down the runway. Kasey slammed the close door button, just as a second river of cold water chased after them.

Warda screamed in agony as she pushed the doors together. Shamp joined in, adding her hands and intact tendrils on her side. A wave splashed through, flooding the tunnel, and just as it rushed towards the jail cells, the doors shut.

Chapter 37

Tsarena

an hour later, in the Irene

Tsarena let Warda's wings and muscles rest along the examination table. Warda didn't have the same rough edges as the others did. She was still obviously traumatized, but Warda wore a strong face. Maybe it was the way Warda consistently thanked her for spraying her injured wings or the way Warda asked *her* questions. The bench, meant for one creature of average proportions in the GU, only fit Warda when she stretched out her wings.

"They're beautiful," Tsarena murmured to the wings. Her four-fingered hands danced along the wings, following their angles and feathers that lost their purpose eons ago.

Warda smiled at the Orchi. "That's the highest compliment you can give a Tayir."

"Is it?" Tsarena beamed. "I'm glad I told you then. I debated saying nothing." Tsarena plucked the gloves off and lathered her hands in moisturizer. Warda's body had cuts and bruises scattered across her.

"How's Mahina holding up?" Warda asked.

A heavy sigh left Tsarena's lips, and her chest rose with a second inhale. "She's okay." In truth, Tsarena wasn't sure. She went to an IV bag, checking the contents, trying not to think of Mahina. "Do you happen to know if this solution—"

"—It works with my biology," Warda said.

Tsarena nodded and drew the IV. "Where do I—"

"—This vein." Warda pointed to a large green blood vessel going from her neck to her wing.

Tsarena's cheeks reddened. "Sorry, I never learned Tayir biology."

"It's quite alright," Warda said, taking a brief pause. "You have no reason to know my biology."

Kasey and Shamp's wounds took a bit of gauze, a bit of intravenous drugs, and a sugary treat. Falisto's wounds, however, took the majority of the medical equipment in the room after his stunt jumping into Shamp's bullet frenzy. He was adamant that he wouldn't leave the mission, and that it was surface-level damage. Tsarena's vocal cords still felt sore since the screaming match about Falisto's fitness to continue the mission, but she'd given in, accepting his plea to push himself past his limits.

"Can I ask," Tsarena started, throwing away the needle packaging, "what happened?" Before Warda could speak, Tsarena qualified the invitation. "You, of course, don't have to."

"No," Warda answered. "I don't mind telling you."

Tsarena rested on a swivel chair with a maroon cushion and silver body but no backing. A true GU seat for the various knees of species. "Why were you there?"

"The planet?" she asked.

"Yes—Porygar."

Warda looked into her eyes, getting lost somewhere in the purple mist. "I fled," she said. "Me and a few others."

"There are rumors the Tayirs set up two colonies, is that true?"

Warda's eyes turned vacant, and she looked at her. "Yes. Two official-unofficial colonies, I was a fringe case."

Tsarena cleared her throat. "I was just curious because the Observers teach—"

"—They do." Warda shifted in her seat, bringing her wings close together and putting a strain on the IV needle. "We believe the Observers, and their belief that species shouldn't leave their home planets."

Tsarena leaned in, asking the question with her body, *so why did you break that tenant?*

"But," Warda started, "we also believe in survival."

"So, you knew the attack was coming?"

"We had faith it wouldn't," Warda said. Her voice lowered as if sharing a secret, and her words slurred out her mouth turning into an ominous chant. "But faith wasn't enough for some of us. For me."

"How many of you came to Porygar?"

Warda looked up at the window above them. The stars glowed brighter, more grandiose, and occupied more space than she recalled. "A thousand?"

Tsarena sprung from the swivel chair, sending it rolling away and nearly out of the medical room. "A thousand?"

"I guess that does seem like a lot," she said. "But it's true."

"H-how are you the only one left?"

Warda's eyes blinked slowly. "Because we served our purpose."

"What purpose?"

Warda glanced away from Tsarena. "Building the ship and," she paused, "as a food source."

Tsarena's heart dropped along with her mouth to the floor and out the hull of *the Irene*. Her fingers wiggled as she drew them to her trembling lips. "Oh God, I-I'm so sorry." Instinctively, she put her hands on Warda's thigh, looking right into her eyes. And for a moment, they didn't say anything, they just stared at one another in the room.

Warda embraced the support of Tsarena's hand before she sighed. "We need to make sure that ship is destroyed."

Tsarena frowned and cocked her head. She'd seen the beam, how it pierced right through the ship and the planet. "Why wouldn't it be?"

Warda cocked her head back. "Because we built it."

* * *

Kasey

"Let's start with the main issues," Kasey said. They sat in the "brainstorming room," a room on *the Irene* that Kasey didn't know existed for the better part of his time with PTF. Lemon-shaded walls gave Shamp's leathery skin a jaundiced undertone as she stood in front of the board with styluses gripped by her tendrils.

"Agreed." Shamp swerved back to the other four at the table.

No one spoke.

"Anyone?" Kasey pressed.

"If we're starting with basics," Tsarena started, "let's put on the Tyol Virus."

"Jasoosi guns," Falisto hummed.

Shamp grimaced but scribed both down anyway. "Planet Exo?"

"Yes," Kasey said. "And Porygar."

"And the terrorist attack," Tsoki said. "Can't forget that one."

"Currently, we have the virus, the attack, Planet Exo, Jasoosi guns, and the missing colony. But what connects them?"

"Shamp," Kasey began, "you noticed these planets were all Rogue Planets, right?"

"Correct."

Kasey looked up at the ceiling. "There isn't a single Hybrid survivor from the colony."

"We should ask the colonists how they died," Tsoki said.

"We should ask how the hell Warda survived," Falisto muttered. "Or if she came alone."

"She didn't come alone," Tsarena added. "But I don't know how she survived."

Kasey gave a weak smile. "Maybe word it a bit differently than 'how you survived.'"

Shamp added an asterisk to the question as written. "Anything else?"

Tsarena wiggled a bit. "She told me about the ship they were building, and about how much energy it needed."

Kasey stood from his chair, pacing around the room. Whenever he needed to think he moved. Concentrating was one of the few things Kasey always struggled with, and moving got his mind focused. "Shamp found a Rogue Planet in the Moncratic System. If the virus killed Hybrids, and it's on Porygar, Tyol, and Planet Exo, it's probably on all those Rogue Planets."

"But we don't know if it was on Porygar," Falisto said.

"Which is why we need to ask," Tsarena countered.

"But more than that, the Apiary are on those planets."

Shamp made a quizzical face as she turned to the restless Kasey. "Kasey, are you suggesting—"

"—I am."

Falisto groaned. "Suggesting *what*?"

Kasey stopped moving, the dots all connecting at once. "The Apiary created the Tyol virus."

Falisto rolled his eyes. "Why would the Apiary create a virus that targets Hybrids? And be on several planets?"

"They might've not even consciously created the virus," Kasey explained. "The same way alien species carry pathogens."

"You think it's some sort of pathogen?" Tsoki asked.

"I don't know," Kasey said.

Shamp leaned against the screen, one of her tendrils clicking the stylus on and off. "So, the Apiary made the virus. But what about these?" Using the stylus, Shamp slapped the other terms, *Warda*, *Jasoosi guns*, and *Kyros Attack*.

Falisto straightened his back and groaned. "Jasoosi's back and they attacked Kyros."

Tsoki rolled his eyes. "Jasoosi killing Psys and other Orchi? How does that make sense?"

"We know the Kyros attackers weren't Jasoosi. They had Sapien marks on them." Kasey sat back down, massaging his temples to keep some form of movement.

Falisto huffed air from his nose. "Then why are there Jasoosi guns, Tsavon, and the Tayir ships on Planet Exo?"

"Add that," Kasey asked.

Shamp scribed the terms quickly, *Tsavon*, *Tayir ships on Planet Exo*.

Tsarena opened and closed her lips a few times, breath escaping them at regular intervals. "Speak, Tsarena," Shamp ordered.

"I just—okay—here's the issue, the person in the Tayir ship was a Human, and had the mark of Sapien." Tsarena cupped her hands in front of her, laying them on the table. "What if Jasoosi is being framed?"

Shamp turned back just in time to see Falisto's fur stand straight up and out of the unitard. Tsarena continued, "The guns on the Tayir ships, the Tayir ships themselves—technology specifically designed by a Human because of the leather seats."

"But then who is Tsavon?" Kasey asked.

"I seriously doubt Jasoosi is being framed," Falisto mumbled under his breath.

"That's a question for the people out there." Tsarena pointed, ignoring Falisto.

Kasey stood up again. "We know, for a fact, that Rogue Planets have something going on with them. If we confirm the virus killed Hybrids on Porygar, we can essentially confirm the Apiary are probably on those planets." Kasey stopped. "Wait—what is the Tayir homeworld?"

"What do you mean? It was called Bustan." Shamp replied.

Kasey fumbled out his pad, typing like a madman next to the ungodly positioned seat. "Bustan—is it a Rogue Planet?"

Shamp looked back at the board. "I'll write that down too."

Chapter 38

Falisto

Falisto had a hundred and one questions for Warda, and a hundred and two accusations to match. The bird-alien-monster hunkered over the table, her face torn into a scowl. She kept her head down.

Shamp and Falisto talked strategy before Warda entered. Shamp wanted to be good cop. Falisto was more than happy to be bad cop.

"What do you know about Jasoosi?"

Shamp slapped Falisto with the backside of her tentacle. "Falisto," she hissed in a low voice. "We talked about this."

"I'm bad cop, remember?"

"Ignore him," Shamp dismissed.

Warda shuffled in her seat, bringing her wings around her in a self-hug. Feathers from her wings fluttered to the floor. Her eyes were black and large, but they never left the base of the table as if she were ashamed of something. Falisto could smell the fear. It was a rancid odor that he couldn't pull away from.

"I remember Jasoosi," she cooed, her voice raspier than Falisto was expecting. Where lower jaw struggled to close, quivering up and down as her eyes hollowed out her face further. "They uplifted you, failed to account for the impacts."

This took the wind out of Falisto, and he did a double-take before becoming stoic again. "That's right," he said. He couldn't help his eyes from glaring at Shamp. Fur on his paws rose with an unexpected breeze rushing from a vent above them. He looked to Warda again. "They attacked

Kyros."

Warda narrowed her eyes. Shamp interrupted her before she could speak. "Kyros is a megastructure, a quasi-capital for the GU."

Warda nodded.

"They attacked Kyros," Falisto repeated. "Jasoosi used Tayir ships."

"Tayir ships?" Warda spread apart her wings with frustration painting her face as her body involuntarily hissed out air. Falisto got a slight rise from it. Her fear. Her confusion. He didn't try to hide the excitement with his dilated eyes and mouth nearly salivating.

"Yes, Tayir ships. Ships from *your* people," he accused. "*Your* people gave ships to terrorists. To Jasoosi."

Warda cocked her head down, her eyes fighting to stay open. "I've been a prisoner for—I don't even know. But I don't know anything about that."

"Before we dwell any longer on irrelevant matters, can you share when you came to Porygar? Who did you come with? You were found alone—well, the only Tayir."

"What year is it?"

Falisto and Shamp exchanged looks. " It's 2150."

Warda pressed her trembling fingers together, her mouth quivering. "Twenty-five years."

Falisto gasped. "Since the Tayir War?"

Her bruised face looked up at him, with Falisto noticing, for the first time, the cuts that adorned her body. Once they healed they'd be battle scars, something any Psys would be proud to have endured. But she tried to cover the wounds with her body, blanketing them in the plethora of shed feathers.

"Alone?" Shamp pressed.

Warda shook her head. "No. Me and a thousand Tayirs."

The whiplash threw Falisto off, unsure of how to reply. Shamp must've sensed this, taking the reins straight away from him. "Where did they go?"

A laugh escaped Warda. It was wry and short, and she paired it with an audible gulp. "Where do you think?"

Falisto's heart raced, painting the image in his head of Apiary hunched around birds and roasting them like chickens. Bugs chipped away at the overgrown fowls that dared to come on their planet.

Shamp pulled him back with her words. "Observer doctrine states—"

"—I'm aware what it states." Warda stared at the two of them. "But when your species—your people—are being executed and slaughtered, you tend to ignore the constriction of religion."

Falisto jumped in. "How did the Apiary come after you?"

"There was an eclipse—twenty-five years ago—they came out and stole us from our homes. Made us build their ship."

"The ship," Shamp said. "The one we destroyed?"

"Why did it take twenty-five years?" Falisto asked Shamp as if Warda wasn't there.

Warda answered despite not being directed. "Intergalactic travel."

Shamp and Falisto snapped their necks back to Warda. "That's impossible," Falisto dismissed.

"Intergalactic travel is centuries away. Even the fastest drives now would take eons to reach Andromeda."

"They knew how to build them." Warda puffed up her chest, restoring her posture.

"It's impossible," Falisto repeated.

Shamp agreed, "It would require an unfathomable amount of energy! The energy of a..." her voice trailed off. "A star."

"One way to avoid getting eaten," Warda started, "was sharing information about our Dyson technology."

The color drained from Shamp's face as Falisto stared at the two of them. "Am I missing something here?"

"Wait," Shamp interrupted, her voice still cracked in fear. "How do they know about your Dyson technology?"

"The Apiary were on our home planet."

Falisto shot up from his chair and slammed his clawed paws into the table, stripping it of a layer of protective film. "You knew?" he roared and his veins pumped pure fire through his body. "You fucking knew they existed?"

"Falisto," Shamp warned.

"She fucking knew! Her people knew! And they just decided to not tell us?" Falisto pointed at her while yelling. "What more proof do you need—these are the bad guys!"

"We tried to warn you," Warda whispered. "No one listened."

"Liar," Falisto spit. His voice was pure venom, toxic as he shot out rhetoric. "You killed *my* people. You killed *my* mother. You killed *my* family."

"Falisto!" Shamp pulled him back with her tendrils, but Warda didn't retreat from the flames spewing out his mouth.

"Qiula?" Warda asked.

"Representative Qiula," Falisto corrected, breaking free of the grip from the Venori's slimy tentacles.

"Captain Bigon planted a bomb on the ship, he was the one that killed your people, not me."

Falisto lunged but Shamp pulled him back further. "You need to cool it!"

But Falisto ignored her, scratching at the tentacles that wrapped around each of his appendages. "You're a liar!"

* * *

Kasey

"I like this room," Tsavon said.

"You're saying that because the walls aren't that awful shade of yellow?" Kasey cackled.

"That and I'm here with you." He flashed Kasey a cheeky smile, despite the fact that they were going to interview another prisoner of war.

"Come in," Kasey yelled.

The knob turned slowly, creaking open and allowing Mahina to enter. Kasey could tell from the dirt in her hair and smudged specks on her face that she hadn't opted for a shower yet. In her hands, she held onto a bag of basji chips, with three or four wrappers coming out of her pockets.

"Thank you for joining us." Kasey stood up from his seat, offering his hand.

Mahina's gaze wandered to him and although a bit hesitant, she shook his hand back. "Thanks for saving us."

Tsoki didn't offer the same gesture, instead opting to stay seated. Kasey's eyes watched as Mahina condensed herself by folding her arms over her legs and wrapping herself into a ball. Slowly, she rocked herself back and forth. This wasn't the woman Tsarena described. The happy-go-lucky explorer.

"We have just a few questions," Kasey spoke.

Mahina nodded. "Okay."

"You came to Porygar to be a Primer, right?" Kasey asked. He knew the answer, Tsarena read the information in the diary and put it in the mission report (which Kasey took the liberty of reading).

"I did," she murmured. She buried her head into her knees and wiped her runny nose along the frayed cloth covering her thighs.

"Do you know a 'Tsavon?'"

She stopped her rocking.

"I did." Her voice fell, cracking and morphing into a guttural cry. "I did."

"It's okay. I know this is tough."

Mahina sobbed into her knees like bony pillows. She did everything in her power to avoid Kasey's eyes seeking hers to make direct contact.

"Who was he?" Tsoki asked.

Mahina tried to swallow air between shrieks, but only after her fourth attempt, she uttered something coherent. "He came from space and helped the colony out."

"Where in space?" Tsoki pressed.

"He said he was a part of some group and they sent him there."

Kasey raised an eyebrow. "What group?"

"He never specified." She rubbed her eyes now, using the bases of her palms and reducing her eyes to stubs.

Kasey slid a cup of water to Mahina, stopping it just short of the table's end. Tsoki exchanged looks with Kasey, and the two had an entire conversation through their eyes. When Mahina managed to wrap herself around her mind again, she swallowed and wiped her eyes. "I'm sorry," she said. "I shouldn't be crying."

"It's okay," Kasey coaxed.

Tsoki dug deeper. "How'd he die?"

Kasey shot Tsoki a new look as if to say *give it a rest.*

"He got eaten." Her lips flapped in the cold air of the room. "He and so many others."

"That's horrible," Kasey said.

Tsoki and Kasey let her cry for a minute, working her tear ducts so far beyond their normal capacity that she had to rehydrate with water just to refill their reservoirs. After another bellowing session, she pulled herself together again, ready to collapse at only a moment's notice.

"Are you *sure* you're ready for more questions?" Kasey asked.

She nodded, her face red and stained with markings from her fingers.

"What were you doing down there?" Kasey asked.

Mahina inhaled, taking the air out of the room and channeling it outward as she spoke in one breath. "They round us up, make us work, and forced us to build a ship. Some others put stuff in rocks."

"What can you tell us about the ship?" Tsoki leaned forward, his pad blinking with no notes so far. "Anything is helpful," he assured.

"It's massive," she explained. She wiped her face again, her tear streaks now leaving behind cleaner lines through the graveyard of dirt that was entrenched in her skin. "The biggest ship I've seen."

"Did you learn anything about the ship?"

"It has a high carrying capacity," she explained. "And can use a high amount of power. There is this big *thing* towards the center like a super magnet."

"Was there a lot of living space?" Tsoki asked.

"No." Mahina swallowed. "We put lots of the rocks on the ship, and make nurseries for their young."

Kasey and Tsoki exchanged looks again before turning back to her. "A generational ship?"

"Maybe?" Mahina said. "So few of us are engineers. They have the plans and we do what their leader says."

"Are they weak to anything?" Tsoki asked. He filled his notepad now, with information appearing on every corner, no matter how trivial.

"Just like any other species," she explained. "But they have hard shells."

"Are they like bigger bugs?" Kasey asked.

"No." Mahina's voice thundered, a hint of sadness obscured by the overwhelming dread carrying it. "Those things aren't just *bigger bugs*."

Kasey caught her present tense. She was still experiencing the trauma of this, living in the nightmare of the Apiary. "What were they like?"

Mahina closed her eyes, almost like she tried to picture the images of the Apiary again. "Some have wings, others have fangs and thorned limbs. But they are more than that," she leaned forward. "They're feral and act without reason except one—the leader is the scary one that strikes without warning."

"I know this is a lot," Tsoki cut in. "But what was going on with these rocks?"

"I don't know," she admitted. "But that's what killed a lot of Humans off."

Kasey angled his head and put his tongue against his cheek. "Were most of the Humans Hybrids?"

Mahina shook her head vigorously. "Yes."

"Blue rocks that turn red?"

"Sometimes purple."

"Tsoki," Kasey whispered. Both of them leaned backward, from Mahina, muttering as if not to scare her. "The Tyol virus is in the rocks."

* * *

Tsarena

Tsarena wasn't thrilled to do her interview alone, but she wasn't going to apprehend Kasey from spending time with Tsoki after he helped save Mahina, and she didn't want to hear the term "Jasoosi" any more than she already had so that cut Falisto.

The chair that held her upright was red and contrasted with her skin from the overhead lighting. Niko and Lulu, the parents of Sola, walked into the room, taking their seats. Their fingers interlocked, and their eyes soothed one another.

"Thanks for coming," Tsarena said.

They nodded, each taking their seats. Scooting over, the two came together, putting both chairs side by side.

"So," Tsarena started, "I'm gonna ask you a few questions, okay?"

"Alright," Lulu said for the both of them.

Tsarena placed both her hands on the table. "First, do you guys need anything? Want anything?"

"We're okay," Lulu said. Niko nodded in agreement.

"Your daughter," Tsarena laughed with a smile. "She's doing great. Really great."

"When can we call her?" Niko croaked.

"When we figure out how to approach the situation with Warda."

"Why can't we talk to our daughter?" Lulu shot, her voice stern.

Tsarena sighed. Of course, she was going at it alone. "Because we need to make sure Warda won't pose a threat to everyone onboard."

"Warda's harmless!" Lulu shouted. "Warda did nothing but help us down there with those bugs."

"I know," Tsarena assured. She licked her lips and shifted in her chair. "But the GU doesn't know that."

"Then tell them," Lulu ordered. "Because I wanna call my daughter."

"I know," Tsarena repeated. "But if the GU finds out there's a Tayir—living—on this ship?" Tsarena didn't finish her sentence and Lulu's face softened.

"I just—" Lulu's voice cracked. Niko sprung his arm around her and brought her close. "I miss my little girl."

Tsarena's heart fell to the pit of her stomach as Lulu's face scrunched up while tears cascaded down her eyes. "I miss her so much," she cried.

Tsarena looked down at the floor before looking back at the two of them. Niko kept his muscles tense as if it were a surefire way to hold back bodily functions. But the facade cracked after thirty seconds of Lulu wailing.

The pad along the desk lit up, calling Tsarena's attention. She quickly opened it up. "I'll give you a minute," Tsarena said. She whipped out of the seat and turned her back to them while still in the room.

Shamp: We located the last colony. They call it "Hadiqa."

Kasey: That's good. I guess we can drop Warda off?

Shamp: What I find befuddling is the ship is so grandiose but merely fell to one beam.

Tsoki: That's a bit reductive, the Irene's beam is no joke.

Falisto: We could just call in GUM and let them handle this.

Kasey: I don't wanna get Respow involved. He made Tayirs public enemy number one. We need to get her out first.

Falisto: Maybe they are.

Tsarena: I'm in an interview with Lulu and Niko now. They wanna talk to Sola.

Kasey: I don't blame them.

Tsarena: What should I say?

Kasey: ...

Kasey: I don't think there's anything you can say. I'm trying to think what the next move is.

Tsoki: If we go to this final colony of the Tayirs what exactly do we hope to accomplish?

Kasey: Warn them about the Apiary, if they don't know already they could be underground.

Tsarena: I don't know if that's gonna work.

Kasey: We sure as hell can't tell Respow anything involving the Tayirs.

Shamp: Our primary concern should be the citizens of the GU. Let's redirect our focus on them, please.

Falisto: We send them back on the Irene and we take the Navigators to the Tayir planet?

Tsarena: I think that's a decent idea.

Kasey: Shamp, how'd you wanna check to make sure the ship was destroyed?

Shamp: A probe?

Tsoki: I'm telling you, it's destroyed.

Falisto: Shamp's right—that ship was built to travel to across the galaxy.

Shamp: If they survived, they are going to where that Dyson Plate is to siphon that power.

Kasey: Okay, let's get everyone together and let them know.

Tsarena: Good.

Chapter 39

Kasey

Kasey headed to the helm of the ship after speaking with Lulu about a request he had. Since it seemed that PTF was heading to the Tayir planet, Amber and Benjo would be left in the dark. Lulu, Sola's mother, and Porygar colonist, waited for Kasey to address the crowd.

All of the colonists were subdued, with only a few mutters coming out. With the absence of a podium, Kasey approached his approximation of the halfway point in the room to address everyone. His voice connected to amplifiers in the room, and he spoke gingerly at first, as to be safe not to blast out anyone's eardrums.

"Everyone," he said. His voice came through the amplifiers a bit quiet for his liking. He cleared his throat and raised his voice. "Everyone." His voice thundered now, rising by a few decibels.

That got people's attention.

"We're heading to Kyros." Some applause came from a few members of the colony. He powered through their sounds, speaking again, "You all were exposed to a deadly virus in the rocks on Porygar. We call it the 'Tyol virus,' and it was discovered about a week ago. It's lethal to Hybrids. They'll quarantine you and make sure you're okay."

A few more murmurs. Shamp joined Kasey now, coming from the back of the room where the rest of PTF hung by. "It is not deadly to non-Hybrids," she clarified. "But that does not mean it is a pleasant thing to carry."

"After that, you should be back to normal." Kasey turned his eyes to Warda who hung off to the right. She held her wings together, her fingers dancing with one another while she looked at Kasey.

"However, I have a request."

With doe eyes, they all looked at Kasey. He didn't like public speaking, not because of fear, but because he couldn't speak to everyone in the room the same way. He was much better at interpersonal communication, adapting from person to person.

"We cannot tell anyone about Warda."

Another set of murmurs. Colonists raised their voices so Kasey practically yelped. "Warda is a Tayir. Her people are being blamed for something they didn't do. There was an attack on Kyros, with Tayir ships Humans purchased from the Black Market."

Colonists looked back at each other and examined Warda as if she was capable of bombing and destroying a Panel of civilians.

"I wouldn't ask this if it wasn't serious—" he said, stepping forward, "—we can't mention her."

"But she was a hero!" someone shouted.

Another voice joined in. "She took care of us!"

"I know," Kasey said, quelling the crowd. "I know. But the narrative has already been spun." Kasey pointed out of a window in *the Irene*, in what he presumed was the general direction of Kyros. "They made up their minds."

Kasey inhaled. "We're gonna take her back on a Navigator, and Mahina, here, has agreed to fly you all back."

Mahina meandered out from the crowd, crawling next to him and Shamp. Her clothes were clean now, replaced with a proper unitard, pink in color and adorned with specks of lime and teal. She'd filed away her trauma for the time being, but she still didn't have the jovial nature Tsarena always gushed about.

"She has experience flying, and she'll get you safely to Kyros."

"What do we say about you?" another person asked.

Kasey looked at the speaker, an older woman reaching forward with her body and spine. After a moment, Kasey responded, "Tell them we needed to take care of something."

The colonists mumbled. Kasey's eyes turned to the Psys faction, who, to his surprise, had been nothing short of cooperative and pleasant. "Thank you," one of them said.

Another added it.

Then another.

Then a shrill scream like a howling wolf and whistle of the wind echoed in *the Irene*. It was a girl's voice, high-pitched and ear-piercing. Kasey and the others grabbed their ears. The child's voice wailed, with a finger pointing out the window to Porygar. Still echoing, she kept the pitch but added fear with each passing hum. "It's the ship!"

Kasey darted to the window, as did the rest of PTF, watching a Kyros' Panel-sized ship tear itself out the core of Porygar. A long, thin sheet of metal, adorned with particles of rock and dirt rose in the emptiness of space. The metal folded in on itself, forming an angular shape resembling a pyramid with the piece sundered by *the Irene's* beam hanging on the side.

"Shamp!" Kasey shouted. "Falisto, Tsoki, Tsarena—prep the weapons!"

Colonists broke into a frenzy, running around in *the Irene*. Warda flapped over towards Kasey and the others. She screeched in horror as the ship jettisoned itself to function without the defunct piece, leaving it behind along with the shards of Porygar.

"Kasey, the weapon's systems are shot!" Falisto roared nearby. "I can't shoot it!"

"Like hell we can't," Kasey hustled over. "Tsarena, Tsoki, what's the status of our FTL drives?"

"Fired up, we can go, but what about that ship?"

"We know where they're going!" Kasey shouted. "We gotta get these people out."

Warda flew closer. "They're going to use the Dyson Plate," she cried.

"Tsarena, launch us out of here!"

As she hit a few buttons, a wall of blue light encapsulated them, and Kasey took a final look at the planet. Millions of rocks burst from where the Apiary ark left, with asteroids of all sizes readying to fall back down like hard rain. Where the colony used to be was now only part of a massive crater, and the entire planet began to deform into shards with varying topography, almost as if the Apiary ark poisoned the core as a final act of defiance.

* * *

Tsarena

Warda sat patiently in the Navigator, blinking every few seconds. Falisto sat in the front, with Shamp joining him. In the docking station of *the Irene*, Kasey waited outside for Tsarena to finish her moment with Mahina.

"You're gonna be okay," Tsarena said to her.

"I know."

Tsarena swallowed. "I just got you back and now I have to leave."

Mahina struggled a smile, noticing tears in her eyes. "You're my best friend."

Tsarena laughed, her voice cutting through it. "I'm so glad you're okay."

"You saved us," Mahina said. "Of course we're okay."

Tsarena looked at the Navigator, Warda's eyes giving Tsarena a somber sensation. "Warda really took care of you," Tsarena said. "And I need to help her now."

"I know." Mahina's forehead came closer to Tsarena's, and the two let their skins touch one another. For two friends, they were close, but Tsarena had accepted that was what they were. Friends, nothing less, nothing more, and she'd have it no other way.

Mahina brought Tsarena in for another hug, wrapping her arms around her so tightly that if possible she would've popped Tsarena's head off her body. Tears in both of their eyes fell past their unitards and to the white ground.

"I wish I had more time," Tsarena croaked. "Just more time."

"Me too," Mahina said. "But when you come back, we're going to the movies."

"Trashy comedy?"

"Of course," Mahina giggled through watery eyes.

Tsarena saw her friend again now, a piece of her old self restored. "Can we also get burgers?"

"Tsarena," Mahina teased. "You said you needed to cut back on the grease."

"I know," she sniffled. "But we need a true celebration."

"And we'll have one." Mahina pushed Tsarena's curly hair back behind her ears. "A majestic one."

Tsarena looked into Mahina's eyes, her friend safe, right there, in her arms. For a moment, the two stood there, enjoying what Tsarena thought could be the last time. The logistics of this mission hadn't escaped her. She realized that she was doing the unthinkable with the rest of PTF: going to fight a hostile alien race with the sheer magnitude to build a ship capable of going across the entire galaxy. Now they weren't just returning Warda. They were going behind enemy lines.

After a long moment of another embrace, Tsarena unglued her arms from Mahina's body and marched towards the Navigator. Kasey greeted her eyes, red and watery, with his own hug. It wasn't the same, but it would have to do.

* * *

Falisto

The journey was further than the crew expected, but it was the perfect excuse for them to get some much-needed rest. Despite the need to sleep, even if for only an increment, Falisto kept checking things: the unitards, the weapons, the fuel.

The rest of the crew fell asleep along the floor, all bunched up together into a line of bodies. Falisto liked the warmth radiating from them, and, if in the right mood, he'd have pretended to dislike it while secretly enjoying the company. But like him, Warda was awake, looking outside the window of the FTL bubble.

Falisto couldn't look at her without remembering what she said. The accusation she made. Falisto replayed it in his mind, occasionally thinking of responses he wished he thought of at the moment.

"I'm sorry," Warda whispered. She turned back from the window to

Falisto. His eyes, slanted and pupils thin, looked right into her own. "I know what I said affected you."

"It didn't," he muttered.

Warda tried to smile which he found creepy. Like all species without lips, mimicking this sort of body language was a fool's errand. "I am sorry," she repeated.

Falisto shifted in his seat then jolted up and walked closer towards her. "You really think Captain Bigon would just blow up a ship of other Psys?"

"I will show you evidence if we have it on Hadiqa."

Falisto was so hot he was surprised steam wasn't rushing out from his nose. "You won't have evidence because it didn't happen. Plus, any evidence you have could be doctored."

"I know that you don't believe me," Warda admitted. "Nonetheless, I appreciate your help."

Falisto's neck snapped back. "I'm not helping you."

Warda nodded as if she understood his statement. "Thank you, either way."

He growled low, a primal response. Maybe part of him had doubted Captain Bigon. Whether or not it was conjecture, speculation, or a straight lie, it made some sense. Captain Bigon never offered to go to the ship, instead Qiula did—as she always volunteered for everything. That was a fact she lived by, like how water should be clear and fish eaten raw.

It didn't make sense. Why target Tayirs as collateral? Captain Bigon—if he did such a thing—could only have done so if he had someone else aiding him. To go undetected and yet execute something so flawlessly—that was cunning Captain Bigon never had.

Shaking his head, Falisto descended to the others, nestling up in the corner where their combined body heat provided the warmth he sought. But on some level, he believed Warda.

Falisto had the dream again aboard the Navigator with his mother. He was his current age, still young by Psys standards but not so much by other alien standards. His honey and cocoa fur poked out his suit, and his Slart attached to his waist. Qiula strutted in front of him, wearing the usual rose gold accents and gripping her pad like a lifeline.

"Mother—" he said.

"—Lady Qiula." She still had her kind expression on her face, the one that didn't immediately make someone cower into submission.

"Lady Qiula," he corrected.

"Come, let's find the incompetent who failed to do their checks on the Nima ship."

"W-wait."

She stopped in her tracks, gingerly turning towards him. They were on the same deck right before they saw Captain Bigon and his quarters on the ship. This ship—he remembered it now—was the royal ship, meant to be traveled on by the higher-ups in the unified Psys clans.

"What?" she barked. "We don't have all day."

"Mom," he said, coming up close to her. She didn't correct him immediately, instead studying him like she'd never seen this side of him. "Mom, I don't think you should go."

She blinked. "Excuse me?"

"Mom—Captain Bigon—I think he might have something to do with this."

She continued to blink. "Falisto, what on Katree would make you say that?"

"Something's not right."

Her eyes flashed downward to her paws on the floor, and they quickly returned to his. There was a twinkle there, a sort of compassionate color to her pupil. Slowly, she closed her eyes and blinked at Falisto before she spoke, "I know."

Falisto moved his eyebrow muscles into a narrow position. "You know?"

"I do," she said. "Something's not right, but it's my job to figure out what's wrong."

Falisto's eyes welled with tears. He knew he was dreaming, he'd listened to that dumb AI and now had control of this moment. But he was acutely aware of what always inevitably happened. "If you go down there you're gonna die!"

She came closer to Falisto, their marigold eyes sharing a stare, connecting the mother-and-son pair. With a blink, her pupils amplified in size, and she kissed his forehead after going on her tippy-paws. "It is not your fault."

Falisto was the one blinking now, staring in confusion at her. "I couldn't save you."

"No one could have," she said. "What happened was out of your control."

A teardrop leaked from his eyes. "I love you, Falisto," she said. "What happened to me, it isn't your fault."

He just looked at her, staring into her eyes and forgetting that he kept trying to pull back the tears. "Mom, I don't want you to go—to die."

Using both her paws she embraced him, wrapping them around his shoulders and neck. "I'm always with you," she said. "Always by your side."

A wave of calmness washed over Falisto, and a pang of guilt he didn't know he carried dropped, and, for the first time in a long time, he felt free. Falisto closed his eyes, and when he opened them back they weren't in the royal ship in his nightmare, they were somewhere else.

He remembered this place, he remembered distinctly the smile on his mother's face. The clothing she wore was translucent and with touches of royalty through pendants and gold accents. She laughed and danced with him in the backyard of their home on Katree, along with his brothers, sisters, and cousins, all partaking in the Nima clan song. His mother never could carry a tune or dance on beat but it didn't stop her. This was how he remembered her. This was his mother. She was a happy Psys, and though she ruled with an iron but fair fist, she loved her family. She loved Falisto.

Both in the Navigator with PTF and in the dream, Falisto smiled, because he knew he would never have the nightmare again.

Chapter 40

"I'm starting to think the bird abandoned us," Powers muttered. He sat by the communication systems for the past week to everyone's disagreement.

Empty pits of mawz dotted where Powers rested his knees. He moved knobs and dials until a signal came through his speakers, coated in feedback. Occasionally, when Powers took a bathroom break or stretched his legs, either Riley or Luke would wander over to try and make any sense of the buttons and sliders. Even though Luke had some training from Zanbaq, it didn't stick to him like it did Powers.

"His name is Zanbaq," Riley said.

Powers didn't look back, instead, he opted to put headphones on that came with the system. "Same difference."

Riley growled. Luke sensed the growing irritation Riley festered with not just Powers but the rest of the Travelers. Whatever optimism she had evaporated after a week without communication or as much as a run-in with the Tayirs.

"He's coming back," Riley said.

Luke eyed her, nodding with a smile to try and brighten her up as much as possible. With a dwindling supply of mawz, spirits were low, and food reserves were lower. A few succumbed to wounds even Tayir technology couldn't fix. Bleak didn't even begin to describe the situation.

"He's coming back," Luke soothed.

"We've been waiting here for a week," a detractor coughed from the back. "He's gone."

"He wouldn't leave us," Riley dismissed.

"I don't think he did," the detractor murmured. His cocoa skin was covered in sweat, and it had a bit of a jaundiced tint to it with his eyes yellowing to match. "I think he might be—"

"—He can't be," Riley said. "He's gonna come back and he's gonna get us back to our ship."

Luke kept the fake smile as hard as he could on his face, but something in him cracked. Maybe it was the thought that he would die with a whisper—through starvation or eventual cannibalism from his other Travelers. Powers would be the first to suggest it. He'd start by joking about it before taking more risks pulling people to the side and making small comments. Maybe even stab someone by accident and say the body couldn't go to waste.

A diet of mawz wasn't exactly the healthiest for a Human, but it was better than scurvy. Despite the searing heat, Luke made it a priority to take a walk around the complex and observe the architecture around the strange planet. Grass was odd here, darker and distinct from the other green he was used to. The rainstorms were brutal, but the humidity and simmering heat when it didn't storm was somehow worse.

"Wanna go on a walk?"

Riley balled her hands up into fists and shot a look at Powers. She exhaled a deep pocket of air and rose from the floor. "Yeah."

People always hyped up planets as "super-earths" or "better-than-earth planets." Catchy headlines were what actually green-lit missions like *the Traveler*. But no planet would ever be Earth. The gravity here was all wrong to Luke, movements hadn't adapted the way he expected them to. "Days" were oddly short and nights endlessly long. The oxygen intoxicated him, convincing him he could run faster than he actually could. No amount of terraforming, no amount of engineering and science could replicate Earth.

"I know he's coming back," Riley said, unprovoked.

"I know," Luke agreed.

"Have you..." her voice trailed off for a moment. "Seen anything?"

Luke cocked his head, peering over Riley's disheveled blue hair and into the rainforest surrounding the building they were in. What they thought was a city was more so a singular structure, almost like a temple of sorts. Sounds of wildlife sang their mating calls in the dark surrounding forest, and the humidity showered Luke in beads of sweat as they cruised. "There was something," he said, finally.

"What was it?"

Luke swallowed. He kept the piece of information to himself for a reason. "I think I know where they keep their ships."

"Where?"

Luke turned back to her and pointed in the distance where a clearing was. At first blush, it was like a bald patch in a head full of hair. Not noticeable, completely natural, and likely just a cosmetic change. But, on closer inspection, reflective metal shimmered with rare blasts of light.

"Why there?"

"Small, but sizable for escapes."

"You've seen them?" Riley asked.

Luke shook his head. "No, but I've heard the sounds from here. There's metal, too."

"Have you told the others?"

"And start a war with everyone trying to leave the planet?" Luke shook his head. Riley was the only person who could know this information. She wouldn't leverage it or come up with heinous ideas like the others would. But even Luke had become slightly suspicious. The diet of mawz began to play tricks on his judgment, and weariness was as common as trees.

"Good call," Riley uttered. "Good call."

"Besides, we wouldn't even know how to fly them."

Riley continued walking until Luke came to a sudden stop. "You alright?" she asked.

Luke turned back to her with a glimmer in his eyes. "I have a plan."

Riley looked at him, her eyes wide and pensive, weary of what he would say next. "You don't wanna storm the castle, right?"

Luke laughed, "No, not that." He took a moment before speaking again. "We need to find Zanbaq."

"You mean like go after him?"

"Yes," he said, anticipating her question. "I know the general direction he went." He pointed straight ahead of him. "They went close to the ships but didn't actually leave the planet."

"You think they're nearby?"

"I hope they are," Luke sighed. "The other option is wait for mawz to dwindle out."

Riley considered this. "We have mawz for, what, maybe two or three days? Four if you're really trying to last?"

"I know." Luke's eyes were large and wide, looking back at the clearing.

"I think you're right." She looked up at the stars. "Do you even think *the Traveler* is waiting for us? Why haven't they sent someone?"

"I don't blame them," Luke said. "If I saw a ship with 95% of my crew leave get pulverized in space and plummet to an alien planet with aliens, I wouldn't assume good odds."

"What if *the Traveler* isn't even there?"

"I have faith it is," Luke said. "But not for much longer. I wouldn't wait more than two weeks."

Riley tore her eyes away from the night sky, the galaxy particularly beautiful that night. "Let's look for Zanbaq."

Twenty minutes later, Luke and Riley told the group they were embarking on a search the following morning. The Travelers all joined in protest when Luke and Riley told them they planned on taking their portions of mawz. Powers, oddly enough, supported Luke and Riley, letting them know they should be given their full portions. With the three loudest voices accounted for among the surviving Travelers, the masses let it happen.

The next morning, they went off. Equipped with handmade archaic weapons of sickles and machetes fashioned from extra metal sheets, Riley and Luke slashed through the forest, clipping leaves and branches that swiped in front of them. The forest housed several odd animals, squirrels with four tails, two-headed foxes, and large insects with guns. Luckily they managed to avoid the latter.

"This forest is dense," Luke whispered.

Rustling from leaves a few meters ahead put them on guard. Both of them raced to the trunk of a nearby tree, occasionally stealing glances at the supposed source. The leaves crunched and loose droplets from hanging branches rippled into scattered puddles

Although obscured, Luke made out Riley's eyes. They looked at one another. The noise continued until they heard something they couldn't understand. Speaking, a language.

Luke stole another glance, this one far more risky, catching the insect they were weary of. Black, hardened skin protected the alien bug, with its translucent wings frozen in place along its back. Teeth-like thorns sprouted from each of its appendages, but it wasn't the one speaking, it was the Tayir.

Riley dared to peer, sneaking a peek just to watch a giant burst of energy from the bug's rifle kill the talking Tayir.

Riley whipped her head back and gulped. She looked to Luke and they both looked back to the building they left behind. It didn't seem like they'd walked as far as they did, but after a few hours, they made a sizable distance between them and the safety of the cruiser's crash landing.

Familiar chirping pleaded. Both of them recognized a few words as the insect lifted its gun to another Tayir. Bewildered, Riley dove out from the tree trunk. "Hey!" she shouted.

The insect whipped back, roaring at her and raising its gun. A burst from the gun hurled through the air past Luke and Riley's tree trunks.

"Fuck," Luke mumbled. "Hey, you!"

The insect screeched, peering at Luke now. It maneuvered its gun to him, shooting down the tree trunk. Luke dove out of the way as it crashed to the ground and scorched the dewy leaves and branches looming over them. Despite the rainfall, another energy blast ignited the forest, forcing clouds of smoke to accumulate in the already dimly lit night.

It stomped forward, moving its chest with each strut. With its arms and tendrils, it swiped the twigs in its way, getting closer to the dirt-covered Luke who hid behind a stump.

The insect found him now, readying another pulse.

"Die you son of a bitch!" Riley shouted, stabbing the creature through where its heart would've been. The shackled Tayir cried in terror from a short distance away. Some of the blood splattered onto Luke's face from the distance, bright green.

Riley pulled the sickle back, letting the insect stumble for a moment before falling over.

"Are you alright?" Riley asked.

The fire around them spread now, igniting other trees and patches of grass. "I almost forgot you weren't a soldier," Luke said.

The three of them didn't speak. Instead, Luke and Riley followed the woman as she frantically waddled over hills. Walking eluded the bird's skill set, she winced with each branch or pile of leaves that crunched under her talons. Smoke from the forest fire billowed into the sky, obscuring whatever moonlight they had. She weaved them through the forest like an endless maze with a thick path until they came to a treeless section.

"Oh my God," Luke said.

Riley gasped at the sight when she came next to Luke.

Cages imprisoned Tayirs outside of a gaping abyss in the planet. What Luke thought was a clearing was actually a rupture, going from one far end of the planet to another, surrounded by trees on both sides to give the illusion of a continuous forest. The cages were made from different materials—mostly metal but some looked like stone. They were primitive, easy to cut with a simple weapon.

The Tayirs inside cooed and whistled, signaling to the group of three. Luke couldn't move, his feet merged with the ground and turned into stone as the wounds on the Tayirs became clearer. Some had bite marks carved out of their wings, while others couldn't even stand properly. The cages kept them huddled together, forced into tiny groups in a cage that could barely fit one. It was like they were cattle.

The unnamed Tayir that guided them rushed them over. She yelped about the lock, pointing to it and speaking so quickly that even if they knew the language, Luke doubted they'd be able to translate it.

Luke's eyes wandered past the array of cages to one in the distance with a familiar-looking Tayir. "Riley," Luke said, swallowing before finishing the thought. His finger, bony and trembling from lack of any substantive calories, pointed to the far away jail. "That's Zanbaq!"

They dashed away from the Tayir who guided them, still waving her arms frantically but flying after them. "Zanbaq!" Riley cried.

His swollen face and featherless features startled Luke. Around his neck, he still had his lanyard, though it looked like it suffered as much of a beating as he did. Bite marks and full chunks of skin were missing from his body, and he coughed trying to speak. "Riley?" he asked.

"It's okay," she shouted. "We're right here, I'm gonna get you out."

Riley used the weapon to dig into the jail cell, cutting away specks and bits. "God dammit!"

"The Apiary are coming back," he coughed. "They're coming."

"I don't care," she spat. "I'm getting you out, that's final."

"Don't—" he said, wrestling with his own voice.

Riley only pushed further into the bars. Telling Riley no was the best way to get her to speed up doing the thing you didn't want her to do. It only took Luke a few days to know that. Luke spun around, looking for something to aid in the cutting. Out to the side of the jail cells was a pile of things, needlessly stacked upon one another with no real sense of rhyme or reason. These things, whatever they were, didn't seem like the smartest creatures.

Luke took a blade, it didn't seem perfect by any means, but it was sharper than his dull excuse of a machete. He rushed back, knife in hand, and dug into the lock like it was butter. It sliced it open, cutting out layer after layer of defense until the jail cell shrieked open.

An ear-splitting transmission screeched in Luke and Riley's ears. "Fuck!" Luke shouted, the sound a mixture of feedback and voices.

"*L-Luke, Riley—if you can hear us—we need help we're getting—*" the transmission cut in both of their ears. "*Killing us!*"

"Oh no," Luke said. Zanbaq limped out of the cage, falling over top of the two of them. Riley quickly grabbed him with her metal arms, sweeping him up before he fell to the ground. The others in the cage ran out, heading to different cells and tugging on the bars separating them.

"I'm gonna figure out what's going on," Luke said. His eyes moved from Riley and Zanbaq towards the structure they'd stayed in.

"That's crazy, don't go!" Riley shouted. "The Tayirs need help!"

"You stay here, I'm gonna go help the others!"

Zanbaq struggled to form words. "Luke," he said. "Be careful."

"Wait—what's the plan?" Riley asked.

Luke gulped. "Survive."

V

The Extinction

Chapter 41

Kasey

The team of six stepped out of the Navigator onto the alien world. The air smothered Kasey closer to the ground with thick humidity. Kasey slapped a mask on from his unitard, choking his coughs and warming his face. New to him, he had a belt wrapped around his waist with several grenades given to him by Shamp. It felt odd having things dangle along his hips, but it didn't help that the gravity made him sag to the ground.

"What now?" Falisto asked, his whiskers sinking.

"We pray we beat the Apiary here." Warda pointed to the walls surrounding the city. "Buildings are a good sign."

"Is this planet," Kasey started, "heavier?"

"By Human preferences, yes," Shamp said. "Minuscule change from Earth. You must hail from a planet with less gravity."

"Glad there's a reason for it," Kasey murmured. He shuffled along the dust-covered ground, kicking up ash and sand.

Towers spiraled skyward, pricking fallen clouds. Stone perches stuck out like thorns on a rose along each building, with a triangular gate surrounding the city.

Hints of sugary mint and black pepper swirled in Kasey's nostrils, bypassing the cloth protection. A double sniff confirmed the scent. He scanned the ground for an explanation, maybe a wildflower, the right mix of chemicals, or hell even peppermint itself. Something to explain the markedly Human flavor of peppermint.

"Eerie," Shamp said, standing behind Kasey. Her eyes mirrored Warda's, starstruck and focused on the fortress city. The sky was a gray-white like a summer thunderstorm waiting to downpour.

Tsarena gazed at the sky for the Apiary ark. "I don't see them."

"I don't either," Tsoki added. He faced towards the blistering side of the planet where lava flooded rocky hills and spilled into rivers of fire. A blanket of twilight inhibited long-range viewing, but dim lights from a distant moon cast away pitch blackness.

Tsarena wandered from the group to a gash in the ground, and the crack continued spreading from one end of the planet to another.

A shock wave along the ground made Kasey's feet dance. "Did you feel that?"

Falisto shook his head. "Feel what?"

The gray, dust-fused soil rumbled and shifted, answering his question. Bobbing like a buoy in water, the schism in the planet ripped further, inviting Tsarena into the depths.

"Tsarena, get back!" Kasey yelled.

Pieces of rock tumbled down to the planet's core. Tsarena scurried back, falling on her glutes. Her fingers gripped the ground, and she propelled herself towards the Navigator, kicking herself back.

"An earthquake?" Falisto knelt low, going on all fours.

Kasey helped Tsarena up, even though his own feet slipped while Warda fluttered above them and the shaking earth, her flapping tearing open the gouge on her wing. Pebbles vibrated rumble after rumble, and Kasey struggled to levy Tsarena up. Warda's talons lurched forward, pulling Tsarena by her unitard. A screech echoed from the crack, followed by quieter howls. The cacophony made Kasey grab his ears, the symphony of screams metamorphosing into a blood-curdling battle cry.

"That doesn't sound good." Tsoki drew his Slart. Millions of footsteps stampeded, and bugs erupted from below, spewing out insects with thorned bodies and worn weapons. Tsoki cried out, "They're coming!"

Falisto and Shamp fired at the crack, retreating towards the Navigator while firing flurries of rounds. These bugs differed from their Porygar counterparts, but they bled and screamed the same. Three blasts from

Shamp's Slart catapulted through multiple Apiary, carving through their reinforced bodies and leaving holes in their chests. Force from bullets pushed them right back down the schism they climbed.

Rolling behind a few cacti, Kasey and Tsarena fired their Slarts. Apiary readied primitive weapons. Bugs pierced the front of the cacti guarding Kasey and Tsarena, cutting through the plant with ease despite rust covering their blades. Some thrusted spears and harpoons, flaying the alien plant. Between slashes, Kasey fired back, landing squarely in the skull of bugs slicing at them. A few Apiary fired musket-style weapons, while the majority rushed the fortress.

Apiary drilled with mole-like claws up from the ground, climbing with a ravenous look in their eyes. Colors ranged from a fluorescent white to an empty black depending on the flavor of insect, and beetle horns protruded from most of their heads, while sharp teeth covered their limbs like hair on arms or feathers on birds.

"No," Warda shouted. "No!" Insects climbed over one another, forming a mountain of bodies. Most Apiary paid them no attention. The city was the flame and the Apiary were the moths following the beacon.

"Get back!" Tsoki waved Tsarena and Kasey inward.

Shamp fired at a few Apiary analyzing Kasey and Tsarena. "They are distracted with attacking the city, hurry!" Crouching, they rolled back, huddling near the Navigator.

"Sons of bitches!" Falisto shouted so loudly it startled the insects. He shot at runners, breaking through their back shells. "Cowards!" He fired another round, then another, and another. Despite fallen allies, they continued mounting each other to reach up the city's walls.

Javelins, spears, and arrows arced to the city from the charging platoon. "What's that supposed to do?" Falisto grunted.

"They're not even close to the city," Tsarena said.

"They are not aiming for the city." Shamp pointed to the sky. "Look!"

Bathed in steel armor, Tayirs hovered and dodged Apiary attacks. Tayirs fired guns, with energy bursts catapulting out in a massive flurry. Outside their wingspans, several spherical ships shot at the crack. In the distance, a singular Tayir flew to a bell tower, grabbed a rope, and wrung it around, ringing throughout the city and towards Kasey and the others.

More Apiary rushed from the crack, but now Tayirs met them, descending like rockets. Bullets rained down from their rifles, penetrating the pests. For each insect that fell, two replaced it, climbing over the carcasses with no care for the remains.

The ground rumbled again, stretching the rip further and revealing more antennae from reinforcements. Clicking sounds from their mouths squealed and Kasey's ears winced, the crescendo interrupted by Falisto's bullets.

"Die you sons of bitches!" A barrage of bullets from his gun plunged into the bugs, as dozens of Tayirs spotted the team.

Warda shouted something neither Kasey nor his converter made out between songs of war on the battleground. A flock of Tayirs snatched each member of the team with only Falisto protesting by thrashing his tail and arms. Kasey shivered involuntarily from the sharp talons scraping the top layer of his shoulder skin, but he let himself get carried.

"We're taking you to the city!" the Tayir clutching Shamp shouted. His wings glowed a deep azure, with a mix of navy and black feathers creeping under metal armor. Like strands of hair, the birds shed feathers in clumps, leaving behind a path.

"I hate being this high!" Falisto shouted. Still wielding his gun, he unloaded a clip into bugs below, staining the ash-colored soil with neon green blood.

Tsoki followed, adding his bullets before pulling out something Kasey had never seen before—a purple grenade that seemed archaic in origin and different from Shamp's gift. He bit off the clip, threw it, and counted. After a four-count, it detonated into a gravity well, sucking everything in a three-meter radius. It dragged Apiary in, breaking apart appendages and making them shriek and cry before exploding a magnificent amethyst and leaving only green guts and a dusting of smoke.

Falisto shouted in glee. "That's what I'm talking about!"

As they entered the city, more Tayirs left it. Armed with weapons and dawning armor Kasey thought would've anchored them, they pointed to a specific tower in the sky. With a silent nod, the Tayirs dropped the team into the building they pointed to.

"That was a rush," Falisto snickered. The room they were taken to condensed the group into a huddle, with the Tayirs leaving them. Gaudy artifacts piled inside. "Not a fan of heights, but that felt good."

"Do Tayirs have a hoarding problem?" Kasey murmured. Golden-rimmed mirrors painted the walls, patterned carpets covered the limestone floors and gemstone-laid tables filled every open space. Sculptures had a dedicated corner, with tiny statues leaning on each other.

Before Kasey could take it all in, an armored Tayir flew in. This one, decorated in red armor with a helmet completely obscuring his head, clicked a button behind him. The suit followed the command, and its protective plating retreated from his feathers and head, creeping backward and revealing a different Tayir silhouette.

Kasey took another look at the room while the Tayir disrobed. In a sense more was less, various art pieces and mediums stuffed the room, with realism clashing against abstract works and color schemes meaning nothing. Enlarged images of foreign landscapes captivated Kasey, their quality better than in person. This wasn't some sort of museum or a lone Tayir's hoard; this was their entire art across history, all stuffed in this one room in a mix of culture and passion.

When the armor finally peeled back, the Tayir stared into Warda's eyes.

Warda clasped her fingers and held them close to her mouth. "I never thought I'd see another Tayir." Her eyes fluttered and twitched with tears.

The two embraced one another, weaving feathers together and sharing warmth. The hummingbird-looking Tayir stood taller and varied more than Warda. Whereas Warda resembled something between a bat and a blue jay, the armored Tayir had a long beak reaching far and decorated with black paint.

Warda sniffled and lingered in the embrace longer than Kasey had with any Human. She savored the electrifying rush of every feather interlocking. Tsarena grazed Warda's back, patting her and whispering soothing affirmations with each touch. The hummingbird nodded, avoiding his beak from poking Tsarena.

"We came to warn you," Falisto cut in, breaking the warmth. "But we might be too late."

Kasey jumped in. "The Apiary, they're coming."

The soldier angled his head towards Kasey. "They're... coming?"

"We found them on another planet, a few light years from here," Kasey explained. "They'll be here soon."

The unintroduced Tayir nodded and turned to Tsarena and Tsoki, then to Falisto and Shamp. "You don't fear me?" he asked.

Three of the four exchanged looks, with Falisto scratching the Tayir's eyes with his glare. "I don't fear you," Falisto hissed. "I'm only here to know why your people killed mine." His claw instinctively drew from his paw and pierced a loose feather dropping to the floor. Falisto's nostrils flared and his eyes widened despite his pupils thinning like a snake's. Almost growling, he showed his teeth, grinding them as he narrowed his stare.

"I appreciate your honesty." The Tayir stepped forward. Falisto's claw held the feather. "General Azalia." The Tayir held his winged hand to where his heart probably was.

"Nice to meet you," Kasey said from behind. General Azalia didn't shift his gaze.

"Falisto Nima," he muttered.

"Nima," Azalia whispered the word almost as if it were taboo. "We never harmed your people." His voice was deep and commanded respect.

"So I've heard." Falisto's muscles stiffened, and his paws trembled.

"May I have your names?" The General turned away, now looking at the two Orchi and Venori.

"Shamp," she said. Her tendrils wrapped around her waist, a sign of fealty.

"Tsoki." He placed his hand over his chest and did a unique bow like a curtsy. Tsarena joined the motion.

"I would ask how you found this place, but I assume Warda informed you."

Warda stirred, a knot appearing like an Adam's Apple in her throat. She swallowed the mass, the sound traveling from her neck. "I'm sorry. They killed everyone in the colony, tortured us, and—"

"—Do not blame yourself," the General murmured. "They know where we planned to go. They were already here long before us." Warda looked up at him, her eyes filled with tears. He spoke again, "You are here now. That's all that matters."

Her body sank back, her shoulders slouching down and her breathing returning to normal.

"Is what you say true?" He turned to Kasey now.

"Yes," Kasey hummed. "They're coming."

Holding onto what Kasey assumed was his comms implant, the General commanded, "Get the front line and Orbital Defense Team." He waddled towards Falisto. "We can talk in a moment. Right now—Kasey, is it?—we have to deal with this."

Kasey pulled out his pad, showing images of the Apiary ship. "This is their ship," he said.

General Azalia sighed. "An ark ship." He held down one of his ears, linking to an ethereal voice Kasey could only make bits and pieces out of. "They're bringing a Queen."

Shamp's tendrils wiggled about. "A Queen?"

General Azalia started, "The Apiary have a Queen. Similar to other insects. When the Queen dies, they lose order."

"How fitting," Falisto cooed. "Bugs have a Queen. Squish them like any other bug."

"Is there a Queen here?" Kasey asked.

"There was," he said. "We killed her several years ago."

"Then how are they still here?" Tsoki asked.

"You saw their weapons," the General said. "They're primitive without their Queen." He wandered to a painting near Kasey, a meadow in twilight. "But they have numbers."

"So, literal bugs?" Falisto puffed up his chest.

"Only massive," General Azalia added. "We speculate they come from a highly oxygenated planet.”

"We think they’re on Rogue Planets,” Kasey explained. He looked to Shamp to jump in, she was the mastermind, after all.

Shamp brought the wiggling tendrils to her side. “They also have a virus through exploding rocks.”

The General chirped, “Maybe they’re more widespread than we thought.”

"Anything else about the bugs that makes them...” Tsoki paused. “... buggy?”

"You,” he said, pointing to Kasey and ignoring Tsoki. “I’ve never met one of you before. But I’ve heard of you.”

Kasey cocked his head. “Human?”

"Human,” he whispered the word, the sound rolling off his tongue. “You look similar to them.” He pointed to Tsoki. “An extra finger and different skin.”

Kasey’s face flushed and sweat dripped down his forehead. “What happened to the Travelers? Where are they?”

He paired a sigh and a shrug. “I don’t know.”

Kasey exhaled, resting back down from his tippy toes. As much as he wanted those answers, he knew the sad reality: he’d never know. Just like how he’d never learn why Musk Station was destroyed.

"Why are you helping us?” he asked. “GUM hates us. Destroyed Bustan and decimated our population.”

Falisto growled. “Well—”

"—We’re not GUM,” Kasey said, cutting off Falisto. “We’re PTF.”

"Sorry, I don’t know what that is.”

Tsarena smiled. “We’re the Peacekeeping Task Force.”

General Azalia did a slight chuckle. “The GU *hates* us.” He repeated it, almost as if this time they would understand him. “They declared war based on a lie. Why should I trust you?”

"Because I’m here,” Warda cooed. She sheathed her wings. “They saved me.”

General Azalia stared at her for a moment then went back to Kasey. “How do I know you won’t give our location to GUM?”

"They don't know we're here," Kasey said. "And we wouldn't come to warn you if we wanted to destroy you."

General Azalia nodded. "Let's get to work."

Chapter 42

General Azalia stood at the war table in front of the PTF members and Warda. Another Tayir next to him, General Batala, typed on a pad. She resembled a parrot, with her beak curved downward and painted with purple markings on her wings. Unlike other Tayirs, General Batala had a cybernetic enhancement with a mechanical eye. It made Falisto think of Benjo.

"What's the plan?" Falisto asked. He looked around the tent. The city, which had been called "the Sanctuary," didn't seem welcoming to him.

General Azalia scooped something up from a cart next to him. "We've been waiting, but I think it's time." Hundreds of milk-colored marbles poured out of his wing. "We use our secret weapon."

"Secret weapon?" Tsoki asked. He tied his hair back in a bun with curly strings sticking out from the sides.

General Azalia took a few steps. "We've been at war long enough to learn about a weakness." He double-tapped a screen, causing a tiny infographic to pop above the spheres. The group's converters struggled at first, but Falisto got the gist.

Falisto groaned. He couldn't help himself after reading the ridiculous secret weapon. "How is *this* a secret weapon?" His tone was sharp.

"It's abundant here," General Batala explained. Her blood-orange feathers cloaked her body, and she spun to the orbs. "And bugs hate it."

"Abundant doesn't mean strong." Falisto crossed his legs before rolling back into the chair. He dared to lean back, keeping one foot along the ground to keep the chair from tipping too far.

General Batala squawked. "It's toxic to them."

"And that's gonna work?" Falisto said incredulously. "Your secret weapon is just peppermint oil."

"It's not just a weapon," General Azalia said. "It's also a solution."

"To what?" Kasey asked.

"The Rupture." His wing moved above the crevice on the map. "If we cover it, they can't attack."

Tsarena cocked her head back. "But how does peppermint help? I have a friend who likes peppermint, but it doesn't fill holes to my knowledge."

General Batala swapped her stare from Falisto to Tsarena. "These bombs have a mixture of polymers to cover the Rupture's surface."

"How long has it been there?" Tsoki asked.

"Years," General Azalia said. "When we formed this colony it was already here. We covered the star with our Dyson Plates, built a city, and the Apiary attacked."

"Why have you not sealed it before?" Shamp asked.

"They break through any seal we place. We've sent blasts through the cracks, but they keep coming." He rubbed his wings together. "We need a seal that's toxic to them, something they can't fight."

"And that's peppermint oil? The things Humans use as candles?" Falisto asked again. He pointed his paw to the bomb. The milky substance seduced Falisto with its creamy consistency, but he remembered the contents.

"It's not that weird," Kasey said. "Psys eat raw fish without any worry. I can't do that."

"That's different," Falisto spat.

"How?"

Falisto stirred in his seat. His general answer would've been "because Humans are weak," but he didn't know if he still believed that. "Who knew one of the most poisonous things to Psys is also poisonous to the Apiary," Falisto muttered through gritted teeth.

"You're gonna be okay, right?" Tsoki asked.

"I just can't get any on my whiskers," Falisto explained. "Or face or paws."

"We actually want all of you here," General Azalia pointed to the floor. "With the Orbital Defense Team."

"What about overhead strikes from the ark?" Kasey asked. "Can't those Apiary planetside just attack us from above if they throw bombs high enough?"

General Batala moved closer to General Azalia, passing by him and coming into Kasey's view. "That's why I'm here," she said. "Our Orbital Defense uses our Dyson energy. It creates a barrier around the city."

Kasey pursed his lips. "And that protects from possible air strikes?"

"It does," General Batala said, her voice unconvincing to Falisto. "But there is a problem."

Tsarena replied, "What is it?"

"Our Orbital Offense System also uses Dyson energy."

"How is that a problem?" Shamp asked.

"Well," General Batala started, "it means we can't have both operational at the same time."

Falisto hummed. "So we protect the city, you protect the skies."

"I'm the General," she roared. "I make those calls."

"We wanna fight," Kasey said. "On the front lines."

"And *you* will," General Azalia proclaimed. He pointed one of his wing fingers to Kasey. "But the others can't."

Kasey blinked. "What?"

"You'll lead the team in the skies. Shamp, you'll be along the barriers."

"Skies?" Kasey marveled.

"I know you won't die from peppermint." He plucked an object from the table and levied it in front of Kasey. "You have experience flying?"

Kasey's face became ghastly white and turned stone cold. His fingers fidgeted, trembling along the pocket of his unitard. "You want me to fly?"

"No," General Azalia said. "I *need* you to fly."

"So, then what, it's just Kasey in the air and Shamp along the walls while we're with the Orbital Defense Team?" Tsarena asked. "That's crazy we can do more!"

"I'll be fine," Kasey said.

"I won't let him go alone," Tsoki interrupted. The passion in his voice caught even Falisto off guard.

"I don't have a ship for you," the General said.

"I'll go back for the Navigator." Tsoki leaned back and looked at Kasey while he spoke aloud. "Everyone wins."

General Azalia exhaled. "Fine, but I still need you here." He pointed to Tsarena.

"I have experience with these systems," she murmured. "It makes sense."

"I don't have any," Falisto uttered. "I can help with the perimeter." He turned to Shamp. "I'm coming with you."

"Fine," General Azalia said. "Kasey and Tsoki, in the skies. Falisto and Shamp, along the walls. Warda and Tsarena, inside of ODT managing the systems."

"Got it," Kasey said, followed by nods from everyone. "How big is the front line?"

"Small," he murmured. "Just under a hundred soldiers."

Falisto's eyes rolled out onto the floor. "Not even a full hundred?"

"We invested in science," General Azalia said. "That's how we've lived as long as we've had in the Sanctuary."

A nervous lump formed in his throat.

"Is there a contingency plan?" Shamp asked.

The General looked in her direction, cockeyed and shifting his weight to one talon. "Bunkers."

"Bunkers?" Tsoki asked. "How's that meant to help?"

"With all the copious energy we're getting," General Azalia said, tapping his talon. "We can power bunkers for decades."

The table exchanged looks for a moment before he spoke again. "We're going to bomb the Rupture in ten hours." General Azalia moved cream orbs back into the cart. "Dinner rations should be ready soon."

Kasey and the others sat at the same war table with a few civilian Tayirs bringing platters of food and drinks. "I know this isn't glamorous," General

Azalia started, "but I promised you I'd answer more questions." The table was dark stained wood, an item they took when they fled judging by the lack of trees on the planet. Each chair was plucked from a different era of art and craftsmanship, with Kasey's chair fit for a king and Falisto's a modern-day soldier.

Using a tendril, Shamp poked at the yellow food on her plate. It wiggled on the platter after a bit of a smack from her. "Is this edible?" Shamp asked. "I am doubtful it is compatible with everyone's biology."

"Mawz is a universal food," General Azalia said. "The drinks, however, are catered to you individually."

Before anyone took their first bite, Falisto started with questions. "What communication did you allegedly collect from Captain Bigon?"

"You're impatient," General Azalia chirped.

"Answer the question." Falisto used his claws to slice part of the mawz.

General Azalia wiped his beak with a hole-filled rag. "Luckily, you're not a soldier under my command." There was something sardonic about his voice. "Fortunately, I understand your passion."

"Can it," Falisto said. "Just tell me what happened."

"Do you know Captain Bigon?" he asked.

Warda sighed. "His mother was Captain Qiula."

The General's beak fell to the floor. "Observers guide her."

Falisto narrowed his eyes. "Tell me what you intercepted."

General Azalia brought forward his pad. After hitting a few screens and pressing a few buttons, an audio log swept across everyone's pads. "I couldn't understand the language," he explained. "Not at first. I have a transcript of it on the side."

Falisto snatched his pad from his waist, turning the volume to the maximum level and reading the transcript along with it.

Unknown Voice: Are the devices placed?

Captain Bigon: Yes, they are.

Unknown Voice: And what of Qiula?

Captain Bigon: She's still on the ship. I got a way to lead her on the target ship, right above the Tayir homeworld, as planned.

Unknown Voice: Good. Soon, our plan will be coming to a close.

Captain Bigon: What of the boy?

Unknown Voice: If he dies, that's a bonus. If not, he won't be able to salvage any power back.

Captain Bigon: Good. Watch for the fireworks.

The audio cut. Falisto's paws gripped the pad so tightly he could've sworn he added new cracks to the device. "How do I know this is real?" Falisto shouted.

"You'll have to just trust us, I'm afraid," the General said.

"Where did you get this? How did you get this?"

"That I do not know. It is in our datasets and assets, collected by someone before the destruction of Bustan."

Falisto's claws scratched the bottom of the pad. He knew it was real. Ever since Warda told him he'd replayed details, small but important details about Bigon he hadn't picked up. The way he conveniently planned the trip's course, how hard he campaigned for a war against the Tayirs, how he, of all Psys, benefited from his mother's death.

The table exchanged looks with each other. Falisto looked to Kasey who was trying to find the words, something to wipe away the crashing down of his world. "Falisto..." Kasey said.

Without a response, Falisto bolted from the table to just outside the tent. Kasey pushed out his chair, but Shamp, with her mawz-stained tendril, stopped him. "Give him some space."

* * *

Kasey

The conversation turned light when Falisto returned. No one acknowledged the dried corners of his eyes or how he frequently blinked or looked to the ground. In fairness, he didn't either. Instead, he powered through the conversation. They talked about simple things: culture of the Tayirs before the wars, humanity's story, and their own lives. General Batala and

Tsarena swapped stories about the Observers, General Azalia and Warda discussed old Tayir books from their favorite authors, Tsoki and Kasey got closer together, and Shamp and Falisto mourned Drake again. For a minute, it was as if the war he unknowingly entered had come to an end. The war that he brought to him and his team.

"So, why this planet?" Shamp asked. "This planet does not appear the most hospitable."

General Azalia's face darkened. He sipped something from his mug, then craned his head up to the stars. "When we found the Apiary we begged for help from the GU." He relived the moments he was recalling, the pain in his voice, the scars burning with old pain. "When it became clear they wouldn't help, we sent three ships out for another type of settlement and sent signals for help to all directions."

"And this is one of the planets?"

"Yes," he said. "There's also Janina, our homeworld Bustan, and this one, ir."

"So there could be more of you?" Tsarena asked.

"Could be," Warda beamed.

"Not likely," General Azalia said.

Warda's elated face melted into a horrified expression. "Why's that?"

General Azalia finished off his beverage and signaled for another. "We've sent our ships, unmanned ships, looking for other Tayirs. We never found anyone. Not even Janina."

"That's what those were on Kyros?" Kasey asked.

"But those attacked people," Falisto fired.

General Azalia put down his food. "Some of our ships got lost. They need weapons to destroy debris so we equipped them."

"Well that solves one mystery," Kasey said. "Boring but it makes sense."

"Anything else?" General Azalia asked.

"That Dyson Plate," Kasey started, "how's that working?"

"It's three large solar panels," he explained. "It takes the energy and gives us it for our technology and weapons. As you can tell, a consequence is that we do not receive light on our angle of the planet. So, we have to adapt to temperature and artificial means of light."

"The Apiary need it for their ship to reach the speeds they want." Warda cracked her neck. "They could barely go faster than light with the fuel they had on Porygar."

"Still can't believe GU doesn't have this tech yet," Kasey marveled.

"I'm sure they do," Tsoki murmured. "But using it would cut so many jobs from the energy departments."

"But think of the tech we could have if we used it," Kasey defended.

"I'm on your side," Tsoki retorted. "I think we should have it."

"It is almost too much," Shamp said.

"It can be," General Azalia said. "We don't need it operational again for another century before we run out of reserves."

"What would we utilize it for? We would have an overabundance." Shamp licked the end of one of her tendrils.

Tsarena put down her fork. "I have three questions."

"Go ahead," General Batala said, filling in for Azalia who was mid-sip.

"Why do you think the GU refused to listen? Warda said you sent messages and reports but they were ignored."

General Azalia put down his cup. "We have enemies," he explained. "Jasyx, for one, fear the Observers. We're heretics to them. We denied the attack on the Nima ship because we didn't do it." Falisto winced. "What's your second question?"

"What do the Apiary want? On Porygar that ship looked like it was supposed to go across the galaxy. Why are they here?"

General Azalia and Batala shared a glance. "If what we speculate is correct," General Batala started, "these Apiary far exceed the population on our homeworld."

"What does that mean?" Kasey asked.

"She means," General Azalia started, "this planet is home to most of the Apiary that we have discovered. This entire planet is filled with cracks where these things crawl out. If the ship is an ark ship, the goal is probably to go somewhere else."

Tsarena nodded.

"Your third question?" General Batala asked.

Tsarena swallowed the mawz in her mouth. "Have you ever thought about frying this?"

Chapter 43

Falisto

The ringing from the bell tower didn't wake Falisto. Neither did the Tayirs rushing out of the barracks nor the whizzing bullets overhead. What *did* wake Falisto was Kasey's shoves.

Warda waddled over to Falisto. "Get up!"

Falisto groaned, his eyes difficult to keep open.

"There's more," Warda said. Her fingers gripped the pad with such ferocity it should've split it in two. "More than we expected."

"How much more?" Falisto asked, hiding a yawn with his arm.

She flashed the image.

It was like a straight cup of coffee that made his hair stand up. "Stay on our comms. General Azalia and Batala have direct ones with us."

He slid into his unitard. With his Slart holstered, he and the others climbed up the stairs, following the sirens wailing above. They came to a crossroads, with three different paths for them to take. Almost with an unspoken seriousness, they looked at each other and nodded.

"Be safe," Kasey yelled over the symphony of sirens.

"Don't drop them until my count!" General Azalia barked. Shamp and Falisto were among a long line of foot soldiers rendered flightless. Some had missing wings, others were mere hatchlings, too young to hold a gun the right way, let alone fire it.

Falisto, using his scope, zoomed in on the legion in the sky passing over the army of bugs. Tayir soldiers approached the Rupture, each gripping their bomb with warm peppermint oil-polymer solution splashing around. They dipped under projectiles, with some hitting it head-on with their armor.

"I don't think this is gonna work," Falisto muttered under his breath, just loud enough so Shamp could hear.

"*Fifteen seconds.*" General Azalia worried, his voice losing that chirp Falisto hated.

In the sky, Tsoki and Kasey soared ahead of the Tayirs, levying bullets into the bugs, disregarding the countdown. Their ships merely bounced spears and javelins thrown at them. It didn't stop the Apiary. The two PTF neared the Rupture, with Falisto mouthing a countdown. *One, two, three.*

"*Now!*" General Azalia ordered.

Countless spheres of peppermint oil cascaded down like a blizzard in a tundra of ash. Bombs released simultaneously, with a few a moment or so faster. The bombs were meant to land on the edges of the Rupture, spilling oil deep into the ground and crystallizing a ceiling. The polymer followed the peppermint's journey, and eventually connected with others at the end. Apiaries hit by blasts burned as if peppermint were an acid melting away their skin and shells.

Shortly after contact, polymer chains foamed around the crack. Bubbles from one another combined to form solid material, reaching over the hole in the planet and bridging the gap. They condensed around the central crack most Apiary crawled out from, cutting several in half at the molecular level, turning it into a frayed cotton ball of peppermint-flavored styrofoam.

Then, the second wave of Tayir with primarily polymer-focused bombs came. They flew through the air a few kilometers behind the others and tossed explosives indiscriminately. The covering hardened the milky base, solidifying like hot glue with a lime tint.

The hint of peppermint Falisto got earlier became an inescapable odor settling into the threads of nanotechnology and fibers in his unitard. Even several kilometers away the stench had spread through the ground, traveling across the soil and towards the city.

A few Apiary attempted to climb up the Rupture still, digging at and gnawing the top, but as quickly as they chewed, they burned from the poison, their bodies raining down the depths.

"It's working," Falisto marveled. His eyes, golden and massive, watched the onslaught, and his flat ears listened to the sounds of the chew-and-fall over the comms. For whatever reason, the insects continued to eat at the base despite seeing one another collapse to their death. He grinned and resumed shooting.

* * *

Tsarena

Tsarena and Warda stood in the ODT, a few meters away from the war table. Pieces and markers sprawled across the map, shaken into loose piles representing the plan. Tsarena stared into an array of screens in front of her. Although most mirrored dark patches of space where cosmic rays lived, a few focused on other vantage points. Feeds from Tayir ships and the Navigator, as well as several feeds attached to the perimeter, populated the displays. The radars next to her would scream if someone—even non-Apiary—dared to enter the airspace.

From an engineering standpoint, the city impressed Tsarena. Four cannons served as the city's defense. Rudimentary in some ways, the system harnessed energy transferred from Dyson Plates into the cannons. In turn, they'd shoot highly concentrated particle beams. Thin lasers that, to the naked eye, were less exciting than a laser pointer. Unlike a laser pointer, this beam contained a plethora of radiation and heat, searing and breaking apart anything in its path.

"How are the cannons?" General Batala asked.

Warda spoke to the pad. *"We can switch to them now."*

"Wait," she said. *"I don't want us to switch off our shield just yet."*

"Kasey," Tsarena said. *"How's it up there?"* She peered at his visual from his ship's camera.

"Good," he said aboard the Tayir ship. *"This ship reacts to my actual*

movements like it's listening to my body."

"*Peppermint bombs,*" Tsoki laughed. "*I can't believe it.*"

"*Leave it to an advanced species beyond our capabilities, coming up with new ways to kill bugs,*" Kasey said.

"*How does it look up there?*" Shamp asked. "*From where Falisto and I are at, it appears successful.*"

"*The polymer bombs worked.*" Tsarena flipped through feeds. A sheet of peppermint material covered the Rupture. Although not perfect, it hardened enough that bullets couldn't pierce through it, though some tried judging by the pecks and bumps along the surface.

"*We're taking out the remaining ones,*" Falisto said. "*They can't hide now.*"

"*This was easy,*" Shamp whispered. "*Too easy.*"

Tsoki muttered, "*We know that ship's on the way.*"

"*I hope it doesn't have any surprises,*" Tsarena flicked back to other screens.

"*This is going to take a while,*" Shamp proclaimed. "*They really have numbers.*"

"*They out-manned the Tayirs pretty abundantly,*" Kasey said. "*Ten to one, and that's being generous.*"

Tsarena flipped to a feed coming from a soldier with General Azalia. An additional rain of peppermint oil solution drizzled down from canisters Tayirs carried in satchels around their armor. Liquid clung to the ground, swimming into the soil and painting a soft white over the diluted gray. The dusting of a third round and last remains of the bombs left few targets for Shamp and Falisto to take down.

"*We're about to head back,*" General Azalia said, dropping the final bomb over the newly sealed ground.

Before Tsarena could speak, sirens wailed from next to her with lights flashing every shade of red. Scarlet. Rose. Cherry. "*Wait, something's happening,*" Tsarena shouted. Her voice was shrill and she shook her head back to move her dangling curls behind her. "*Something's here!*"

General Batala spoke, "*Azalia, get out of there!*"

General Azalia yelled back, "*Copy that, we'll begin heading—*"

A ray of red energy shot down from the sky, piercing through the Tayirs along the Rupture and even the Apiary underneath the polymer layer. They disintegrated into nothing more than smoke, and the camera feeds cut.

"*Fall back!*" General Batala yelled.

Panicked, Tsarena swapped back to Kasey's feed. From the air, Kasey zoomed towards the overhead ship. Obsidian and raven in color, the ark covered most of the sky and cast a darker shadow over the Rupture and Tayirs through sparse moonlight.

From the center of the ship, a second boiling red beam jolted down, piercing another crater in the peppermint and polymer layer. Pieces of the top coat burnt instantly, and fire rampaged along the Rupture spreading like gasoline. More Apiary, burnt from either peppermint or the beam, crawled up like zombies with their bodies ignited and deformed.

Kasey shot at the crisped insects. "*Bastards!*"

Tsoki swooped towards the Tayirs soaring away. "*I'm gonna get the injured ones I can!*" Dashing through fire harpoons and flaming spears, Tsoki flung open the Navigator door. A flood of Tayirs piled in. One, in an attempt to reach the Navigator, received a spear to the throat and dragged the Navigator from its high altitude before Tsoki shook him off.

Tsarena couldn't move her body. Instead, her hollow eyes could only watch the sky in both awe and horror. Another red flash punctured the defensive line, spreading this time towards the shielded Sanctuary. Energy in a dome shape repelled the beam, absorbing portions of it while riposting a chunk. The craft, as if alive, grew enraged at the defense, and fired a series of rockets at the crevice. Explosions increased its length, chipping away at the ground, even if it meant killing Apiary in the process. What remained of the polymer base struggled to meander through the soil, until it puttered out. The mothership inched closer to the city, flickering off its beam like an effortless spotlight.

General Batala commanded, "*Switch to offense and fire the cannons!*" Tsarena shook herself. Next to her were the buttons, one meant to activate defense, the other meant to activate offense. She slapped the button. The entire Sanctuary responded with a groan so loud it reverberated through the building, moving the dust and loose pebbles on the ground.

"Get a good aim!" Warda cried.

"Where do I aim?" Tsarena said.

The cannons groaned, loud enough that the screeching metal ate away at Tsarena's ears. "Where do I aim?!" she shouted. Her heart beat out of her chest. A cold sweat broke her connection to her body.

Warda didn't answer, instead yelling, "Just shoot it!"

Tsarena locked on the center of the ship as it readied another blast. Cursing, Tsarena hit the button. Four cannons shot condensed particle beams at the ark. The ship responded with a wave of bright red fire, spewing pieces of the ship and breaking off like a chunk of a boulder. Avalanching down, the pieces of the Apiary ship fell on Tayirs still in range.

Just as the ark entered the atmosphere, it retreated, smothering the fires in the airless void above them. It split into pieces, with vines between three large chunks forming as it left space. Tsarena could only gasp as the radars picked up hundreds of tiny ships splintering off the ark ship, heading straight for the city.

Chapter 44

Kasey

Kasey twitched his fingers, commanding the craft to chase a slew of ships spilling from the ark and retreating into space. Tiny vessels shot rockets and blasts from manta ray-shaped wings. Scattering, they split in every direction, unleashing their barrage of ammo into fleeing Tayirs. Their bodies catapulted to the ground like pellets while others burst midair.

"*They're everywhere!*" Tsoki cried.

"*Tsoki, there's still a lot coming from space!*" Kasey rotated the ship. "*On your six!*"

Tsoki's Navigator veered away and sent a defensive rocket backward. It whizzed through the air, intercepting an alien rocket and exploding into a puff of green-gray smoke.

"*Kasey, Tsoki,*" General Batala's voice chirped. "*The Queen is somewhere!*"

Kasey moved the ship towards the cloudless sky. "*I doubt they'd send her on one of those ships.*"

Outside the atmosphere, the ark withdrew further. Sliced wires, shattered metal plating, and sundered escape pods leaked out from holes in the ship where the energy cannons pierced with the particle beam. Remnants formed a breadcrumb trail followed by charcoal smoke left from the suffocated fire.

"*Can you fire another blast?*" Kasey propelled the ship higher, leaving behind the planet's gravity.

"*We need to switch to defensive measures or the Apiary will kill everyone!*" Tsarena's voice echoed.

Kasey's forearms stuck to the edges of the ship as he hung in space. The ash-colored planet below him didn't have the same ethereal blue that Mars or Earth did. It didn't look much like a home but it was someone's. The system beeped a warning Kasey already knew: this one Tayir ship couldn't surmount the behemoth ark ship. Even though it limped away in space, severed into several smaller sections, two polymer bombs wouldn't do it. But, the Queen was still there, and Kasey intended to kill her.

"*Don't shoot it anymore*," Kasey's voice thundered. "*I'm gonna go after the Queen.*" Already hearing the naysayers, he disconnected from the comms and went forward.

The odds were stacked against him: a single-man invasion of an ark ship sounded about as fruitful as negotiations between a Hyoose Psys and Nima Psys. But odds weren't ever in Kasey's favor.

The ark decelerated the further it distanced itself from the planet. Curiously, it approached a nearby moon. It entered its orbit, barreling around slowly in a predictable arc, whilst sliced into three large pieces. Loose metal and wires fell out from each portion. That's when the chain of nanobots began healing the ship. They pulled together wires so small Kasey wasn't even sure they were actually there until he got closer. Albeit slowly, the three pieces magnetized one another, with the centerpiece calling on its two sister sections to reform into one being. *That's how it made it back from Porygar, it heals.* Kasey scanned the ark using the Tayir ship, looking for some indication where the Queen was.

He reconnected to the comms. "*I'm gonna find where the Queen is hiding,*" he said.

Tsoki was the first to respond. "*Kasey, stop! Don't go in there alone!*"

"*It's suicide!*" Falisto echoed.

"*Don't do it!*" Tsarena cried.

"*Kasey...*" Warda said.

"*Shamp's comm isn't working as well but she—*"

"*—Kasey do not go!*" her voice, painted with static and feedback, pierced his ears.

"*Guys,*" Kasey started, "*I'm gonna be fine. It looks like they're keeping the*

Queen here with only a few soldiers."

"*Even if it's just you and the Queen you can't go alone. All those ships could come back at any time.*"

"*Don't worry,*" he said, trying to calm his nerves. "*I'll see you all soon.*" With a click the call disconnected and he opened a private channel with Tsoki.

"*When this is over,*" Kasey said, "*can we take a break from PTF? A vacation?*"

Silence followed, with Kasey tapping his knee as he approached the ark. His tongue traced his teeth, and blood pumped ferociously through his veins.

"*Where to?*" Tsoki asked.

Kasey exhaled the concern that he'd gone too far. "*I hear Poseidon's got surfing.*"

"*Never been.*"

"*I'll take you.*"

He swapped comms off.

A positive to the ark ship having entire chunks missing meant Kasey didn't struggle to find an entry point. All he did, was weave through some debris left by parts the nanobots hadn't cleaned up yet. He wiggled inside, the Tayir ship practically invisible as it hid behind bits of metal orbiting the moon. It was like the ship was meant to break to absorb the damage. Like a malleable piece of metal that could serve many functions if beaten right.

The entry point was between a large hallway of sorts, with one door sealed tightly and, from Kasey's deductions, still pressurized. His suit came with a slight head covering that could oxygenate him for a few seconds, but not long enough for him to dilly-dally. But the inside had to be breathable, or, at the very least, manageable.

With the ship as close to the door as possible and nestled between two portions where vines hadn't reached out from, Kasey headed to the door. It hissed air out in front of him. The chamber sprayed his suit and body with some ventilation. He was still floating in zero-g, in the mist in the airlock.

Gravity slammed him to the ground, landing him on his back. Kasey groaned. The mask that covered his head and face as part of the unitard didn't have any cracks so it was a win in his book even if the slam came with pain. The next door opened to the main shard where he was met with total darkness.

Of course. He slipped in, drawing his Slart and using the light. A white glow illuminated the floor, a murky purple and gray combination mixed with rocks from Porygar. Kasey held up his pad and re-scanned the area, also using it as a secondary light. Pads were powerful, especially the military-grade ones. But they couldn't map alien structures.

Rocks, all condensed into torpedo-like missiles, filled the ship. Kasey frowned, but his questions only multiplied as he continued down the hall. No single light, dancing flame, or window appeared. Everything was just... dark. Part of him wanted the alien bugs to have something like a hive nest or super advanced technology he'd seen in science fiction films. But, by all accounts, this was normal, and that terrified him.

He passed writings and paintings strikingly similar to those on Planet Exo, and more loose rocks laid in suspension. Their colors ranged from bright indigo to deep violet, like the rocks from Porygar when he brought his light to them. As he touched them, they darkened, almost reacting to heat from his suit's fingertips.

Sounds echoed ahead of him. Countless footsteps slapping the ground and coming closer. Kasey gulped. He determined the source: a giant ant hurling towards him at enormous speed.

Switching to lethal mode, Kasey dove to the side and shot in the general direction. The beast shrieked in pain, with blood slapping the ground. It let out a few cries but succumbed. Kasey crept to the body, flashing his Slart of it.

This Apiary didn't seem like the others. It certainly didn't seem regal, but Kasey wasn't sure what a regal insect would look like. This one *did*, however, have armor in addition to its body's exoskeleton. Its body reverberated, loose neurons making twitches come out. Some twisted part of Kasey wanted to scoop up the gun, a jade green with a thick trigger that didn't have the same musket quality the primitive ones used on Hadiqa. He resisted the urge but found himself looking back as he continued.

Kasey passed through rooms filled with rocks like gravel. Absent were any sleeping quarters, mess hall, med bay, or anything for what Kasey assumed would be on an ark ship. Hell, he couldn't even find suspension pods or something similar. But what he did find, made him realize just how feudal of a society the Apiary were: a throne room.

Fitting, Kasey chuckled to himself. Inside this section of the ship, ceilings went high like a cathedral, and paintings Kasey couldn't fully discern covered the walls. Columns, both decorative and necessary, separated a raised platform with a singular chair. Notably, however, there were *no* rocks filled with the virus. Instead, this room was full of nothing but things of value. Heat signatures hadn't picked up anything in this part of the ship either.

The thought of an advanced species—or at the very least—powerful species creating something so barbaric and nearly juvenile made Kasey want to crawl out of his skin. This was an ark ship so hauntingly empty it was like a spectral hand scratched him with nails tougher than a Psys. He took a step closer to the throne, his footsteps bouncing off the walls.

Then he heard a voice.

Chapter 45

Benjo

Benjo hated Kyros' lighting. No such thing as a "soft" white light on Kyros, it was always harsh and unforgiving. Autonomously, he shielded his eyes with his hand. That made him realize he actually *had* a hand. A pleasant change from his last moment of lucidity.

"He's awake!"

Benjo groaned, pain emanating in every part of his body. Pain wasn't usually a good sign, but becoming a triple amputee in the backseat of a Navigator wasn't usually a good source of treatment. The pain meant he *had* something. "This isn't my arm?"

Amber's ginger touch quickened his heart monitor. He wiggled his toes—or rather, his new toes—waiting for the nerves to respond to his commands. Slow, at first, but they listened. The fingers did the same, twitching with a slight nudge from his brain after a delay. "Did I get completely rebuilt?"

Benjo followed Amber's warmth from her bronze hand. Half-hoping he had enhanced eyes, Benjo let the light gnaw at his face, unprotected by his hand. Amber eclipsed it, the light haloing around her figure. Her blonde hair, back to one holistic blonde, shined a shade of platinum he could've sworn she'd sworn off.

"I'm right here," she soothed. She hushed him, giving a few gentle pats. "Don't worry, I'm right here."

Benjo went to wipe his eyes, but his arms resisted. He'd just had them in front of his face, now they were giving him trouble? He shivered, a chill scratching the top of his head. He sent his arm to investigate, but it was still anchored to the bed. In the distance, he caught a glimpse of his reflection along a metal plate. Against his will, he'd gotten a buzz cut.

"How long was I out?" he asked. Although physically unwell, his brain functioned fine. Hell, better than fine. But the rest of his body stiffened—not in the way people have stiff knees in the morning—stiff in that he couldn't *actually* move them without an internal struggle. Intensive reconstructive surgery wasn't something Benjo ever did, and his body reminded him of that.

"Two days." Her voice cracked with uncertainty, almost as if she'd lost count. Purple bags sunk beneath her eyes, and her nails were noticeably short, jagged with bite marks. She was just as beautiful, but he'd seen sleep deprivation signs.

Benjo winced and his shoulder twitched. Flesh still covered his hand, so that was good. His fingers moved better than the metal counterparts. "What happened?"

"Kasey cut off your parts, remember?" She sat on the bed, moving the covers to the side.

"I do." Benjo coughed, his lungs trying to keep up with the weight of the metal. "But, I meant after coming here."

"They traded your parts," Amber said. "Gave you some new ones."

"But what about Kasey and the others?"

Amber turned back to a TV dangling along the wall. A ginger-haired news reporter interviewed a shy woman. "They found them," Amber said with a smile. A woman—Mahina—flashed on the screen. Various bandages swaddled Mahina's body parts, wrapping in different directions.

"What happened on Porygar?" the reporter asked. Without much respect, the journalist shoved the microphone in the girl's face.

"Can you turn that up?" Benjo asked. He shifted in the hospital bed, his body beginning to make peace with the titanium. Amber flicked the volume button.

Mahina spoke low, the pandemonium transforming her voice into a whisper. The lone microphone became an array, each mic fighting off other mics jabbing at her.

"What happened?" the reporter asked again, this time almost accusing her as if she decided to go missing.

Mahina looked into the camera and stared into Benjo's eyes through the lens. "We were abducted."

"By whom? By what?"

Before she could answer, a tall man dressed in black pinched her arm and answered for her. "No more questions." The colonists rushed them off, all guided in different directions with reporters following and shouting halfheartedly.

"Those guys looked like military—not a branch I've seen, though." Benjo turned towards a table next to him where a glass of water rested. Using his new hand, he plucked it, accidentally shattering it apart with two fingers.

Amber's eyes bulged. "Yeah, you're gonna need physical therapy."

A knock at the door caught their attention. Benjo exchanged looks with Amber. "Were you expecting someone?" he asked.

"No," she said with a puzzled look. "I'll see who it is." She rose from the end of the bed and approached the door. She peeled it back slowly.

"Oh, Sola," Amber exhaled. "It's just Sola." The slow movement sped up, becoming a yank.

"You're awake." Benjo coughed.

Sola clutched two things: a hand of a taller woman next to her, and a stuffed sheep. "You're Benjo, right?" the woman asked. Her skin was tawny like Sola's, but her hair dangled in far less concentrated curls.

"I am."

"I'm Lulu," she said. "I came to you, per request."

"Request?" Benjo's eyes narrowed and his mouth hung open. "Who—" he stopped himself. "Kasey."

Lulu nodded back. "Bingo."

"Where is he?"

She looked up and eyed the doctors in the distance of the room, too busy studying something on a microscope. Cupping her hand and coming to his ear, Lulu whispered, "I don't know if we should talk here. They're taking the colonists away."

Benjo didn't respond immediately with words, but rather a slight nod.

"I'll tell you more but we have to go," she explained.

"Excuse me miss!" one of the Jasyx doctors shouted. Its eyes blinked rapidly as it crab walked towards them. Amber quickly intervened, jumping to the Jasyx's attention.

"*The Irene* got impounded," Lulu said. "Read the note."

"Are you family?" the Jasyx spat, pointing to Lulu and Sola, ignoring Amber haphazardly waving her arms.

"They are," Benjo assured. "They can stay."

"Sir, we have rules, not for your safety but for theirs. If you aren't family you can't be here. Please leave," the Jasyx said to Lulu.

"Fine, just let me give my *family* a hug." With an unusually tight hug, Benjo's skin quivered from crinkled portions of a paper note sliding down his upper back.

The note may as well have been an essay given how detailed the instructions were. First, leave the hospital, second, meet at a street by the docks, third, escape Kyros aboard *the Irene*. Unfortunately, no details explained how they would do this. Benjo had to improvise.

During rounds, a nurse with pink hair, short and curly, wandered into his room at his request. Benjo distracted her with questions, a mix of standard questions and creative ones to keep her occupied ranging from philosophical "what is the meaning of life" to the mundane "are there any side effects with new parts?" Amber had an opening to disable the security in his room, which, to his chagrin, was quite robust for a triple amputee.

When the nurse left, Amber slid back in, got their temporary IDs and a change of clothes, and bolted out. Benjo didn't know how surveilled they were, but judging by the additional host of guards outside he figured it was more than the average GU citizen.

"You got your original scanner?" Amber asked, already out of the hospital.

Benjo checked his pocket anyway. "I do," he paused, "Why are we going this way?"

"It's quick!"

The hospital on Panel C equipped itself with the inner pipes of Kyros. Such an area was off-limits for good reason: getting electrocuted was just as easy as stepping on a crack. Pipes delivered everything from water to waste, nanotechnology to electricity, and everything in between. It made for an excellent maze, albeit a deadly one with electrical components close by, waiting for a Hybrid to step on it.

Benjo leaped onto blue and green pipes, jumped over red and yellow ones, and took short breaks on the whites.

"I feel like a kid," Benjo laughed. "Like leapfrog."

"Yeah, except if you die here you die for good," she fired back.

Benjo shook his head. "The note said to meet outside near the street, how far are we?"

"Not terribly far," she said. She ducked under some overhead pipes that were purple and black.

Benjo exhaled. "I didn't think I'd become a fugitive the second I woke up."

"It sounds to me like Kasey's harboring a fugitive."

"I wouldn't put it past him." Benjo laughed. "But I'm sure there's more to it. What happened on Porygar?"

Before she could answer, their tunnel ended with Lulu's car waiting with Sola in the backseat. "This way!" Lulu howled.

Benjo shrugged, then immediately piled into the back with Amber and Sola. Lulu caught the attention of a soldier who recognized either the escaped hospital patient or the stolen car.

"Eek!" Lulu shouted. "Sorry!" Slamming on the pedal, they blasted away. "Buckle up!" Lulu commanded. Using the throttle, she flung forward, weaving out of traffic and leaving the pipes in a trail of dust.

"You drive like you're crazy!" Sola shouted with her eyes closed. She screamed with each minor movement, the seat belt crossing her stomach and gluing her to the car.

"It's about to be bumpier." Lulu's foot slammed the accelerator. Inertia shot Benjo and Amber into their seats, the strain choking Benjo.

"She's better than you at driving at least," Amber said to Benjo.

Cockeyed, he shook his head no. "Just cause I don't speed doesn't make me a bad driver."

"We're only a few minutes away," Lulu yelled. "Almost at *the Irene*."

Sola squeezed Benjo's hand, her entire palm fitting around two of his fingers. A speckle of guilt, mixed with equal portions of sadness and regret, filled Benjo's heart. Fear dripped from Sola's eyes, but when she wrapped her fingers tighter around Benjo, some of that fear went away. If it were up to him, she would've bled out on Porygar, holding only onto the paw of the stuffed sheep for comfort. *Kasey was right to save her.*

"That was a rush." Lulu had a sinister grin, curved upwards and her eyebrows narrowed.

"Will someone tell me what the hell I missed on Porygar?" Benjo asked.

Lulu made a silent glance at Amber in the rear-view mirror. "Do you want me to tell him or do you?"

Amber sighed. "Better from you."

The PTF ring of *the Irene* was smaller than Benjo remembered. Guarding it was a singular man. His curly hair was short, and he had three piercings, all along his nose. He smacked bubblegum in his mouth, blowing little balloons of air and popping them with a chomp.

"Tunde," Lulu shouted.

He squinted and put a hand over his eyes like a visor. "Lulu?"

"Yep," she said.

"I didn't realize they found the colony." His voice was a complicated mix of excitement and nervousness.

"I need a favor," Lulu said.

Tunde frowned. "That's the first thing you say to someone after going missing for weeks?" Now his voice teetered to nervousness.

Lulu sighed. "Before I say it," she began, "I'm cashing in my one-time redemption of 'you owe me.'"

His eyes widened. "Must be pretty serious."

"Yeah, I need you to let us go on *the Irene*."

Tunde's face turned to stone but cracked with a laugh. When no one in the group changed expressions the stone face returned. "You're not serious?" he asked, his chewing gum barely hanging in his mouth.

"I am," she said.

"That's, like, mega illegal."

"We're PTF, that's the PTF ring," Benjo said. He tried to speak with authority, show Tunde that he at least embodied the role of belonging on *the Irene.*

Amber levied her Slart. "See?"

Tunde backed away. "Still, I was given strict orders."

"And we're giving stricter orders," Benjo said.

He raised an eyebrow. "I can't just let you on *the Irene.*"

"We need to leave," Amber said. "Please, we don't want any trouble."

"Who said anything about trouble?" Tunde's fingers danced along his pistol on his belt.

Benjo drew his Slart and shot him in the shoulder with a tranquilizer. Tunde looked at his injury with the vial draining into his body. "Oh God—"

Using only his metal arm, Benjo shielded Tunde from his fall, gently lowering him to the ground. "Sorry, PTF needs us." Benjo carried the body back to the stand. "Okay, now all we need is to get on the ship and figure out where they went."

"Just sent it to your pad."

A smile crept across Benjo's face. "You're amazing."

"When you leave, you probably wanna just straight FTL out." Lulu turned back now, holding onto Sola's hand. As Lulu jogged to the car, Sola stood still, spinning a tad with her sheep in her hands.

"Be safe," she said. "Tell the bird lady thank you."

With a nod, Benjo and Amber entered the PTF ring. "Get your husband and get out of Kyros. Something's not right."

Chapter 46

Kasey

From all directions, the voice boomed, "You should not have come here." The high pitch carried a regal authority, and a shiver crawled up Kasey's spine. It made his teeth chatter and fingers twitch. Though he could not see it, Kasey felt eyes puncturing his skin like daggers from somewhere in the room. Someone—something—was here. Watching him.

The voice exploded again, repeating the line, this time with more ferocity. "You should not have come here."

Kasey's mouth dried. He swallowed, finding his voice. "Who are you?" he said, while in a turning motion, hoping he'd make contact with the disembodied voice.

It answered, this time from a more defined direction, "I am Queen Fraxay Gol Ruchs, leader of prisons FP-131, FP-144, FP-145, and now FP-291."

Kasey brought his Slart to his chest. Those combinations of numbers and letters reminded him of exoplanet designations. Kasey narrowed his eyebrow. He glared in the direction he thought where the eyes were stabbing him from. "Those the planets you're on?"

The Queen uttered a sound that invited goosebumps to cover Kasey's body like scales. "Yes. Prisons."

"Didn't know they made Queens for that," Kasey shouted. He waited for a retort of some sort but it never came.

"I have no quarrel with you."

Kasey tightened his grip. "I find that hard to believe."

There was a pause. Panning his Slart, Kasey expected to find some sort of breeding ground with boils of insect larvae or honeycombed sections with various overgrown bugs. But the ship was empty, except a missing piece of metal here or there.

Kasey shouted again, "What do you want?"

There was a moment of silence before the clicking and clacking of the mouth parts uttered in a thunderous voice a singular word: "Revenge."

Kasey's finger hovered over the trigger. Revenge sounded like a ruse. Revenge was reserved for someone who was wronged. A way to establish equilibrium, not a justification for genocide. "On who?"

"The Watchers."

He stopped turning and focused on a thought. *The Watchers?* That sounded like a comical villain organization. "Who're the Watchers?"

"You do not know them." The unseen bug licked its teeth, the sound of saliva coating each tooth whistling in the echo chamber. "Yet."

That didn't sit right with Kasey. "Why don't you talk to me face to face?"

The alien laughed. "I have not conversed with another being in years."

This made Kasey raise an eyebrow. Come to think of it, he didn't recall any Apiary saying anything to him or others. He thought back to General Azalia's statement that the Queen was the intelligence. "Apiary don't talk much?"

"No, we do not. I give commands, they listen."

Like pets. It dawned on Kasey, a thought that he hadn't realized until that very moment. The Apiary couldn't act on free will because they were acting on instinct—orders from their master. "Are you the only sentient one?"

A deafening pause told Kasey the answer was yes.

Squelching from slime rubbing against the metal floor made Kasey flinch, his ears practically caving in on themselves to avoid the horrid sound accompanying the putrid smell. Kasey clutched his Slart as a figure obscured the striking light. Hunched over, the Apiary crept forward. Dormant wings rested on her like a hunchback and thin bristles covered her limbs. Her wings had perforations, microscopic holes with the color unevenly spread. Bronze painted across her outer shell, similar to Amber's arms. Six appendages shot out of the ant-like body, with her teeth slicked down from a wash of her tongue. Patterned fabric covered parts of her body, weird shapes that told a story somewhere between the threads sewn together by one of her non-sentient servants.

"My species," she began, her voice no longer echoing, "will go extinct."

Kasey's finger left the trigger, the word "extinct" practically pulling it off. For a moment, the Queen wasn't a killer bug, slaughtering the lives of innocents. She was just trying to survive. Up close, her eyes filled with sorrow and burden, and the mantle of responsibility she wore degenerated her body into the shriveled mass it became.

"You're killing the Tayirs." Kasey shook off the unnerving tingle prickling his body. "If you kill them, *they* go extinct."

The Queen's mouth hung ajar, and her eyes sucked Kasey's soul right out. "I must prioritize my people."

"I can't let you kill them." He pushed his hand forward holding the Slart. His hand trembled slightly before he added his other hand to stabilize it, and he caught himself breathing through his nose in short increments. "I won't let you kill them."

"Necessity," she reminded. "Necessity." Her face hollowed, her expression neutralized and her eyes blinked. "It is out of necessity." She repeated the word as if it would make it true—as if it made it okay. She needed this, her people needed this, her species needed this.

"There has to be another way—"

"—There is no other way." The Queen shifted her weight to four legs, rising. She towered over Kasey now, her head cast in darkness where his Slart's light couldn't reach. Kasey took a shot, but the bullet sent ripples through a force field in front of her that Kasey hadn't detected. *Oh fuck.*

With one of her appendages, she swiped at Kasey. He rolled along the side, hitting a column with his oblique and thigh. His Slart spun across the floor with the white light still brightening the room. Kasey sprinted to it like a moth to a flame, galloping over holes in the ship's floor.

Something snagged Kasey's foot, bringing him to the ground with a slam. Pushing himself up, a tibia with some rancid flesh on the bone met him at eye level. Kasey gagged, but it sped him up and closer to his gun.

"I will not let my people die!"

Still running, Kasey scooped up his Slart and discharged rounds into the force field. More ripples. The Queen sneered and jabbed forward. Kasey dodged to the side, but the Queen's bristled appendage sliced Kasey. Sidestepping a follow-up, he unsheathed his combat knife.

The Queen lowered to all six appendages now in a stance like a runner as she roared in the light of Kasey's Slart. Kasey grabbed the hilt of his knife, the golden light shimmering along the edges. It pierced the shield, sending ripples, more concentrated than the bullets did. *That's it!*

The Queen headbutted, sending Kasey a few disorientated steps away. Kasey stabbed forward, but this time a hole carved out the shield.

"Just let my people live!" she paired her proclamation with an "X" shape cut from two limbs. Kasey screamed in agony, and blood spurted out in the same shape. His suit hissed out a cocktail of elements, the smoke obscuring his view momentarily. From the side, Kasey plucked a broken-off piece of the column and chucked it at her. As with the knife, the ripples along the shield appeared later than the bullets.

He turned to a column and looked back at the Queen. *Now or never.* Standing his ground, Kasey waited for her horizontal slash. He ducked underneath, letting the bristled limb chip the column. Kasey rolled to the side and fired useless shots at the barrier.

Avoiding a series of strikes, he went around the column, mapping it out in his head. One step this way, one step that way. Another slash from the Queen brought him to his knees. He howled, and punched her, forgetting the wall. It greeted him like a concrete barrier, crushing his fingers. Using another thorned appendage, she slashed at his shoulder, sticking pricks into his body like thorns on a rose.

Kasey shoved it off and limped to the angle he mapped out. He held his Slart at the top of the column and did a quick approximation. He took the grenade Shamp gave him that he'd attached to his belt loop and held it in his hand. Kasey bit off the clip—*one, two*—Kasey threw the grenade to the top, blowing off the connection of the column to the ceiling. The Queen stumbled back from the blast of fire in the sky. The column wavered, and he kicked it to her with all the power he could.

The Queen grimaced, but before she could register what was happening, the column slammed the barrier, ripples multiplying across until it shattered, knocking her down to the floor and pinning her. Dust rose into the area and blood from her limbs burst outward with each crash of rubble. She cried in agony, bellowing out expletives Kasey didn't understand.

Bleeding himself, Kasey struggled towards her while grasping his gun. Blood dripping out the "X" of his body and the shoulder injury, he swallowed the pain, trying to form a facade. He held his Slart out at her. "You have no idea what you have done," she cried.

"I can't let you just kill an entire species." Kasey's hand didn't shake anymore, now steady and facing the head of the Queen.

"They are dead anyway." Her body twitched, and she groaned. "When I die, the others lose all their orders."

Kasey didn't pry, ignoring the statement.

"I have given explicit orders to all of them to hold back, to not destroy the Dyson energy centers so we can harvest it." She spit blood. "Without me, they'll revert back to instinct, feral instinct. They will kill you."

He readied the gun.

"When the Watchers come, remember: I warned you."

Kasey pulled the trigger.

Kasey carried himself through the ship, past the throne room entrance and an array of poisoned rocks with the virus festering inside. Clicking onto his comms, Kasey connected back online.

"*Guys!*" Kasey beamed. "*The Queen is dead!*"

Silence.

A crashing sensation weighed him down. "*Guys?*"

Kasey stumbled and forced movement despite the burning "X" crossing his chest. He winced, falling to one knee as his shoulder tingled. He took shallow breaths, trying to calm his body. "*Guys?*"

This time feedback.

Not a voice, but better than silence. Through the darkness, he stayed in the oxygenated room, the zero gravity lifting him. Although easier on his body, the blood pooled and seeped out before forming clumps in front of him.

His suit was crippled, and without a source of oxygen, he'd have to brave the false vacuum of space. He knew the distance, how fast he could travel, and how little time he'd have without a space suit.

He closed his eyes and took a deep breath, ordering his diaphragm to relax. Another breath, this time longer than the last. The blazing gashes across his body cooled with each exhale, the heat and inflamed skin constricting as he breathed.

Kasey opened his eyes. His mouth opened and his jaw would've hit the floor had gravity been reinstated. "Is that *the Irene?*"

Chapter 47

Benjo

There was something odd about being one of two people inside *the Irene* ring Benjo didn't like. Too much space made him feel like he should be using it, filling it with grenades and guns or even more energy for *the Irene's* cannon. But, when faced with little time, he only had his Slart and unitard on his back.

Amber sat at the helm with him, speeding in the FTL bubble. Benjo never really appreciated the sapphire sphere before and how it covered the ship like a gemstone. Amber took it upon herself to fly the ship as Benjo still hadn't mastered the art of aviation, even with his new upgrades he couldn't install skills.

Amber interrupted his thinking. "What do you think we'll find?"

Benjo raised his hand to his chin. "Honestly?" He turned to her, eyes wide and mouth open. "No clue."

"Well, we know what Lulu said," Amber began, "if it's true, then we're walking into a literal battlefield."

"I was going to say war zone," Benjo murmured. "But we won't know until we get there."

"There's something I'm worried about," she said.

"What?"

"The virus, it's in those rocks."

"Didn't you get the same primer coat as me?" Benjo looked at his hand, made with similar paint from the scanner his mother gave him.

"Viruses mutate. There's—what—a thousand variations of the flu?"

Benjo smirked. "I don't think it mutates in days."

"We don't know though. I mean it's a man-made biological weapon."

"Bug-made," Benjo corrected.

Amber rolled her eyes. "You know what I mean."

"Look, we'll be extra careful and see if we can distance ourselves from it."

"You don't understand." Amber's voice cracked like a mirror hit with a bullet. "I almost lost you."

Her eyes stared into his skull, past his skin, and into his essence. "I can't do that again," she sobbed.

With a sigh, Benjo rose from his seat and embraced her. "I don't want you to cry while you fly this thing."

Amber let out a mixture of a cry and laugh followed by giggling. "I'm serious."

"I know," he paused, "but we're going to be fine, I promise."

She swiped away tears dribbling out her eyes and took a quick inhale. "Okay, I'm holding you to that."

Benjo sat back down, pulling the radar out. Outdated in some respects, the radar provided a decent two-dimensional visual of objects in three-dimensional space. Other stars they passed by faded along the map, while their destination got closer and closer. The FTL bubble shimmered before coming to a halt. Now, a planet, gray like ash, popped up on the radar, with thousands of little satellites. The radar boomed in the cockpit, practically screaming every picosecond to inform Benjo and Amber of space junk in orbit.

Amber shielded her ears. "Turn it off!"

Benjo didn't need to be told twice to find the manual override (also known as the power button). The slew of beeps came to a screeching halt. His mind stable, Benjo realized *what* the debris was as it became clearer.

Chunks of metal floating in space came from something else, a part of something much bigger like a singular piece of a thousand-piece jigsaw puzzle. But after another moment of analysis, Benjo realized the metal wasn't floating, it was *moving*. Slowly, sure, but moving nonetheless.

"Looks like some sorta trail." Benjo traced his finger along the window. "Where's it lead?"

Benjo shrugged. "That's the mystery."

"Let's try the comms?" Amber suggested.

"This is Benjo to all PTF, please come in."

A minute passed.

Then two.

"Try again?" Amber asked, breaking the agonizing silence.

"This is Benjo to all PTF, please, anyone, come in."

A third minute passed.

Amber and Benjo's expressions morphed into apprehensive messes, with their lips trembling and mouths open. Benjo rubbed his shaved head, letting the prickly texture tickle his hand.

"B-Benjo?" A defeated voice shivered.

Benjo bolted up from his seat, *the Irene* shaking with his jump. *"Kasey?"*

"Good, you're actually there," Kasey said between coughs and a weak laugh. *"Thought the Queen poisoned me."*

"Kasey, where are you?"

"The Apiary ark." Kasey coughed again, this time wet and more guttural.

"I'll triangulate his location." Amber pushed up the console, bringing a menu Benjo had never seen before.

"Kasey, hold on, we're coming."

"Where are the others?"

Amber turned back to Benjo before hitting her comms. *"They're not with you?"*

"They're on the planet," his voice dragged and his tone softened.

"I got his location, we'll take a Navigator."

"Kasey, we're on our way to you."

"No—help the others."

Amber looked into Benjo's eyes for a split second. "You get him, I'll establish comms with the ground team." Amber went back to the console. "Don't forget our promise."

"You know I'm not good with flying," Benjo said.

"Use autopilot, it's safer," she assured.

"I remember being told that before."

* * *

Falisto

Falisto fired rounds into the heads of Apiary galloping towards the bunkers. Bullets whizzed in the air, and Falisto looked up at the sky. Remnants of the ark ship descended, hurling like asteroids to the ground.

Falisto stood outside the bunkers with Shamp, Tsoki, and Tsarena. Without the barrier protecting the Sanctuary, what remained of the Tayir soldiers and PTF became the bulwark. Tayir soldiers were far and few between, with the vast majority blasted away from the ark's beam. Falisto pushed the thoughts aside. The Apiary changed from earlier; now, their eyes were bloodshot and their fangs dripped with saliva. It was almost as if they became mindless savages with one thing on their minds: food.

Shamp whipped her tendrils across an Apiary jumping towards her. "We must retreat!"

"Hold them off as long as possible!" Falisto commanded. A beetle-shaped bug rushed Falisto with its horns drawn. He uppercut it, slashing through metallic skin and drawing blood out. Falisto forgot how fun it was to kill the way nature intended him to: with his claws digging into the barrier of his prey, pouncing on them, and savoring the hunt.

Tsarena hit one with the hilt of her Slart before reloading. With a new magazine, she sprayed into a trio of bugs in various appendages. "I'm with Shamp, we can't do this for much longer."

"Where's Kasey?" Tsoki shouted in frustration.

"He's fine!" Falisto yelled back. He dug his claws into a body too close for Falisto's liking. Pulling his claws out, he allowed himself to enjoy the carnage.

"*Everyone's inside!*" General Batala cooed. "*Get in the bunkers!*"

The group receded, but Falisto stayed in the fight, swiping at nearby Apiary. But one bug found an opening while Falisto focused on a single enemy. The insect jumped out, flinging its thorned appendages at Falisto. Caught off guard, Falisto dashed back, but tripped over a carcass and fell on his butt. The bug jabbed at him, hitting the ground as Falisto scurried backward. Slash after slash, the insect kept stabbing between his legs. Then Falisto hit the wall. Nowhere to go. The bug loomed over him, ready to finish off Falisto.

A bullet came through the other end of its head before falling aside. Lime green blood splattered in front of Falisto, hitting the concrete slab behind him and the upper part of his face. Tsarena stood, her gun still raised. "You ready now?"

"*We're coming.*" Using a tendril, Shamp helped Falisto up while Tsoki shot at the Apiary.

After a moment, Tsarena spoke to the comms, "*We're on our way.*"

No response.

"*Warda, General Batala, come in.*"

The bunkers were maybe about half a kilometer away, in the heart of the Sanctuary. Falisto's stomach churned from fear. "They're fine," he assured.

"It is unusual," Shamp began, "we just contacted them."

Tsoki fired a flurry of bullets into a series of bugs hurrying to them. "Just keep going."

Darkness blanketed the Sanctuary, suffocating out the lights once dangling from ropes around the city. Fire from Apiary airstrikes replaced the lanterns; they burned what little vegetation had grown without the sunlight, their black leaves crisping into soot. Gashes in overhead towers produced rubble that crushed stalls from merchants and vendors who didn't move in time. Rock-tipped spears and other crude weapons dotted the inner Sanctuary like a graveyard of fallen soldiers.

Falisto paid attention to Shamp's gait. Her left leg lagged behind her right, and she relied on her tendrils to stabilize her from toppling over. "Shamp," he said, rushing ahead of her, blood still covering his face.

"What?"

"You're hurt." Without asking, Falisto examined her leg. Blood leaked out the side of a deep wound with sand dusting the sides of her gray skin. She shook her leg out of the way, but not before Tsarena joined Falisto.

Tsarena's face drained. "Shamp, my God."

"We can't stop, guys," Tsoki said. He fired bullets, his eyes shifting from one direction to the next. "They're everywhere."

"Then let us go," Shamp grunted, shaking her leg out of Tsarena's grasp. "I am fine."

"Let me help carry you," Tsarena suggested.

With a pensive frown, Shamp agreed and wrapped her tendrils around Tsarena's shoulder and arm. Falisto took Shamp's other arm. He couldn't reach her shoulder height, but he presumed some support was better than none.

"We're almost there," Tsoki said, holding out his pad. "Just a little bit longer."

"Let's hurry." Falisto shouldered more of the Venori. "Don't worry, we're gonna make it," he said. His eyes looked up at the stars, and, for a moment, he could've sworn he saw *the Irene* above him.

* * *

Benjo

Benjo parked the Navigator in the wreckage of the ark. Plates of steel attracted loose bolts and screws dripping from it. With some sort of authority or refusal to die, the ship pulled itself together by its bootstraps and forced parts back together. Venori-like tendrils extended across the triptych of the ship, magnetizing back to one.

"*Kasey,*" Benjo said. "*Where are you?*" He held onto the suit he brought from *the Irene*, the singular size would have to work, even if it squeezed every organ like a corset.

"*I'm inside.*" His distant voice, frail and tired, came through the comms.

"*Hold on, I'm coming.*"

"*Be careful.*"

"*You're the reckless one,*" Benjo snarled.

Kasey didn't laugh. Benjo shivered with fear from the silence.

The door standing between them unlatched with air and loose molecules spewing into the void. Benjo gripped suit parts as he floated into the airlock. Behind him, the door slammed, and gears echoed as they twisted into a lock.

Artificial gravity surprised Benjo, nearly causing him to face plant the floor. Intuitively, he avoided the floor by hitting the wall and accidentally smashing the helmet. "God," he said to himself. "Fucking bugs." Glass covering the helmet had cracked, with the incision becoming a jagged maze in the mask. He cupped his view and looked through a peephole in the door. *"Kasey, I'm here."*

New air flooded the chamber, cleansing him of cosmic radiation space bathed him in. Tiny holes sucked back the polluted air and an audible *click* confirmed the unlock, and he pushed it open.

Kasey's fingers twitched with his body sprawled out on the floor, speckled with blood. A giant "X" was sliced into his chest, and his shoulder had pricks where loose gas from his suit dripped out. His eyes wavered between states of lucidity. Benjo rushed to him and levied him against the wall. "Kasey!"

"Amber, come in."

Static.

Benjo shouted an expletive and examined Kasey's body, his suit torn to shreds and helmet cracked. Neither of them had metal lungs, and, without a breathing apparatus, it'd be next to impossible to make it through space without a helmet.

But it *was* possible.

Air lingered through Kasey's nose and mouth. Benjo unhooked his helmet, letting heavily oxygenated air creep through into his lungs. With trembling fingers, Benjo snapped his old helmet around Kasey's neck. Undoing his suit, Benjo wrapped Kasey in his external armor, leaving Benjo with only his unitard on. Barefoot and frigid in the near blackness of the room, he lit the room up using both their Slarts.

"Okay, Kasey, you gotta trust me." He was talking to the unconscious, but it brought him some comfort. This way, he could at least tell Kasey he warned him.

Going into the airlock, Benjo breathed deeply, sucking in all the air and oxygenating blood flowing through his veins and metal pipes. The movement of his diaphragm aided him, nullifying his anxiety. A byproduct of necessity. Before he'd open the airlock he'd have to exhale all the air in his lungs, spare not a single molecule so it wouldn't get slurped right out.

He recalled lessons during the Sapien War—the training and science behind the vacuum of space. Most training didn't address this certain predicament. Not a lot of sense in educating an entire platoon on what to do when their ship got blown up and they had to linger in space for a few seconds. He had some facts: he had less than ten seconds before passing out and risking brain damage, it would be cold but not freezing, and, of course, Newton's first law. One move and he'd go in that direction until something stopped him.

Closing his eyes, Benjo mapped a route in his brain. The idea made him scoff, the need of a plan to traverse from the inside of a ship to another just a few meters away.

"Okay, Kasey, here we go." He pushed the air out of his lungs for a final time and kicked the door open. *Ten seconds to do this.*

The warmth of the distant sun and the lingering heat from the explosions of the ships kept him from quickly solidifying. *One.* He choked on nothing and gasped without making a sound. *Two.* He tried to calm himself amid the cacophony of fears running freely in his brain, and he focused on pressing the Navigator open. *Three.* Gripping Kasey, Benjo reached the button, hitting it with his elbow. *Four.* The door creaked open and salvation shined Benjo right in his eyes. *Five.* Benjo dumped Kasey inside, Benjo's body gasping again. *Six.* A vignette formed around Benjo's vision. *Seven.* Benjo slipped inside, and, with his metal toe, hit the close button as the door was still opening. *Eight.* The doors closed and his eyes shut. *Nine.* The Navigator door nearly reached the top. *Ten.* Oxygen and gravity flooded the ship.

* * *

Kasey

Kasey willed himself awake despite the harsh light forcing him to squirm. Adrenaline pumped through his veins. Placing his weight on one leg proved to be a challenge, immediately forcing him to grapple onto the bed he just exited.

Benjo rushed into the room, with his new arms so bright it was the first thing Kasey noticed. "You're awake," Benjo said with a smile.

Scooping underneath him, Benjo shouldered Kasey back upright, his other hand still gripping the bed. "How long was I out?" Kasey asked. His mouth couldn't keep up with his words, firing off faster than his lips could move.

"Just a few hours," Benjo said.

"Hours?" Kasey coughed. "Where is everyone?"

"They're okay," Benjo said. "They're in the bunkers."

"The bunkers?"

"The Apiary broke through their shield, they're still down there with limited comms. Amber thinks that big ass ark ship's magnetic pull is fucking with it."

Kasey touched his comms implant. "*Tsarena, Tsoki, Shamp, Falisto, Warda, come in?*"

They all responded in a flurry.

"*How're you feeling?*" Tsoki asked.

"*Not great,*" Kasey admitted. "*Not horrible either.*"

"*That's good,*" Tsarena sighed. "*I'm so glad you're okay.*"

"*You gave us a worry,*" Falisto spat.

"*What's your status?*" Kasey coughed and grasped the new grooves in his body. A sharp pain rode up his oblique, hitting his shoulder where bandages covered a series of stinging holes.

"*Oh you know,*" Falisto cooed. "*Stuck with a bunch of Tayirs in a bunker with no ammo.*"

Benjo spoke off his comms. "We might want to consider calling Respow."

"We can't do that," Kasey said. "You know we can't."

"I think he'd understand," Benjo defended. "He's an opportunist, but he isn't evil."

"I don't think he's evil either, but I told General Azalia I wouldn't." Intrusive thoughts of General Azalia's death gnawed Kasey, and he tried to swallow it down.

Benjo shrugged. "All I'm saying is there's a real possibility that without Respow there won't be any Tayirs left." Kasey winced, grabbing his oblique.

"You're in no condition to fight. We need reinforcements and a proper way to fully establish comms again."

"We can't get Respow," Kasey said.

Benjo sighed. "Well I suggest you enlighten me with an idea on how we exterminate—

As if all Kasey's neurons fired at the same time, the solution hit Kasey. "—I know how we beat them."

"Uh—okay, but Kasey—"

But Kasey was already limping away with a plan forming.

Chapter 48

Tsarena tried to not pay attention to Tsoki's footsteps as he paced near the door. The rapid taps made her uneasy, but with limited room in the bunker, it was between Tsoki nervous-walking and Falisto's comments about how they should've packed more ammo. At least with Tsoki she could think. Usually, Tsarena hated tight places because it always suffocated her, but something about being around civilians comforted her. Maybe it was a shred of Imposter Syndrome, but she never identified as a soldier—she never faced true combat.

Apiary banged on the doors outside interconnected tunnels between bunkers and paired it with shrieks and screams. Young Tayirs cried into their mothers' bodies who tried to calm them, despite crying themselves. Children were fine for a while, unaware of the gravity of the situation. It was easier to put everything on the back burner when reality wasn't barging at your door with hungry eyes and salivating mouths.

Tsarena's eyes wandered to Tsoki, who had his pad out. He typed away as if writing his last will, his fingers slapping the keys faster than his feet hit the ground. From behind Tsarena, Shamp limped over, trying to hide her slouch. Tsarena briefly acknowledged her with a weakened hand wave before Tsoki's footsteps finally hit a nerve.

"What're you doing?" Tsarena asked Tsoki. He didn't look up from his pad, instead completing more sentences and words, stringing them together into what she could only presume was his magnum opus.

Shamp tapped Tsarena. "Falisto and I are investigating access points to the bunker's armory."

"Is that a good idea? Kasey said to just give him a few minutes."

Shamp bent down, her tendrils weaving around both her and Tsarena to create some sort of secretive wall from the other Tayirs listening. In a whisper, she spoke, "The Apiary are breaking through here." Tsarena went to move her eyes but Shamp quickly snapped. "Do not look. There is a crack in the seal. We have approximately eight minutes until the door breaks and they storm us."

Tsarena's heart dropped out of her body. "W-what are we gonna do—"

"—If we get some of the guns from the armory we can probably kill off a good portion and buy Kasey more time for whatever his plan is."

Tsarena looked to Tsoki, now off his pad and joining in the tunnel after Shamp tugged him in by the unitard. "I'll tell Kasey."

"Already did," she said.

Tsarena gulped. "Do we tell Warda and Batala?"

"I think we must," Shamp said.

Tsoki, Falisto, Warda, Shamp, General Batala, and Tsarena stayed incognito as they meandered through crowds of Tayirs. They passed sections of the bunker through tunnels bridging another series of bunkers. The armory sealed off after the cannon shots inadvertently triggered a lockdown.

The door stood in front of them, golden metal with a slit underneath allowing a harsh light to peer out. Tsarena's watch ticked down. Tsoki stood next to her with his pad experiencing an influx of messages.

"Who'd you call?" she asked.

Tsoki's face struggled to form a solid expression, oscillating between several reactions. "Uh, no one, just messaged a few people."

"Well stop," Falisto said, brushing against Tsoki's shoulder. "We have less time than we do ammo."

Tsoki pouted but subsided, letting Falisto size up the door. He poked and studied it as if there was some sort of science or magic passcode. Tsarena let him prod it, beginning with his claw scratching the metal.

"Maybe we should ask the actual Tayirs how to open it," Tsarena said.

The group turned to them, General Batala a shell of herself with her eyes vacant and her body slouching. Warda had the same empty stare, but she stood tall and radiant despite it. Maybe having big eyes rendered the lifeless stare common among the Tayir, or maybe the shared trauma of survival pried the vision receptors open to their maximum.

"Shamp," Falisto commanded. "Use your tail thing to open the door from the other side."

Shamp looked at him, stupefied. "Tail? How do you think my body works?"

Falisto shrugged. "You can't reach the door?"

"No!" she admonished. "I cannot thin it out like a tongue!"

"Keep your voices down," Warda said. "We don't want to scare the children anymore."

"You do realize they're gonna be scared in a few minutes when those things break in!" Falisto whisper-shouted.

"Will all of you just stop!" Tsarena punched her fists down by her side. "I think," Tsarena started, "I can widen the gap."

"With what?" Falisto growled.

"Force."

Warda's jaw dropped. "I just said we don't want to scare anyone!"

"The words stick in my throat like a bone but Falisto is right. A momentary scare is better than death."

General Batala and Warda exchanged looks. Warda stepped closer. "What do you suggest?"

Tsarena pointed to General Batala. "Tell everyone they're gonna hear an explosion—"

"—Explosion?!" General Batala blurted.

"Look, this door was made by you guys, right?" Tsarena said, practically accusing them.

"Yes," the General said.

Tsarena held out her grenade. "Do you think there's any other way inside?"

"Of course there is," the General said halfheartedly.

"There's a way that we can get in within the next few seconds?"

With an exhausted sigh, the General shook her head. "You're right."

"Just go and tell everyone there's gonna be a small disturbance but it's nothing."

The General shook her head. "I hope Kasey knows what he's doing."

"He does," Tsoki said. "I know he does."

* * *

Benjo

Benjo didn't have as much trouble in the darkness of the ship as Kasey undoubtedly did. Benjo, back in his suit and standing where Kasey's dried blood stained the black floor of the ark ship, had a few options for where to go. *The Irene* and Navigator mapped parts of the ship, but the only thing interesting they detected was some great attractor on a lower floor. Whatever it was, it hated communication, splicing together comms and sending out jumbled messages or sometimes no messages at all.

Part of Benjo wanted to go with Kasey and Amber on their mission to "kill all the bugs," but he had to destroy the jammer. Although the temporary probe acted as a communicator and translator, it was limited in capacity. Without proper channels of communication, a battle, much less a war, was impossible, and Benjo didn't take bets with shitty odds.

At calculated points, Benjo placed charges across the floor and walls. He'd expected more—well, frankly, at least *some* pushback by the Apiary—but he practically walked in as a guest.

Using fancy tools in his new eye, Benjo surveyed a long corridor he came across. Pads were light years behind this technology, and Benjo loved being the advanced one. It reminded him of when he was a kid, ahead of his friends whose parents didn't let them get upgrades. Areas he placed charges highlighted in yellow despite shadows swallowing the hall. He couldn't shake the feeling that something about this whole thing was wrong. Something *had to be* wrong. This couldn't be this easy, nothing like this ever was. An advanced species with no protective safeguards?

Sticking explosives to the sides, Benjo neared his final destination: the attractor. Mapping from his eye suggested something massive was protected by the walls below him, and whatever it was, it was vulnerable enough to warrant three layers of insulation.

Finding a staircase proved challenging, but after a few turns, jumps, and bends, Benjo found the insect version of an elevator, a narrow, vertical tunnel. Despite the lack of visual stimulation through the ship, something new peppered the darkness. Little bits of technology, like mini pads and chips carrying data, stemmed through the insulated room. It piqued his interest, and Benjo tried Raking with his fingers. Red streams of energy jumped onto the computers, draining information in a language Benjo couldn't understand. With one hand sucking in loose bits of information, the other planted more charges around layers of insulation.

After placing the final charges and storing the information, Benjo hurried back to the alien elevator tunnel. His mind sifted through the bits of data he'd drained while he scaled the walls. Something about it felt gooey, almost adhering to him like liquid glue. Some sounds beeped in through the comms, but it was too far gone to be coherent.

By the time he reached the Navigator, the comms had gotten only worse, now completely silent, and for the first time in a long time, Benjo didn't like the silence. The Navigator set a course to *the Irene* and followed its direction, weaving past bits of loose metal still hurling towards the attractor.

Following a quick and dirty calculation, Benjo approximated he was at a healthy distance to pull the trigger. With a sense of curiosity, Benjo let the autopilot do its thing while he went to watch the fireworks.

With the window in front of him, Benjo held the trigger and pushed the button. The ark became a momentary fireball in the night sky, so bright that it would have even lit up a black hole. The vines that once pulled the parts together shriveled up, snapping in half, and the tiny bits of metal traveled in millions of different directions, never to return without the attractor. To Benjo's surprise, a large section barreled straight into his Navigator, ripping it apart.

* * *

Kasey

Amber held her hands on her hips. "You realize this is the stupidest, craziest, riskiest—"

"—And if it works," Kasey interrupted. "We'll save the day." A grin stretched from ear to ear. Even if for some reason Amber disagreed and changed her mind, it was too late. *The Irene* was already in motion and going too fast.

Amber shook her head with a smile. "You know, I wouldn't have guessed you'd gamble an entire species on an idea that *might* work."

"The light from this star will take around six minutes to reach them," Kasey reiterated. "Shamp told me the Apiary will breach the bunker in eight."

"And we're exactly one minute and thirty seconds away." Amber looked at the star map. *The Irene* yelped emergency calls, asking for constant overrides. "Override emergency stop," Amber shouted.

"Let's get to the Navigator."

"So, how exactly did you deduce that sunlight was the Apiary's weakness?" Amber asked. She nestled in the Navigator, the only one left on *the Irene* now that Benjo went to plant explosives.

"Think about it," Kasey started, "where have the Apiary been on?"
Amber shifted her eyes. "I dunno."

"Rogue Planets," he answered. "But not just any Rogue Planets, the ones either the Tayirs are on or that have a complete tidally locked side that's always in darkness."

Amber sighed. "But that doesn't mean they're weak to it."

"True, but their ships don't have light or windows. They only came to the colony on Porygar during the eclipse."

"Mako, if you're right about this, what do you think is gonna happen? They burn up like some sort of vampire or something?"

"Maybe," he said. "Or maybe it disorients them so much they have to retreat. Now that the Queen is dead they've lost all sense of order. They're acting on instinct."

The Irene issued its final warning. "DANGER: PATH AHEAD BLOCKED."

"Override!" Amber yelled.

"OVERRIDE REQUIRES ALL PASS—"

"—Override!" Kasey shouted.

"OVERRIDE ACCEPTED: CRASH IMMINENT."

"Now!" Kasey ordered.

Out the hull of *the Irene*, Amber flew the Navigator, letting the PTF ring pierce into the Dyson Plates. *The Irene* unfolded from its ring shape into a curved arc. In the silence of the crash, the metal of *the Irene* scraped apart the energy siphons, splitting away chunks of glass and wires, and allowing light to shine towards both Kasey and the planet. Shards of the mirror catapulted toward the ball of plasma. Once beacons of energy, the mirrors burned up into nearly nothing, leaving only its light, heading straight home.

Chapter 49

Tsarena

The crack in the bunker spread into a series of tears, dust coming through the new ruptures zig-zagging along the walls. Tsarena stood with the team, each wielding a gun from the armory. She held a Tayir rifle, an assault weapon with a flimsy trigger that felt alien in her featherless hands. Tsarena took a breath, said a prayer to whoever listened, and closed her eyes. The darkness outside invaded the bunker as lights flickered on and off inside from Apiary gnawing on cords and other generators. Wavering, the bulbs made no promise of staying on.

"Whatever Kasey's doing better hurry the hell up," Falisto spat.

"We have around ten seconds," Shamp said from behind Falisto.

Tsoki stood with Tsarena and General Batala. "This is the only entrance they're making progress on," General Batala said. "They can only come through here."

Tsarena opened her eyes. Bulbs died out, cloaking them in darkness. Luckily, the PTF's Slarts illuminated the bunker. More thrashing at the doors caused Tsarena to gulp. The cracks and ruptures in the door and walls worsened, and, like a thin layer of ice covering a body of water, the jagged lines multiplied and were ready to shatter with just the force of a breeze. Then something happened.

Golden sunlight beamed down, illuminating the outside and seeping through the lightless bunker. It cast their shadows behind them and fully enveloped the gray world, giving tints and hues to the colorless Sanctuary. The Apiary's ravenous banging morphed into screams and slams against the doors, seeking shelter instead of food.

General Batala scurried to a live feed from one of the tower cameras. Tsarena kept an eye on the door, making sure an inconspicuous beetle didn't rampage through the compromised barrier. Along the feed, Apiary murdered one another for spots of shade, even going so far as to shoot runners huddling in. Those unfortunate enough that didn't scatter in time sizzled, cooking in the newfound brightness of the world.

Tsarena put her gun away and clasped her hands together. "He did it!"

General Batala couldn't help but sob, embracing her and the others in a hug. "He did it!"

A screech over their comms confirmed the lines were back, with Kasey in the middle of a transmission.

"*Kasey!*" Tsarena yelled. "*You did it!*"

Kasey exhaled over the line. "*It worked?!*"

"I'll get the others," General Batala said.

"Tell them to be careful," Shamp cautioned. "Some Apiary are in the shadows. We should probably play exterminator."

General Batala nodded before flapping off, changing positions with Warda.

"*Thank you—all of you—for everything,*" Warda said. "*I owe you my life, and my peoples'.*"

"*It was a team effort,*" Kasey said. "*This time credit goes to Benjo, he saved me.*"

"*I need to meet Benjo,*" Warda cooed.

"*We're looking for him now,*" Amber replied. "*Having some difficulty finding him, I think his comms got fried by the attractor.*"

"*Do you need help?*" Tsarena asked.

Shamp took her gun. "If we plan to disembark, we should help extermi-nate."

"Agreed," Tsoki said. "Don't wanna leave the civilians open."

"It's tidally locked so we won't lose daylight, but no sense in letting the bugs live."

Falisto stepped up. "Don't gotta tell me twice." He flung the door open, greeting the team inside with the stench of rotting flesh mixed with hints of peppermint. Although only open for a second, the odor had already established a home inside the bunker.

"Smells fucking horrible," he roared.

"I wouldn't expect it to smell good, exactly." Tsarena tried to stomach a gag.

Falisto covered his nostrils with a paw. "Maybe I'll stay in the bunker."

"How about we go help find Benjo?"

"So, Tsarena, Warda, Falisto go help find Benjo. Tsoki and Shamp stay with the local population?" General Batala confirmed.

"I'd like to see Kasey," Tsoki murmured. "But I don't wanna leave Shamp and General Batala alone."

"Don't take any risks," Tsarena reminded. "Warda, you wanna come too, right?"

She nodded. "Very much so."

"*Kasey,*" Tsarena began, "*we're on our way up to you now.*"

"*We can use the help, this is like trying to find an invisible needle in an invisible haystack.*"

"*Scratch that,*" Amber sighed. "*We actually need another ship this Navigator's out of energy cells.*"

"*Just send us your location,*" Tsarena said.

As she emerged outdoors with the sun rays hitting her cheeks and bathing her in light, she closed her eyes. It recharged her, almost like she was a flower in desperate need of photons for photosynthesis.

Heat rose slowly as the sun blanketed the planet, but it had already made a marked difference. Warda flapped next to Tsarena, holding a gun like a novice the way it hardly fit in her finger-wings. Falisto put on a helmet and suit, protecting him from the rancid odor permeating the air.

Apiary snarled at one another in shade spots. Weapons and insectoid bodies littered the ash ground, giving the gray a green tint like grass. Beetle-shaped Apiary argued with ants who tried to dig holes inside their protected areas.

* * *

Kasey

An hour of searching nearly drove Kasey mad. Space was big—lots of people knew that, but not a lot of people knew *how big* it was. Finding Benjo felt like a fool's errand in some regards, like using a spotlight to find a pin in an ocean of pins. Kasey stood in the center of the Navigator, with Amber, Warda, Falisto, and Tsarena. He peered out the ship's windows and clicked the radar, praying to find the same beat from Benjo's radio. The problem wasn't that the radar wasn't picking things up. Indeed, the radar picked up every slim piece the bombs and blasts jettisoned off.

"*Benjo, come in,*" Kasey said. After a few seconds, Kasey spoke to the team, "Maybe they aren't going through?"

Amber swallowed. "It came through on my end." Her fingers quivered as she paced back and forth in the limited space of the Navigator. "I have a bad feeling."

"Amber," Tsarena started, "it's gonna be okay. He's alright, his Navigator just got messed up from the blast."

She bit her fingernails and paced further into the body of the ship, past Warda and going around her spread wings. "Benjo should be showing up."

Kasey didn't say anything to this. Instead, he tried his comms again. "*Come in, Benjo.*"

The Navigator had a healthy distance from the planet, somewhere between the now sunny gray world and the wreckage of the ark ship. With the sun hitting the planet where the Dyson Plates were, the Sanctuary was a singular colorful dot on the world. The litter composed of asteroids and the Apiary ark ship's shards not recalled by the attractor spun in a predictable orbit of the planet, making a headache for travel.

"I'm picking up something," Tsarena said gleefully.

Amber raced to her side. "What is it?"

"I dunno, a sorta object coming really fast. Like, *really* fast." Tsarena moved her gaze towards the window, pointing where the object would materialize from. "It'll be there in five seconds."

Static from a different source other than the five of them rang over the comms. Kasey jolted, his hands damp with sweat and his eyes open as wide as could be.

"*Benjo?!*"

More static emanated from their device until...

"Is that classical music?" Amber asked.

"That's classical?" Falisto grunted. "Sounds pretty underwhelming."

"*Benjo?*" Kasey repeated.

Tsarena looked out the window with Kasey. The beep came again, and the object materialized right before their eyes. Its three rings in sequential order surrounded a cylinder in the middle with x-bridges branching out. The ship's vibration made a groaning sound like a whale in the ocean passing by a sardine. It spun and hurled through the vacuum until it slowed to a halt, its rings still spinning as it anchored to the position. Smack dab in the middle of space was *the Irene* in all its glory with a missing PTF ring.

Kasey shivered. It was like a blast of cold air rode his spinal column to his neck. *What's it doing here?* Nauseous and frigid, Kasey stammered, "*This is Kasey to the Irene.*"

The music continued, until a voice silenced it, overpowering the stringed instruments from a time long passed. "*Kasey?*" The voice sounded shocked, perplexed by the presence of another person with comms. The inflection, the pitch, the way it sounded like an accusation. It was Respow.

"*Respow! What are you doing here?!*"

He didn't answer the question. Instead, he asked his own. "*Why'd you have to come here?*"

"*To find out about the Tayir ships, we discovered them on a planet and that they're being made by the Black Market and—*"

"*—Spare the details.*"

The snip in his voice made Kasey recoil, still watching *the Irene* in its uncompleted state without the PTF ring. "Something's wrong," Kasey murmured off comms. Tsarena glanced at him as he plucked his pad out, fumbling it open. Making spelling errors with his commands, Kasey switched from public comms to the private PTF chat.

"*Tsoki, Shamp,*" Kasey said on the private channel. "*Get off the planet NOW!*"

"*We're almost done exterminating the bugs, don't worry we'll have our moment,*" Tsoki flirted.

"*No—listen to me, Respow's here and he's acting funny. He has the Irene I'm worried he's gonna do something!*"

A second of silence that felt like an eternity ensued. "*Kasey, there is something I need to tell you.*"

"*No, we don't have time for that, you need to get your asses on a ship and leave!*"

"Kasey," Falisto murmured. Kasey didn't respond at first, now shaking every part of his body. "Kasey!" Falisto yelled.

He whipped his neck back, tearing his eyes off *the Irene.* "What!"

"You need to listen to this."

Kasey plugged into the PTF chat again, listening in to Respow's words. "*Those birds down there are a virus. They're threatening everything we built. They were destroyed for a reason. They will be destroyed again.*"

"What does he mean by that?" Warda's eyes were the biggest they'd ever been.

Amber shook her head violently in the negative. "He's joking—Respow wouldn't..." her voice trailed off.

Falisto sat motionless while Amber went to the helm of the ship. Warda hyperventilated, each breath merging with a cry until the two distinct sounds became indistinguishable.

Kasey swapped back to the private channel. "*Tsoki, Shamp, go!*"

"*We will not make it, I am afraid,*" Shamp said. "*Please tell my sister, Kviya I am sorry.*"

"*Shamp, stop, you can get to a Navigator and leave!*"

The Irene's rings began to violently spin now, generating a red charge like lightning from a Hybrid Raking.

"*Kasey,*" Tsoki choked. "*I wish things were different.*"

The light of *the Irene* condensed in front of the cylinder, the size of the shot now tremendous enough it covered one of the rings. Kasey's heart quickened, skipping beats faster and faster. With a flick on the pad, he swapped back to the public comms.

"*Don't do this! Please!*" Kasey pleaded to Respow. "*We have options! They're harmless people!*" It was like throwing spaghetti and hoping something—anything—would stick.

"*You should've never come here.*" *The Irene's* rings spun faster, almost like a drill screwing into the ground. Tsarena clasped her mouth with her hands, tears welling her eyes. Warda banged on the window, begging to escape so she could warn her people and get them to evacuate on ships they didn't have the time they ran out.

Kasey switched back to the private channel.

Tsoki spoke again. "*Kasey.*" The beam of *the Irene* evolved into a ray of fury, aiming for the planet. "*There's something I have to tell you. I'm not who you think I am.*"

The crushing beam went through the center of the planet, vaporizing its entry point. It struck through the mantle, and to the solid core. It condensed for a moment, then spread out millions of tiny pores like light shining out of a perforated lampshade. Fire burst from the light, connecting lines over lines until flames cloaked the ash in a burning storm. Shards of the planet splintered off, and for a moment, Kasey swore he heard the screams of everyone, terrified of certain death. Then the planet exploded, with nothing more to show for it than the trillions of rocks that spawned from the onslaught, rushing to the Navigator.

Chapter 50

Falisto

Falisto jumped in the cockpit, plucking Amber away with little resistance in her catatonic state. He flung her to the copilot seat, his primal urge to survive overpowered his learned sense of manners. Falisto dragged the throttle without warning, forcing the Navigator away from the shower of debris rushing to them. He flicked up the switch for the FTL drive but doing so alerted Respow. *The Irene* turned to the Navigator and readied another beam.

Then something happened.

A distortion, tiny by cosmic proportions but large enough for their Navigator, opened in spacetime. A portal, a wormhole, whatever it was, it was an escape. Falisto shot them through, traveling along the bridge of stars and planets condensed into a cylinder. "Buckle up!"

The Navigator shuttered, rocking violently and throwing Falisto like a ragdoll in his chair. He gritted his teeth and checked behind him. Kasey gripped the top for dear life, Tsarena held her knees while strapped to the chair, Amber trembled with fear among the shakes from the bridge, and Warda sat on the floor of the ship, her giant eyes glistening with tears.

When they reached the other end, the wormhole snapped shut, leaving behind only a blanket of darkness. Their surroundings changed dramatically. Gone was the ash planet or remnants thereof. There were no satellites, no visible celestial bodies or nearby stars, just space with dots of light so infinitely far away.

For a few seconds, no one said anything. They just breathed. Falisto thought of Benjo, lost somewhere in space, and Tsoki and Shamp. He'd just been with them not too long ago. Shooting bugs. Hiding in the bunker. Being together.

But radars picking up something above them disrupted his thinking. Something massive, irregular, and out of view approached. The behemoth awakened Tsarena and Warda from their trances, while Kasey and Amber continued disassociating. Falisto's claws prodded menus and systems sprawled out along the console, looking at diagnostic reports that could be summarized as: the Navigator was screwed.

"Our systems are fried, the wormhole fucked it all up!" Falisto hissed.

A large *clunk* came from above.

Everyone looked up at the Navigator's ceiling. A blue flame burned through, lasering out a wide box. The cut section of the ceiling fell to the ground, mere inches away from the unresponsive crew.

"Pirates?" Tsarena asked.

A delicate sphere lowered into the Navigator's atmosphere before it shot out its golden ray, scanning through the Navigator from the top breach. A voice spoke from the ball, "Confirmed lifeforms authorized by Tsoki Vanjo."

Falisto's shoulders loosened. *Tsoki.* Then he turned to the motionless Kasey who stirred at the mention of the name. Falisto took a step forward, leaving the pilot seats and Amber behind as he investigated the hole. His Slart drawn, he pointed at the square connecting the two ships. *Who the fuck is up there?*

"Don't worry," a voice shouted from above. "I'm not gonna hurt any of you."

"Who the fuck are you?" Falisto yelled. He knew better than to trust a person who wouldn't show their face.

The voice scoffed. "Oh, yeah, don't mention me saving you, skip that part."

"Thank you," Tsarena said, seemingly leaving her trance.

"Don't say thank you," Falisto spat.

"Orchi are always so much nicer," the voice laughed. "Look, we got a lot to talk about. Come up here."

A chain link ladder rolled down the hole in the ship to them. Excess ladder toppled over itself, piling towards Kasey's feet. He walked closer, almost like it summoned him.

"What are you doing?!" Falisto yelled to Kasey.

Kasey didn't respond, he just kept climbing until he reached the top. Grunting, Falisto followed, climbing over and up the new ship. With each step he took, the darkness overhead became clearer. But what he saw at the top confused him: clashing metals welded together, monitors and displays of unequal sizes, and various species dotting the atrium, even another Tayir.

A Hybrid woman stood by the chain ladder with her hands on her hips, the metal gripping her abdomen. Her eyes were red, almost like she'd been crying, but she carried an unmistakable radiance with a beaming smile. She wore a golden bandanna wrapped around her forehead, with two, bright-blue, twin braids coming from her scalp. "We got a lot to do," she said. "I'm Riley."

"What is this place?" Falisto said, turning around and staring at the ceiling.

"This is the *Conglomerate*."

"Weird name," Falisto cooed.

Tsarena ushered Amber and Warda up the ladder, each joining Kasey who was also enthralled with the ship. "Is that a Tayir?!" Tsarena yelped, pointing to a withered Tayir with its feathers gray and thin.

"Yes—his name is Zanbaq." Riley took a step towards Tsarena. "You must be Tsarena."

"Who are you?" Kasey asked.

"Kasey," she smiled. "Tsoki spoke about you a lot." Riley's voice waned, and her radiance flickered off for a moment.

"Who. Are. You?"

"Look, we have a lot to talk about. I promise I will answer anything, tell you anything, the whole nine yards." Riley pointed to a room in the distance, entirely different from the current setting. Instead, that room glowed a deep purple.

"Zanbaq?" Warda yelped, now making eye contact with him.

Riley stepped in front of her. "Be careful," Riley warned. "He's... ill."

Warda's eyes returned to the floor, and she retreated to Tsarena.

"How do we know you aren't gonna kill us?" Falisto hissed.

Riley chortled. "Well, it would've been easier to just drop a grenade in your ship." Her metal finger pointed to the hole she made.

"Who are you? How do you know Tsoki?" Kasey's voice turned into a scornful growl, and the words that left his mouth thundered the entire ship. Falisto had never seen Kasey like this before. He knew Kasey could get angry, but he didn't know the extent of that anger until that moment.

"I'm a Traveler," she said.

* * *

Kasey

On any other day, Kasey would've been grateful some random woman with blue hair saved him and his crew from certain death. But with the Tayirs essentially extinct, Benjo presumed dead, Tsoki and Shamp actually dead, Kasey wasn't exactly grateful. The phrase "I'm not who you think I am" clung to his brain. His mind fixated on the phrase, reiterating it, again, and again, and again.

They sat at a table, lined with refreshments including mawz and water. It wasn't a meal, at least, not in the sense that they needed plates and were being waited on. Most of the crew or passengers or whoever they were came and went, adding some food of different varieties. Kasey's stomach growled from the aroma of warm bread, but he couldn't bring himself to eat. His body craved it, but anguish weighed too heavily on him that any movement would compromise him.

Every chair at the table was different, each from unique sets and teetering with broken legs, missing armrests, or torn cushions. Paintings on the wall were slanted, and lights glowed different shades of white and yellow with their bulbs at different wattages. Everyone's eyes dried from crying at one point or another, and the table didn't say a word. Falisto even had tear marks, crawling down his fur and equipping his eyes with red veins.

"Benjo is out there," Amber proclaimed. The others looked at her, listening in. It was the first word she said since the blast of Hadiqa. "He has to be. His comms just didn't work." Amber looked at everyone, seeking someone who would entertain her idea. "Right?"

The blue-haired woman turned a corner and walked in. "Okay," she said. "I'm sorry, this is not how I wanted us to meet." The skin just under her eyes was drier than the rest and had a bit of a shiny sleekness to them. She sniffled getting close to the table. "But we got things to discuss."

She tapped the pistol tucked along the holster on her side and placed it on the table. The handle was a stark white, with an orange trigger. Falisto simmered and let out a low growl from his whole body.

"My name is Riley. I'm a member of Jasoosi."

Falisto lunged up from the table. "I knew you were an organization!"

She held out her robotic hands in a way as if to suggest she meant peace. "I understand, but hear me out."

"Why?" Falisto growled.

Kasey would've reacted to the news, but his brain kept repeating "I'm not who you think I am" in the background. But then it made sense.

"Tsoki was Jasoosi," Kasey said.

Riley nodded. "That's right."

"Why would we trust you, thug?"

"Because I just spent half my exotic matter opening a wormhole to save you."

Falisto shut his mouth. After a moment, he sat back in his chair and swiped a piece of mawz.

"Thank you," she said. He didn't look at her, instead chomping into the food, juice exploding onto his face after the first bite. "That man you call Respow," she began, walking around with her hands behind her back, "is a power-hungry maniac. He's the one leading Sapien."

This got Kasey's attention. "That's an extraordinary claim that requires extraordinary evidence."

She smirked. "He just killed one of only two Tayir colonies left in the Universe. If he knew about the other they'd be next."

"There's another?" Warda gasped. "Where?"

"Part of Jasoosi. Protected by the *Conglomerate*. Right here." Riley pointed to the ground.

"What about Tsoki?" Kasey said. "What was his role?"

Riley's face contorted, the mention of the name a knife in the heart, Kasey presumed. "Tsoki was recruited to give insight on how close Respow was getting to know we exist."

"Jasoosi has been wiped away for centuries," Tsarena said. "Besides it was never even proven!"

"The Jasoosi you all know was destroyed." Riley rested her hands on the table and pushed herself forward. "This one—this new one—formed shortly before the Tayir War, when Qiula and the Nima heirs were assassinated and the Tayirs got framed."

"Why did you just let us lead Respow right to the Tayirs?" Kasey shouted. "Why didn't you have Tsoki tell us about you? About Respow?"

"Tsoki was given specific orders to never communicate the plans." Riley took a seat now, leaning back in a chair fit for an old woman knitting. "As to how Respow found you, I think it was from that big ring ship leaving a trail."

Color drained from Amber's face. "You mean Benjo and I brought them?"

Warda turned to her, her eyes wide and mouth open. Kasey couldn't tell from the body language of the Tayir immediately, but he was certain she was angry for the first time. "It's your fault?"

"It's no one's fault," Riley snapped. "The only person to blame is Respow."

"What's his motivation, what does he want?"

"It's him and Representative Bigon. They wanna quietly kill off the Tayirs, and it just so happens Apiary resided on Rogue Planets. Now they wanna kill them off. They say 'peace' but peace doesn't involve war in my book."

"But why do Tayirs and Apiary pose such a threat?" Kasey asked.

"If we believe what they say is true," Riley started, "then there's some super predator out there. Not just warring with lower civilizations but actively punishing them by placing them on Rogue Planets. Apiary call them the 'Watchers.' Kind of a boring name if you ask me."

"So, what, we're supposed to just set aside our differences and work with my people's executioner?"

"No," she said. "But, it means if we wanna prepare—the right way—we need to take out Respow and Bigon."

"I'll never, *ever*, join Jasoosi." Falisto pushed his plate away and got up. As he stomped away, Riley did a slick movement with her hands, shutting the exit points.

"You're free to leave," she confirmed. "Only after you watch this reel."

"Reel?" Kasey asked.

"An old piece of technology banned for privacy reasons." She turned to Kasey. "This might be of particular interest to you." She looked back at the rest of the group. "If, after watching this, you wanna leave, you are not only more than welcome to leave, but I will personally help you leave."

A screen behind the table fluttered awake, and Kasey squinted. His heartbeat intensified. He dashed from his chair to the screen. The features became clearer: the brown hair, the eyes with crow's feet, the dimples his mother always talked about. The man was looking at his reflection in a puddle of water. He was surrounded by trees, and a howling gale pushed away the remaining bits of hair covering his face. "Dad?" Kasey said.

* * *

Luke

Running. Sprinting. Racing. Luke followed branches from trees on fire, twigs inching out of the ground along the path, and landmarks he recalled. He swore he had seen that patch of grass and strange tree stumps before. The burning forest evolved into a tidal wave of flame, eating away at mawz growing from the top and forming a cloud of smoke to block out the lightning.

A root in Luke's way snubbed him, bringing him to the grassy ground. He face-planted, his entire body stinging from impact. He cursed, pulling himself back up, his newly acquired wooden spear now sliced in two. His hand grasped the sharper section, ignoring jagged pieces of bark wedging splinters in his skin.

Luke tried to make sense of what was going on—but he couldn't—something was happening, someone was killing the Travelers, the people he left behind. The linguists, the soldiers, the specialists, all of them were in danger. Faces of his other Travelers flashed in his head and played like a slideshow. *How did the Apiary find them?* Then, a horrible thought crept into his brain. *What if it wasn't the Apiary?*

He hustled, keeping his knees high and increasing his stride involuntarily. Familiar branches and patches of grass became more memorable until he reached the base of the structure. He gulped. As he closed in, screams and pleas from Travelers inside got louder. It didn't deter Luke, instead, he called upon his bravado and climbed the stairs. He heard pops and bangs like muffled gunshots that didn't sound like they should.

At the entrance, Luke crouched and slowed his pace. He took shallow steps and prevented his weapon from dragging along the ground. The element of surprise was the only thing on his side, and he had to keep it at all costs. He only had this one primitive weapon that he grabbed along the way from the clearing with Riley, and he wasn't certain that it would aid him much in a gunfight when he didn't have as much as a slingshot.

Slowly, the loud yelps died out. Luke mapped the building in his head, trying to remember the columns he could use as cover and the location of other possible weapons. The filers they used to cut into the mawz were promising, but the Travelers likely grabbed those to fight off whoever was attacking them. Some were soldiers, after all. He crept until the torch's fire formed a shadow.

The silhouette stood tall, with arms, hands, and knees that bent the right way. Luke tightened his grip around the wooden spear, sending the creaking bark in every direction from the pressure of his fist. Whoever was responsible for this was a Human, and he could only think of one person. After a countdown from three, he turned the corner, seeing Powers standing over the body of his fellow Travelers.

"What have you done?" Luke cried.

Powers turned to him with an unfamiliar pistol in one hand and a knife in the other. Crimson blood spotted Powers' face, and with a sick smile, he stared at Luke. "You really shouldn't have come back." Scratches decorated his face, blood spilling out of them and dirt dotting areas that didn't have marks. He limped towards Luke, taking a shiv of sorts out of his right thigh.

"You killed them," Luke managed to utter through chattering teeth. He kept his stick weapon tucked behind him.

"I'll be honest," Powers said. "I didn't plan to."

"That gun says otherwise."

Powers looked down at the gun in his hand. Tossing it to the side, it hit the chest of someone he'd killed moments earlier. "Out of bullets, anyway."

Luke narrowed his eyes, keeping his hands warm and ready to move at a moment's notice. "Who's 'they?'"

"The winners," Powers said. "The other aliens."

"The others?" Luke stammered. "You called the people that destroyed their world?"

"They made contact with me, back on *the Traveler*."

Luke blinked. "You had them blow us out of the sky?"

"That was a pure accident," he said. "And I tried to get us to leave."

"You called the other aliens here to do what? Destroy the planet with us on it?"

Powers frowned. "I tried telling them," he said. He pointed to the dead among the Travelers with the stained knife. "I tried to tell each of them we needed to talk to the *winners*."

"Do you hear yourself? You're crazy! You just killed a bunch of Humans and probably an entire species and yourself!"

"No," Powers said. "Captain Bigon's got a plan. With my help, I just secured humanity's future."

"Who's Captain Bigon?" Luke spat.

Powers shrugged. "Someone who wants power so he can keep peace."

"You're going to die," Luke said, flatly. "They're going to come here, and they're going to kill us."

"I secured my safety," he said. "Back along *the Traveler*, when they contacted me, I sent one of the escape pods back with everything. They need to give me a ship to retrieve it if they don't want it reaching humanity."

"You're blackmailing them?"

"I'm securing my life." Powers held out his hands. "You and Riley, you guys can join them too."

Luke took a step back. "Join them?"

"I think it would be a great showing of humanity, that we, as a species, are united in the logical decision."

Luke's body went cold, and static came through his comms. Riley said something, garbled to the point he couldn't quite make it out.

"Luke, you're a nice man," Powers said. "You might not agree with my decision, but we need to side with the winners, whether or not they're right."

Luke dug his shoes into the ground. He waited for Powers to step forward. Luke's hand gripped the splintering wood so tightly it drove bark into his skin.

"You can even take credit for this," Powers said. "I bet they'd like to see my intellect, your strength, and Riley's tech. Assuming you want her here. They're benevolent, they'll understand."

Luke gulped. "After destroying an entire planet and having you kill your crewmates you call them benevolent?"

Luke didn't wait for his response. He lunged at him, unsheathing his stick from his back, slashing a scratch from Powers' lower chin up to one of his eyes, cutting the cornea. Powers stumbled back in anguish, holding his eye and shouting. Luke kicked with his foot, sending Powers back further. Rage overcame Luke and he ran forward, slashing overhead. Powers veered out of the way, dodging behind a column. Luke sprinted, slashing again, this time cutting Powers across the chest and ripping the cloth covering it.

"You fucking monster!" Luke cried. He kept slicing through the air, trying to make his attacks hit. Powers fumbled something in his hands, and Luke bolted to him, ready to swipe at his neck and end him.

BANG!

Luke stopped in his tracks, his stomach burning and bleeding. It didn't hurt at first, his body pumped all the adrenaline left in him. He tried to will himself forward, but another *BANG* stopped him to a halt. Powers stood in front of him, his new scar going up from chin to eye.

"I wish it went differently," he murmured. He rushed out of the room, leaving Luke bleeding with two bullets in his body. Luke coughed, the pain settling in now. A flame-like heartburn radiated from his stomach across his body. He tried to put pressure on it, tried to stop the blood seeping out, but he couldn't force his body any more than he already had.

The room spun, and Luke lay on his back, staring at the ceiling. Willing himself to put his fingers to his comms, Luke trudged his hand towards his neck, dragging blood around it as he tapped.

"*R-Riley—*" Luke whispered.

"*—Luke! Powers called the other aliens, they're coming here, we have to go!*"

"*Riley,*" Luke struggled to say.

"*Luke!*"

As the darkness made a vignette around his vision, Luke thought of Kasey and Daphne, together at the table, playing some game. Maybe they were talking about how Daddy was seeing the aliens, how he was going to be one of the first people to meet the extraterrestrials. *Time slows when you die.*

After a series of blinks, Riley appeared overhead with Zanbaq looming over him on the opposite side. Luke coughed a mix of blood and spit, savoring the taste of iron in his mouth.

"Tell Kasey and Daphne—"

"*—Luke, save your energy!—*"

"I love them." He closed his eyes, choking on his last breath of alien air, and envisioned his happy place. He sat at the table—the dinner set in the kitchen, dingy from raising Kasey but still the nicest thing in their home. Daphne's parents gave it to them, as a wedding present. Luke drew a card from the deck, Kasey and Daphne allying to take him out so they could go to battle, just the two of them.

* * *

Kasey

The video feed ended with a younger Riley taking the chip out of Luke, sobbing the entire time. Just as then, she stifled a cry in the back of the room, looking away from the screen the second Luke's dying voice murmured.

Kasey was motionless. He wanted to shift his body, punch with his arms, and kick with his feet, but he couldn't move. The only part that did move was his trembling lips and eyes soaked with tears. They traveled down his face, and once they started they couldn't stop. He thought of the Tayirs, Shamp, Benjo, Tsoki—God, Tsoki—all lost to one man's selfish belief he knew best for the universe. Then he thought of his father.

He imagined a future where his experiences with Tsoki, Shamp, and Benjo weren't taken away from him. Tsoki and him going on dates and maybe eventually falling in love, Benjo and him getting on each other's nerves with different worldviews, and Shamp and him talking for hours and learning new words from one another.

Then Respow entered his mind. Powers, Respow, it didn't matter what anagram he went by. He did this to Kasey. He killed his friends. Killed countless Tayirs. Usurped the role of Representative by rampaging an orchestrated alien attack. It was him, all of it, even the death of his father and the Travelers. Kasey slammed his eyes shut, moving his body for the first time with his own volition. His trembling lips curved into a smolder, and his eyebrows narrowed into a stern face. An image of Respow flashed in his mind, that was his target, and he hated him.

Kasey looked to Riley, wiping tears from his eyes, and spoke with a newfound conviction. A creed steeped in hatred and revenge but dressed up as justice. "I'll join you."

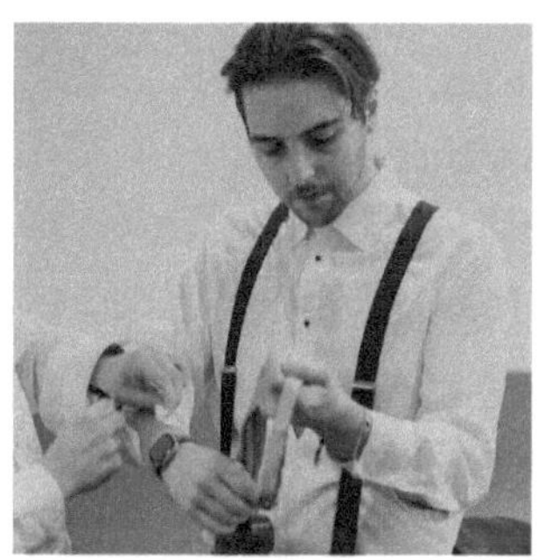

About the Author

Eddie Pittman is a multi-talented individual whose journey through law school led to a successful career as an attorney in Alexandria, Virginia, has been equally complemented by a fervent passion for literature and writing. With a dual background in Criminal Justice and English, Eddie was primed for creative storytelling.

Eddie resides with his partner and three feline companions, who he often finds inspiration from (in fact one Falisto is based on two of his cats if they shared a body). While Eddie's professional life revolves around the intricacies of law, his passions extend far beyond the courtroom. A dedicated aficionado of science fiction, Eddie found his gateway into the genre through the captivating universe of the Mass Effect series. From there, his love for speculative fiction blossomed, culminating in the release of their debut science fiction novel.

When not immersed in the realm of literature, Eddie can often plays video games, binge-watches RuPaul's Drag Race, and, of course, writing.

You can connect with me on:

🌐 https://eddiepittmanauthor.com

🐦 https://x.com/eddiepittmanaut

📘 https://www.facebook.com/profile.php?id=61556840249060

🔗 https://www.instagram.com/eddiepittmannovels/?hl=en

🔗 https://www.goodreads.com/user/show/171325871-eddie-pittman

Subscribe to my newsletter:

✉ https://673f5c1c927611ef825eb5b573eedea6.eo.page/z2z66

Also by Eddie Pittman

The story continues in Revolution Among the Stars! Available on Kindle Unlimited and physically at your favorite book store July 31, 2025.

Revolution Among the Stars

Kasey Mako thought surviving the Galactic Union's genocide was the hardest fight of his life—until he joined Jasoosi, a resistance group determined to bring the Union to its knees. But revolutions aren't won with bloodshed alone; they're won with the truth.

The Galactic Union is creating something—a weapon so devastating it threatens everyone across the Galaxy. As Jasoosi clashes with the Union, Kasey and his team race to expose the conspiracy. if they fail, the Union won't just crush the revolution—they'll annihilate everything. But the deeper Kasey digs, the more he unearths secrets that were never meant to see the light.